DOWN THESE STREETS

JAMES SCOTT BELL

Compendium Press

ISBN: 978-0-910355-63-6

CONTENTS

INTRODUCTION

I've always considered short stories the hardest kind of fiction to write and —at the same time and in the right (write) hands—the most powerful form of storytelling.

I can still feel the emotional jolt of many Hemingway stories. "Soldier's Home," "Hills Like White Elephants," and "The Short Happy Life of Francis Macomber" come to mind. Even the work that got Hemingway the Nobel Prize, *The Old Man and the Sea*, is really a novella, coming in at a modest 27,000 words. But you're knocked out at the end. *The old man was dreaming about the lions.*

Another 20th-century writer whose best work was short form is William Saroyan. After years of rejection, he burst onto the literary scene with the unforgettable story "The Amazing Young Man on the Flying Trapeze." His *My Name is Aram* is my favorite among all short story collections.

Stories such as these belong to the "literary" genre. They are primarily about characters, relatively "quiet" about plot. In college I was fortunate to get into a workshop overseen by an acknowledged master of literary short stories, Raymond Carver. From him I learned the value of "the telling detail," a small item in a story that reveals a universe of a character's inner life.

The term *literary* is used primarily to distinguish such stories from other genres, like *pulp fiction.* Oh, how I love the world of classic pulp (1920-1950), so named because these magazines were printed on cheap, wood-pulp paper so the publishers could sell them for a dime or a quarter on newsstands. Writers like Dashiell Hammett, Raymond Chandler, Carroll John Daly, and Erle Stanley Gardner ushered in the hardboiled school of pulp writing.

Another legendary pulp writer was Robert E. Howard, most famous for introducing Conan the Cimmerian (aka Conan the Barbarian) in the pulp mag aptly titled *Weird Tales.* But Howard also wrote action stories featuring "Sailor" Steve Costigan, a seafaring scrapper and former champion boxer. The main draw was not boxing but Costigan's humorous, first-person narration.

In junior high, I found another kind of short story in Ray Bradbury's *The Illustrated Man.* Here were flights of imagination mixed with sparkling prose and a "kicker" ending. Man, I wanted to be able to write like that (a desire not uncommon to nascent writers reading Bradbury). He seemed to be saying to me, "The door is open to my story world. Come in! But keep watch, for you never know what's waiting for you at the end."

Plus, my favorite TV shows as a kid were *The Twilight Zone* and *Alfred Hitchcock Presents,* with their delicious twists. (*"It's a cookbook!"*)

This collection, then, is my homage to all these styles. Here are stories with a twist, stories with a heart (the "literary" type), and stories with a punch (about a 1950s boxer in L.A. named Irish Jimmy Gallagher).

My title is taken from a Raymond Chandler essay which every pulp writer knows practically by heart. For those unfamiliar with it, here's how Chandler described the detective hero:

> Down these mean streets a man must go who is not himself mean, who is neither tarnished nor afraid. He is the hero; he is everything. He must be a complete man and a common man and yet an unusual man. He must be, to use a rather weathered phrase, a man of honor—by instinct, by inevitability, without thought of it, and certainly without saying it. He must be the best man in his world and a good enough man for any world.
>
> He will take no man's money dishonestly and no man's insolence without a due and dispassionate revenge...If there were enough like him, the world would be a very safe place to live in, without becoming too dull to be worth living in.

This perfectly describes my own series hero, Mike Romeo. Indeed, this imbues everything I write. And when I write about the other kind of man (or woman)—the criminal, the *femme fatale*—then justice is sure to be swift.

I've also included some of my flash fiction (stories under 1,000 words). These are perfect when you need some quick escapism, or are fighting boredom in a waiting room or grocery store line.

In fact, there are stories here for any occasion—except, perhaps, rock climbing.

The door is now open. Come in, enjoy, but keep close watch—because you never know what's waiting for you at the end…

Jim

STORIES WITH A TWIST

As I mentioned in the introduction, I'm a great fan of stories with twist endings. I have the utmost respect for the many writers who were and are masters of it. I've tried to honor that craft with the following stories.

HEED THE WIFE

"I think we can do it," Susie said. "I think we can steal the money and no one will ever know."

Frank Dabney looked away from the Chargers game long enough to make a face at his wife. "Hey, babe, can you grab me some more Doritos?"

"I'm serious," Susie said. "Will you put the stupid game on mute a second and listen?"

Uh-oh. Frank knew what it meant when his wife said *listen*. It meant you paid attention right now and took two minutes of annoyance, or you'd pay for it with two days of freeze-out. And the Arctic didn't have anything on Susie Dabney when she got mad.

But Frank knew how to play his wife when she was like this, and if he did it skillfully he could maybe cut down the annoyance to a minute and a half.

He had to. It was the fourth quarter, the Chargers were behind, and Herbert was moving them up the field.

"Baby," Frank said, "you don't really mean that, so I don't think we need to—"

"I do mean it. I'm tired of this. Tired of you being out of work and all the lousy jobs I have to take to keep us in this stinking place."

Frank agreed the place stunk. It was the worst house on the worst street in this crummy neighborhood in San Berdoo. But it was a roof. On the other hand, if they didn't make some money soon . . .

They'd been homeless before, sleeping in the van, and he didn't want that again, no sir. But what his wife was suggesting was wack.

Frank said, "I promise I'll go out looking tomorrow. I'll really look this time. Really."

"No, no good. We've been down that road. We can take the money from Brewster and make it look like some Mexican did it. I've planned it all out. And I figure it's worth three hundred thousand, maybe more."

On the silent TV, Justin Herbert completed a pass for twenty-five yards.

"I'll think about it," Frank said, intending to do no such thing.

Susie got up, huffed, and went to the kitchen. Frank turned the sound on again. The crowd was going nuts.

But off in the distance in his mind, in the far corner of the stadium in his cranium, Frank heard an ominous echo, over and over—*Yes, you will. Yes, you will.*

The next day Frank looked for work in earnest. He got the runaround at Pep Boys and a "We'll let you know" from Home Depot. Staples was a dead end and OSH was a graveyard. Walmart had too many old people and Starbucks had too many young ones.

Frank Dabney, at 38, was a loser, and he knew it.

But he was determined to fight on.

Last night he'd been inspired by Mr. Justin Herbert. The Chargers superstar had led his team to a fourth quarter comeback. With one minute, three seconds left, the Chargers needed a touchdown and a two point conversion just to tie. Justin got it for them.

Then he led the Chargers to field goal range in OT, where they won it. Magic.

So Frank Dabney decided he and his prospects, and especially his marriage, were in the fourth quarter, and he was going to drive down the field, Manning-like.

Had to, because Frank knew he was not the greatest looking of men. He knew he was lucky to have Susie. Even after her affair with Spike Trancono at the Harley shop, Frank eagerly took her back in. He wasn't exactly God's gift to women, and if she were to leave him he didn't know what he'd do.

That night Susie said to him, "We can do this. I know the combination of the safe, of course, and also how to rig the security cameras." Susie worked doing the books for old Hal Brewster who ran an equipment rental company in town. He'd been there almost forty years. He was one of the last of the old-time businessmen, who ran things on trust and a handshake.

Susie had been working for him part time for three years now. Brewster trusted her.

Frank said, "But he's a nice old guy, been good to you."

"What does that matter? Nice isn't going to cut it for us anymore. What's wrong with you? What happened to the man I married?"

He hated that one. Hated when she questioned his manhood.

And then she went to the nuclear option. She threw her arms around his neck and pulled him close, and ran her tongue over his ear.

The firehouse of Frank's nervous system sounded all alarms. Every muscle jumped to attention. His blood slid down fire poles, jumped into trucks and revved the engines.

Then Susie whispered, "You need to listen to your wife," and gently nudged him toward the bed.

"Dude, you're talking grand theft."

Arch Renfro popped another Budweiser and put his feet up on the scuffed coffee table in his garage. This was his "man cave" and only a few friends, like Frank, were ever allowed in here.

In part, it was because Arch had served a nickel in Pelican Bay, and wasn't exactly open to a lot of socializing. He didn't trust people. Except Frank, because they had grown up together.

"You're looking at jail time, maybe the big house," Arch said. "You really want to do that for a run at three hundred large?"

"Susie wants it," Frank said. He sounded pitiful, even to himself.

"Man, you got to stone up."

"She'll leave me. I mean, she really will this time."

Arch reached in the cooler, pulled out another Bud and tossed it to Frank.

"I'm going to say this once," Arch said. "You need to listen to me, you hear? Your ol' buddy. I'm telling you this is a bad idea."

"Look at me, man. You think I can just go out and find me another woman?"

"She's playing you."

"Maybe I want to be played. Maybe that's the whole thing."

"I want you to look at my lips," Arch said. "Listen to me and not to her. Got that?"

"You're killing me."

"I'm trying to save you, man."

Frank popped open his beer and drained it in three long gulps.

He was buzzed when he hopped the Red Line without paying, and rode the train to Pershing Square. He got out and started walking, trying to sort things out.

Susie or Arch? Who should he listen to?

Arch, his friend who would never steer him wrong.

Or Susie, who might leave him.

But grand theft?

He thought about what Arch said to him a few hours ago. *Listen to me and not to her. Got that?*

He heard Susie's voice in response. *Yes, you will.*

What to do, what to do?

Frank looked up then and saw an odd building. Here in the middle of Los Angeles, where office buildings of glass and steel rose high above the streets, was a squat little structure made of stones. Like some medieval church. Yes, that was it. It looked as if a collector of Scottish chapels had moved this, stone by stone, from the highlands to Hope Street.

Stepping closer, Frank saw a brass plate near a rounded, oak door. The plate said, Ecumenical Bible Society.

Bible. His grandmother always told him the Bible had the answer for any problem, any question he had.

He went inside.

Cold as a crypt it was. The only light appeared to be coming in through stained-glass windows. The place was a patch quilt of colors, on the floor and the walls.

Straight ahead of him was a large open room. In the middle of the room was a huge table. Surrounding the table were shelves of books.

He took a step toward the books.

"May I help you?"

Frank almost jumped out of his skin. He whipped around to find a woman with gray hair, perhaps seventy years old, dressed in a plain suit and wearing what looked like black orthopedic shoes.

"I, um, came in to see if I could find a Bible," Frank said.

The woman smiled, and Frank thought at first it was justifiable derision. What a doofus he was. Like walking into an antique shop and asking if they have any old stuff.

But her face and eyes were warm, and Frank decided she was only being nice.

"I would be happy to help you," the old woman said. "Would you like to step into our reading room?"

She motioned him forward.

For a second Frank thought of a good witch bidding him to enter her cave.

Whatever.

In they went. The woman turned on the lights and the room lit up like normal.

"Did you have a particular translation you'd like to see?" she asked.

"Uh, English?"

"What I meant is, there are several translations from the original languages, Hebrew and Greek, into English. Are you familiar with the King James Version?"

"Not really."

"That's the one with all the *thees* and *thous,*" she said. "But don't let that dissuade you. Was there a particular book of the Bible you wished to see?"

Frank started to get a little nervous. He didn't want to go into any of the reasons, he just wanted to hear from God.

"No," Frank said. "Just sort of wanted to see what you had."

"If you'd like to browse, please go ahead," the woman said. "We here at the society encourage folks to open up the Scriptures, and discover God's Word for themselves."

"Exactly what I was thinking," Frank said.

"I'll be in the next room if you have any questions. Our Bibles for reading are on this shelf." She pointed to a serried row of leather and hard-bound volumes. Then she smiled again and left the room.

Friendly sort, Frank thought. If she only knew why he was here.

He looked at the Bibles. Which one?

Did it matter?

Couldn't God speak through any one of them? Hadn't he? Didn't he speak to saints and popes and jazz like that?

He closed his eyes and ran his finger along the spines. His fingernail made a clicking sound. He stopped at random and pulled the Bible he'd selected off the shelf.

It had a worn, black leather cover. That was a good sign. It felt, well, important. It said *Holy Bible* on the spine in faded gold. At the bottom of the spine, also in gold, was printed *1561 facsimile.*

What did that mean? Could that be the *year* 1561?

What did it matter? It said *Holy Bible.* If it was an oldie, maybe it was a goodie, too.

He put the Bible on the burnished wood table in the center of the reading room and sat in a hard, wooden chair. Maybe that was all part of the Bible reading experience, he thought. Hard on the tush but easy on the soul.

Whatever.

For a full minute he looked at the Bible. It looked back. And then he offered up what he supposed was a prayer.

Okay, God, I'll give it one try. You tell me what to do. I got no other place to go. You da man, God. Here we go.

Frank closed his eyes again and opened the Bible at random. He stuck out his right index finger and made a grand loop with it in the air, then let it touch down on the page.

He looked.

His finger had come down on the side of the page, but very clearly his fingernail was directly under a line. He bent down to read it.

Heed the wife, and no other.

If a bolt of lightning from the hand of God himself had hit Frank

Dabney then, it would have felt the same as the jolt that coursed through his body.

God had given him an answer, in his Holy Book.

God had answered his prayer!

There had to be a reason for the theft now. Perhaps this was God's way of punishing old man Brewster for some secret sins.

Maybe the old guy drank or was a serial killer or something.

It didn't matter. God had told him what to do. *Heed the wife, and no other.*

"I want you to take a weapon," Susie said.

It was three nights later, three wonderful nights. Susie could have asked Frank to eat his own head, and he would have tried.

Stealing three hundred grand seemed a very small price to pay for a life like this.

Only—

"Why do I need a weapon?" Frank asked.

"There are some real undesirables down there at night. I don't want us held back because some lowlife stumbles in."

"I can't get a gun, at least not legally. Maybe Arch could, but I don't think he will."

"I don't mean a gun. A tire iron will do. Something like that."

"Oh, okay, I get it now."

"Just do what I say, all right?"

Heed the wife, and no other.

"I will, babe. I will forever."

Brewster's U-Rent was just outside the official town line. It had a chain link fence with razor wire on top. Inside were the trailers, tractors, loaders, trenchers, tillers, dollies and just about anything a do-it-yourselfer might need.

In the middle of the yard was an office, a converted mobile unit that old man Brewster had added to over the years.

Inside the office was a safe with three hundred thousand dollars cash in it.

Outside the office, outside the fence, Susie Dabney drove her ancient Ford Escort. Frank was in the back seat, lying down to avoid being seen. He had a pillowcase in his back pocket and a head full of Susie's planning. She knew what she was doing all right.

She zipped past the front entrance and turned left on the easement road between Brewster's and the play yard of the *Tabernaculo de Nueva Vida*, the Pentecostal church that had thrived for twenty years in town.

Susie stopped at the back of Brewster's.

"We're here," she said, and Frank got up. He grabbed the tire iron in his gloved right hand and looked out the window.

The light was muted here, just as Susie said it would be. Frank had been to Brewster's during the day but never at night. The only light was from the one hanging on the utility pole at the front corner. It gave the whole place an eerie shade of luminescent gray. Frank felt like a shadow moving under the moon, only tonight there was no moon.

"Hurry," Susie said. She'd already popped out of the car and was unlocking the big chain that secured the gate.

According to her plan, the security cameras had been set to *reset* at precisely this hour. The auto-reset would take five minutes. But Susie, who was the only one besides Brewster who could work the system, had manually set it for twenty minutes.

That was the amount of time Frank would have to get in, get to the safe, open it, take the money and get back out.

Where Susie would be waiting to pick him up.

She handed Frank the key to the back door of the office.

"I'll be back in eighteen minutes," she said. "Check your watch."

He did.

"Go," she said.

He heeded her.

Using the small flashlight, Frank found his way quickly to the safe. It was right where Susie said it would be, between the metal filing cabinet and the credenza with an autographed photo of Derek Jeter on top of it.

Like a thief in one of those old caper movies, Frank put the flashlight in his mouth and spun the combination on the safe.

It clicked open as easily as a cupboard.

His nerves were tingling with excitement. He felt more alive at this moment than at any other time in his mediocre life. And all because of—and for—Susie.

He didn't know why God was answering his prayer this way, but he was. And when he and Susie were clear with the money—she also had a plan about hiding it until they were ready to use it—he would spend his life making her happy. Maybe he'd even pull another job.

Whatever she said, he'd listen to.

There was only one part of the plan he was unclear about. That was the Mexican fall guy part. But Susie said she had rigged the system so that, upon reset, it would replay some old footage she'd found in the archive. There was a laborer who had been in the shop four months ago and got into a shouting match with Brewster. He was later caught on camera in the early evening, loitering outside the front gate. He looked drunk.

Susie knew how to manually timestamp that footage. She had archived it just before doing the reset.

The suspect would be seen in proximity to Brewster's at the time of the theft.

And both Susie and Frank would say they were at home, blissfully sleeping together.

Frank took the pillowcase out of his back pocket and started stuffing the cash into it. Susie had assured him old man Brewster kept the stacks of twenties, fifties and hundreds in his compulsively neat way. That proved to be the case.

Another reminder that he could listen to his wife. She knew what was going on. Down to the last bill.

Frank closed the safe and spun the dial.

And turned around when the lights went on.

"What're you doing?" old man Brewster said.

Susie Dabney drove to the am/pm market on Pike and parked outside the door. Shadi, the night counter guy, young and firm, was right where she knew he'd be.

"Hello there," Shadi said, his deep brown eyes perking up.

"How're you, darlin'?" Susie said.

"I am most fine tonight," Shadi said. He had hair the color of pitch. Susie couldn't remember seeing anything so black.

"Well Shadi, I just came by to see if you've seen my husband tonight."

"Mr. Dabney?"

"He's the only husband I've got, Sugar."

Shadi smiled a mouthful of gleaming white teeth. "Oh yes, yes, I know, oh my—"

"So have you? Seen him?"

"He has not been into the store since I have been here."

She shook her head. "He took off without telling me where he was going. I really can't stand that."

"I do not think you should," Shadi said.

"Well now, Shadi, if I was married to you I don't think I'd have that little problem, now would I?"

His dark brown skin began to lighten around the cheeks.

"How about a pack of Kool Filter Kings, Shadi? And I'll go cruise around and see if I can find that dipstick husband of mine."

"I hope he learns to treat you nice, Mrs. Dabney."

"Call me Susie," she said. "We know each other well enough for that."

Shadi smiled and turned to get the smokes.

Oh no oh no oh no.

Brewster was standing right there, swaying in the doorway. The smell of bourbon was so strong it crossed the room like an extended jab and hit Frank in the nose.

"Who the hell are you?" Brewster said. "And give me one good reason not to shoot your sorry butt."

Frank stood. As he did, he picked up the tire iron from the floor and held it behind his leg.

"You better answer!" Brewster said, his words slurring.

Frank took two quick steps, swinging the tire iron like Derek Jeter himself.

The preliminary hearing in the case of the People v. Frank Dabney got underway on a bleak Monday, Judge Arturo Rios presiding.

It took only two hours for the prosecutor to put on its minimal showing. The arresting officer and a forensic serologist testified, placing

Frank at the scene of the crime with the blood of the victim on his clothes.

Barton Suffington, Frank's lawyer, stood up, buttoning the coat of his Brioni suit. "Your honor, at this time we will challenge the sufficiency of the People's allegation, and submit that there is no culpability for the actions taken that night."

Judge Rios looked at Suffington over the glasses perched on his nose. "This ought to be interesting."

"Everything my client did on that night was under the direction of God."

At that, Rios closed his eyes. "Mr. Suffington—"

"I have an offer of proof."

"I was afraid of that."

"Unless," Suffington announced, "your honor is going to state that God does not exist. The God every witness in this courtroom swears to before they take the stand."

Rios sighed. "Counsel, the court is well aware of your theatrics. But just to get this out of the way, what's your offer?"

"I call my client, Frank Dabney, to the stand for the sole issue of laying a foundation."

"Make it fast," Rios said.

Frank walked to the stand and faced the clerk, who told him to raise his right hand. The clerk said, "Do you solemnly swear that the testimony you are about to give in the cause now pending before this court shall be the truth, the whole truth and nothing but the truth, so help you God?"

Frank stuck out his chest. "I do, so help me God!"

Judge Rios rubbed the bridge of nose.

Frank sat on the witness chair, relieved at last to be able to tell his story.

And tell it he did, about how he found the phrase from God that told him to listen to his wife, and nobody else, and how he believed everything that happened at Brewster's was what God would have him do.

Then he added a bit about his lying, stinking wife, but the judge ordered that part stricken from the record as irrelevant.

The prosecutor did not ask Frank a single question, preferring to sit at his table with a smirk.

Then Suffington said, "I call Mrs. Harriet Wright to the stand."

The old woman from the Bible society stepped forward, holding a volume in her hands. She was sworn in and sat in the witness box.

Suffington began. "Mrs. Wright, what is your occupation?"

"I am curator of the Ecumenical Bible Society in downtown Los Angeles."

"How long have you worked in that capacity?"

"It will be fifteen years next January."

"And were you working there on October 14 of this year?"

"Yes I was."

"Do you recall my client, sitting there at the counsel table, coming into the society on that day?"

"Yes I do. He wanted to read a Bible."

"And what did you do?"

"I showed him into our reading room, where our reading Bibles are located, and left him there."

"Now, my client has testified that he pulled out a Bible that said *1561 facsimile* on it. Are you familiar with such a Bible?"

"Yes I am," the witness said. "I've brought it with me as you requested."

She placed the Bible on the rail of the witness box.

"Now my client testified that he found a verse in that Bible that said *Heed the wife, and no other.* And you called me this morning to say that you had found that verse?"

"Sort of," Harriet Wright said.

Frank gripped the arms of his chair.

"Please clarify," Suffington said, obviously miffed.

"Well, I used a concordance and found all references to *wife* in the Bible, and did not find that particular wording. But I was curious. This edition of the Bible was originally published in 1561 in Zurich, Switzerland, by a small group of English expatriates. It is an edition that includes commentary in the margins. And I was able to find the phrase your client found, in the notes next to Proverbs, the Twelfth Chapter, Fifteenth verse."

Suffington smiled. He looked at the prosecutor who was, suddenly, quite interested. Then Frank's lawyer said, "Will you please open to that passage?"

Mrs. Wright did so.

"And isn't it true that it says *Heed the wife, and no other* exactly as my client as testified?"

"Not exactly," Harriet Wright said.

What was going on here? Frank had been so certain, especially with the assurance of his expensive lawyer, that Harriet Wright was the slam dunk witness in his favor. Even if the judge did not toss out the case, they were laying a foundation for an insanity defense at trial. It was essential to get all this on the record now.

But this woman was hesitating. Why?

"Mrs. Wright," Suffington said. "Will you please read for us the phrase that you have found?"

"Objection," the prosecutor said. "This whole line is irrelevant and immaterial. It goes beyond the scope of a preliminary hearing."

The judge took in, and let out, a labored breath. "We've come this far. Let's finish up. The witness may read the phrase."

Mrs. Wright adjusted her glasses and picked up the Bible and read. "Heed the wise, and no other."

Frank couldn't stand it. He shot to his feet. "That's a lie!"

"Sit down, Mr. Dabney!" the judge said.

He did, but trained his eyes on the treacherous woman.

Judge Rios said to the witness, "Am I to understand, ma'am, that the word you just read is *wise* and not *wife?*"

"Yes, your honor," Mrs. Wright said. "You see, this was written in old English, and back then the letter *s* looked very much like our letter *f.* It's the same thing you see in the handwritten script of the Declaration of Independence."

Frank's heart dropped to his stomach and burst into flames.

For a long moment no one said anything. And then, up from the silence, like a slow boil, came the laughter of Judge Arturo Rios.

"I'm sorry," he said. "I'm sorry . . .this is just . . .I'm sorry . . ."

Not as sorry as Frank Dabney, who was bound over for trial.

———

She looked at him through the Plexiglas, as serene as a boa constrictor enjoying a freshly swallowed rabbit.

"What are you even doing here?" Frank said into the handset.

"I just had to look at you one last time," Susie said. "I had to have one last look at the stupidest man in the world."

Frank bit down on his cheeks and tasted blood.

"What idiot looks at an *s* and gets an *f* out of it? And thinks it's God talking to him? You deserve everything you get. An *f* out of an *s!*" And then she started laughing.

Frank hit the Plexiglas with his fist. And hit it and hit it.

The deputy in charge rushed over and grabbed Frank's arm. Frank screamed and jerked away and hit the Plexiglas again, and again.

It took three guards to rip him from his stool.

That night, one of Frank's four cellmates, a meth head named Stanley "Bad Snort" Thompson, leaned down from his top bunk and said, "I heard what happened, man. About your wife and all."

News travels fast in jail, Frank thought.

"You want a chance to do something about it?"

Frank sat up, almost hitting his head on the underside bunk above. "Like what?"

"There's a whole lot of risk involved," Bad Snort said. "A whole lot. I mean, if you break out of here you can get into a whole lot more—"

"Just tell me about it," Frank said.

The night was soft, and so was Shadi. Susie loved his silky skin against hers. He was an able lover, but more than that he had a head for investments. He was going to take the three hundred grand and run it up for them, as soon as it was safe. A little at a time, here and there, and then they could get out of this place. A place that reminded her too much of Frank. He'd been on her mind a lot lately, and she couldn't stand that. Like he was going to haunt her dreams forever.

Shadi kissed her ear at the precise moment the door of the bedroom banged open.

Susie screamed.

The lights came on.

It was Frank. In his hands was a sawed-off shotgun.

"Where's the money?" Frank said as he stepped to the foot of the bed.

"Frank, listen—"

"The money, Susie. Where is it?"

"Storage locker. Frank—"

"Where's the key?"

"Frank! You can't do this."

"Please," Shadi said. "This is not as you suppose!"

Frank laughed and raised the shotgun.

Susie screamed. "Frank!"

Frank held the shotgun on the unhappy couple. He said nothing, just stood there, laughing it up.

"Take all the money!" Shadi said. "We do not want it."

"Yes," Susie said. "All of it!"

Frank laughed harder.

"Frank!" Susie said. "Say something!"

Frank stopped laughing and caught his breath. He looked at his wife through the shotgun sight. "You played me for a fap," he said.

She blinked. "What?"

"Fo long, Fufie."

NO LAUGHING MATTER

He died.

Pete Harvey, "The Harv" as he billed himself, just flat out died in front of the 11 p.m. crowd at the Comedy Zone.

He sucked, he blew, he bit. The new cutting edge material didn't work the way he was sure it would, the way it had to.

He'd given four months to the new stuff. It was his final bid to break out of the huge ocean of sludge that is the stand-up scene in L.A. He'd even, as a good luck move, put it all on a CD first, so sure was he that he could capitalize on this new way of doing comedy.

But he died just now, and it was chewing away at his insides as he sat at the bar.

Adrianna, the bartender, came over with her encouraging smile.

"How'd it go, kiddo?" she said.

"Gimme a double Jack," Pete said.

"It can't be that bad."

"Make it a triple."

"Funny." Adrianna put a napkin on the bar top. "Let me start you with a single."

"When's it gonna happen for me?" Pete said.

Adrianna put a glass on the napkin and poured a shot of Jack Daniels.

Pete said, "You think I'm good, don't you?"

"You work hard, Pete."

"Not what I asked." He took the drink and downed it. "I needed to kill tonight. I died."

"It happens," Adrianna said. "My dad used to say that which does not kill us makes us stronger."

He stared at the empty glass. Thoughts popped and zinged across the wasteland of his brain. *Career over. What now? Car wash management? Will I ever make it? Can I sell my soul? What would that even fetch?*

He grinned. Yeah, maybe it was time for the devil—the very devil, Satan himself—to come sit next to him and offer to buy his soul in exchange for getting him to the top, or at least some outright, sustained laughter at some of his freaking jokes.

The man who sat next to him did not look like Satan. He was big, like a football player, around thirty-five or so. He wore a crisp blue suit and burgundy tie.

"Not exactly a good night for you, was it?" the guy said.

Jerk. Just what a comedian who bagged wants to hear. Pete ignored him, signaled to Adrianna for another.

"He's had enough," the guy said.

Pete snapped him a look. "Where do you get off—"

"You got potential," the guy said. "Let's talk."

Adrianna said to the guy, "Can I get you something?"

"Give us a little privacy," the guy said. "If you don't mind."

Adrianna nodded, sauntered to the other end of the bar.

"What's this about?" Pete said.

"I know what it's like to struggle in this town," the guy said. "Been through it myself. Now I got me a job that pays great, doing what I like to do. What if I told you I got a way for you to do your act and make five grand in one night?"

Pete coughed. "What?"

"Five large. For you. For one performance."

"Right! Got it. And I'll host the Oscars next year, right after I do the Golden Globes. Gee, where do I sign?"

"I'm serious."

Pete looked into the guy's cold blue eyes. He did look serious. "But you just said I sucked."

"No, I said you didn't have a good night. But it's not over. There's a party that needs some laughs, and you're the guy who can do it. The money's no problem. Five large."

"Okay, who put you up to this? Jimmy? Was it Jimmy?"

The guy reached in his coat and came out with a crisp $100 bill. He put it in Pete's shirt pocket. "Here's an advance."

Pete took out the bill and looked at it. "You really are serious."

"Dreams happen in this town, pal. And it just so happens this is your shot at the dream. We go down the street, not too far, you perform whatever your best stuff is, and if you score, the sky's the limit. But you get the five grand anyway."

"Just down the street?"

"Five minutes."

"And five thou is guaranteed?"

"Absolutely."

"Who can afford to pay me that?" Pete said. "And why me?"

The guy leaned toward him. "I think you got potential. And the somebody is a somebody who can take you to the top. Are you in or out?"

Well, Pete thought, these things do happen. Guy in a small club just happens to be "on" when a big-time producer shows up because he had some free time that night, and boom, the guy gets a national TV spot. Maybe this is one of those times. And he could sure use the five Gs.

He put the Benjamin back in his pocket and stood. "Let's go."

"You made the right choice," the guy said. They got up.

"I got a gig," Pete said to Adrianna as he walked by her.

"Go get 'em," Adrianna said.

The guy drove a black Caddie. In a twist of comedic irony, he told Pete his name was Guy.

"I got one for you," Guy said as they pulled onto Sunset. "Why didn't the skeleton go on the roller coaster?"

"Um," Pete said. "Why?"

"It didn't have the guts."

"Oh," Pete said. "That's...funny."

Not.

"Maybe I should do a little standup," Guy said. "What do you think?"

Pete was not about to tell him what he thought. So he said, "What kind of work do you do?"

"Me? Oh, a little of this, a little of that. Security you might say."

He sure was built like the bodyguard type.

"Here we are," Guy said, pulling into the underground garage of a high rise. He punched in a code and the gate opened. They went down into the garage and stopped at an elevator door.

They got out. Guy punched a keypad and the elevator opened.

And Pete's nerves fired on all cylinders.

"Look, wait," Pete said. "I don't know, I appreciate this, but I don't think I want to do it." He took out the bill from his pocket. "You can have this back."

"Hey, now," Guy said. "You've come this far."

"I just...I'll walk back."

"Listen, Pete—"

"No, really."

Guy sighed. "Let me give you a little incentive."

He pulled open the left side of his coat, revealing the butt of a serious-looking gun in a shoulder holster.

Pete's chest tightened. He tried to find words but they were all jumbled in his dry throat.

Guy gently pushed him into the elevator. "You're gonna be fine."

As they went up, Pete said, "Tell me what this is about, man. I mean, a gun?"

"You'll find out."

"You know, scaring the snot out of me is not exactly the way to prep me up for comedy set."

"All comedy is based on pain," Guy said with a smile. "I'm doing you a favor. I'm rooting for you, pal."

The elevator dinged at the top floor of the high rise and the doors opened. "After you," Guy said.

Pete stepped into an opulent corridor. There was a big door in front of them, with a keypad beside it. Guy entered a code and opened the door for Pete.

The penthouse apartment must have taken up half the top floor. It looked like a movie set.

"Nice crib," Pete said.

"Sit here," Guy said, pointing to a large chair in the center of the room. And what a room it was. Pete had done his act in clubs smaller than this place.

Pete went slowly to the chair, like he was approaching Old Sparky, the infamous electric chair they used in southern prisons years ago. Guy walked with him—the guard escorting him on "the last mile."

When he sat, Pete almost let out a howl of relief that he didn't feel snap, crackle, and pop.

"Take a couple deep breaths," Guy said. "Like it's your first time on *The Tonight Show*."

The standup comedian's ultimate dream. Could this be a real audition of some kind? Was he in any way ready for it? After bombing at the club?

Okay, Pete told himself. Pressure's on. This is what you signed up for when you made comedy your life. Well, maybe not *this*. He'd been heckled plenty of times, but never threatened with a gun!

He took the deep breaths.

Another man entered the room.

He was dressed in a red silk bathrobe. Around forty, he was trim, with a full head of black hair, neatly combed. He kept his hands in the pockets of his robe and stood for a long moment staring at Pete.

Pete tried to stay cool but the robe guy's glare was like police lights in some old cop movie.

Finally the robe guy said, "So you are The Harv."

"Uh," Pete said, "yeah."

"In order to distinguish you from all the other Harvs in this world?"

"I guess. Who—"

"I mean, there's Harv down the street, and Harv the school teacher. There's Harv the basset hound and Harv the who-knows-what. But you are *The* Harv."

"That's my handle, my brand," Pete said, failing in his attempt to keep his voice from shaking.

The man in the robe stepped in front of the fireplace with no fire in it. "Do you have any idea who I am?"

Pete shook his head slowly.

"Of course. Why should The Harv care about anyone else? Or anything else besides his precious career?"

What was this going to be, an insult fest? Pete started to stand. Guy pushed him down.

"Come on, man," Pete said. "What am I doing here?"

"This is your moment," the robed man said. "That's what you're doing here. Your chance to rocket to the skies. You see, I am someone who has the power to make you a star in your chosen profession. That's what you want, isn't it?"

"Well, yeah," Pete said. "Of course."

"Then all you have to do, within the next half hour, is make me laugh."

"Make you laugh?"

"That's it. Not smile. Laugh. Think you can do it?"

"I have no idea—"

"Come on. Are you any good at what you do or not?"

"Yeah, I'm good. I worked the last ten years to get good."

"That's not all you worked on," Robe said.

"Excuse me?"

"You're quite the ladies man."

Pete put his hands out, as if to say, *So what's that got to do with anything?*

"Come on," Robe said, a fake smile on his face. "You can level with me." He bobbed his eyebrows. "The comedy thing is a chick magnet, isn't it?"

"You know, I don't know."

"We're a couple of guys. Come on, level with me. A lot of action, am I right?"

Pete could not think of a more uncomfortable conversation, unless it had *hemorrhoids* and *sandpaper* in the same sentence.

"Am I right?" Robe said again.

"I do okay."

"Sure you do. With all kinds, huh?"

"Sure, yeah."

"Even other men's wives."

Uh-oh.

Robe's eyes were narrow now, and the fake smile was gone. What was this about? Had Pete had this guy's *wife?* Please no.

Pete said, "I really think there's been a misunderstanding." He tried to stand again, got pushed down again.

"No, Mr. The Harv. There has not. You slept with my wife. On more than one occasion."

Okay, Pete thought, who, who? More than one occasion? How long ago? Someone from the club?

"I honestly think there's been a mistake," Pete said, having no idea if there had been.

Robe nodded at Guy. Guy reached in his coat and pulled out some photographs, which he tossed on Pete's lap.

They were clandestine photos of Pete in his car with . . . what was her name again? Yes, he remembered her now.

"Bring back memories?" Robe said.

Pete swallowed hard. "Look, man, I didn't know she was married. Honest! She came on to me."

"Ignorance of the law is no excuse. And neither is ignorance about another man's wife. Her name is Melissa, you'll recall. Do you recall that, Mr. Harvey?"

"Um, I really don't—"

"Melissa Rockwell. The last name is the one I gave her. The one you have dishonored. But she won't be needing it any more."

Oh man! What was going on? One of those pregnant pauses, the kind just before the perfectly delivered punch line, descended on the room.

Finally Pete said, "So what do we do now?"

Rockwell sat in the stuffed chair next to the fireplace. "Now? Here's what we do. You have thirty minutes to make me laugh. Do that, and I will give you five thousand dollars and I will see to it that you make it to the top. But if I fail to laugh, you will just, well, die."

A shudder like a drunk's DTs coursed through Pete's body. "You cannot be serious."

"Oh, I am, and that's your challenge. I am a serious man, and you better make me laugh, and you better do it in—" He looked at a wall clock. "Twenty-nine minutes. Now you can stand up. You're a standup comedian, after all."

Pete's legs were shaking. He didn't even know if he *could* stand up. But if he was going to get out of this sick joke, maybe bolt from the room, he had to.

Slowly, he stood.

And gathered himself. Let's go with this, baby. This is the challenge of a lifetime. The sort of thing a real performer or athlete lives for.

Pete's dad was a ski enthusiast, and used to talk about an American skier named Bud Werner. In the late 50's and early 60's Werner became the first world-class skier America had ever produced. Made the Olympic squad three times. Then retired, and was doing a ski film in the Alps. He was skiing down a mountain when an avalanche happened. Instead of taking safety behind a tree or rock, Bud Werner decided to race the avalanche. The race of a lifetime.

One he lost, Pete reminded himself. Werner died that day.

What choice did he have now? There was nowhere to hide, nowhere to run. He had to beat the avalanche. He had to make the guy in the robe laugh.

"Hey, death," Pete said. "What can you say? It's crazy. You ever read the obituaries? People die in alphabetical order. How's that happen?"

He paused, looked at Rockwell's face. It was made of pure granite.

"Tough living room," Pete said.

No response. Not even a twitch.

He cast a quick glance at Guy. Guy winked at him.

"I don't know," Pete said. "You on drugs? Because if you're on drugs that's unfair. I used to do drugs, but I stopped when I saw what it did to my friends. I'd get high, and they all looked weird to me."

The sound of imaginary crickets chirped in Pete's head.

"But I would never advocate the use of drugs. Because I'm not an athlete and can't get my hands on the good stuff."

The silence in the room was like the cold, merciless indifference of a tomb.

At which point a click sounded in Pete's brain. It was the opening of a file in the synaptical network that held the jokes of other comedians. Some good stuff there. Go ahead and borrow a few.

"And what's the deal with dogs?" Pete said. "You own a dog, sir?"

Rockwell was like a mime imitating a statue.

"I got me a pit bull on Monday. On Tuesday I got me a prosthetic arm."

The clock ticked.

"Hey, I must be horizontally parked in a parallel universe."

Nothing.

Pete's dad had given him a Henny Youngman joke book for Christmas when he was thirteen, and Pete memorized the whole thing, to get a handle on rapid-fire delivery. Save me Henny!

"Are you a gambler, sir? Because I only gamble for laughs. Last week I laughed away my car."

.

.

.

"Hey, what do you send to a sick florist?"

.

.

.

"I went to see a psychiatrist. He says, 'Tell me everything.' I did. Now he's doing my act."

.

.

.

Pete tossed out five more one liners, the best of the best.

Nothing but dead air in return.

Fifteen minutes to go. Pete hadn't even gotten a nose wrinkle out of Rockwell.

The avalanche was cascading. Closer, closer.

Pete cast a desperate look at Guy. Who winked. Was that encouragement?

Okay, time to bring out the jokes about wives. Considering the context of this whole performance was a cheating wife (and a comedian who'd just made a mistake, right?), maybe he could eke out one sardonic laugh from Mr. Rockwell. It was worth a shot. Nothing else was hitting the mark.

"And what's the deal with wives?" Pete said. "My ex kept complaining she didn't feel wanted. So I went down to the post office and put up her picture."

Wait. Was that a crack in Rockwell's face?

"Yeah, my ex, what can I say? She should go into earthquake work. She can find a fault quicker than anybody."

Did Rockwell's cheek just move?

"I decided one day I wanted to get something for my wife, but nobody started the bidding."

Rockwell's eyes narrowed. Was he trying hard not to laugh?

"You know how I proposed to my wife? I said, You're gonna have a *what*?"

Rockwell's lips tightened.

"I met her in college, where she was voted Most Likely to Succeed With Anybody."

Rockwell's face returned to its former stoic aspect. So what had just happened? Why did his face do all that. It was almost as if the guy had simply passed gas.

Passed gas . . .

"Hey, did we just have some thunder from down under?"

No laugh, no smile, no twitch, no mercy.

"Is somebody hunting ducks?"

Nothing.

Ten minutes left.

Pete tried sex jokes for two minutes, ethnic jokes for three, channeling Don Rickles. He did some Seinfeld, some Steven Wright.

"I used to work in a fire hydrant factory. You couldn't park anywhere near the place."

Nada from Rockwell.

With one minute left Pete's heart was pounding like a bilge pump. His mind went blank. He opened his mouth but nothing came out.

He looked at Guy. There was almost something like sympathy in the bodyguard's face.

He looked at the clock.

Fifteen second to go!

He didn't have anything left. He felt like the man in the desert, desperately crawling toward an oasis that turned out to be a mirage. He was spent, finished...dead.

And that's when Rockwell laughed.

Pete looked at the clock. Five seconds left!

"Well, well," Rockwell said. "Look at that, will you? I laughed. It doesn't matter that it wasn't at your jokes. It doesn't matter that I was laughing at your pitiful, unfunny, slimy, worthless self. I laughed." He got up from the chair and strolled to the French doors leading to the balcony and opened them. "And so I'll say good-night. Guy, show The Harv out, will you?"

Wait, what?

It came to him then, the whole thing, the set up, the torture, the false relief...and now a push over the ledge.

He felt Guy's hand grip his arm.

Pete pulled it away. "We had a deal."

Rockwell sighed. "I said I'd get you to the top. Well, this is the top. Show our guest out."

Survival instinct kicked in. There was only one way out, the front door. But that meant getting past Guy, standing there like a brick wall. No matter. This was life or certain death. When he played basketball in high school he was known for his quickness. He thought of Guy then as a lumbering opposing player. The element of surprise might do it. All this clicked in Pete's mind in a millisecond.

He made his move. A head fake to the right, a dash to the left and—

—the big, meaty hand of the bodyguard grabbed his shirt and pulled him to a dead stop. Guy held him now like a sack of cats.

"Go on," Rockwell said.

"Hang on a second," Guy said.

"What?" Rockwell said.

"I mean, you did laugh. That was the deal. And besides, I think he's kind of funny."

"I don't pay you to think. Throw him out!"

"I don't think I will," Guy said.

That thing about time standing still, it was real. Pete's arms and legs were hot jelly on a summer picnic table.

And when Rockwell pulled a gun out of his robe pocket, the rest of Pete melted, too.

Guy dropped him.

Pete hit the floor and covered up, like a trench soldier waiting for a bomb to go off.

Bam.

Bam.

Pete didn't move. What just happened? The only sound now was moaning. He dared a look, and saw Guy sprawled on the floor, his gun in hand and a red splotch soaking his shirt. Guy was the one moaning.

Rockwell was across the room, crumpled on the floor, the gun by his side.

Guy's guttural voice slid out of his mouth. "Get...out..." His eyes closed and his head lolled to the side.

Pete got out.

Adrianna was wiping down the bar top when Pete came in. He went to a stool at the other end, sat, stared straight ahead.

"Hey there, kiddo," Adrianna said.

Pete said nothing. She went to him. His face was as pale as a cocktail napkin.

"Pete? You okay?"

"Okay?" he said distantly. A smile creased his face, then he laughed. He rocked his head back, looked at the ceiling and laughed some more.

"So it went good?" Adrianna said. "Your set?"

Pete's laugh hitched up another notch. Then he lowered his head and took a deep breath.

"I killed," he said.

"Sweet!' Adrianna said. "You're on your way!"

AUTUMNAL

Mullin heard the man before he saw him. The crunch of sticks, meaning the man was off the trail and coming through the trees.

The soft whisper of the stream, where Mullin had just dropped his line, was the only counterpoint to the disturbance of nature's floor.

Mullin turned in the little camping chair he'd just set up a few minutes before.

The man was about Mullin's size, six one or two, and maybe in the same ballpark age-wise, forty. He wore hiking boots and short pants, in keeping with the warmth of the September day in the Los Padres National Forest. His shirt was red plaid and his face and skin tanned and leathery. He wore a black baseball hat with an Oakland Raiders logo on it.

On his back was what looked like a full pack with sleeping bag on top and a fishing pole attached to the side. He wore a sheathed knife on his belt, standard for fishermen, along with a dangling cloth strip with several fishhooks on it.

"How you doin'?" the man said.

I'm doing just fine alone, Mullin thought. Fine and dandy and not wanting to talk to anybody else right now, thank you very much. When his father had taught him to fish as a boy, he'd told Mullin it was the grandest way to calm the nerves and the soul. His father had been right about that. And ever since his father died Mullin always fished alone.

"They bitin'?" the man asked. He took off his pack and set it down, as if he was going to pitch camp right there with Mullin, as if they were old high school buddies out on a trip together.

"Not today, it seems," Mullin lied. He hadn't been here long enough to find out.

"Well, sometimes you got to tickle 'em so they come out laughing."

What did that even mean?

"You from around here?" the man said.

Mullin didn't answer. He wanted the hesitation to work as a hint, a nudge to the guy to move along.

"I'm from San Jose," the guy said. "Rob's my name." He put out his hand.

Well, a guy puts out a hand, you have to take it, or risk being seen as a total jerk. And Mullin never liked being taken for one of those.

"Greg," Mullin said, shaking the guy's hand. It was a firm grip Rob had, and skin like a leather glove.

"Let me see if I can stir up a party," Rob said. He unloosed the pole from his backpack and checked it. A red lure, maybe a Jacobin, flashed in the sunlight. "The trout just love these," Rob said. "They're new, and I'm betting the fish down here don't know about 'em yet. You do know the fish get together every night and talk about the latest lures and bait and gimcracks being used, don't you?"

"Didn't know that," Mullin said.

"Why do you think they're called *schools*? So you have to keep one step ahead of 'em, and that is sure what I do. You might say keeping one step ahead is what I do for a living."

"Oh?"

"I'm in real estate. Talk about having to keep ahead of the game. The way things are."

So what are you doing on a Wednesday, up in the mountains, fishing?

"I guess you're wondering what I'm doing out here with a fishing pole in my hand," Rob said.

Now that is seriously weird, Mullin thought.

Rob said, "I'll tell you. The way I work it, I go sixteen, eighteen hours a day, maybe a month at a time. Including weekends. I go and go and then I take two days off. Two whole days. And this is one of them."

"Sort of like a super Sabbath," Mullin said.

"Huh?"

"You know, the Sabbath."

"I'm not Jewish, if that's what you mean," Rob said.

"I didn't mean that. What I meant was, God knew what he was doing when he instituted the Sabbath rest. Once a week, no work, just thinking about God."

"I guess you're Jewish then, huh?" Rob asked.

"Half Jewish," Mullin said. "My mom."

"Well, that still entitles you."

"To what?" Mullin asked.

"Jewish humor," Rob said. "You Jews have all the best jokes. And Yiddish, too. I can't tell jokes about you getting things wholesale, 'cause that'd make me seem like a bigot. But you can, because you're making fun of your own people. Man, I envy you."

"I've never even thought about that."

"You should. It's a great thing to have, boy, all those jokes. Like, what does a Jew get if he touches a frog?"

"What?"

"Schwartz."

The only sound was the river, and it wasn't laughing.

"So you think I'm a bigot?" Rob said.

"I don't know you," Mullin said.

"I'm not. I'll tell you, I hate all races pretty much the same."

Again, the river did not laugh.

Rob said, "Okay, tell you what. I'll stop with the jokes if we can have a little conversation."

"You know," Mullin said, "I was really hoping—"

"I know, I know, but we're out in the middle of nowhere, and frankly I'd feel a little more secure with some company. You heard about those two hikers about thirty miles from here?"

"No."

"Oh man!"

"What?"

"I don't even want to talk about it," Rob said. "I get all I can take in my stories."

"Stories?"

"I like to read crime stories, mysteries and stuff. In fact, it's funny, you and me meeting like this."

"What's funny about it?" Mullin asked.

"It's like a story I read once, by a guy named Lawrence Block, about two guys fishing and . . . there I go again. I wasn't going to run off at the mouth. I wanted a little conversation."

He'd finished attaching his lure and now cast it, with an expert flick of the wrist, into the waters of the river.

And said nothing.

It was Mullin who broke the silence. "What about . . ."

Rob turned his head toward him. "Hm?"

"What about those two hikers?"

"You really don't want to know."

"Now I do. Come on. You have to tell me now."

Rob paused, then said, "All right, look. This is a strange world we live in, it never ceases to amaze me. They found these two hikers, a guy and a girl, students at Stanford. They'd gone missing, so they sent out a search team and they finally found them. Bodies decomposed, of course, but the forensics people said they'd been murdered."

"Murdered? How?"

With his index finger Rob made a quick cutting motion across his throat.

"Whoa," Mullin said.

"But that's not all," Rob said. "They found something really awful."

"That's not awful enough?"

"They found that they'd been gutted—"

"Oh no—"

"I told you wouldn't want to hear it, but now it's out, so there it is. They'd been gutted and there was a little fire pit nearby."

"Fire pit?"

"You know, like a campfire."

"Don't tell me . . ."

"That's right," Rob said. "They found a couple of sharp sticks and, well, they determined that the killer had himself a little meal."

Mullin said nothing. He guessed now this guy was here to stay a long while, and there was no getting around that. All you want to do sometimes is be alone. You want to plan who joins you, not have to make talk with an intruder. Especially when he starts talking about a killing like that one.

Rob said, "I mean, what does it say when you can't come out here and enjoy nature without worrying about something like that happening? That someone will take a knife and, well, you know." As he said this, Rob put his pole on the ground and smoothly slipped his knife out of its sheath. "I mean, doesn't that make you think twice?" Rob held the knife, about a four inch Buck from the look of it, up in the air.

Mullin took a deep breath, let it out.

Rob smiled.

"Not really," Mullin said. "The killer was more likely to use this." From under the chair, Mullin pulled out his own knife, a nine-inch fillet.

Rob's eyes went wide, wider still as Mullin plunged the knife into the middle of Rob's gut. His mouth opened but no sound issued. Mullin cut upward with the knife, turned it within the flesh, then sliced horizontally. Rob's eyes and mouth closed for good.

Rob had been pretty close, Mullin mused. The actual distance from the last time Mullin had performed his surgery was precisely twenty-eight point two miles. And he had a nice spot picked out thirteen point eight miles to the east. But it would be Mullin who chose who was next. He did not like having such choices thrust upon him.

That was not restful at all.

Mullin reeled in his line and started making preparations for a fire.

MY FIRST MURDER

When she came through the door I almost dropped my mocha latte.

"Is Mr. Beddoe available?" she said through her floral-design face covering. Her smooth black hair was straight and long. If I'd had to guess I would have pegged her at twenty-three or four.

"Not at the moment," I said, fumbling to a standing position. I'd had my feet on the desk and managed to knock over a stack of files. "Maybe I can help you."

She hesitated, her lavender eyes giving me the once-over. She looked at the scattered papers on the floor. "You really think so?"

"Please have a seat." I motioned to the one client chair in the office. She was wearing a white-lace, cold-shoulder top over blue skinny jeans and black leather pumps.

I'm a detective. I notice things.

Plus, she was hard not to notice.

"My name is Kyle Cullen," I said.

"Tiana Raven."

"You can take off your mask if you want to. We believe in oxygen."

"Are you sure?" Tiana Raven said.

"If I keel over, you don't have to pay me."

I couldn't tell if she smiled. Masks are taking away our ability to figure out our fellow human beings.

She slipped her mask off.

And I figured her out in a hurry. With full lips to go with high cheek-bones and those eyes, I knew she could get a guy to do pretty much anything.

And I was a guy who needed something to do.

———

For the record, I was working for Don Beddoe, middle-aged and paunchy owner of Beddoe Investigations. *Nobody Snoops Better Than Beddoe.* I'm twenty-eight and after three years trying to get somewhere with an electro-funk band I decided to do what I always dreamed of—become a private investigator.

They still exist. Most do insurance work. In the old days divorce work was common, but that was before no-fault divorces, when adultery actu-ally meant something. Sure, every now and then you get a girlfriend who wants to find out what her boyfriend does every other weekend in Laguna. (Hint: It's usually not fishing.) But those are rare. Even rarer now with the woohoo virus keeping everybody locked up.

I got the bug to be a PI watching old movies with my grandfather. He was a fan of 1940s film noir. Bogart, Dick Powell, Robert Mitchum. He was a Korean War vet who settled in the lush San Fernando Valley of Los Angeles and worked for Rocketdyne when the aerospace industry was booming.

My mom and dad live in Downey, though not in the same house. They got divorced when I was in middle school. The split did a number on me, and visiting Grandad was one of the things that got me through it.

Of course the reality of PI life is completely different than in the old movies and TV shows. Most of this work is dull. That is, when you get it. And we needed to get it. Since the pandemic hit, and the protests and riots, things were dicey for our little office on the second story of a strip mall in Hollywood. The landlord was making eviction noises. The boss was out of town and I was left watching the store.

Then came Tiana Raven, who looked like someone who could pay.

"So tell me what brought you here today?" I said.

She paused. "Do you really work here?"

Okay, so I don't exactly look like a typical professional snoop. I was wearing a Def Leppard T-shirt, shorts, and flip-flops. Suffice to say I wasn't expecting any walk-in clients.

"I assure you I am licensed and experienced," I said. "I've been with this firm six months."

"And you've handled actual cases?"

"If I don't, I don't eat. What kind of case is yours?"

She crossed her legs. "I want you to find a certain person and beat him to death."

I just stared at her. Her face was emotionless and stunning.

Then she smiled.

Oh, that smile. It shot into my bloodstream and spiked my pulse.

"Of course I'm kidding," she said.

"Did you come here to joke around?" I said.

"You don't have to get snarky. I just wanted you to know how I feel about this guy."

"And what guy would that be?"

"His name is Tommy Ludlow."

"I take it you don't like him."

"I hate him."

"What has he done to deserve your ire?" I like using words like *ire* every now and then. Makes people think I went to college.

"He's spending my money!" Tiana Raven said. "And I want it to stop."

"How does he have access to your money?"

"It's like this," she said. "My dad was very rich. He built up his own company during the internet boom. He sent me to private schools and then to Dartmouth, but I dropped out. I didn't see the point. I didn't need a college degree to do what I want to do."

"Which is?"

"Design clothes. Do you like what I'm wearing?"

I cleared my throat and tried not to stammer. "Very … nice."

"You can do better than that."

"Really very nice."

She sighed. "Anyway, my mom died when I was sixteen. Daddy married again, a woman much younger, of course. What they used to call a trophy wife."

"What do you call her?"

"A witch. We never got along. I knew she was after Daddy's money."

"Unfortunately, your father gets to make his own choices."

"Used to," Tiana Raven said. "He died last year."

"I'm sorry."

"He was a Type-A personality, like me. His heart gave out. Anyway, come to find out he set up a trust for me. A trust! I get an allowance, but the bulk of the estate doesn't come to me until I'm thirty."

"How many years away is that?"

"Seven," she said.

"How much are we talking?"

"Six million, give or take."

"You can't wait seven years for six mil?"

"That's just it," she said. "I don't think the money will be there, the way they're spending it."

"Your stepmom and this Tommy guy?"

"Don't call her my stepmother! Her name is Kira Hobbes. She calls herself Kira Hobbes-Raven. And yes, she and Tommy Ludlow are spending the money."

"Which means Kira is the trustee, with access to the funds?"

"Bingo."

"There are laws on the books for that," I said. "Breach of fiduciary duty, for one thing."

"Lawyers! All tangled up in court, and Kira can afford the best! She claims it's all for my benefit, too! Daddy had a little startup company when he died. Tommy worked for it. Kira was vice president. Controlling interest went to her. Now she's calling Board meetings in Cabo, and Tommy is urging her to buy a couple of private jets. In seven years, what will be left? I just want somebody to scare off Tommy and warn Kira. Can you do anything like that?"

"I can have a talk with one or both," I said. "I can lay out a pretty good line of talk. We have a relationship with a lawyer down the way. He's an animal. If they don't listen to reason, I can unleash him. For a fee, of course."

"Of course," Tiana said. "How much will this cost me?"

"For something like this, a retainer of fifteen hundred. Part of that will be for the lawyer, if needed. If not, you'll get that portion back. Then we'll have per diem expenses. I can write up a—"

"Do you take Visa?"

———

Ever since the MeToo movement morphed from helping victims of sexual assault into an attack on masculine biology, guys my age are not supposed to notice beautiful women. Or mention it if we do.

Too bad. I'm mentioning it. This was the greatest credit card payment I've ever taken, and not because her plastic card was good looking.

Transaction done, I asked her where I could find Tommy Ludlow.

"I'll take you to him," Tiana said.

"You want to be there when I talk to him?"

"Why not?"

"It might be uncomfortable for you."

"I want him to see me. To know I'm serious. Any objection?"

"You're the one who's paying."

"We'll take my car," she said, and five minutes later we were on the freeway in her Jag.

As we headed to the Valley, I said, "What else can you tell me about Tommy?"

"He's about ten years younger than Kira. Not too smart. But then again, neither is Kira."

"Any chance it's true love?" I said.

"If you believe in the Tooth Fairy."

"What? There's no Tooth Fairy?"

"Shut up," she said. "You should know that Tommy's in shape. He's around thirty, works out all the time. I wouldn't let things get physical if I were you. You're half his size."

"I prefer to use superior brain power," I said.

"That won't be an issue," she said. "Tommy's a few peas short of a casserole."

I filed that away as we drove on. She took the Vineland off-ramp and headed toward Burbank. At California Street she took a right. The street was lined with well-kept, middle-class homes. She pulled to a stop in front of a Spanish-style house. There was a black Escalade in the driveway.

"This is it," she said. "What's the plan?"

"We could start by knocking on the door," I said.

"Good plan."

There was no answer after three knocks. I took a look through the front window. The curtain was open just enough so I could see inside. Things were a little dim, but I made out two comfortable chairs, a sofa, and a body. The body had a knife sticking out of the back.

"Take a look," I said. "Is that our guy?"

Tiana came over and peered through the window. "That's him," she said with no particular emotion.

"We need to call the police," I said.

"I suppose," she said.

A voice said. "Why? What's wrong?"

It was a man in a T-shirt tucked into his shorts. He had a copious gut, which means he should never tuck his T-shirts into his shorts, or anything else for that matter. He was around fifty. Maybe twenty years ago he'd had the build of a bull. He was soft now, though he looked like he could charge in a pinch. He was wearing a mask.

"Who are you?" I asked.

"I got the same question for you," he said.

"Neighbor?"

"I might be," he said. "Now who are you?"

Tiana said, "None of your d—"

I put my hand up to stop her. "I'm an investigator, and the man inside is dead."

"Dead?" the man said. "Tommy?"

"I have to call the police," I said.

"Do it."

I made the call. As we waited for the cops, the man told me his name was Carl Huston. Then a woman came out of the house next door and joined us. Carl introduced her as Hayden Willingham. She was quite a bit younger than Carl, with blonde hair and pale blue eyes. Her figure was plentiful. She had a mask on, too. Carl told her what was happening.

"So upsetting," Hayden Willingham said. "Such a nice neighborhood."

"How well did you know Tommy?" I said.

"Just to say hi to," Carl said. "Seemed like a nice guy."

"And you?" I asked Hayden.

"And me what?" she said.

"How well did you know Tommy?"

"What is that supposed to mean?" she said.

"Yeah," Carl said, "what is that supposed to mean?"

"I'm an investigator," I said. "I ask questions. I'm good at it."

Carl said, "Now you can start answering a few."

He pointed at the LAPD SUV pulling into the driveway.

———

The two uniforms wore masks. A man and a woman. Latino. I gave them the rundown. They each looked in the window. The male officer took out his gun and told us all to stay where we were. He went around the side of the house.

The female officer stayed at the window, looking in, hand on her sidearm.

A couple of minutes later the male officer opened the front door. "Clear," he said. "Call homicide."

Ten minutes later a homicide detective arrived. His name was Caravaggio. He was dressed in a black shirt and black slacks. He was as lean as a felt-tip pen. He wore a mask.

I introduced myself and gave him a card.

"You work for Beddoe, eh?" he said.

"Nobody snoops better," I said.

"I don't like private snoops," he said. "They make things complicated."

"You'll get no complications from me," I said.

"We'll see," he said. "Stick around."

He went inside for a look at the body. A few minutes later the crime scene unit rolled in. It was like being on the set of a CSI show, only without the donuts and free coffee.

Eventually, Caravaggio came back out and took statements from Tiana and me. I asked him if he knew the time of death, and he said the ME put it at between eleven last night and two this morning. He gave us his card and told us he'd be following up soon.

As we drove away Tiana said, "So what do we do now?"

"You talk like you're my partner," I said.

"I'm paying you, aren't I?"

"I prefer to work this alone, if you don't mind."

"What if I do mind?" she said.

"Then you can have your money back," I said, but did so with a lump the size of a wadded hundred-dollar bill in my throat.

Tiana didn't say anything. She cast me a glance. I thought I saw something in that glance. Something Lauren Bacall-ish. I'm no Bogie, and it was probably just my imagination, but was there a hint of admiration in that look? Probably not.

"Keep the money," she said. "What will *you* do next?"

"With Tommy dead," I said, "part of your problem is solved. That still leaves Kira and the spending. It also leaves her, I would venture, as a suspect in Tommy's murder."

Tiana said nothing.

I said nothing.

"What is it?" Tiana said.

"What's what?"

"You look like you want to say something."

"I do."

"So say it."

I said, "You may turn out to be a suspect."

For a long moment she was silent, her mesmerizing eyes fixated on the road. "I guess you're right. I better have an alibi. How much will one cost?"

"Huh?"

She laughed. "I love kidding you. I didn't kill Tommy. I was with friends yesterday. I spent the night at Leila's. We made a pitcher of margaritas and watched a movie."

"What movie?" I said.

"What movie?"

"That's what I said."

"Oh yeah. I get it. Alibi. Okay, it was *Bridget Jones's Diary*."

"An oldie," I said.

"So?"

"Did you stream it or DVD it?"

"Um, I think DVD."

"You *think*?"

"I was drunk!"

"Okay," I said, "were there other people you know of who Tommy was involved with? Criminal types?"

"I don't know."

"Where did he work?"

"At a health club."

"You know the name of the club?"

"I think it had the word Spartan in it."

"Spartan Dan's?"

"That's it."

"See? I'm a pretty good detective after all."

She smiled. "You'll do."

"Where is Kira now, if you know?" I said.

"Still in Daddy's house, of course. Prime property."

"I should give her a visit."

"I'll let you do that one on your own," Tiana said. "I can't stand the sight of her."

She dropped me at my office and drove off. I stood there wishing she hadn't.

I wrote up a report for the chronology on the new case. Then the walls started closing in. I drove home to my apartment on Ivar and mixed myself a drink—milk and Bosco. I played Madden for a couple of hours, cooked a frozen pizza, and watched *Pitfall,* a 1948 noir with Dick Powell, Lizabeth Scott and Raymond Burr. Such is the glamorous life of a detective.

———

Next morning at the office I found my boss, Don Beddoe, sitting at the front desk and tapping away at the computer.

Without looking up, he said, "Is she hot?"

"What?"

"She. The girl. Tiana Raven."

"How did you—"

"Sit down, kid." He turned from the computer and faced me. Don likes floppy Hawaiian shirts, and this one was all splashy yellow flowers and green palm trees. Bald on top with a goatee that is mostly gray, Don Beddoe would make a great lawn gnome.

He said, "You left the client retainer letter on the desk. I saw you also got us a Visa payment. Your car is still out front. I figure you had to be with this Tiana babe. She is a babe, right? Anybody named Tiana Raven has to be."

"I'm not going to lie," I said.

"And what was the first darn thing I taught you?"

"Never get personally involved with a client."

"And the second?"

"Get the money up front."

"So it sounds like you're one out of two," Don said.

"Hey, I can handle it."

"You recall our agreement? It states I can take over any case in the office, right?"

My face got hot. "I said I can handle it!"

"Okay," Don said, raising his hands. "Cool down and tell me what the case is all about."

I told him.

"Murder, eh?" Don said. "Technically, that's not our problem. Unless, of course, the police consider you a person of interest."

"Why would they think that?"

Don shrugged. "They think a lot of things to cover their behinds. But you will have an alibi, right?"

"Of course."

"Not of course. Do you know what time the crime was committed?"

"The ME says between eleven and two in the morning."

"You showed up at this house with Tiana Raven."

"Yeah."

"And the neighbors saw you."

"Yeah."

"Do you know if they saw you drive up? Or walk up to the house?"

"I don't know any of that."

"How do you propose to proceed?"

"Tiana wants to protect her trust money from her stepmother. She doesn't want to go to court about it, which is what she should do. I was supposed to try to convince Ludlow to lay off the spending spree he was on with Kira Hobbes-Raven."

"I can't get over these names," Don said.

"Guess that leaves me with a murder to solve and a runaway trustee to rein in."

"Wait just a darn minute," Don said. "You don't have to solve any murder."

"I don't?"

"Why would you?"

"Because…"

Don smiled. "Because it's a murder, and you're a PI, and you just assumed. But you were hired to talk to a guy, and now he's dead. You have no reason to look into it. It's a police matter now."

I shook my head.

"I know it's disappointing," Don said. "Nothing like a real, honest-to-goodness corpse to get the blood flowing. Don't worry. There'll be other stiffs."

Just then the office phone rang. Don waited for me to do my duty and answer.

I picked up. "Beddoe Investigations. Nobody snoops better than Beddoe."

"Kyle!"

"Tiana?"

"Help me!"

"Where are you?"

"Arrested! At the Hollywood Police station. They say I killed Tommy! Please come help me!"

She hung up.

Don saw my blanched face. "What is it, kid?"

"Tiana's been arrested for the murder of Tommy Ludlow."

"What?"

"Yeah," I said. "I guess now I really do have a murder to solve."

"Your first."

"Have to start sometime," I said.

"Be careful," Don said. "Be very, very careful. Don't let this little vixen tempt you into her web."

I had to smile. "You make this sound like a real film noir."

He smiled, too. "Isn't that why you and I got into this business in the first place?"

————

At the Hollywood Station I gave a card to one of the two uniforms at the front desk. He said I had to put a mask on. I whipped out my bandana and put on my Old West bank robber look. He told me to wait, then went through a door into the bowels of the station. He came back and took me to an interview room where Tiana sat at a table.

"Kyle!"

"Hang on," I said. I waited until the door was closed and sat in one of the two chairs on my side of the table. "Have you talked to anybody yet?"

She shook her head. "Kyle, get me out of here. There's—"

I put a finger to my lips. "Don't say anything. They've got this place wired, and anything you say can be used against you."

"But—"

I shook my head.

A minute later Detective Caravaggio came in. "Smart boy," he said.

"Just protecting my client," I said.

"You mind if I ask her some questions?"

"Is she free to go?"

"No."

"Then she is invoking her right to remain silent, aren't you, Tiana?"

"I guess," Tiana said.

"Don't guess," I said. "You have to be unambiguous about it, or Detective Caravecchio—"

"Caravaggio," he said.

"—will be able to use anything he gets. So tell him you wish to remain silent, and you wish to get an attorney."

"Who?" she said.

"Remember that lawyer I was telling you about?"

She nodded.

"I'll give him a call," I said. "Meantime, don't say anything to anybody, understand?"

She nodded.

"Smart boy," Caravaggio said.

I went outside and called Mark Turnbull, who has a one-man law office a few doors down from Beddoe Investigations. You may have heard his radio commercials. He calls himself "The Hammer." His tagline is "Don't let them nail you." His voicemail picked up. *You've reached the law office of Mark "The Hammer" Turnbull. If you're in jail, tell me where and don't talk to anybody till I get there. If you've been in an acci-*

dent, don't talk to any insurance company until I talk to you first. Leave a
message."

"Mark, Kyle Cullen. Got a client, Tiana Raven, being held at Hollywood Station. Suspicion of murder. Bogus. She's got an alibi. Get down
there soon as you can, and we'll work out our usual details later."

———————

I drove over to Studio City to Spartan Dan's Health Club. Like most of the
health clubs in California, it had spent tens of thousands of dollars when
the governor said they could reopen. Then the governor yanked the rug out
from all the restaurants, gyms and salons, going back to lockdown. He
issued his orders after working out in the gym at his 12,000 square foot
mansion in a gated community.

When I walked in, the purple-haired and masked receptionist said,
"Sorry, we aren't open. But we are taking reserv—"

"I'm not here to break a sweat," I said. "I want to talk to the owner. Is
he around?"

"Um, I'll see," she said. "Would you mind putting on a mask?"

"I would mind, yes. I'm about eight feet away from you. If I start to
sing an aria, I'll back up a few more steps."

Her eyebrows formed the downward arc of disapproval. She picked up
a handset and spoke into it.

A moment later a guy with biceps the size of soccer balls came
through an inner door. He wore a tank top over his tanning-booth skin. His
mask was black with a skull on it. He was my height—six feet—but if I
curled up I could have fit into his chest.

"Can I help you?" he said.

"My name's Kyle Cullen. I'm a private investigator."

"Yeah, sure."

"Are you Spartan Dan?" I said.

"So?"

"You're not going to kick me into a cistern and shout 'This is Sparta!'
are you?"

If I'd had X-ray vision, I think I might have seen a slight smile under
his mask.

"You like *300*?" he said.

"One of my favorite movies," I said.

"You could use some training," he said. "A lot of it."

"Maybe I'll take you up on that," I said. "What I'm here about is Tommy Ludlow."

Spartan Dan shrugged his shoulders.

"Didn't he work here?" I said.

"I don't have to answer your questions," he said.

"Is there a reason you won't?"

"Privacy," he said. "I believe in it."

"Me, too. I also believe in justice."

"What's that supposed to mean?" Spartan Dan said.

"Tommy Ludlow is dead," I said.

The receptionist yelped.

Spartan Dan stared at me for a moment. I wished I could have seen his jaw muscles. You can get some good tells that way.

He said, "When?"

"Some time yesterday."

"How?"

"Murdered."

The receptionist yelped again.

"Maybe you better come in my office," Spartan Dan said.

"Maybe I'd better," I said.

———

His office had framed photos of bodybuilders all over the walls. He sat behind a desk with some trophies on it.

"Tommy was a good guy," he said. "A little wild sometimes, but everybody here loved him."

"Did he have any run-ins with anybody?"

"Not that I recall."

"How well did you know him?"

"We didn't hang out a lot together. It was mostly just here at work. But we had some talks."

"What did you talk about?"

"Lots of different things."

"As for instance?"

"I don't know, sports. Food."

"Women?"

"Sure."

"Did he have a girlfriend?"

"He did mention seeing someone. I got the impression she was an older woman."

"What gave you that impression?"

"He said he was dating an older woman."

"Ah," I said. "Did he mention her name?"

Spartan Dan shook his head.

"Does the name Kira Hobbes-Raven mean anything to you?" I said.

He shook his head again.

I said, "Let me ask, and this is just me being a private investigator, with a license and all, but did you ever get sideways with Tommy Ludlow?"

His eyes narrowed. "No."

"Never?"

"I just told you," he said.

"Would your receptionist out there say the same thing?"

He didn't answer. He looked like he wanted to power-lift me and spin me around a few times. He opened a drawer and took out a set of nunchucks. He placed them on the desk.

"That's all for today," he said.

I put one of my cards on his desk. "If you happen to think of anything."

"I won't," he said.

As I drove toward Brentwood I got a call from Mark "The Hammer" Turnbull.

"Well, I talked to her," he said. "Her alibi didn't fly."

"What!"

"Yeah, they questioned her friend, the one she supposedly spent the night with, and the friend cracked. Said Tiana left about eleven, and was tanked on margaritas. So they're holding her overnight. She'll see a judge tomorrow, and she'll probably be denied bail."

"So what did she tell you? Did she do it?"

"I never ask my clients if they did it. I get their story and find the evidence that fits. If we don't find any, I may have to recommend she plead to manslaughter."

"This is so crazy."

"You're stuck on her, eh?"

"Did I say that?"

"You didn't have to. Where are you headed now?"

"I'm going to talk to the stepmother."

"Whoa."

"What?"

"Hold on there."

"Why?"

"We need to talk," he said.

"About what?"

"You're going to be talking to someone who may or may not be helpful to my client."

"*Our* client," I said.

"Whatever. Pull over somewhere and let me call you back with some strategy. This is where I shine."

So I got off the freeway and drove through a Jack-in-the-Box. I parked on the street and ate curly fries and drank a Coke.

The Hammer called me back. We strategized. He suggested a few questions for me to ask. I was ready to ask them.

———

Kira Hobbes-Raven lived in a house in the hills of Studio City, overlooking the Valley. It was an obviously remodeled, mid-century modern showcase home, fit for a very rich man with a hot young wife. Two perfectly matched palm trees near the front door looked like they'd been planted by a studio prepping a set for a *Gilligan's Island* re-boot.

I gave the big oak door a healthy knock.

A moment later a voice came out of a hidden speaker. "Who is it?"

"Kira Hobbes-Raven?" I said.

"What do you want?"

"My name is Kyle Cullen. I'm here on behalf of your stepdaughter."

"What's this about?"

"She's in jail," I said.

"So?"

"I thought you might be able to help."

"I have nothing to do with Tiana."

"You don't even know what she's in for," I said.

"I don't care to," she said.

"It's for the murder of Tommy Ludlow."

There was a long silence. Then the door unlocked and opened.

Kira Hobbes-Raven had blond hair, cut into a bob with wispy layers that flared out at the ends. Her face was round and smooth, a testimony to a surgeon's touch. I would have advised her collagen implanter to pull back a bit on the lips. The pouty look would have been much better if she were twenty years younger. She was wearing a cotton shirt with a leopard print, white pants, and white sandals. She looked ready for a yacht party.

Except that she had astonishment in her brown eyes. "How?"

"You mean you don't know?"

She shook her head.

"Can I come in?" I said.

"You're not wearing a mask," she said.

"No."

"Why not?"

"Because I'm sane."

Her eyebrows went up.

"I need to know," she said, and let me in. And then, for a moment, I thought she might faint.

"Are you all right?" I said.

"No," she said. "Who are you again?"

"Kyle Cullen. I'm a private investigator."

"I have to … what do you …"

"Can we sit down?"

She showed me to the spacious living room. Everything was white except the black, curvy furniture and all the fixtures. Sunlight poured in from big windows that looked out at an infinity pool in the back yard.

I sat in one of the plush chairs. She sat on the sofa.

"I didn't hear anything about this," she said. "When did it happen?"

"Some time yesterday," I said. "Tiana and I went to his house to talk to him. When we got there, I saw through the window that he was dead. The police came and took over. And later arrested Tiana."

"That little b——"

"She didn't do it."

"How do you know?"

I really didn't know, did I? Don Beddoe would not be pleased with me. But Mark "The Hammer" Turnbull would be.

I said, "I am just trying to find out the facts. It's no secret to anyone that you and Tommy Ludlow were more than just friends."

"So what? That's nobody's business."

"It is if you were draining trust funds."

Fire flashed in those brown eyes. She stood. And cursed like a stevedore.

"Get out of here!" she said.

"This is not a good reaction—"

She cursed like a longshoreman then, which is very similar to a stevedore.

I got up. "I advise you not to touch those funds."

"I advise you to get out of my house!"

It was a pretty good comeback line. I got out.

And when the door was closed I went around to the side of the house. Don Beddoe taught me a favorite trick of his, checking garbage. People throw away the most interesting and revealing things. The only downside is you have to root around in trash. Not my favorite thing, but Tiana was in jail and hey, I just happened to be here. I just hoped Kira Hobbes-Raven wouldn't stroll out and curse at me again. My ears hurt.

I checked the black receptacle. There were a couple of plastic trash bags in there, tied neatly at the top. I tore them open and got a lot of coffee grounds on my hands for my troubles. Nothing of interest there except that Kira apparently had a thing for Kashi 7-Grain waffles.

There was nothing in the blue recycle bin. Maybe I'd have to report her for not being more careful separating her refuse.

There was no reason to check the green, but just to be complete I took a look. It was full of cut grass. I started digging around in it. I moved a bunch of grass to one side, then the other.

And saw a white cloth. I grabbed it by the corner and pulled it out. Blades of grass clung to it. I shook it hard once and most of the grass fell off.

It was a white hand towel. Nothing very interesting about it, except for the blood.

———

Of course I should have notified the cops, but they're not exactly speedy in the analysis department. I was, because I knew Anthony Morrelli.

Tony Morrelli used to be a doctor. Then his license was taken away after he was discovered to perform surgeries while high on cocaine. None of the surgeries were unsuccessful, but the medical board did not see that as a mitigating circumstance.

Now he runs an under-the-table crime lab for people like me. His lab is in his garage in a house out in Eagle Rock.

Tony answered his door holding a shotgun. He's about five -four, with a spray of gray hair and permanently hunched shoulders.

"Don't shoot," I said.

"You never know," he said. "Come in."

I explained the situation to him and showed him the towel.

"You want the blood type, right?"

"DNA if you can."

"DNA'll cost you five thousand. Blood type, two hundred."

"Let's go with blood type," I said.

"Somehow I knew," he said. "Now get lost so I can work."

———

A detective's mind works overtime. It keeps moving around the puzzle pieces and tries to see the bigger picture. There was one forming in my mind, but too many pieces were missing.

I went back to the office and tried not to think of Tiana. That was a no go. Her face kept popping up in Dolby Vision on my brain. I finally had to go out for a walk.

Which was like a visit to the zombie apocalypse. In our little strip mall there were five spaces available for rent. The little mom-and-pop Chinese restaurant I liked to frequent was gone, a victim of the irrational ham-fisted lockdown rules in Los Angeles. It's okay to get on an airplane and, when you eat, not wear a mask, even though there's someone one seat away from you. But you can't go inside a restaurant, sitting further away from people than on a plane, and eat?

Two of the empty shops had plywood over their windows, which were shattered during a peaceful protest.

Depressed, I thought about picking up some bourbon at the liquor store —one place that is apparently "essential"—but was interrupted by a phone call.

"The blood is Type AB positive," Tony Morrelli said.

"How rare is that?" I said.

"Not the rarest, but still pretty limited. About three-and-a-half percent of the population."

"I'll come over and pick up the towel," I said.

"Bring me two hundred smackers," he said.

———

Now it was time to really play detective. I got the towel from Morrelli, then called a contact Don Beddoe had with the coroner. I was trembling with excitement as I waited for my answer. The contact came through. Tommy Ludlow's blood type was AB positive.

Feeling like a combination of Sam Spade and Phillip Marlowe, I drove to Hollywood Station and went in and asked for Caravaggio. They told me to wait on a bench by the bail ATM. I played Mario Kart on my phone until Caravaggio came out.

"This better be good," he said.

"You don't like private snoops, huh?"

"Whaddaya want?"

"Always getting in the way, right?"

"Spill it."

"Unless they help you solve a case."

"Never happens," he said.

"Until now," I said. I gave him the rundown and handed him a plastic bag with the towel in it. I told him I was ready to give a sworn statement, and testify in court when the time came.

He was momentarily speechless.

"How soon can you spring Tiana Raven?" I said.

"It's all worked out very conveniently for you, hasn't it?" he said.

———

"You brilliant, wonderful thing!" Tiana threw herself into my arms.

"I won't argue with that," I said.

"You magnificent dumpster diver!"

"That's so sweet," I said. We walked out of the station to my car, which is a very modest Sonata.

As we buckled up I said, "What did Caravaggio tell you on the way out?"

"He told me I was lucky," she said.

"Did he tell you why?"

"Because I was free, I suppose."

"Did he tell you why you were free?"

"Huh?"

"What were his exact words to you, all of them."

"What's got into you?"

"It's important," I said.

"Nothing. I hardly spoke to him. Some uniformed officer brought me to his desk, and Cara—whatever his name is, said, 'You are one lucky lady.' He handed me a paper, some kind of release form. It's here in my purse."

"That was it?"

"Uh-huh."

"Let me see it," I said. She took out the paper and I looked it over.

"What's next?" Tiana said.

I took out my phone and started thumbing a message. She leaned over then and kissed my cheek. My cheek got hot. I finished the text, started up the car. I took the long way back to the office. Tiana didn't seem to mind. Me neither. I enjoyed her telling me what a genius I was.

———

Back at the office we walked in on Don Beddoe, at his desk, chewing a toothpick.

"There's my boy," he said. "And our satisfied client."

"In every way, I'm sure," I said.

Tiana gave me a quizzical look. "What's that supposed to mean?"

"You got everything you wanted out of this," I said. "Kira's out of the way, the money goes to you. And unless I miss my guess, Don here gets forty percent, and ten percent will go to The Hammer."

Don Beddoe sat up straight. "You crazy?"

I said, "You knew if I went to question Kira Hobbes-Raven that I'd take a look in her trash. You drummed that into me. The Hammer tipped you off that I was going to her house. Then he stalled me while you got there first and planted the towel."

Don spat his toothpick onto the floor.

"You killed Tommy Ludlow," I said. "Tiana stole one of the hand towels from her father's house last time she was there. You snuck into Tommy's house at night. Stabbed him. Bloodied the towel and left. Tiana let herself get arrested with an alibi that didn't hold up. That's when I march in with this towel, and the cops go get Kira. If she becomes a convicted felon, that removes her as trustee, so the funds go directly to Tiana. And you and Tiana enjoy the money and, maybe, each other."

Dead silence.

To Tiana I said, "It was you who gave me the last piece of the puzzle. Caravaggio didn't tell you where I found the towel. But you knew. You called me a dumpster diver."

"You idiot!" Don shouted.

"Don't call me that!" Tiana said.

"Then shut your face," Don said. "He'll never sell that story to the cops."

"What story?" Detective Caravaggio said. He'd just walked in, accompanied by a couple of uniformed officers.

"Your text said I'd find the real killer here," Caravaggio said.

"It's a duo," I said. "I suggest you separate them before you grill them."

"It wasn't me!" Tiana said. "It was him! He made me! He killed Tommy!"

Don didn't even blink. "Women," he said.

I said, "Don't let this little vixen tempt you into her web."

Don Beddoe snapped. He jumped out of his chair, climbed on his desk, and dove at me with outstretched hands. His hands got my throat and his bulk knocked me to the floor. It took both cops and Caravaggio to get him off me.

After something like that happens, a good detective needs a snappy line. As I got to my feet and smoothed my shirt, I said, "I guess that means no bonus this year."

Philip Marlowe would have been proud.

———

Don and Tiana were charged with murder, and Mark The Hammer Turnbull got pulled in as an accessory.

And me? I'm now sitting in my office alone, sipping a mocha latte. The sign guy is putting the finishing touches on the door:

Cullen Investigations
"No Dumpster Too Deep for Me to Peep"

LUCKY PENNY

The guy says, "It's a lucky penny."

He was sitting in the back of my cab. He owed me $7.50, which he gave me in cash, including the two quarters. No tip.

So I give him my best glare and that's when he holds up the copper disc.

He was young, mid-thirties, light brown skin and a turban on his dome. I think it was the turban that did it, actually had me thinking this guy might be some sort of holy man. But the stuff about the penny? C'mon.

"Keep it, cheapie," I said.

He smiled. "I am in earnest. This penny is lucky for the holder. I would like you to have it, as you have brought me to my appointment in plenty of time. Therefore, I'd like you to—"

"Just leave it on the seat and get out," I said.

"Remember me," he said, "when this penny brings you luck."

And with that he was out the door. I watched him disappear into the bowels of Grand Central Station.

———

You get all kinds as a cabbie in New York, and that's for certain. I once picked up a guy who claimed to be the reincarnation of Mary, Queen of Scots. He rattled on about being misused by the 4th Earl of Boswell. Kept it up all the way from 34th and 3rd to Tribeca. When he paid me and got out, he said, "I'm going to lose my head over this!"

Another time I picked up this young couple at Columbus Circle. They were headed to Chelsea. They seemed like the nicest couple you'd ever want to meet. Then at 41st and 9th they start fighting. Not verbally, either. It was a full on MMA cage match in the back of my cab. I pull over and have to yank them out. The man's face was bloody. He fell on the sidewalk and the woman starts kicking the holy fishcakes out of him. I pull her away from the guy and she turns on me! I managed to duck a punch and scrambled back into the cab. I was about to call the cops when I see the woman helping the man to his feet. Then they hug and kiss. Then the woman comes to the passenger window and taps it, like I should unlock the doors and let them in again. Instead I peeled out of there. Some business I don't need.

But the worst is when you get stiffed. That's money you're owed in good faith. That's money that puts beer in your refrigerator, lets you go out to a movie now and then.

I grumbled a few choice words about the turban guy and rumbled on down 42nd Street. A block later a guy in a nice suit and overcoat hails me. He gives me an address on the upper East side and off we go.

Like most single riders today, he's not interested in chit chat. He's glued to his phone. I see him in the mirror, thumbing a text, scrolling, making a call. At least he's not one of those loud talkers. That kind drives me crazy. I had a loud talker once, a middle-aged guy carrying a *Wall Street Journal*, who went on for ten blocks about what he was going to do to his wife when he got home. He was going to teach her a lesson "once and for all." He was going to "skin her alive." He was going to "rip her hair out." And various other actions of the same ilk. I was sweating and breathing hard when I got to the drop. As he was counting out bills I said, "Don't do it, man. Anybody'd do that to a woman is lower than pond scum."

He paused, then hands me the fare plus a twenty-percent tip, says, "Thanks, pal" and gets out.

I tell you, I think I lost a day of living with that trip, but at least I had some good dough to show for it.

But this guy was nice and quiet, and so was the drive to East 72nd. So I go up 8th and then cut across the park at 65th. I like that drive. Gives me a little green comfort after banging around in the gray and black asphalt jungle.

I dropped him in front of one of those nice buildings with an awning out front. The fare comes to $15.27. The guy uses the credit card reader. When he finishes the total is $50.

As he starts to get out I say, "Sir, I think you made a mistake."

"You mean the tip?" the guy says.

"Yes, sir."

"No mistake. I'm feeling good. My dad's surgery went great. He's going to make it. He worked three jobs when we were growing up, so I know what it's like for the working stiff. You caught me at the right time. Consider this your lucky day!"

And with that he was out of the cab.

I was feeling all warm inside and—

Lucky day...

Nah, couldn't be.

I got out and went around to the passenger side and opened the rear door. Was that penny on the seat? No. The floor? (Better not to look too close at the floor of a cab, but this time I made an exception.)

Nothing.

It had to be a coincidence. I just happened to pick a guy up who got some good news and wanted to throw some financial love to a working stiff.

But don't luck and coincidence wear the same clothes?

I don't know why, but I gave the back bench seat one last look when I saw it. The penny. Half of it anyway, as it was wedged in the seat crack.

"Hot dog!" I said.

Yeah, I actually said *Hot dog*.

I pinched the penny and removed it. I looked at Honest Abe and smiled.

"How much luck have you got for me, Abe?" I said.

I was about to find out.

———

I set the penny in the empty change tray in my console, making sure Abe's face was up. Didn't feel right to have him face down, fighting for air.

I was feeling so good I flicked on my *Off Duty* lights and drove up to 79th for another leisurely drive through the park. It was right across from the Turtle Pond that I heard the unmistakable *bam!* of a blown tire.

I pulled to the side and got out. A jogger loped by and said, with a big smile, "You got yourself a flat!"

"You got yourself a mouth!" I said.

He gave me a one-finger salute and jogged on.

Now I had a choice. I could call it in and get our in-house fixit truck out here. They'd take a fee out of my wages for that. Or I could put the spare on myself.

Uttering a few of my favorite curses, I popped the trunk and got out the jack.

And dropped it.

On my foot.

This time my curse was loud enough to be heard on Fifth Avenue.

An old woman walking hand-in-hand with a little boy was suddenly right there, and she let me have it.

"How dare you!" she said.

The little boy said, "Gramma, where's another trucker?"

"I will be reporting you to the taxi company!" Gramma said, and started fishing around in her purse. As I positioned the jack I saw her writing something on a piece of paper. My taxi number, I assumed.

"And the name's Mickey Partridge!" I said. "Like the bird!"

She jotted that down, took the boy's hand and walked on.

It took me ten minutes to change the tire, during which time a big wad of grease somehow got on my shirt, the new one I'd bought at Nordstrom Rack two days ago!

When I finally got back in the cab I was ready to run down a nun.

Which is when my eye fell on the lucky penny in the change tray.

"Abe!" I said. "What happened?"

He didn't answer.

So I drove on, wondering about luck, fate, life, chance, and whether the universe just liked playing jokes on all of us.

———

At 81st and Amsterdam I picked up a young man, early 20s, carrying a musical instrument case. Clarinet or horn. Wants to go to Lincoln Center. It's a short trip, $8.85, and I wonder about the tip. It's what I call a 'tweener. You can easily round up to a common bill—like a ten. But that can sometimes get you a tip lower than 15%. It'd be nice for the kid to peel me a ten and a one. That'd be a classy 24%. Instead, he gives me two fives. For those of you playing at home, that's a 13% tip. I find myself hoping the kid gets chapped lips.

Then, before the door closes, a guy hops in the back and says, "Drive."

I look at him in the mirror. He's got bug eyes and a shaved head. Wearing a leather jacket, which is strange in this heat.

"Where to?" I say.

"Just drive!" he says. "I'll tell you where."

I've had fares like this before. Anxious types who just want to get somewhere, anywhere, that isn't the place they are. Could be they had a fight with the girlfriend, or got depressed over some bad news. Once I had a guy, nicely dressed, wedding ring on his finger, get in at 96th and 2nd and says to drive him to the Brooklyn Bridge. That's 7.3 miles and the traffic on FDR is killer. Guy doesn't say a word the whole way. Every now and then I check the mirror and see this faraway look in the guy's eyes. I even start to wonder if he is going to the bridge to jump off it. It happens. But when we get there he tells me to drive him right back to where he picked me up. Which I do. "I feel better now," he says, and gives me an 18% tip.

But I don't pick up a generous spirit from the guy who jumped in my cab. I just start driving down Columbus, then 9th. The guy is a real nervous type, looking through the back window like somebody might be following.

Finally he gives me an address on West 44th. Hell's Kitchen. I can't wait to get the guy out of my cab. The only question in the back of my mind is what he's going to tip me on a $7.10 fare.

The answer this time was a big, fat goose egg.

Because he gets out and comes around to my window. I lower it to take the dough.

Instead, I get a 9mm semi-auto pistol in my face.

"The money," he says. "All of it."

It happens. You get robbed. Even though a lot of fares are by credit card, you still carry a good amount of cash. When it reaches a certain amount, you're supposed to take it in to dispatch, so the word gets out that robbing a hack isn't worth the risk.

This punk didn't get the memo.

So instead of dying over forty bucks and change, I open the mini-safe and pull out all the cash and coin and hand it over.

The guy stuffs it the pocket of his jacket.

"Is that all?" he says.

I'm feeling surly now. I hold up the lucky penny. "Yeah, this."

Next thing I know he clocks me on the head with the butt of his gun, and I go night-night.

———

When I come to, my head feels like a sliced bagel. My vision is fuzzy. There's caked blood in my hair. And this being New York, no one is asking me if I'm okay.

There's a bottle of water on the seat. I open it and drink. My temples throb. It's all coming back to me, what happened. I put the bottle back on the seat and see it—my lucky penny—sitting there, Abe side up.

And then it hits me. Lucky? What if it's *bad* luck that this thing holds?

Yeah, cheapie, I'll remember you all right!

I snatched the penny, got out of my cab, still a little woozy, and issued a full-throated New York oath.

Then threw the penny as hard as I could.

I watched it sail over 44th Street and come down...on a woman's head!

———

There's this urban myth about a penny being dropped off the top of the Empire State Building. They say it can go right through a pedestrian's skull and kill the poor slob. Only it can't. Not enough velocity against the air pressure. But it can sure ding you pretty good.

Well, I'm here to tell you that a penny thrown across the street can do some dinging, too, if it hits the right spot.

Which it did with this woman. She was carrying a bag of groceries. When my penny hit her, the woman staggered, grabbed her head, dropped the bag. The groceries went everywhere.

There was a guy next to her. He caught her to keep her from falling.

My gut instinct, born of survival skills picked up on the streets of Manhattan, pushed at me to get in the cab and drive away. Nobody could possibly connect me with this weird and totally unlucky event. And now that the penny was away from me, I could get back to normal life.

But from somewhere deep inside, maybe down there with the manners my mother tried to teach me as a child—with varying degrees of success —there was an override of the street smarts. Almost without willing it, my legs ran me across the street.

When I got there, the woman was telling the man she was stunned, didn't know what hit her.

"Can I help?" I said. I got down and started picking up the groceries.

"Thanks, pal," the man said.

The woman had a pained look on her face. Even with the pain she was pretty. Maybe forty years old. I felt like a piece of old lettuce from the gutter.

"I'm really sorry," I said.

"What?" the man said.

Instinct fought mother.

Mother won. "I'm afraid I caused this."

"Whattaya mean?" The man was a little younger than the woman, and looked like he could handle himself.

"That's my cab over there. I drive a cab. I was mad and I got out and threw a penny across the street."

"You did *what*?"

"I know, I know—"

"You threw a penny?"

"I'm sorry, I really am, I..." Looking down, I saw that devil coin lying in the sidewalk, right next to the guy's left shoe.

He followed my gaze, and picked it up. "You mean, this?"

"Well," I said. "Yeah."

"You know what you just bought with this penny? A lawsuit, my friend."

The woman said, "It's okay, Jeremy, I'm not—"

"Shut up Rachel," he said. "Wait here."

The guy took out his phone and ran across 44th. He took a couple of pictures of my cab.

"I'm sure it was an accident," Rachel said. Her eyes were blue and friendly.

"I shouldn't've," I said. "I'm just having a really bad day."

"Been there," she said.

"I hope you can see your way to forgive me," I said.

Before she could answer the guy was at her elbow. "Don't say anything else to this guy."

"But Jeremy—"

"He's gonna pay all right. And it'll be more than a penny!" He grabbed the groceries from me and took Rachel's arm and started leading her away.

Yep. If it weren't for bad luck I'd have no luck at all.

———

A week went by. The old lady who confronted me at the park issued her complaint to the company, and I got suspended for a couple of days. Instead of looking at my four walls, and putting the hurt on a couple of bottles of bourbon, I did something I hadn't done since I was a teenager.

I went to The Cloisters.

It's a place my mom took me to a couple of times. It's a branch of the Metropolitan Museum of Art constructed out of sections of French medieval monasteries. It's got this collection of statues and stained-glass windows, and these tapestries. They used to weave these pictures back in the Middle Ages, when there wasn't a lot else to do, I guess. The one I remembered as a kid was of a unicorn in a pen about to jump out.

It was still there, of course. Looking at it again, I thought that could be me, all fenced in, and maybe I'd catch a foot on the fence, fall flat, and stab myself with the horn.

Outside there's places to sit and you can look out at the Hudson. I sat and looked. And said a little prayer to my dear departed mother. A prayer for help.

When I got back to my apartment there was an official letter waiting for me in the box. I'd been served. The woman was suing for ten grand.

Then the company called me, because they were served, too.

I was canned.

Well, so much for prayers. And pennies.

————

Of course I couldn't afford a lawyer. The verdict would be a foregone conclusion. Any job I got after that I'd have my wages garnished to pay.

Well, there was one way to keep them from collecting.

I decided gas was the way to do it. It'd be easy to seal up the door and windows, then just fall asleep and never wake up. I went out and maxed my credit card on a lobster dinner. Then came back home, nicely warmed by my last meal.

I duct taped the kitchen window. I was about to start on the door when I got a buzz.

I ignored it.

Then it buzzed again.

I pressed the button. "Yeah?"

A woman's voice said, "Mr. Partridge?"

"Yeah?"

"It's Rachel Walling."

What could she possibly want?

"May I see you a moment?" she said.

"What for?"

"It will only take a moment."

"You packing heat?"

"Excuse me?"

"Have you got a gun?"

Pause. "Oh my, no."

"Joking," I said. "Not too funny. I'll be right down."

She was waiting at the bottom of the steps.

"Thanks," she said.

"For what?" I said.

"Seeing me."

Actually, seeing her was a pleasure to the eyes. But I couldn't say that.

"Okay," I said.

"I just wanted to tell you, I'm dropping the lawsuit."

"You're...what?"

"It was my brother. He just wouldn't quit. I went along with it, but there's one thing I couldn't get out of my mind."

I waited.

"Your face," she said. "The look on your face when you ran across the street to tell me you were sorry. It had such...anguish. You were suffering, and from more than just that penny."

"Lady, you don't know how right you were."

"I just couldn't go through with it. I wanted you to know. And I wanted to see your face when I told you. I was hoping it would bring you some peace."

Well, ol' Mickey Partridge, tough guy New York cabbie, felt tears welling up.

"I think you've answered me," she said.

I stood there a moment, just breathing. Breathing! Suddenly the air was sweet again.

"I'm really glad you came," I said.

She smiled as sweetly as the air.

"This may sound crazy," I said, "but can I buy you a cup of coffee or something?"

————

And that's how we ended up talking for two hours and discovering we liked the same old movies—*The Quiet Man, Meet Me in St. Louis, Singin' in the Rain*. And made a date to see *The Maltese Falcon* at a revival theater.

Four months later, after I landed a job driving for UPS, we were married.

On our honeymoon night, in the Poconos, Rachel gave me a present. I opened the little box and saw the penny. There was a chain attached, through a little hole at the top. I'm happy to say the hole was *above* Abe's head.

"See?" Rachel said. "It was lucky after all."

A NEW NAME

Dirk Connors was the best right-handed pitcher in baseball. A fireballer for the Arizona Diamondbacks, he regularly brought the heat, sometimes reaching 101 mph on the meter. Once he hit 103. His nickname, Rocket, was well earned. Combining his heater with a killer curve and nasty slider, his ERA was 1.54 six months into the season. His record was 7-1, that one loss owing to an error by the left fielder.

But in a game in Los Angeles against the Dodgers, Dirk was pulled in the fourth inning after feeling a twinge in his arm. The next day, the Diamondbacks placed Dirk on injured reserve so he could rest his most valuable asset.

Instead of returning to Phoenix with the team, Dirk stayed in L.A. for a while. It was his favorite city, the main reason being "the babes." That very night Dirk headed to a club downtown, GhostBar, getting past the velvet ropes because of his fame.

He sat at the bar and ordered a bottle of Cristal, served in an ice bucket, with two glasses.

And waited to be approached.

He didn't wait long.

At twenty-seven, with chiseled features and flowing curly hair, Dirk Connors reveled in considering himself "a chick magnet." (He actually used those words to describe himself to his teammates, without embarrassment.)

So when a shapely beauty sidled up to him, he flashed his pearlies and said, "Hi."

The woman giggled. "I just thought...I wondered...are you..."

"Yep, I am."

"The pitcher?"

"Call me Rocket. Would you like some champagne?"

"Really?"

"Have a seat."

———

Two days later, the young woman, Julia Thomas, presented herself to the Los Angeles Police Department, Central Division. She was accompanied by her attorney, Sylvia Millford Rollins, the prominent Civil Rights lawyer. Julia Thomas's face and neck were black and blue. One of her eyes was swollen shut.

At a press conference called by Ms. Rollins, she stated, "Dirk Connors raped and nearly killed my client, Julia Thomas. We are calling on the District Attorney to institute prosecution, and for Major League Baseball to immediately and permanently suspend Mr. Connors."

———

After a series of conference calls between Dirk and the Diamondbacks, it was decided that Dirk should be represented by a Los Angeles attorney known for his defense of celebrities—Jim Josephson.

"It's her word against mine," Dirk told him at their first meeting in Josephson's downtown office. "You can't get around that."

"Maybe," Josephson said. "But these days, maybe not."

"Make it that way," Dirk said. "Make her squirm on the stand."

"Listen to me," Josephson said. "I'm a trial lawyer. The jury is going to have a bias for the victim."

"Alleged victim," Dirk said.

"Sure," Josephson said. "But any cross-examination has to be handled delicately. Yes, it's your word against hers, but we have to establish that quietly. Let me handle it."

"Be sure you do," Dirk said. "This is my career. Major League Baseball is run like a crime family. They're out to get me. Don't give them a leg to stand on."

"Or a right arm," Josephson said.

"Ha ha," Dirk said.

———

Six months later, the trial began on a Tuesday in the Superior Court, Judge Melinda Johnson presiding.

"A chick judge!" Dirk said to his lawyer.

"And you be on good behavior," Josephson said. "Make no faces. Sit here like a choirboy. Think you can do that?"

"Easy peasy," Dirk said.

The prosecutor, Stefani Munro, made her opening statement to the jury. She painted a picture of a sexual predator. "A man using his celebrity to do with women whatever he will."

Dirk ground his teeth but didn't let it show in his face. He put on his best choirboy expression, which, while he hadn't much practice at it, satisfied him as more than adequate.

Then it was his lawyer's turn. Josephson was calm and quiet as he told the jury about Dirk Connors' hard work to become a top pitcher in baseball. He admitted that as a single guy with his looks and money, Dirk was attracted to women, but they were also attracted to him. And this case would come down to his word against hers, and they, the jury, would be the ones to judge who was telling the truth.

The prosecutor called Julia Thomas to the stand.

Oh, what a performance, Dirk thought. It only took three questions before Julia turned on the waterworks.

Dirk, disciplined through all the years of hard work to get to where he was, kept his expression serene.

But every now and then he stole a look at one of the jury members. A young barista from Starbucks. And he found her looking at him. He knew what to do with that. He put on a slight smile, looked away, and returned to choirboy.

When the prosecutor was finished, Jim Josephson stood up for the cross.

"Ms. Thomas," he said, "just a few questions. On the night in question, you were at GhostBar with a friend, yes?"

"Yes," Julia Thomas said.

"You often go to clubs?"

"I like to, yes."

"Isn't it true that one of the reasons you go is to meet men?"

Pause. "Well, sure."

"It's nothing to be ashamed of," Josephson said. "It's what young people do."

The prosecutor said, "Objection."

"Sustained," said the judge. "Rephrase, Mr. Josephson."

"In your opinion, is that what young people do?" Josephson said.

"Objection."

"Overruled. The witness may answer."

"I suppose so," Julia said.

"And you recognized Mr. Connors, is that right?"

"Yes."

"And you approached him, not the other way around, correct?"

"Well, yes."

"And when he offered you a glass of champagne, you gladly accepted, yes?"

"I guess I did."

"Ms. Thomas, I know this is hard for you, but please don't guess. You were happy to accept a chance to have a glass of champagne with Mr. Connors, weren't you?"

"I...yes."

"Now, isn't it true that during the course of your conversation with Mr. Connors, you asked him if he enjoyed rough sex?"

"No! I never said that."

"Isn't it true you wanted to tempt him?"

"No!"

"The great pitching star, Dirk Connors, could be yours?"

"Objection!" the prosecutor said.

"I have no further questions," Josephson said.

When it was time for the defense case, Jim Josephson called one of the

GhostBar bartenders, Blake Tunney, who was on duty the night in question. He testified that Julia Thomas had approached Dirk Connors and seemed "very interested." He further testified that he overheard Julia say the words "Rough sex."

On cross-examination, Stefani Munro hammered Blake Tunney, eliciting the admission that the place was crowded and loud and that his recollection might be suspect.

Jim Johnson called Dirk Connors to the stand.

He took Dirk through his background, his dreams and aspirations, his hard work to become one of the best pitchers in baseball. He asked Dirk to face the jury and tell them what happened that night.

As Dirk turned, he made eye contact with the barista. He told the jury he went to the bar just to relax, how Julia Thomas had approached him, how he offered her some champagne.

"After a couple of glasses," Dirk said, "she says to me, 'Do you like rough sex?' I laughed it off. But she said she was serious, did I like it? And I said, 'I don't really know.' And she said, 'Do you want to know?' I didn't say anything, and she said, 'My place isn't far from here.' And she was very attractive and I was feeling good and, you know, I'm a guy."

He looked at the barista. "So I went with her to her loft. We smoked a joint and started kissing, and then she told me what she wanted me to do."

Dirk paused and sighed. "So I gave her what she wanted. Look, I'm not proud of it, but I did exactly what she wanted me to do."

"Objection!" Stefani Munro said. "Speculation as to what she was thinking."

"Sustained," the judge said.

"Thank you, Dirk," Jim Johnson said. "No further questions."

The prosecutor came at Dirk like a lioness protecting her cubs. Dirk, who knew how to take coaching, had been well prepped by Jim Johnson. He kept his composure, resisting the urge to get angry. He answered every pointed question in a soft, velvet voice.

And then it was time for closing arguments. Jim Johnson stood and, without notes, faced the jury.

"Ladies and gentlemen, on behalf of my client, Dirk Connors, and myself, I want to thank you for your attention over these two, difficult days. Being a juror is no easy task. I want you to know that your attention is greatly appreciated, as is your willingness to serve here and carry out the duties of a jury."

Dirk gave the barista a fetching look.

"You're here, ladies and gentlemen, because the wisdom of a thousand years says you are to be here. It's the wisdom that says that only a sworn body of people selected from the community can be completely trusted to do what is right, what is fair. You are the only ones competent to pass on the guilt or innocence of my client."

Jim Johnson stepped closer to the jury box.

"Did you know that the right to a jury trial is the only right mentioned twice in our Constitution? Yes, twice, so important is this right. Why is it so important? Because you, ladies and gentlemen, stand between the accused and the accuser. You are not here for the benefit of the prosecution. She doesn't need a jury. You are here for the benefit of the defendant."

The lawyer walked back to the defense table and held out his hand toward Dirk.

"You are here to see to it that the government does not ride roughshod over a citizen accused of a crime. This isn't like most other countries, where an accused is arrested and presumed guilty. No, under our system of justice, which is the greatest ever devised, an accused is presumed to be innocent. And you, ladies and gentlemen, make sure that presumption remains unless the government is able to overcome it, beyond a reasonable doubt."

Jim Johnson returned to the middle of the courtroom.

"Ladies and gentlemen, as her honor will tell you, a reasonable doubt exists when you have a hesitation to act, that is, a hesitation to vote guilty. You may go back into the jury room and say to yourself, 'I sort of believe Ms. Thomas.' But in that moment you have hesitated. And the judge will tell you in such a circumstance, you must vote to acquit Mr. Connors. Both my client and I thank you for your attention to our case, and your commitment to your duty."

The jury was out two hours before returning a verdict of not guilty.

———

With a couple of months before Spring Training, Dirk rented a house in Silver Lake. He figured he could have himself a good time before getting serious about playing again. His arm was feeling fine, but the only workout he wanted to give it was lifting a glass.

He got to know some new clubs. His favorite was Jax on Melrose. They treated him like the star he was.

On a Tuesday night in December, Dirk parked himself at the Jax bar, ordered a bottle of Cristal and two glasses.

He didn't have long to wait.

She was wearing a tight red dress that accentuated her positives. Of which her body was only one. Her green eyes and blonde hair were two others.

She sidled up to him—oh, that telltale sidling—and sheepishly said, "Are you...?"

"Maybe," Dirk said. "Are you?"

She giggled. "Sissy. And you're that baseball player."

"Guess my name," Dirk said, "and you can have a glass of champagne."

"Kirk," she said.

"Oh, so close."

"Oh, wait, wait! Dirk?"

"Bingo. Sit down."

He poured her a glass of champagne.

They both drank.

"I want you to know something," Sissy said. "I saw you on TV in that trial. I was glad they found you not guilty."

"That's because I wasn't," Dirk said.

They drank some more.

"Sissy," Dirk said, "let me ask you something."

"Sure!"

"Do you think two adults should be able to enjoy themselves however they want to?"

"Of course."

"I mean, this is America, am I right?"

"Uh-huh."

Dirk lifted his glass. "To America!"

Sissy giggled, they clinked, and drank.

Dirk filled their glasses. "Now as I was saying—"

Somebody tapped Dirk on the shoulder. He turned and saw a guy in a cowboy hat. A cowboy hat! Maybe in Arizona, but L.A.?

"You're Dirk Connors," the cowboy said. He wasn't a bad looking guy, about Dirk's age, could have been an actor.

"Howdy, Hoss," Dirk said. "You want an autograph?"

"You're scum," the cowboy said.

Great, Dirk thought. One of those guys. Wanting to challenge the Big Dog.

"Go ride your pony," Dirk said.

"You wanna make me?"

"You want to step outside?" Dirk said.

"Let's do it!"

Dirk wanted to. He was sure he could take this punk.

But his arm! All it would take was one wrong punch. He might even break bones in his hand.

He signaled the bartender, a big man named Walker.

"Yes, Mr. Connors?"

"Can't a guy have a drink without some loudmouth calling him out?" Dirk said.

Walker looked at the cowboy. "Whattaya think you're doing?"

"None of your business," the cowboy said.

"I'm the sheriff here," Walker said. "Drift."

"I ain't goin' nowhere."

Walker raised his arm and motioned someone over.

That someone was 6'7" with shoulders as wide as a dugout.

"Or I can have my bouncer escort you out," Walker said.

The cowboy issued a couple of choice words, then stormed across the bar and out the front doors.

"Sorry for the disturbance, Mr. Connors," Walker said.

"No harm done," Dirk said. He turned back to Sissy. "Now where were we?"

"We were drinking to America," Sissy said.

"Oh, yeah."

Dirk lifted his glass. Sissy lifted hers.

They drank.

A few minutes later, Dirk decided it was time. He was getting a little tired, and that wasn't like him.

"Let's go to my place," Dirk said.

"Okay," Sissy said.

"I'll get us an Uber."

"Oh, my car's in the lot across the street!"

It was a pain to get there. Dirk was feeling sick and Sissy had to hold his arm. When they got to the car, Dirk felt like he was on some spin ride at an amusement park. He saw Sissy, the car, Sissy, the car...and then thought he saw...the cowboy!

And then he saw nothing at all.

———

He woke up to the smell of antiseptic and clean sheets. A bed. A hospital bed. His vision was blurry, but he made out the walls, the countertop with various items of medical use.

Then a voice. "You had yourself quite a night."

A man appeared through the fog of Dirk's sight. He had a white coat and stethoscope around his neck.

"How..." Dirk said.

"Easy does it," the man said. "How are you feeling?"

"Not...so hot."

"You're going to be just fine."

Dirk tried to scratch his nose. His arms were...restrained!

"Hey!" Dirk said.

This man...a doctor? His face. Where had he seen that face before?

"I know you," Dirk said.

"You do indeed. Call me Doctor Fred."

"Fred?"

"Dr. Fred Thomas."

Cogs and wheels turned in Dirk's head. "Her...?"

"Father," Thomas said. "Julie's father. I sat in the back of the court-room throughout the trial. Or what I like to call a perversion of justice."

"Now hold on...why am I tied down? Let me up!"

"You'll be up soon enough."

"Where am I?"

"My own little private office. No one knows you're here. And no one knows I'm here, either. No one will ever know. I'm at a conference in Ottawa."

"Huh?"

"It's called setting up an alibi."

Dirk tried to free his arms again. No dice. "What are you doing?"

"You deserve to know," the doctor said. "I hired a PI to follow you. You met her. The fetching woman who approached you at the bar."

"A PI?"

"And her associate, the man in the cowboy hat."

Dirk's head started spinning again.

"When he started insulting you, a little something was put in your champagne. You would call it a date-rape drug."

"She....you...kidnapping?"

"It's a wild story, isn't it? Who would believe it?"

"The cops, that's who!"

"But I'm not here, remember?"

An ominous chill ran from Dirk's neck down to his toes.

"Look," Dirk said. "I'm sorry, okay? I didn't mean anything bad to happen to your daughter."

"But it did," Dr. Thomas said. "She's not been the same since the verdict. She's been trashed as a liar all over social media. She's in heavy-duty therapy."

"Oh, man, I'm sorry, really."

"Sure you are."

"What are you going to do?"

"I'm going to give you a new name."

"You're what?"

"They call you Rocket, right?"

"Yeah, so?"

The doctor wheeled over a canister with a hose and face mask attached.

"You won't feel a thing," he said. "But when you wake up, you'll have a new name."

He placed the mask over Dirk's nose and mouth. The last words Dirk heard before he went to sleep were, "They'll call you Lefty."

A DISH SERVED COLD

After I killed a guy I always liked to go out for a nice meal.

My go-to place was Mastro's on Pacific Coast Highway. They knew me there, knew I liked to toss money around. I tipped like an Arab sheik vacationing in Vegas. All the servers wanted my table.

On this night I got Madison. Sweet, beautiful Madison, an actress who's going to make it big someday.

"The usual, Mr. Hackford?" she asked.

"Bring it on, sweetie," I said.

If I'd've been twenty years younger I would've made a play for her. But I already had two on the side I was bouncing between, and at fifty that's about all a guy can handle. Especially in my racket.

You don't set out to become a hit man. It's not your dream job out of high school. The occupation finds you, not the other way around. It picks you just like nature selects a mutation for survival. So when I fell in with the O'Hanlon crew in Boston, as a leg breaker, nature knew I was hard and heartless, which is what you get to be growing up in Roxbury.

Blackie O'Hanlon took a special liking to me. He was a Sox fan and I knew more than any of his crew about the Boston boys. I knew all about their history, from Tris Speaker to Ted Williams to Carl Yastrzemski to David "Big Poppy" Ortiz. Which is why Blackie loved talking to me. And why, after my first murder, which was an accident, he molded me into the killer you see here today.

Madison came back with my usual—a Hendrick's martini with a twist. I ordered an appetizer—half a dozen oysters on the half shell.

Like I said, the first time I killed a guy I didn't mean to do it. But this florist, a runt named McPherson, was way behind on his loans and needed some incentive to pay up. In his office he begged me for more time.

"Just a week, Dave, honest!" he said. "I got some things in the works."

"Well, Mac, one thing that ain't gonna be working for awhile is your left leg."

I was holding a baseball bat—a Louisville Slugger with a Nomar Garciaparra autograph.

"No, no! Please!"

It's funny how often they beg me with the word *please*. As if rules of common courtesy apply when you owe the big man money.

I got the bat ready, just like Carlton Fisk about to hit that famous homer in Fenway during the '86 World Series.

But as I swung, McPherson dropped to the floor and the bat hit his head.

I knew he was dead the second I made contact.

Not good. Blackie O'Hanlon only wanted his seasoned pros doing the hits. He planned them out carefully, to keep the cops in the dark.

Now things were messy.

Madison returned with my oysters.

"How's the acting going?" I said.

"Pretty good," Madison said. "I just got cast as Rosalind in *As You Like It*."

"That's a Shakespeare, yeah?"

"One of the best roles."

"You'll kill it," I said. A little inside humor. I lifted my martini in a toast. "Here's to success in everything we do."

But success was not certain as I stood over McPherson's dead body. I had to think fast. Long story short, it was good the florist shop was closed for the night. McPherson kept his delivery van keys on a pegboard in his office. I grabbed them, put on gloves, dragged the body out to the back. I unlocked the back of the van and put the body inside. I went back in the store and got my bat.

I drove the van out toward Wollastan Beach, parked in an alley, then walked up to Harvard Street and hailed a cab. The bat was in my overcoat.

Next morning I called Blackie O'Hanlon, fully expecting to be taken down several pegs.

Instead, he said, "Stuff happens. You did good. Lay low for awhile. I'll get back to you."

Madison returned to check on me. I ordered my meal—a rib-eye medium rare, grilled asparagus, and a glass of Caymus cabernet. That night I slept like a baby. That's another thing that made me tops in my line. I never lost any sleep over it. Not a wink.

When Blackie called me into his office a few days later, he said, "You've got the stuff, kid. You're ready."

And that's when I became a hit man. Three kills for Blackie, before Blackie himself got lead poisoning from the Harrington gang.

I got out of Boston, but quick, and headed to L.A. to go freelance.

After my meal, and a nice tip for Madison, I went out into the cool Pacific night, where the valet, a young guy named Nicky, fetched my car. I tipped him a ten.

"You da bomb!" Nicky said.

I laughed. I could have told him I never use bombs. Too complicated and unnecessary. Of course, all I said was, "Thanks, kid."

Full and happy I was as I pulled out of the lot. I drove home, listened to some jazz, and had myself a deep, refreshing sleep. I dreamed of warm, white beaches and Piña Coladas.

———

My first job in L.A. was to take out a guy named Tony Santucci. He was a do-gooder, working with troubled teens on the street. He had a thing about drugs, a vendetta you might say, and that's what got him on the wrong side of the cartel and a supplier named Vincent Cruz.

Cruz called me in for a meeting. And let me tell you, Cruz knew how to live. His house was one of the biggest in Whitley Heights. That's a classic neighborhood in the middle of Hollywood, up on a hill above Franklin. A lot of the old-time movie stars had mansions up there.

Cruz was a handsome guy in his late forties. He wore an open-collared shirt with plenty of bling on his chest. He sat behind a big desk. He picked up a humidor, opened it, and held it out for me to take a cigar. I dared not refuse. He took one for himself and used a gold cutter to snip off the end over a large, glass ashtray. He handed me the cutter. I clumsily went through the same routine.

His bodyguard took a lighter off the desk and fired up Cruz's stick. The bodyguard came around to where I was seated and did the same for me. With a nod, Cruz dismissed the guard.

Cruz said, "I hear good things about your work in Boston."

"Nice to be recognized for your work," I said.

He nodded. "I got a job for you. If you do good, there'll be more."

"I appreciate that."

"Of course..." Cruz took a lingering puff of his cigar. "...if you mess it up you won't ever work again."

He smiled. He was sizing me up, seeing if I showed any hesitation or nerves. Truth is, I was a little twitchy. But I knew how to hide it. Another natural selection mutation I was born with.

"I don't mess up," I said, then quickly took the offensive. "How much?"

"I like that," Cruz said. "Right to the point. Ten grand, since this is your first with me. Do it right, and you get more next time. Call it the Vincent Cruz incentive plan. You want in?"

"As far as I can," I said.

Cruz put out his hand and I shook it.

"Now, I want you to put two in the back of his head," Cruz said. "I want it to look professional. I want it to be a warning. I got the piece for you, untraceable."

"Works for me," I said.

And it so was settled. Cruz gave me the skinny on Tony Santucci and off I went.

Santucci lived in Silver Lake. Scoping out his house I was able to determine he had a wife and three kids—a boy and two girls. Sociopath that I am, and proudly so, I didn't care a bit that I was going to hit a family man. It'd be no different than if Santucci got hit by a car. Life's tough all over. You got to learn to live with bad stuff.

I caught Santucci one night coming out of the building downtown where he went to help kids. I sapped him and put him in the trunk of my

Caddie, the first of several I've owned. I used zip ties to secure his hands behind his back.

I drove up to place on Mulholland Drive that I'd found before the hit. A nice, secluded spot with plenty of scrub on the hillside. Perfect place to dump a body you want to be found.

He was coming around when I opened the trunk. He knew right away what was about to happen. "Please!" he said.

There was that word again.

"I got a wife and kids!"

At least I made it quick.

For my first reward meal in L.A. I chose Musso & Frank Grill in Hollywood. A house martini, then a bone-in pork chop. Loved it. I went there two more times.

The years went on and the hits just kept on coming.

———

Now to the waking nightmare that nearly sent me to the loony bin. I'd been given a contract by one of the cartels to hit a federal prosecutor named Samuel Simpson. That's no easy job, let me tell you. There's layers around the feds. But O'Hanlon had taught me how to plan, and plan I did. It took me three weeks of tailing Simpson, watching his every move. I finally got him outside a late-night drugstore. A garrote was my choice, the Sicilian necktie.

I drove my Caddie up to my favorite spot on Mulholland and dumped the body.

Then went out to Mastro's for another fine meal. Chilean Sea Bass with rosemary garlic sautéed button mushrooms.

At home I fell into a deep sleep....until knocking on my front door jolted me awake. It was a cop knock. You get to know those in this work. My clock read 3:22.

More knocks.

I threw on a robe and went to the door. I peeped out at two suited guys with *Fed* written all over them.

Like a good citizen, I opened the door.

"Mr. Hackford?" the front guy said.

"Yeah?"

"I'm Agent Dave Crowley," the front guy said. "This is my partner, Agent Carl Stern."

"Uh-huh."

"Mind if we come in?" Crowley said.

"Yeah, I do. I was asleep. What's this about?"

"Murder," Crowley said. "Professional."

"So?" I said.

"We know you have certain...associates."

"Look, fellas, I'm just a working stiff trying to get along."

"What's your line of work?" Agent Stern said.

"Freelance accountant," I said.

"I've never heard of that," Stern said.

"It's a growing field," I said.

Crowley said. "Would you mind if we took a look in your car?"

"You want to search my car?"

"Just a quick look," Crowley said.

"You know you can't search my car, or my house, or me for that matter, less you got a warrant."

"You can give us consent," said Crowley.

What were they looking for? I knew enough of the law—you have to in my business—to know a cop or a fed can't start poking around unless you give them permission. If you don't, they may get testy and try for a warrant. If you do, you're showing you got nothing to hide.

There was nothing in my car except the registration in the glove compartment. I keep things tight.

"Sure, have a look," I said. "Just make it fast."

"Will do," Crowley said.

"I'll unlock it for you."

I went to the kitchen counter and grabbed my keys, then went out to the Caddie. I hit the fob and unlocked the doors. Crowley looked around the front, including the glove compartment. Stern eyed the backseat.

"Pop the trunk, please," Crowley said. I didn't like the way he said it. It was an order. So I gave him an eye roll, then opened the trunk.

Stern and Crowley went around and looked.

"Mr. Hackford," Crowley said. "Can you explain this?"

"Explain what?" I said

"Come look at this, please."

I went around and looked.

And my heart whammed against my ribs.

In the trunk was the body of Samuel Simpson.

There was nothing I could say, nothing I could do. They took me in and shoved me in a cell. I kept screaming I wanted my lawyer.

But not even he, the best criminal lawyer in the city, could help me. He tried the insanity defense. No dice. I got life.

I went batty not knowing how this all happened. There was no way on earth that body could have been in my trunk.

Except there was.

Six months after I arrived at the federal pen in Mendota, I had a visitor. When I sat in the pod I recognized the face on the other side of the Plexi-glas. It was that valet from Mastro's.

"How you doing, Mr. Hackford?" he said into the handset.

"Nicky, right?"

"That's right," he said. "Nicky Santucci."

Santucci? Santucci!

"That's right, Mr. Hackford. Tony Santucci was my father. When I was eight years old you murdered him. It took me fifteen years to find out it was you."

My mouth opened but no words came out.

"I made you my project," Nicky said. "Found out everything I could about you. All the way back to your days in Boston. The feds were very helpful. When you take out a federal prosecutor, they tend to take it hard, especially when they've got no evidence to nail you."

My hand shook so bad I almost dropped the handset.

"It didn't take much to find out you love Mastro's. So I got a job as a valet, waiting for you to show. And then, there you were. I do computer work. I paired your fob. And I put a tracker in your wheel well. That's how I found out where you lived, and how I kept track of your movements on my laptop. Kept watching, until the night you drove to a remote part of Mulholland Drive. I knew you must've been dumping a body there, the same way you dumped my dad's body all those years ago."

I bit my lip so hard it drew blood.

"I drove my truck out there early the next morning. Found the body in the weeds. I wrapped it up and hauled it home. I told the FBI all about it. I was the one who suggested a sting. Has there ever been a sting with a dead body? I don't think so. First time for everything. You must have been having a good sleep as I popped your trunk with the fob clone and put the body in with the agents' help."

That's when the clouds parted and the sun appeared. If Nicky was waiting for me to crack up, he was in for a shock.

"I got to thank you, kid," I said. "I haven't been sleeping good, not knowing how that body got in my trunk. You've taken a load off my mind. I actually feel better, much better."

Nicky's face didn't change one bit. "You know, there's an old saying —'Revenge is a dish best served cold.' I've had a lot of time to think that through."

"Good for you," I said.

"My father worked with gang kids. Helped a lot of them. But others ended up dead, or in places like this. Even so, they all respected my dad."

"That's a great story, kid. Sell it to the tabloids."

He smiled, cold as ice. "There's a couple of those guys doing life right here. They know you now. You're going to know them, too. But not yet. Maybe next month, maybe next year. Maybe ten years from now. The only thing sure is, you won't know when it's coming."

He hung up the handset and was gone.

That's the worst of it. Not the bodies. Not the families. The worst of it is I can't sleep anymore. When I manage to drop off from sheer exhaustion, I don't dream of white beaches or Piña Coladas or a pretty waitress named Madison.

All I see is the ice-cold smile of Nicky Santucci.

CAREER MOVE

"You wanna run that by me again?" Fireboy said.

"A bomb," Franklin Tolliver said, "that won't go off, but could have."

They were sitting at a corner table in Miceli's in Hollywood. It was 3:17 p.m. The lunch crowd was mostly gone and the dinner crowd hadn't yet come in. That's how Tolliver had planned it. No listening ears.

"But what's the freakin' point?" Fireboy said.

All Tolliver knew about the one they called Fireboy was what his cousin—doing a dime up in Soledad—told him. Though Franklin Tolliver was the "success of the family," he and his cousin Dix, who had gone down a more destructive path, had always been close. That's why Franklin was able to make this contact. And Dix would never tell anybody about it.

"That's up to me," Tolliver said.

Fireboy sat back and smiled. Tolliver did not like that smile. It was knowing. For a second Tolliver considered calling the whole thing off. But then he thought of the adulation, the once-in-a-lifetime event that would elevate his stalled career to heights he'd never reach on his own.

For the last three seasons on the hit show *Domain,* Franklin Tolliver had a recurring, though minor role. Though the producers kept plans for season four close to the vest, Tolliver was getting the vibe that his character was going to be written out. Maybe suffer flaming death. And then what? The business was fickle. Once you were off a hit show, you never knew where the next gig would come from.

Franklin Tolliver, at thirty-one, had paid his dues. Ten years of acting classes, little showcases, scrambling for commercial work. He was *this* close to going up a tier because of *Domain*. To have this rug pulled out from under him now was a fate he could not allow to happen.

Besides all that, he deserved stardom because he was a *great*, not just good actor. He had no qualms about saying so to anyone—you have to have confidence to succeed in this business, he'd long ago learned. He was going to win two, count 'em, two, Oscars over the course of his long career.

"You wanna be a star, huh?" Fireboy said.

"So what?" Tolliver said. "You'll get paid, handsomely."

"I'm not as handsome as you, am I?"

Sure enough. Fireboy had stringy hair, pockmarked skin, and was probably in his early forties.

"Don't make this difficult," Tolliver said.

"I like to know what's going on when I do a job," Fireboy said. "Gives me a sense of peace. I work better when I have a sense of peace."

"Dix said you'll do your job and keep your mouth shut."

"That's right," Fireboy said. "My career ain't worth nothin' without people know I can keep quiet."

"Okay then."

"But I still want to know. I can walk out of here same as you."

"And lose twenty large?"

"There'll be other jobs."

Well, Franklin Tolliver thought, you wanted to do this deal. So do it.

"All right," Tolliver said. "Yes. To be a star."

"But you're on a hit show."

"Minor role."

"That fits," Fireboy said.

Tolliver felt his stomach roil. And not from hunger. "I'm no minor actor. You don't know anything about me. You have no idea how good I am, so why don't you just shut about that?"

"Whoa," Fireboy said, leaning back.

"Do we have a deal or not?" Tolliver said.

"If you buy me dinner," Fireboy said. "I always wanted to have dinner with one of the world's great actors."

"You got that right," Tolliver said.

"Aces," Fireboy said, and smiled. He was missing one of his lateral incisors.

For two days Franklin Tolliver couldn't sleep. The show was on hiatus, so he wasn't filming. There were no appearances scheduled by his PR firm. He didn't place much hope in his firm anyway, since the last time he made an official public appearance was at the opening of a refurbished strip mall in Studio City three months earlier.

To deal with the nerves, he decided to go back to his old acting teacher and do a few scene exercises.

Jocko Freeman was a highly respected acting coach in L.A. He'd been at it for thirty years, with dozens of working actors having sat under his tutelage. Tolliver studied with Freeman for two years before getting his big break on *Domain*. After that he no longer took classes. He didn't need them. He knew he could act.

But Jocko was pleased to see him. A bearded bear of a man, he opened his arms wide as Tolliver entered the space where he held classes.

"Bring it in!" he said, and pulled Tolliver to him.

Tolliver saw about half a dozen acting students sitting in the theater chairs, looking his way, wondering in the semi-darkness who this was.

"A prodigal has returned!" Jocko Freeman announced to the other students. With his arm around Tolliver's shoulders he said, "You all know Franklin Tolliver from the show *Domain*."

A couple of the students broke into smiles and applauded.

One of the men folded his arms and glared.

Envy, Franklin Tolliver thought. The occupational hazard of the acting world. The guy is envious of me, and why not? I'm on a show!

"We were just about to do some improvs," Jocko Freeman said to Tolliver. "Care to join us?"

"That's why I'm here," Tolliver said.

And so it was arranged. Tolliver took the stage with one of the women and one of the men—the one who had glared at him.

Good. I'll bury him.

Jocko announced the next improv game. He called it "Space Work." Tolliver remembered the game from when he played it in Jocko's class. One person announces a situation and a character, and begins to do something. When Jocko says, "Now!" the next actor joins in as a character of his choice. There is one more "Now!" and the third actor steps in.

Jocko gave the beginning to the man, whose name was Rob.

The next to join would be the woman, Heidi.

Tolliver was designated number three.

"Begin!" Jocko Freeman said.

Rob went to center stage and said, in a Peter Lorre voice, "Now it is time to unleash my master plan! To take over the city of New York so I can stage my own production of *Hamlet* and star in it myself, since nobody else thinks I can act!"

There were titters from the other students, but not from Franklin Tolliver. He thought, Is that a dig? This guy's throwing shade at me! This little—

"Now!" Jocko Freeman said.

Heidi joined Rob at center stage, pretending to chew gum and acting like a little girl. "Watcha doin'?" she said.

"I'm taking over New York," Rob said.

"Why?"

"Because, you little nosy thing."

"How you gonna do it?"

"I'm building a great, big bomb!"

The words slammed into Tolliver's head, ringing in his brain, so much that when Jocko Freeman yelled, "Next!" Tolliver didn't move.

"Franklin!" Jocko said. "Next!"

Tolliver didn't move.

Rob, moving back into himself, stood straight and said, "Yo, pretty boy! You're on."

At which point, something snapped inside Franklin Tolliver. He rushed at Rob, fists forming.

Heidi moved like a mother lion in between them.

A stream of expletives poured out of Tolliver's mouth, met by a similar torrent out of Rob's.

The voice of Jocko Freeman shouted, "Enough!" Then he was on the stage holding Tolliver back.

"Everybody," Jocko said, "take a twenty-minute break!"

"Some actor," Rob muttered.

Tolliver said, "You wouldn't know good acting if it bit you in the—"

"That'll be all," Jocko Freeman said, gently pulling Tolliver off the stage.

When they were alone, Jocko said, "What's got into you, Franklin?"

Tolliver said, "Where does he get off talking to me like that?"

"Is something wrong? You seem out of sorts."

"I didn't come here to get insulted."

"You came here because you're hurting," Jocko Freeman said in his grandfatherly tone.

Franklin Tolliver felt like his soul had been ripped out of him and hung on a line. He quickly stuffed it back in. "I just got bored and wanted a workout."

Jocko cocked his head.

"You don't believe me?" Tolliver said.

"You're holding back," Jocko said. "An actor can't do that. Why don't you come back to workshop?"

"I don't workshop anymore!" Tolliver said. "I'm beyond this place!"

He ran out of the building, only half sorry he'd said those words.

"Listen good," Fireboy said.

It was two in the morning, and Tolliver was in Fireboy's crib in East L.A. His combo sleeping quarters and lab, more precisely. To be completely accurate, it was a shack backing up to an alley with a strip mall on the other side.

A dim yellow light bulb dangling from the ceiling coated the place in dull illumination.

"I'm listening," Tolliver said.

Fireboy pointed to a gray block of what looked like clay, sitting on a wooden workbench. "This is Composition 4," Fireboy said. "C-4 to you. Plastic explosive."

"That stuff's dangerous," Tolliver said.

"Oh, thanks for telling me," Fireboy said.

"I mean, it could go off."

Fireboy shook his head. "You don't tell me how to blow things up, and I won't tell you how to do Hamlet. How's that sound?"

"But what if I jostle it?" Tolliver said.

"This isn't nitro. You can drop it, you can play with it, you can mold it into a statue of George Washington if you want to. It's not gonna explode. It has to be detonated. You got to have enough shock to kick off the chemical reaction that makes it go boom. Capiche?"

"I guess," Tolliver said.

"Well, I don't guess," Fireboy said, with more than a little boom in his voice. "This is my business, see? This is what I do. Nobody knows how much skill this takes."

As nervous as he was at the moment, Tolliver understood Fireboy completely. To not be appreciated for whatever it is you do in life, when you're really good at it. Tolliver, the actor. Fireboy, the bomber. Both had skill sets.

And right now, Tolliver knew the most deadly skill set was Fireboy's, and so he'd better listen.

"All right," Tolliver said. "Tell me what else I need to know."

"I'm gonna design you a detonator that'll blow people away," Fireboy said.

"What!"

"Let me rephrase that. Anybody who looks at it, and I'm talkin' bomb squad guys, they'll think it's sophisticated and deadly, but didn't trigger because of an electrical malfunction. They'll be like, Man, you are so lucky. One little electric charge and you would've been spread all over Fantasyland."

"So no matter how I handle it, it won't go off?"

"That's what I'm telling you. But it's got to look like it could. This is genius, what I'm doing here. You good with that?"

"I guess I have to be."

"Hey, man, that's not good enough. Tell me you trust me."

Tolliver's mouth was dry.

"Tell me," Fireboy said.

"I ... trust you."

"Aces! Now, where's the money?"

Tolliver took an envelope out of his inside jacket pocket and put it on the workbench. Fireboy opened it and counted out the Benjamins. Fifty of them.

"You get the other five thousand after," Tolliver said.

"If you don't blow up," Fireboy said.

Tolliver's head started to go light.

"Kidding!" Fireboy said. "You'll be as safe as newborn baby in a crib at Fort Knox. And then, my friend, you'll be gold."

Yes, yes, Tolliver thought. That's what this is about. Risk and reward. And the reward was worth it all.

D-Day.

Disneyland Day.

The day that would be the first day of the rest of his glorious life. Franklin Tolliver felt oddly serene as he approached the courtyard between the two parks—Disneyland to the left, California Adventure to the right.

And in the middle the huddled masses yearning to breathe fun.

It was Friday, and school was out, so there were lots of kids with their parents. The excitement of the little tykes was a joy to Franklin Tolliver. He loved Disneyland, always had. He'd come with his mother a lot. His father was not a presence in his life, so it was just a time when he and Mom would be together having fun in "the happiest place on earth."

Mom, who had done her best to raise him a good, church-going boy. He was never very good in that role. After college, when he told his mother he was going to be an actor, she said, "I don't like that business. People only look out for themselves."

He'd told her, "Don't you worry, Mom. I'm a great actor, and I'll prove it to the whole world. And then I'll buy you a new house."

"I just want you to be happy," she said.

"Acting makes me happy," he said.

And he was starting to act now, here at Disneyland. Just another visitor, with a hat and shades. He didn't need any autograph seekers this day.

He ambled toward the Disneyland gates—noting that his ambling was perfectly nonchalant, sort of like Montgomery Clift in *Red River.* Now there was a great actor! Franklin Tolliver was in that league for sure, and it was time people knew it.

The trash can with Mickey on it was right where he'd spotted it a week ago. Just to the left of the first turnstile.

He also spotted a couple of screeners. In his research he discovered that Disneyland had specially trained security to watch both sides of the gates. If anybody seemed suspicious, a screener would follow that person around for further observation.

That's why Tolliver had selected this location, just far enough from the gates so the screeners wouldn't come into play.

His palms were sweaty. But it was a good sweat. The kind he got when the cameras were about to roll. Time to start the scene. He put his phone to his ear and paced, as if talking to Steven Spielberg. He mouthed some words every now and then so any security guard would think nothing of his presence.

A little girl with Minnie Mouse ears smiled at him. He smiled back. The girl's mother gave him a look and smiled. An all-smiles bonus! It was a good sign.

And then he spotted him. Fireboy. Walking casually his way out of Downtown Disney. Dressed, for once, in clean clothes. But a cowboy hat! Could he have been more conspicuous?

But then Tolliver remembered what Fireboy had told him. A good bomb planter did not dress like the Unabomber, for heaven's sake, as in shades and a hoodie. You've got to *look* conspicuous, not like somebody trying to hide in plain sight.

So on he came, and Tolliver turned away from him, still moving his lips in his faux convo with Spielberg. *"Sure, Steve, I can start filming on Monday. See you on the set!"*

After ten seconds or so he turned back around.

Fireboy was just standing there, smiling at him!

What the—!

Then Fireboy took a step to the left and Tolliver saw it.

The bomb.

The ever-loving bomb.

In all its deadly glory.

Fireboy started walking back the way he came.

And it was time.

It was now or never.

And it couldn't be never.

Except in one respect.

His life would never be the same again.

As per their plan, Tolliver counted down from ten.

Nine.

Eight.

Seven.

Six.

Not enough children around!

Five.

Four.

No, wait. A woman with a stroller.

Three.

A double stroller! Two babies!

Two.

One.

An extra second, letting the woman get closer. Then—

"Look out!" Tolliver screamed. He dropped his phone and charged, sweeping up the bomb, about five feet away from the woman and stroller.

The bomb itself was a mess of exposed wires and a square casing. Inside, he knew, was the C-4.

And now it was in his hands.

When Walt Disney first conceived of Disneyland, he wanted it to be a magical place. Kids and adults could come from all the corners of the United States—and the world, eventually—to be transported to an environment of pure enchantment.

So heralded was the opening in 1955 that it was run live on the ABC television network, with host Ronald Reagan. Sure, there were mishaps. Mr. Toad's Wild Ride overloaded the circuits, which didn't help considering the record-level heat.

But the crowds were enormous, and within the first ten weeks a million visitors entered through the gates.

The numbers only went on from there, even in the wake of several tragic events. Kids injured, even a few deaths. Which were all covered by the Disney lawyers who were as cold and hard as the Queen from *Sleeping Beauty*.

But never had there been a bomb.

Until now.

Tolliver headed for the Mickey Mouse trash receptacle, screaming, "Call security! Call security!"

He heard a wonderful sound—the screaming of two frightened children—and sensed the beginnings of current cultural herd activity: the taking out of phones, the recording of video.

Now only ten feet from the refuse can.

Tolliver heard a *boom.*

And then realized the *boom* was his heart, spiking with anticipation.

Three steps, and then he was there.

He shoved the bomb into the Mickey bin and, for good measure—and as rehearsed a hundred times in his mind—he flung himself upon it, sending it to the ground, with him on top, as a soldier throwing his body on a live grenade would do.

And there he stayed.

Now it was a matter of the supporting cast.

First on the scene was a young woman in Disney colors, with a shoulder mic.

"Sir!" she said. "Do not move!"

That was Tolliver's cue to roll off the receptacle and say, "Bomb! There's a bomb!"

A look of panic spread over the young woman's face. This was no lost child scenario, no missing purse left at Space Mountain. After a moment's hesitation, she spoke into her mic as she waved an arm at the gathering crowd.

Tolliver got to his knees, then his feet. A good twenty or thirty people, including kids, were gawking. Waving his arms, Tolliver shouted, "Get back! Get back!"

Several people followed his instructions, but three or four held up their phones, recording events.

Good, Tolliver thought. You're on!

"Back! Please!" he said. "There's a bomb!"

A woman's voice said, "That's Franklin Tolliver!"

A hand caught his arm. It was the security woman. "Stay with me," she said.

"We need to get everybody back!" Tolliver said. He yanked his arm away and went to the young couple closest to him. High schoolers, from the look of them. The girl had her phone up, trained on Tolliver's face.

"Please, get back," Tolliver said. "There's a bomb in the trash can."

The boy said, "Hey, you're Franklin Tolliver."

"Get back!"

"Cool," the boy said.

Tolliver turned his head slightly to the left so the camera would catch his good side.

Three black-shirted men raced out from the park. Two of them grabbed Franklin by the arms and hustled him away from the crowd. The other black shirt joined the security woman to keep the crowd back. The last thing Tolliver saw before being yanked through a gate was at least five phones trained on him.

That's a wrap, he thought.

It was five hours before Franklin Tolliver got away from the Happiest Place on Earth. In that time he sat in a security office just a stone's throw from Main Street. He told his story four times. The last time was to an Anaheim police detective named Andreesen, who gave Tolliver his card and said he might have a few follow up questions for him.

"We've got to catch the guy who did this," Andreesen said.

"I'll do whatever I can," Tolliver said.

Back at his apartment, emotionally and physically drained, Franklin Tolliver fell asleep. When he woke up it was nearly five p.m.

He turned on the TV and went to Channel 5, the local news.

A commercial for Liv-A-Snaps doggie treats was just ending. Then the news desk, with the man and woman co-anchors giving a tease for the broadcast.

"A TV star becomes a real-life hero at Disneyland," the man said.

"And a potentially dangerous gas leak near a megachurch in North Hills," the woman said.

"All that, and the latest on the Dodgers shakeup, coming next!"

Tolliver looked at his muted phone. Fourteen calls, ten voicemails. He listened to the one from his agent. *Are you kidding me? Are you freaking kidding me? I'm asking, ARE YOU KIDDING ME? Call me!*

There were messages from CNN and Fox News.

The Tonight Show.

And from someone working for Malpaso Productions requesting a talk about movie rights. Malpaso...yes! Clint Eastwood's company!

A big smile spread across Franklin Tolliver's face.

The last message was a familiar voice

That smile pretty much stayed there for the next two weeks. Franklin Tolliver was not only the toast of Hollywood. He was a national phenomenon unlike anyone since Lindbergh. And Tolliver didn't even know who Lindbergh was!

The only sour note was from a gadfly Hollywood blogger who said that it all seemed too pat, too perfect. He was swarmed by social media blowback, so much so that he had to suspend his Twitter account.

Which made Franklin Tolliver very happy.

The last message was a familiar voice. "Aces! You are the man of the moment. You're gold. Just a reminder about our meeting tonight."

Anxious little firebug, Tolliver thought. But he guessed he deserved the next payment, for sure. The five grand was in a shoebox in Tolliver's closet. A small price to pay for the unlimited future now stretching out before him.

He spent the next two hours setting up appearances on TV and talking to his agent about Malpaso. His agent said it was time for Franklin Tolliver to think about setting up his own production company.

Tolliver had fun thinking up possible names for his company as he drove to East. L.A.

"Genius," Fireboy said. "Didn't I tell you?"

"You told me," Tolliver said.

"You hear the bomb guy on Channel 9? You hear how lucky every-body was it didn't go off?"

"Lucky, all right."

"Luck had nothin' to do with it." In the dim, yellow light of the shack, Fireboy's eyes trained on Tolliver. "But you get all the glory."

"It all worked out," Tolliver said, quickly adding, "Just like you said."

Tolliver put the envelope with the five grand on the workbench, just as he had before.

Fireboy just looked at it.

"It's all there," Tolliver said.

Fireboy looked at Tolliver again. "Yep, all the glory. All the money ..."

"You want to count it?" Tolliver said.

"Movie deals," Fireboy said. "Big movies. They pay, what, twenty million for somebody like you?"

"I'll go visit Dix and tell him what a good job you did," Tolliver said.

"I gotta figure that five grand is a good number from now on."

"I don't think I'll be needing you again," Tolliver said.

"But you do."

"Huh?"

"To keep quiet."

Fireboy smiled. The hole where his tooth was missing seemed like the entrance to a dark abyss.

Tolliver's voice trembled as he said, "You want another five thousand?"

"A month," Fireboy said.

"You ... we ... that wasn't our deal."

"New deal," Fireboy said. "And for that I won't let the news hounds know how you hired me to make a fake bomb."

"But ... you can't do that without getting in trouble yourself."

"What trouble? A misdemeanor? But then I'll be famous, too. I'll show 'em all how I did it, and everybody'll know I'm a genius, and you're a fraud. And they'll hear it, too."

Fireboy took something out of his dirty shirt pocket. It looked like a small phone. There was a little red light on the thing, illuminated.

A digital recording device!

Franklin Tolliver's head went into automatic improvisation mode. He was now in a role, a master assassin, like Jason Statham. Indeed, Tolliver had a small, non-speaking role in a Statham movie when he was just starting out, and one day on the set he studied Statham as he went through his choreography for a fight scene with four stunt men.

The way Statham had used his elbows to simulate the smashing of two noses simultaneously. How fast he was, too.

Which was how Franklin Tolliver's right elbow went plowing into Fireboy's face. It landed with brutal and satisfying force. Fireboy crashed to the floor.

Improv class! I am Jason Statham!

That's an assassin on the floor!

He must die!

The first time he'd been here, Tolliver noticed an awl among Fireboy's tools. It had been on a small table by the door.

It still was.

Franklin Statham Tolliver grabbed it.

And plunged it into Fireboy's neck.

And again.

And again.

Tolliver didn't know how long he stood there, motionless but for the rising and falling of his chest. At some point he moved into another role, from one of those CSI shows. He thought about evidence. He hadn't touched anything except the awl, which was still in his hand.

A hand that was covered with blood.

He bent over Fireboy's lifeless body and wiped his bloody hand on Fireboy's shirt. He cleaned the blood off the awl the same way.

There was a canister of Fresh Scent Wet Ones antibacterial wipes sitting on a corner of the workbench. Tolliver took two out and wrapped them around the awl. Then he took another wipe, picked up the envelope with the five Gs, and walked carefully to the door, avoiding the pool of blood on the floor.

Using the wipe, he opened the door, went out, and closed it.

His body was buzzing with adrenaline as he drove away. But he calmed himself with the assurance that he'd gotten away with it. No one could associate him with Fireboy. The only time they could have been seen together was at that lunch at Micelli's. But what detective was going to think to canvass all of Hollywood to find out if anyone knew a low-life criminal who was dead in East Los Angeles?

By the time Franklin Tolliver got off the freeway at Gower, he was feeling more confident than ever. This was just another acting role, the cool lone wolf who killed a bad guy. The only thing he needed was a memorable catch phrase, like *Hasta la vista, baby!*

Then inspiration struck. *That's awl you get!*

Franklin Tolliver started laughing hysterically.

Two blocks from his apartment building, Tolliver pulled over to the curb on the opposite side of the street, so his driver's door was next to it. There was a storm drain there. Tolliver opened his door and threw the awl and the wipes into the drain.

Except the awl hit the top of the curb and didn't go down.

Cursing, Tolliver leaned out of his car and flicked the awl with the back of his hand. Down it went.

But when he sat up again something flashed in his rearview mirror.

It couldn't be!

But it was.

A cop car was pulling up right behind him, its colored light bar flickering.

No!

Think!

Another acting job. You can do this. Stay cool.

Tolliver closed the door but put the window down.

A uniformed officer approached with an illuminated flashlight.

"Are you all right, sir?" the officer said.

"Feeling a little sick," Tolliver said. "I thought I might throw up."

"Been drinking?"

"What? No. I had kind of a big day and I'm not feeling right."

"Would you mind stepping out of the car for a moment?"

"What for?"

"I'd just like to make sure you're all right to drive."

"I am, officer. I only live a couple of blocks away. I just need to get to bed."

The light flashed in his eyes.

Tolliver blinked, covered his face with his hand.

"Put your hand down, please," the officer said.

Better do as he says.

Tolliver lowered his hand.

"It *is* you!" the officer said. "You're the guy who saved those kids at Disneyland!"

After two weeks of glory and acclaim and a contract to star—star!—in a big-budget action film, Franklin Tolliver got a call from Detective

Andreesen, asking if he wouldn't mind stopping by the station for a few final questions.

"Thank you for coming in," Andreesen said, taking Tolliver to a quiet room with a microwave and small refrigerator. He motioned for Tolliver to have a seat at a round table. "Can I get you something to drink?"

"A Diet Coke if you have one," Tolliver said.

Andreesen brought the can to Tolliver along with a Styrofoam cup.

"Are you any closer to finding out who planted the bomb?" Tolliver said at the same time he popped the can open.

"I'm afraid not," Andreesen said, sitting at the table and plopping down a pad and pen. "Which may mean, at this point, we never will."

"That's terrible!"

Andreesen nodded. "But thanks to you, something worse didn't happen. Your actions were, well, amazing. Just amazing."

"I didn't think about it," Tolliver said. "I just did it."

"It's a good thing you were where you were."

"Just luck. If you can call it luck." Tolliver chuckled, the way a modest hero might chuckle. He wished he was in acting class for this, to show that Heidi chick what he was capable of.

Andreesen said, "Now, just to go back to the beginning, you were getting ready to go into the park?"

"Yes."

"What were you doing just before you saw the bomb?"

"I was just talking on the phone."

"To who?"

Oops. Phone records! They could check. Why hadn't he thought of that?

No matter. Act cool.

"Tell you the truth," Tolliver said with a shy smile, "I'm kind of embarrassed."

"Don't be," Detective Andreeson said. "What you say here, stays here."

Tolliver leaned forward, holding the Diet Coke in both hands. "See, I didn't want people talking to me, asking for autographs and all that. I know that sounds arrogant, but I get that all the time."

"So the old pretend-to-be-on-the-phone trick?"

"Exactly."

"How'd you notice the bomb?" Andreeson said.

"Well, like I said, I was pretending to talk and waiting for the park to open, just walking up and down, and I looked and, well, there it was."

"How did you know it was a bomb?"

"I've been in some thrillers. I know what a homemade bomb looks like."

"It's funny," Detective Andreeson said. "Most bombers hide these things in a backpack or some such."

"Sure."

"And it was placed sort of to the side, not where it would do the most damage."

"I didn't even think of that. I didn't even think at all."

"So you scooped it up?"

"Yeah. I saw it was near a trash can, and just stuck it in there. I really didn't think."

"No thoughts at all?"

"Just that there were some kids around."

"It was an incredibly brave thing you did."

"I don't know. Sometimes you just do something. That's all. I don't want any credit."

"But you're sure getting it. You're all over the place."

Tolliver took a sip of his diet Coke.

Andreesen touched his lip with the top of his pen. Then said, "I had this wild thought."

Tolliver thought that was an odd choice of words.

"If somebody wanted to get really famous," Andreesen said, "he could set up something just like this. He'd hire some low-level bomb maker to make a bomb that looked like it could go off, but wouldn't. And then find some public place. Like Disneyland."

Tolliver felt his pulse pounded his neck. "That'd be a sick thing to do," he said.

"I agree," Andreesen said. "You're sick."

"Excuse me?"

"Why'd you do it, Mr. Tolliver?"

Keep cool. "That's a terrible thing to say."

"I'm just asking."

"You honestly think I set it up?"

"I do."

"But why?"

Andreesen put his pen on the table and looked deeply into Tolliver's eyes. "Because," he said, "you're just not that good of an actor."

The jolt of the insult hit Franklin Tolliver like a high-voltage wire. His body jerked from the chair. "What do you know about acting? You cop, you nothing cop! I am the greatest actor of my generation, and now everybody is going to know it because I saved those kids at Disneyland! You didn't! I did! I'm the one who's all over the place, not you! And you sit here and accuse me of doing a thing like this! Like I'd make a fake bomb and pretend!"

"That's what actors do, though, isn't it?"

"I'm leaving now," Tolliver said.

"One more thing," Andreesen said. "Why'd you say fake bomb?"

Franklin Tolliver had to use ever fiber of his actor's being not to let his face betray him. His shoulders, quite on their own, shrugged. He'd never studied shoulder action in acting class.

"Because," Andreesen said, "we had an expert from the LAPD bomb squad give us a hand. He said that bomb was expertly made ... expertly made not to go off, that is. He was impressed. And he said he knew of only one guy who could do such a job. He actually called this guy a genius. Name of ..." Andreesen looked at his notebook "... Lyle Fitz, known in the trade as Fireboy. Does that name ring a bell?"

"Never heard of him," Tolliver said. But his voice cracked when he said *Never*.

"Yeah, so we paid a little visit to his pad, and what do you know? He's lying there dead. Some ugly puncture wounds to his neck. We're going over the scene right now with that proverbial fine-tooth comb. Would you like another Diet Coke?"

Franklin Tolliver shook his head slowly.

"You can quit acting now," Andreesen said.

Three years after pleading guilty to manslaughter, Franklin Tolliver was paroled from prison. He no longer had an agent or a show. During that first year of incarceration, however, he became a Twitter hashtag: #WorseActorsThanFranklinTolliver. Over eight thousand Twitterati had responded with answers, likes, re-tweets, memes, and scorn.

Relying on his cousin Dix, and some of the other contacts he'd made in prison, Franklin Tolliver purchased a false ID under the name Enrique Angel Escobar. He had an underground plastic surgeon rework his face. He then moved to a small town in Louisiana and got a job at McDonald's.

In August, the local theater company held open auditions for its upcoming production of *Show Boat*. Enrique Angel Escobar auditioned for the part of Gaylord Ravenal, the dashing riverboat gambler. He did not get the part.

Confronting the director, a woman named Cecilia Cummings, after the audition, Enrique Angel Escobar demanded to know why he wasn't cast.

"I felt you were trying too hard," Ms. Cummings said. "Why don't you join our acting workshop?"

MISS MAGENTA

OCTOBER

"Oh, dear," Millicent Magenta van Slayton said, looking out at her flower garden. She said this because there were no flowers. Indeed, nothing had bloomed there for twenty-three years.

Yet each day Miss Magenta, as she had been known since she was a teen, would venture from the house into the small, walled patch of ground and poke at the dirt with a trowel, as if to magically induce a horticultural rebirth. As if to prove to herself there was life somewhere outside the old house which challenged her with encroaching death.

It was the soil, Dr. Severen had once told her. The soil, he said, needs aeration and fertilization, and perhaps a chemical compound. "Which must," he said, "be just about three feet below the surface."

The mention of a chemical anything horrified Miss Magenta, for she believed only in the purely natural.

Indeed, sixty years earlier she had danced *au natural* in the Folies Bergère in Paris. For three nights running, drawing massive crowds, who were not scandalized by the view (being French) but were instead awed by Miss Magenta's Can-Can-kick finale. Her kick leg was able to reach a position perfectly straight up, as if she had no hamstring at all.

But when her mother heard about all this she demanded Miss Magenta's return to the family home in Suffolk County.

Once Miss Magenta was back in the fold, the matriarch of the van Slayton family, widowed and embittered and (it was said) more than a little batty, proceeded to mold her only child into a facsimile of herself, using all the psychological weaponry of past van Slaytons, who had come to the shores of the new world with slaves and an iron-fisted will which they passed on to generations of offspring—a line which finally died out with the death of Manfred van Slayton shortly before the cultural event known as Woodstock.

The result of the widow van Slayton's program of emotional coercion —fueled in large part by the threat of withholding the family fortune from her daughter in preference to a bequest to Sarah Lawrence College, from which the widow had graduated in 1940—was that Miss Magenta never left the grounds of the old house again.

And what was in that house, people increasingly wanted to know. There was a report from a lineman who was working a nearby power pole, and who carried a convenient set of binoculars (rumors that he had been paid by the *Suffolk County News* to take a peep), that the house was crammed with all manner of items. From stacks and stacks of newspapers and magazines, to a pile of stuffed animals, to floor to ceiling books. Books, that is, not shelves.

The story that ran in the *News* used the term *hoarders*.

Through the family lawyer, the widow van Slayton instituted a libel suit. It was thrown out in summary judgment, and before the appeal could be filed Miss Magenta's mother died.

That had been sixteen years ago.

There was some trouble about the will and the funeral arrangements. A couple of distant cousins came out of the woodwork to contest the will. Miss Magenta called in the family lawyer once more, Mr. Harrison Bonteller of Bonteller, Bonteller, Macready & Phitts. The litigation took eighteen months, and Miss Magenta did not have to appear in court. Harrison Bonteller was completely victorious and Miss Magenta was suddenly worth, after attorney's fees and estate taxes, twelve million dollars.

Eleven million of that she placed in a simple savings account, despite the advice of Harrison Bonteller.

The other million, in various denominations, was spread out in different nooks and cubbies in the big old house.

Any needs she had, including visits from a private physician, were paid for in cash.

Which led to rumors in town that Miss Magenta was sitting on a ton of raw bills in her stuffed house. And if anyone ever got in there and was able to look around, he might find a goodly chunk of change.

The rumor was given voice one day in Suffolk Station Coffee, a high-end java place a mile from Miss Magenta's home. The speakers were two local teenagers—Brianna and Dakota—offspring of two high-end Suffolk County couples.

Sitting at an adjoining table was a transient named Eddie Kagle, twenty-eight, who had skipped out on his probation in Nebraska and was trolling the rich neighborhoods of the east for an easy score.

What could be easier than a crazy old bat living alone?

Eddie Kagle was no dummy. He'd finished high school and was accepted by the University of Nebraska. But a drug habit sent him in another direction, the trajectory of which landed him in the jug for two years. Which Eddie Kagle used to (as his dear old granny used to say) turn lemons into lemonade. He learned from his cellie the fine art of breaking and entering, and how to research a target.

Which was what Eddie was doing on a fine October day, on a bluff with a pair of stolen binoculars. He could see the grounds from the east side. The place was ringed by a high, ivy-covered wall. The only entrance was gated.

There was a massive security warning sign posted in front of the gate. Two camera stanchions were positioned on either side of the drive.

Another stanchion rose out of the back yard, its electronic eye gazing down at the hillside behind the house. Eddie, who had once been good at geometry, calculated an angle of approach that would give him the best, stealthy route to the back wall. From there, he'd be able to scale it relatively easily. He'd have to be careful about hidden spikes or electrified wiring. But something in his gut told him anything like that was as obsolescent as the old bag inside the house.

But as far as Eddie could determine, the wall in the rear portion could be scaled by someone with the right equipment and the right moxie.

His granny always told Eddie he had moxie.

And in the slam Eddie also learned patience. For four days he watched the house, looking for patterns. Only twice did he see a car pull into the property after the driver punched a code at the gate.

The first time it was an older man carrying a black bag. He went inside the house and stayed twenty-seven minutes.

The second instance was a delivery van with SIPE'S MARKET stenciled on the back. A young man got out and carried a box to the front door. The door opened and he went inside. Four minutes later he came out the same way.

That was it for the daytime.

And no one came at night.

The only other form of life Eddie saw down there was the coffin dodger herself, who came out of the house once a day, into the back yard. She seemed always to be muttering to herself. She would look at the dirt for about ten minutes before going back inside.

On Tuesday night Eddie, in his sleeping bag, looking up at the stars, decided the next night he would make his move.

His only unresolved question was whether or not to kill the old girl after he got the money.

Miss Magenta sat at the kitchen table. Her companions were seventy stuffed animals from various years in her life, piled up on the elaborate, curved bench of carved mahogany. As was her custom before going to bed, Miss Magenta selected one of the animals as her primary friend for the evening.

Tonight it was her black mohair Scotty dog, which she had received for Christmas, 1941. Only five years old at the time, Miss Magenta was aware enough to know that something "big" had happened recently, something about "Japs" and bombs, and everyone was listening to the radio all the time. And she knew the one voice, the comforting voice that belonged to the president of the United States, and she also knew he had a Scottish terrier named Fala, which her developing brain interpreted as *Fella*. Which is what she named her new toy.

Tonight, eating her instant Cream of Wheat, Miss Magenta talked of the old days with Fella, who stood attentively on the table.

"Do you remember Rory Calhoun?" Miss Magenta inquired. "He had such dreamy eyes. He was a real man, I can tell you. If only I had met him before running off to Paris. I could have landed him, you know. In those days, I could have landed anybody."

Fella did not say anything.

But something fell in the house. A distant noise. A thump. Near the French doors?

"Oh, dear," Miss Magenta said. It was probably a stack of newspapers. They went down periodically, having taken on, over time, the character of the Leaning Tower of Pisa. Gravity inevitably caught up a pile, and down it would go. Once it was the *New York Times* of roughly three years. Another time a beautiful stack of *Life, Look,* and *The Saturday Evening Post.* It would mean at least a day of re-stacking. More if she found herself caught by some old issue or other, like the time she looked with jaundiced eye at the *Look* cover story on Liz Taylor shortly after her first split with Richard Burton.

Ah, well. Tomorrow she would have a look at the new mess. It would give her something more to do than poke around in the useless garden. Perhaps she would—

"Did you hear that, Fella?" she said.

Fella merely stared.

"I think ... I think someone may be in the house!"

Eddie almost cursed an amplified blue streak. Only the rigid self-discipline of the former incarceree kept him from it. He had a plan and it did not include making more noise than a falling pile of newspapers. His pen flashlight illuminated the clutter and his nose took in the musty scent of old, printed broadsheets. What almost took his breath away was what remained. A veritable forest of stacked reading materials taking up what looked like every livable space in the room. Except for a corridor about a wingspan wide.

He hadn't counted on having to find the old lady's bedroom through a labyrinth of junk. If the whole house was like this it would take more than a little dexterity to get through this place. His thought was to surprise her in her sleep, get the max out of shock value. Get her to talk with the fear of death staring her in the face.

Now he was wondering if he'd even find her in the first place.

And then he didn't have to worry anymore, for she found him.

"How dare you!" Miss Magenta said. From the beam of the little flashlight Eddie saw that she was tall and rather thin, a bit stooped over, her gray hair long and brushed smooth. She wore black silk pajamas with gold stitching along the sleeves and pants.

Her face was angular and pasty and at the moment held an expression of wide-eyed rage.

"Get out!" she said.

"Hold it, lady," Eddie said.

"You are not allowed in here!"

"You just stay chill and you won't get hurt."

"Come, Fella!" The lady slapped her thigh. "Come on, boy!"

Oh great, a dog. Well, if it came to that, he'd use the .38 to plug the mutt and then he'd have to get rough with the old hag.

"Get him, Fella! Get him!"

Eddie waited. Heard nothing. No approaching paws or snarling lips.

Was there a dog at all? Or was she as crazy as a soup sandwich?

"And all the fires of hell and gone will rain down upon you!" she said.

Soup sandwich, definitely.

Eddie said, "This doesn't have to be hard. You just tell me where the money is and I'll be on my way."

"Evil, evil!" The lady waved her arms around. Then turned her back on him and shuffled into the shadows.

Now he'd have to get physical. What a mess. Not just the house, the whole plan.

You can't reason with a nutcase. He'd have to use pure terror to get her to talk.

If, that was, he could find her.

Following the last known direction of the shadowy gray hair, Eddie lit his way down a corridor lined on either side with plastic tubs and cardboard boxes, piles of books and vinyl albums—on top of one stack was a Frank Sinatra album called *Come Fly With Me,* with an illustration of a jaunty Sinatra in a hat taking an unseen woman's hand—two piles of neatly folded towels, with hotel monograms, a great big silver bowl filled with matchbooks, an actual wooden orange crate with ... bobble head dolls! And one of the doll heads bent backward so it was staring right back at Eddie. It was a ballerina bobble head and she looked ticked off at having her dancing days ended.

Eddie got a chill. If this was a horror movie, those dolls would soon be after him.

But this wasn't a horror movie. This was just a plain old nightmare of a job, and he was getting plenty hot about it. Maybe he'd just kill the witch and take whatever collectibles seemed valuable. In the joint he was allowed TV time, and watched that show *American Pickers* all the time. He'd be able to figure something out.

No, he wanted the cash.

Now which way did she go?

Miss Magenta, circa 1959, could tap, dance on toe, and give Cyd Charisse a run for her money. Everybody said so! She was still limber, and if it came down to it she could outrun this criminal, this hooligan, this intruder, and what was he doing here, anyway?

Surely not something ... unmentionable! But she would well understand if that were the intent, for she had never lost her looks! No, nor her allure! Men had always been jelly at her feet, even though it had been quite some time since Yves Montand drank champagne out of her shoe.

Shoe!

She had slippers on.

As she padded up the spiral staircase, she thought about dancing shoes. Yes—ballet pointe! It had been years since she'd attempted toe, but that wasn't what this was about now. It was about something else entirely, if it should come to that.

Eddie heard the creaking of the stairs. But he was unsure of the direction of the sound. He was a rat in a maze. The old lady was the cheese. Oh, she would be sorry when he got to her. This rat had teeth. At least one big tooth—a six-inch Buck knife. She'd feel it. She'd talk. Or he'd fix it so she never talked again.

The smell of the place. Like old nightgowns. Like stale perfume that had soaked into the walls. Like a coffin must smell after two weeks in the ground, and why did he think of that particular image?

Sweaty desperation bit him, made his underarms wet. Eddie had never believed in ghosts but he was starting to reassess. If a skeleton jumped out from behind one of the piles of junk he would have been scared, sure, but not surprised. Not now.

He found the stairs. It was a jumble of items, things like porcelain cats and large colored rocks and old candy boxes—at least a dozen of them. A crazy person's idea of decoration!

Up he went, and at the top of the stairs his flashlight hit on a Buddha statuette, the fat thing sitting and smiling, as if it knew something Eddie did not. He felt like smashing it in the face.

But he heard something.

Movement.

He shot his beam quickly to the right and there she was! And she moved ... quick and lithe, and to his astonishment her right leg was coming up, up, and fast and he took a foot to the bottom of his chin and in that flash between pain and falling he thought *She kicked me!* and then down the stairs he went, backward, neck and head and shoulders banging, nose crunching, legs overhead then underneath, until he thumped on hard ground and then into blackness.

And then awareness.

He couldn't breathe. He couldn't move. Pressing down on him, what was it, an avalanche of smelly ... what? ... newspapers! And a force pressing it all down. Like someone pressing ... no ... jumping on top of the odious pile.

Can't breathe.

Can't breathe!

Can't ... breathe ...

MAY

Dr. Severen said, "I must say you are looking quite well."

"I am feeling quite well," Miss Magenta said.

"You won't need anything more from me today, nor perhaps for a month."

"Yves Montand once drank champagne out of my shoe."

"Yes, I know, dear. You've told me that."

"But have you seen?"

"Seen?"

"Come!"

He followed her through the labyrinth and to the French doors. She opened them wide and spread her hands. He looked beyond and saw something wonderful. Flowers!

"This is fantastic, Miss Magenta," he said. "Utterly fantastic."

"All I needed was the right fertilization below the surface," she said. "And purely natural."

"Really? May I ask what it was?"

"I don't know the name," Miss Magenta said. "It was something I found in the house."

THE TIP

Lily knew the guy would be trouble.

Last customer before closing was always trouble. Usually some drunk coming in to get pancakes and coffee to soak up the booze in his gut. Dave's Flapjack House was at the edge of town, with a liquor store and tavern across the road. Locals who worked at Henderson Farms and the new Motel 6 frequented Dave's, mostly in the morning. Truckers rolling on Interstate 80—hauling freight to Des Moines or Omaha or Salt Lake City—loved the last-stop feel of the place and, truth-be-told, flirting with Lily, who worked graveyard until Dave's shut down at 2 a.m.

It had been a quiet night, if you didn't include the three college kids who drove down from State and, reeking of marijuana, came in for stacks and couldn't stop laughing and talking in what Lily's mom called "outside voices." It got so noisy that Frank Stallings, a regular, sitting at the counter, told Lily he wasn't enjoying his buckwheat cakes because he wanted to stuff them in his ears.

Lily went over to the table and politely asked if they might keep it down a bit. The kids–two boys and a girl, if you were allowed to make that assumption anymore–looked at each other and nodded, then cracked up again. Fortunately, they downed their flaps in record time, fueled no doubt by the hunger pangs induced by the hippie lettuce. That got them out of there faster than the usual patron, but they paid with a card and left Lily only a five percent tip.

So she was feeling less than cheerful when the man in the leather jacket waltzed in at 1:57 and parked himself at the booth by the door.

This meant she and Carlos, the night cook, would be here at least until three, what with the side work and cleanup. Three, that was, unless this guy was one of those casual eaters who took his own sweet time finishing.

The man—around forty, Lily guessed—looked sour and in no mood for chitchat. Which was fine with Lily, who merely said, "Coffee?" when she got to the booth.

"Definitely," the man said. He had a low voice with some gravel in it. With his slicked-back black hair and bushy eyebrows, he looked like an east coast city guy, not somebody from here in the heartland.

Lily handed him a menu and turned to go, but the guy said, "Hey."

She turned back.

"No friendly hello?" he said.

"Hello," Lily said.

"Nah. Say it like you mean it."

He smiled then. His teeth were small and white.

"It's been a long night, sir," Lily said.

"But the customer is always right, am I right?"

No, not always right. Not the college kids high on weed, and not you with your stupid demand for friendliness at...what...1:59 in the morning.

"Can I bring you something to eat?" Lily said.

"Stubborn lass, aren't you?" the man said. "Doesn't say much for the service in this joint."

Joint? Who uses the word joint anymore? Maybe those college kids, but in a much different context.

"Sir, I'm happy to serve you whatever you order. I'll go get your coffee."

"Hope you're a little less sour when you get back."

Sour doesn't begin to describe it, Mac.

Lily went to the coffee station. She didn't dilly dally. Years of experience taught her that the sooner you get a customer his coffee, the better all around. Your tip could depend on the one transaction.

She filled a cup and brought it to the table, put it down.

The man was studying the menu.

"See anything you like?" Lily said.

He looked at her. "I do now," he said.

Maybe some jocularity was called for. Lily actually liked bandying with the truckers, and they liked it, too. She had a sharp wit, which her mother always said meant she was smart. She could have gone to college, Mom said, if she didn't have to drop out of high school to help with expenses after her father ran off with a florist from Boise.

"Honey," Lily said, "that little item's not for sale."

He didn't say anything. He gave her a full body scan with his eyes that made Lily's skin crawl around her bones.

"Just bring me a short stack of buttermilk cakes and bacon, crisp." He tossed the menu on the table. "And a better attitude."

Lily snatched the menu and made a beeline for the window.

"Short stack of butters and a side of bacon, crunchy," Lily said to Carlos.

The cook made a face and cursed in Spanish.

Lily went to the far end of the counter, as far away from the booth as the diner would allow, and began filling the sugar shakers.

The sameness of the side work brought with it the feeling of emptiness she often felt now. Turning forty a week ago, she'd come to the realization that this was it, her life, looking at salt and sugar and cream containers, and the passing headlights on the road, and she stuck in a cul-de-sac of routine. Really, all she had to show for it was a set of wrinkles and strong, shapely calves chiseled from years of being on her feet.

Her one chance to get out had been James, the rock drummer, who could melt snow with his sweet talk. Fifteen years ago it had been, a week in his motel room, promises of touring the world—New York, London, Sydney, Tokyo! And then one day he was gone, gone, gone. No note. Nothing. And she was stuck with the bill and no way to pay it. Her pleading and tears to the manager at least got her off the financial hook. In return, she worked a month at the place cleaning toilets and changing linens and wishing she were dead.

She was wishing the same thing now.

She gathered up all the ketchup bottles and cleaned them up. Clarice, who worked the early shift, would do the refilling. Clarice, all of twenty-two, who dreamed of going to Los Angeles to break into the TV biz. Dreams. At least Clarice still had them.

"Order up!" Carlos said.

Lily went to the window and picked up the plate of pancakes and bacon. She grabbed the coffee carafe and went back to the table.

The man was smiling with those ferret teeth. Lily put the plate down and refilled his coffee cup.

"Anything else I can get you?" Lily said, out of habit.

"You can sit down and keep me company," he said.

"Aw, thanks. But I've got to get ready to close up."

"No you don't," he said.

"Some other time, sweet thing," she said in her best kiss-off banter, and quickly went back to work. It was a relief to be away from him. But she felt his eyes on her with each salt and pepper shaker she filled.

The check still had to be delivered. Her nerves vibrated like a blender as she approached and set it on the table.

He didn't say anything. Didn't make eye contact. Just kept eating.

That was a relief.

Ten minutes later the guy got up. He pulled out his wallet and put some bills on the table and walked out.

Lily gave him a moment, then went to the table and checked the amount he'd left there.

The bill had been $16.08.

He'd left a ten, a five, and a one-dollar bill.

And a quarter.

A quarter!

A tip of 17 cents!

It was 3:02 in the morning and Lily's rational faculties were unable to hold back the fire of rage in her head and heart. It was the tip that broke the camel's back, she'd later tell the troopers.

She took the quarter, burst through the door, and caught up to the guy as he was opening his car door.

"You forgot this!" She threw the quarter at his feet.

That was supposed to be her mic drop, her walk-off-the-stage moment. But it turned into something else when the man's fist pummeled the side of her face.

As she fell she was conscious of the moon in the northern sky, almost full, bright. Then somebody flipped a switch in her head and everything went dark.

———

She came to, feeling soft vibrations under her body. Her face was aching. But when she tried to touch it, she couldn't. Her hands were bound behind her back. Felt like tape. Her ankles were bound, too.

Adrenaline rushed to her head and she knew she was in the back of a car and the car was moving and it was dark.

"Help," she said.

"You okay back there?" It was that man's voice. "Want some music?"

"What?"

"Music. You like country or jazz or what?"

"Why…"

"How's that?"

"…are you doing this?"

"Relax, Tiger."

"You…hit me."

"You got a real attitude problem, that's why."

She tried to sit up. Her throbbing head was like an anchor, keeping her down.

"What are you going to do with me?" she said.

"I shouldn't tell you, but it's so good. I mean, I gotta love myself for this. And maybe I want you to think about it for a while. Think about how rude you were, and what that's gonna cost you, seeing as how you killed the Mex."

"What...did you do?"

"Nothin'. You did. Poor guy. Just thought he was closing up. He didn't expect the crazy waitress to shoot him and take all the money from the till."

Blood pounded Lily's temples. What was he saying?

"But you felt bad about it," the man said. "Couldn't live with what you did. So down the road they found you with the money, and with the gun you used to kill him, then turned on yourself."

Fear shot through her veins like scalding black coffee. And with it a sense of powerlessness, of inevitability.

Well, she had wished she was dead, didn't she? Maybe this was the way it was all supposed to go.

But no, not this way. There arose within her an animistic desire for survival, an incipient need to fight.

But fight how? She was immobilized, completely at his mercy.

"Don't worry about it," the guy said. "I'll make it quick, if you play ball. You want to play ball?"

Not knowing what he meant, Lily said nothing.

"First, you're gonna apologize to me. You're gonna say you're sorry. And you're gonna mean it."

Lily drew her knees up to her chest. It struck her that this was a fetal position, something you retreated to when you gave up. No, not this way, not this day.

She calculated she would have only one shot at this. The plan forming in her mind was a thin reed of possibility. But what else was there? It would be what the truckers called a "Hail Mary" pass in football.

Reminding her to pray. Which she hadn't done in years, except for the little "Please don't let there be trouble" kind. Her grandmother once told her there were two prayers God always heard. "Help me, help me, help me" and "Thank you, thank you, thank you."

She uttered the first one.

"What's that?" the guy said. "You got something to say? 'Cause the second thing you're gonna do is get down on the ground and kiss my feet. Then I'll make it quick."

Ronny Winkleblack. The name shot to her brain in an instant, and the feeling of dread with it, the feeling she'd had at nine years old when Ronny Winkleblack threatened to electrocute her.

She'd been walking in the hills by her house, a summer's day, holding a stick and pretending it was a sword, like Xena Warrior Princess, when she came around a tree and saw Ronny Winkleblack from school, sitting with another kid, Terry Porter. They were a class ahead of her, and Ronny smiled and called her over. Ronny, the most popular guy in school, and he was calling her over.

When she got there Ronny said, "Hey, you, you go to Melvin, don't you?"

"Yeah," Lily said.

"Sit down, look at this."

She sat and looked. He pointed at a black, brick-like thing with wires coming out of it, and Ronny asked her if she knew what that was and she said no.

"It's a battery," Ronny said. "And it has enough electricity in it to shock you to death."

Terry Porter laughed. He was standing behind her.

"If you try to run away," Ronny said, "I'm gonna electrocute you."

Lily wanted to cry, but made herself not.

For what seemed like an hour–but was probably only five minutes–Ronny and Terry told her what she was going to have to do, and part of it was taking her clothes off, and when she couldn't stand it anymore she bolted and started running. Her legs were strong even then, and fueled by fear they pumped and pistoned and she did not dare look back.

She got to the dirt road, ran down the road, ran until Bob Altman, a neighborhood boy near her house, he was in high school, saw her from his front yard and asked her what was wrong, and she ran right to him and told him about the boys on the hill who wanted to electrocute her, and Bob said, "You go home," and then he ran off toward the hill.

She was afraid to go to school after that, she made herself sick for a couple of days, but her mother made her go and when she saw Ronny Winkleblack on the playground he had a black eye and wouldn't look at her.

All that came rushing back to Lily now, being tortured by another Ronny Winkleblack, and the same desperation filled her, shifted her position, got her upright with legs folded under her, and she pushed...she *launched*...like a missile, between the front seats, her head striking the guy's arms, and she heard him yell as the car swerved. She brought the back of her head up hard, into his chin, and made solid contact as she felt his hands on her trying to push her away.

Then they were bouncing, turning over, and she was tossed, head thumping, shoulder, arm, legs, head again.

The car stopped moving. They were upside down.

The smell of gasoline.

A groan.

Not hers. His.

Could she move? All her parts working?

Pain shooting through her, but she could wiggle her fingers and move her feet.

The guy wasn't moving. It was dark, she couldn't see.

Help me help me help me.

She closed her eyes and tried to envision where she was in relation to the passenger door. It reminded her of when she was seven and her mom read her the Little House on the Prairie stories and how a little girl went blind, and she feared that could happen to her, so she would walk around the house with her eyes closed to practice, just in case.

Another groan from the guy, louder, then a word that sounded vaguely like "Help."

Backing like a crab, she felt the panel with her hands, felt around until she found the latch, pushed, heard a click!

Pushed.

The door opened a crack. But no more.

Of course! Because the car was crushed somehow.

It *had* to open!

And then it came to her. Legs. Her superpower. Her Xena Warrior Princess legs!

She rearranged her body. It came into contact with the guy's shoulder.

He said, "Hey. Help."

She thrust her legs out like a battering ram.

The door opened with a metallic shriek.

The interior light went on.

He grabbed her arm.

———

His grip was weak.

One more thrust of her legs and the door opened all the way.

She pulled away from him, slid, bumped her head, but was out on the ground.

Her neck and shoulders were on fire.

She righted herself. And looked back in the car.

The guy was pinned under the steering wheel.

Blood trickled from his nose. He turned his head.

"Help," he said.

Help? *Help*? A flurry of words came to her mind, words you would hear in bar fight, and she wanted to shout them at him, but she had to get free and get gone before he himself got out, if he could.

But she was bound.

Wait. Duct tape would rip if you could get the right leverage on it. She knew all about duct tape, it was Dave's favorite miracle fix-it, in everything from the bathroom to the freezer door.

If she could get a little tear started...the car door...a sharp point. Maybe...

She turned her back, felt for the door's corner, positioned her wrists on either side... thrust herself up.

And almost dislocated her shoulders.

"Please," the guy said. "Money. I'll give you...money."

She couldn't help thinking, *Like that lousy tip*?

Once more she tried to tear the tape. This time she heard...felt?... a rip.

She tried to pull apart, but nothing gave way.

How long would this take?

How long before the guy got out?

Five more times she put the tape to the metal.

And then she was free.

She tore the tape off her wrists. She sat on the ground and ripped the tape off her ankles.

"Help me, will you?" the man said. "Money, in my coat..."

Too late for that, pal. You should have given me money before, a real tip, and this wouldn't have happened.

You lose.

She heard the sound of a passing car on the highway. Saw the evanescence of the headlights. Painfully, slowly, she made her way up the incline.

The next headlights that came were heading in the right direction, back toward Dave's.

Lily stood on the shoulder and waved her arms. The lights were big. A truck. Would it stop? Or was it behind schedule and determined to cannonball right by?

When she heard the groan of air brakes Lily almost burst into tears.

Squinting into the bright lights she could only see the silhouette of the driver coming toward her.

A big guy.

"Lily?"

She knew that voice. "Bucky?" One of her regulars.

"What are you doin' out here? You okay?"

"Down there," Lily said. "In a car. A man. He was going to kill me."

"What?"

"The car rolled over. He's down there, wedged in."

"Kill you?"

"Yes."

"Why would anybody..."

"Don't ask me now. Get me out of here."

"Yes, sure. We need to call this in. Is he the only one down there?"

"Yeah," Lily said.

"Come on," Bucky said. "Wait in my truck."

He took her arm and walked her to the cab, opened the door, helped her in. He grabbd a flashlight from behind the seats.

"Stay right here," Bucky said.

"Bucky—"

"I need to check."

"Be careful."

And then he was gone. Lily put her head back against the seat. She close her eyes and slowed her breathing. It's over. It's all over...

She opened her eyes to the sound and vibrations of the truck. Bucky was driving.

"What..." she said.

"Hey, how you feeling?" Bucky said.

"I...I'm okay."

"Need a doctor?"

"I…don't think so."

"I'll take you home then."

"But what's going on? Where is he?"

"I called it in. They'll find him. You can tell 'em what happened tomorrow."

"But what if he—"

"He's not going anywhere," Bucky said. "You rest now. Everything'll be all right."

———

Lily woke up. She was in bed. She looked at the clock. Close to noon. Had she dreamed it? It did feel like a nightmare, but her aching limbs told her it was all too real.

"Bucky?"

A moment later her bedroom door opened and a woman said, "Ms. Benson?"

"Who are you?" Lily said.

"Trooper Maria Amato. I'm here to help. May I come in?"

"Of course."

She was young, around thirty maybe, with a face Lily liked.

"How you feeling?" Trooper Amato said.

"Like a tossed salad," Lily said. Good. Her sense of humor was okay at least.

"I think we better get you to the county hospital, to be safe. I'll have an ambulance—"

"Where's Bucky?"

"We talked to Mr. Harrison and got his statement. He had to finish his run. We'll let him know how you're doing."

"Can you tell me what's going on? The man in the car…"

"He didn't make it."

"Dead?"

"You are one lucky gal, Ms. Benson. The man was a person of interest in a robbery-murder."

Lily lost breath.

"He killed three people at a high-end poker game," Trooper Amato said. "Salvatore Spinelli was his name. Out of Las Vegas."

Lily moved her mouth, but nothing came out.

Trooper Amato said, "There'll be plenty of time to get your statement, Ms. Benson. Right now you just—"

"Carlos?"

"The cook? I'm so sorry Ms. Benson."

That's when Lily wept.

———

When Lily walked into Dave's one Tuesday morning, the whole place applauded, including Dave, who was doing the cooking.

How she wished Bucky was there.

A week later Dave let her come back to work. She needed it, she said, she needed to get busy again, to do something, and this time the work was welcome, the sameness was a comfort, the banter with customers made her feel like herself, her true self, serving and making people happy. Coffee and pancakes and bacon, the universal comfort meal.

Two days later, Bucky came in.

Lily ran into his arms.

"Easy there!" Bucky said.

"Thank you thank you thank you!" Lily said.

"Back to normal, I see," he said. "Bring me the special, huh?"

He kissed her forehead and went to the far end, the table by the door.

For a half hour, with her duties and all, Lily could only snatch bits of conversation with Bucky.

When he finished his meal, she told him that Dave said it was on the house. Bucky laughed and put two twenties on the table. "One for you and one for Dave."

He stood.

"Can't you stay awhile?" Lily said. "I'm almost off. There's so much I want to ask you."

"Lily," he said, "I'll be coming back this way tomorrow. How 'bout you and I go out for a big steak dinner, on me, and we'll talk about life and the future?"

Life and the future? What did he mean?

"Is it a date?" Bucky said.

"Oh, it so is a date," Lily said.

Bucky put one of his big arms around her and drew her in, leaned over and whispered in her ear. "The guy left you a tip."

"Huh?"

He kissed her again, this time on the cheek. Then he was out the door. Lily watched him get into his rig. He waved at her. She waved back. And he was off.

Her legs were light as she walked back to the counter, floating on a cloud.

Only then did she realize something was in her apron side pocket.

She pulled it out. A big white envelope. Thick.

"Order up!" Dave said.

Lily put the envelope back in her pocket and served Barney Rouse, the eighty-year-old Vietnam vet who taught fitness training and poetry at the old folks home on Ridgeway.

Then she went into the bathroom and opened the envelope.

Hundreds and fifties and twenties. Had to be at least five grand!

Oh Bucky, what happened down there? And then Lily knew, just knew, there would be lots of time to find out, and years to talk about it.

Life and the future.

Tomorrow.

FORE

Jimmy McCarren saw her from across the room and knew she would be next. She was just how he liked them. Black hair, form-fitting dress, dancing eyes, perfect smile.

She was standing by herself, sipping a martini. He, of course, was drinking a Coke. He had the tournament tomorrow and never drank anything stronger than a soda the night before.

As for some on-the-road extracurricular activity, he hadn't planned on it.

Until now.

Moriarty, the CEO of a Fortune 500 company, said, "So what should it be?"

Jimmy McCarren, his eyes on the woman in red, said, "Excuse me?"

"My putting," Moriarty said. "You think I should go to a long putter?"

Jimmy looked at him. The exec was one of those 55-year-old type-A personalities who made golf their substitute religion. And Jimmy was their high priest. That's why they paid ten grand to get into this reception. The clubhouse dining room was packed with rich men and their wives—or girlfriends—all of them wanting one chance to hobnob with Jimmy, swap a few lies, maybe get that one secret that would change their golf game forever.

Of course, Jimmy knew there was no such thing as "the secret." It was nothing but sheer, raw hard work mixed with talent that made the champion golfer. Jimmy had known that since he was three, when his dad first put a club in his hands.

But you humor guys who lay out ten large, so Jimmy said, "Long putters can solve a lot of problems."

"You think I should putt sidesaddle with it? Dave Pelz says it's the best way."

"Is he God?"

"Of course not," Moriarty said with a laugh. "There can only be one you."

Jimmy smiled. Being number one in the world did have its metaphors.

And perks. Jimmy looked back at the woman in red who at that very moment was looking his way. She smiled, then looked away and walked toward a display case of golf memorabilia.

"...sidesaddle or not?"

"Huh?" Jimmy said.

"That's all I want to know," Moriarty said.

Jimmy said, "You know what? I think that's a great idea. Pelz knows what he's talking about. You putt sidesaddle for awhile, will you do that for me?"

"Well, sure, I—"

"Excuse me. Nice talking to you."

He made it across the room despite several attempts to stop him with pats and *Hey Jimmy*, even from the PGA Commissioner.

She was still standing at the display case, looking at the top shelf, which held a vintage photograph.

"That's Sam Snead," he said.

She turned. She had green eyes, too, which sealed his fate. Black, red and green, in that combination . . .

"I know," she said. "You think I rode in on a load of golf shoes?"

Her voice had a whispery, Marilyn Monroe quality, but also a hint of toughness. An irresistible combination. It meant competition and the thrill of the hunt. Jimmy put out his hand, which gave him an excuse to look down at her left hand, holding the empty martini glass. He homed in on her ring finger. No ring.

Not that that would have stopped him.

They shook. Her grip was firm.

"I'm Jimmy McCarren."

"I know."

"And you are?"

"Thirsty." She held up the glass.

"Allow me," he said. "What is it?"

"Ketel One, dirty. But only if you join me."

"I'm sorry, but I play tomorrow."

"I don't drink alone. Nice meeting you, Mr. McCarren."

"Wait," Jimmy said. "I'll make an exception."

He went to the bar and ordered two martinis. He knew people were watching him. His rep was that he loved to flirt, but that's as far as it ever went. He had a gorgeous wife at home, and two adorable kids.

Oh, there were rumors about him having a little "on the side." But whenever something like that popped up on the Internet, his team of lawyers went to work.

The truth was kept nicely under wraps.

And it would be so tonight.

Jimmy returned with the drinks.

"So I never got your name," Jimmy said.

"I never gave it," she said.

"Let me guess then," he said. "Clarissa."

She smiled.

"Hortense?"

She laughed.

"Come on, help a guy out."

"If I must," she said. "Dawn."

"I like that."

"I'm glad." She took a lingering sip of her drink, peering at him with those emerald orbs. He went weak in the knees, like the time he lined up that last putt for his first amateur title. Somehow, he made it. And he would make it again tonight.

"You have people to talk to," Dawn said. "I shouldn't take up too much of your—"

"But I want to talk to *you*."

"You're a charmer," she said. "What about your wife?"

Jimmy shuddered at the memory of his last big fight with Keely.

"Is it true?"

"Is what true?" Jimmy was peeling a banana in the kitchen. The kids were in bed.

"You know what I'm talking about. I got a call."

"What do you mean, a call?"

"Pretty detailed. About your trip to Dubai."

"Keely, I don't know what—"

"It all took place on the jet. The mile high club."

How did she know all this?

"Look at me, Keely. You know what the tabloids try to do. You know they're trying to start something. We've had two kids together. Don't you think you can trust me with that?"

It was a good line and he made it sound sincere. But it took another half hour to convince her. It had been very close . . .

This will have to be carefully managed, Jimmy thought. The way you make your way around Augusta National. Strategy, baby.

"I don't know what you've heard," Jimmy said, "but most of it's a lie. I'm just a guy playing golf."

"A married guy," she said.

"A lonely guy," he said.

Pause.

"I'm sorry," Jimmy said. "That wasn't appropriate." He made a half turn.

She put her hand on his arm. "Your secret is safe with me."

If she had told him then she wanted him to jump into a pothole bunker at St. Andrews and eat up all the sand, he would have booked the flight that very night.

"I just wish . . ." Jimmy said, letting his voice trail off as he looked away.

"What?"

"That I just had someone to talk to for awhile."

"You do," she said.

Jimmy spent another hour glad-handing the rich, but remembered nothing he said. All he could think about was the magic hour of eleven, when she would be there.

It was precisely eleven, too, when she knocked on his door.

———

Jimmy teed off just after noon the next day. His drive went 325 yards straight down the fairway. He used his 60 degree wedge to fly the ball ten feet past the pin. It sucked back and went in the hole for an eagle.

He took that as a sign. Life was going to change for him. Radically and forever.

Jimmy won the tournament going away.

He flew home to Orlando and spent a couple of days with Keely and the kids. It was fine. But when he dreamed, he dreamed in blacks and reds and cool, liquid greens.

———

His major sponsor, the sporting goods company that had been with him ever since he'd gone pro, needed Jimmy for a commercial shoot in Big Bear. He flew in his private jet out there on a Monday.

Dawn was at the Inn of the Crags, the most exclusive mountain resort in America, in a room Jimmy had booked under the name of his swing coach, Bart Laidley.

When he got to her room they said nothing until they were spent.

Lying in Jimmy's arms, Dawn said, "We can't do this."

"What are you talking about?"

"Sneaking around, you flying me in. I can't keep this up."

"Why not? I have the resources—"

"It's not a question of resources," she said, lightly tracing a line on his chest with her fingernail. "It's a question of I feel cheap and I have no idea if you'll throw me over."

"Come on, Dawn, I'm not like that."

She pushed away from him. "Convince me," she said.

"How?"

"By telling me the absolute truth." Her eyes were green laser beams burning into his brain.

"What truth?"

"About your women."

"Dawn—"

"If you want me to trust you, tell me. How many have there been?"

"Please, Dawn."

"Tell me. If you want us to be together, tell me."

"I don't know!"

"More than a dozen?"

"Don't."

"Estimate."

"Dawn—"

"Too many?"

"I don't count—"

"Two dozen?"

"No. Not that many."

"Paid for?"

"Only sometimes." He quickly added, "That was a different me. I'm different since I met you. Since I first laid eyes on you. You have to believe me."

"Then you'll marry me?"

The words whammed him in the head like a wayward 7-iron.

"Dawn, this is all so sudden."

"Who cares?"

"But what about—"

"Your wife?"

"What am I supposed to do? Just go home and walk in and say I want a divorce? Out of nowhere?"

"It happens," she said.

His chest tightened. The way it did the first time he won the Masters, on the last hole, by one stroke over Scottie Scheffler. The pressure was so intense. But that was just a tournament. This was his very life hanging in the balance.

"She'd never go for it," he said. "She won't go quietly. She'd make this thing so loud."

"There are other ways to make her go," she said.

He lost breath. His hands shook like he had the yips over a five-foot putt. He was finally able to say, "You can't mean that."

"How much?" she said.

"How much what?"

"How much do want me?"

———

Jimmy shot the commercial the next day. In it, standing the edge of the gorge, he was supposed to drive a ball to the other side. It was a two mile divide, but CG would take care of that little detail.

It was an eight-hour shoot. Jimmy went back to the Inn for a meal with the main crew. He tried to be friendly, jovial. But his thoughts were a couple of floors away. So much so the director asked him if he was feeling all right.

"No," Jimmy said. Then he excused himself and slipped out the back.

The sun was setting over the mountains, and she was there, at the rail, looking as majestic as the mountains.

"This is nuts," he said. "Someone might see us."

"You see that sunset?" Dawn drew close to him. "This is where I want you to ask me."

"Ask you what?"

"To marry you."

Jimmy looked at the sky. Did it represent the loss of something? Or the beauty of a new beginning?

"Give me your phone," Dawn said.

"What?"

"I want to take a picture."

"Of what?"

"Of you against the sunset, as a memorial of this moment."

He gave her the phone.

Pushing him over the rail was easier than she expected. She'd worked out, of course. The leverage was just right, as was his unpreparedness.

She estimated the fall to be at least five hundred feet into the gorge.

But what if there were people at the bottom?

"Fore," she whispered.

————

From SI Online's story, "The Last Days of Jimmy McCarren":

According to the director of the commercial, George Flannigan, Jimmy seemed "distracted and distant. I guess he knew what was coming with all the tabloids and stuff like that. It must have been heartbreaking for him."

Indeed, the sordid details of Jimmy McCarren's extra-marital escapades came out on TMZ the day after his suicide. Even so, many are calling the text message he wrote to his wife and children, just before he jumped to his death, a redemption of sorts.

I love you all so very much. I just can't deal with what I've done.

Keely McCarren, now in seclusion with her children somewhere in France, could not be reached for comment.

———

Keely poured Dawn another glass of Bordeaux, then slid the envelope across the table to her.

"Final installment," Keely said.

"Thank you," Dawn said.

Keely sighed. "You know, if it had only been the women, I don't know if I'd have gone through this."

"I understand completely," Dawn said. "I've had cases just like this. When the husband starts thinking about murder, divorce is usually out of the question."

Keely closed her eyes and nodded.

"But it's all for the best," Dawn said. "This way the entire estate is yours, the pre-nup null and void."

"The kids will be well taken care of," Keely said.

Dawn sipped her wine.

"So where do you go from here?" Keely asked.

"New York," Dawn said. "There's a Yankee who's being a bad little boy. His wife is not pleased."

NEO-NOIR

"There's room for the both of you," Boss said. "And the PR'll be killer!"

Johnny Diamond shook his head. "No way, Boss. This is a one-man gig. For fifteen years!"

"Which is my point," Boss said. His full name was Henry Jay Boston, but everybody called him Boss. Which was fitting, as he was in charge of all aspects of the Petit Palais Hotel in West Hollywood, including the rooftop venue known as the Candlelight Bar. It was in that room on Friday nights that Johnny Diamond—formerly John Stutz of Pico Rivera—held court with his one-man tribute to film noir. Just Johnny, drumming on a table, riffing one-liners and making up stories in the crime-genre style. Quintessential Los Angeles. *L.A. Weekly* had given him a glowing review seven years ago—heck, he'd made the cover—calling his act "an intimate, sexy and artfully rhythmic experience that's unlike anything else in town." The *Weekly* dubbed him "The Film Noir Soul Man."

"Your point I don't get," Johnny said. He crossed his arms and looked at the wall of Boss's office. It was covered with framed, autographed photos. Brad Pitt. Nicolas Cage. Angelina. The Candlelight Bar had always been hip.

"Johnny," Boss said, "he's your *brother.*"

"Stepbrother. And we don't exactly get along, you know." It wasn't just that Robert Stutz had taken to calling himself Bobby Diamond, though that was bad enough. It was that he was so obviously trying to copy John-ny's act. They'd had a big fight about it at their father's funeral two years ago. Johnny's biological father, that was. Robert, almost fifteen years younger than Johnny, got tanked up on red wine and started poking Johnny in the chest. "He was just as much my old man as yours!" Robert kept saying. The two had to be separated.

"That'll add a good vibe to the show," Boss said. "Conflict, right? Noir, see? And Bobby's got a gal pal who plays piano. Imagine that! A piano behind you and Bobby and—"

"Quit calling him Bobby," Johnny said. "And there's no way."

"He admires you," Boss said.

"You've talked to him about this?"

"Well, a little."

"Behind my back?"

"Johnny, I got to think long term. We got a younger generation out there. Aren't you turning forty-five in a week or so?"

"So?"

"I'm just saying Bobb...your brother really connects with the hipsters."

"Forget it," Johnny said, standing.

"Sit," Boss said, and not in a friendly way.

Johnny lowered himself back in the chair.

"The decision's been made," Boss said. "I was hoping you'd go along. But Bobby—yes, Bobby Diamond—is going to be part of Noir at the Bar, with you or without you. I'd rather it be with you, Johnny. We've had a lot of good years together."

"So that's it?"

"That's it."

"What about my cut of the gate?"

"We split it up, but Johnny, I say there's going to be more people. We will fill this place. And up the cover, too. More money all around."

Yeah, Johnny thought. Just like in those capers where the plan goes bad and a fall guy goes down. He was not going to be anybody's fall guy.

"Gimme a couple days to work this through," Johnny said.

"Sure, Johnny. Talk it over with Bobby. He's got some great ideas."

"Anything else?"

"Yeah," Boss said. "Have a drink before you go. Tell Chris I said it's on the house."

. . .

Johnny ordered a double Maker's, neat. Bartender Chris small talked a little, then thankfully left Johnny alone. He embraced the warmth of the bourbon and the amber lighting of the bar. This was a noir moment. Guy gets bad news from his boss. Could cost him. Could change his life completely. Blows up a decade-and-a-half of hard work. But worst of all, somebody is coming up behind him, to try to take his place. To steal his act. Somebody who doesn't deserve the attention...

And somewhere in there, swimming along in a stream of conscious-ness, the idea of murder floated by, and Johnny Diamond reached for it. Pondered it. He thought then he should toss it aside. But he didn't let go. Because under these circumstances, wouldn't it be the ultimate noir move? Only not like the movies, where the guy doesn't get away with it. Johnny Diamond, the Film Noir Soul Man, knew how every criminal blew it. All he'd have to do is make a plan and avoid the obvious mistakes.

Now, what would be the method?

Not a gun—to easy to trace. Not a knife—too messy.

What was the best death in film noir? That was easy. Ann Savage in the classic *Detour.* Drunk and deliciously vicious, she takes the phone into a bedroom, locks the door, starts calling the cops to turn Tom Neal in for murder. She's lolling on the bed, the wire getting tangled around her throat. Neal grabs the wire on the other side of the door and pulls with all his might, choking Ann Savage to death.

One of Johnny Diamond's favorite scenes in all of film noir.

"Chris," Johnny said to the bartender. "Hit me again."

"Sure, Johnny," Chris said. "Feelin' good tonight?"

"Better'n Robert Walker in *Strangers on a Train.*"

"Whatever that means," Chris said with a laugh as he refilled Johnny's glass.

Back in his third-floor loft in Pico Gardens, feeling good—no, more like invincible, after four solid shots of bourbon and driving across town without once giving a black-and-white an excuse to pull him over—Johnny texted his stepbrother.

Hey, Bobby. Just talked to Boss. Good for you! No, good for us! Let's get together and work it out.

Three minutes later came the reply: *Yes! I've been hoping we could do this thing together. When?*

Johnny: *Tomorrow night? Seven? My place?*

Bobby: *Aces!*

That "Aces" sealed the deal, if it needed any more sealing. Johnny had originated that word as his signature catchphrase! Hearing it from his rival —that's what he was, not a blood relation, and not in any sense a brother at all—only set Johnny's resolve in concrete.

The next night, Wednesday, at seven on the nose, Johnny opened his door and there he was. Robert was decked out in black pants, black sweater, and black porkpie hat, looking more neo-hipster than classic film noir protag. More Jared Leto than Charles McGraw, which should be at least a misdemeanor in Los Angeles.

"Bro!" Robert said, and wrapped Johnny up in a big hug.

The overwrought enthusiasm! This was not cool. The act would be completely ruined by this type of hyper display.

And then it hit Johnny. This was Robert's way of gaining the upper hand. A passive-aggressive show of brotherly affection. It repulsed him. In noir, you should come right out and say something. Lay your cards on the table, as the saying went. Raymond Burr would never hug anybody. Torture them, yes. Embrace them? No, unless he had a knife in one hand.

"I have never been to your crib," Robert said. "Wow!"

He was looking at the framed posters and classic lobby cards Johnny had collected over the years. All originals. There was a title card from *Born to Kill* starring Lawrence Tierney and Claire Trevor. Another from *The Asphalt Jungle*. A complete set—eight—of lobbies from *Gun Crazy*.

But the star of the display was a full one-sheet from *Out of the Past*, the movie all noir aficionados considered the greatest of the genre. It had a big head of Robert Mitchum, cigarette dangling, and a deadly Jane Greer off to the side, holding a gun.

"This is so cool!" Robert said, almost putting his nose on the glass of the poster.

"Calm down and have a seat," Johnny said. "And let's do this right. I have some rye, and we'll drink it straight."

"Aces!" Robert said.

Just pound a nail into my temple, why don't you?

Johnny went to the kitchenette and poured a couple healthy shots of Dad's Hat 100-proof rye. He came back, handed one to Robert. Johnny held up his glass and said, "Here's to the floor, which will hold you when no one else will."

"For reals," Robert said.

As they clinked glasses, Johnny thought of all the ways he could kill anyone who said *For reals.*

They sat in leather, wingback chairs. Between them was a classic cherry-wood end table. On the table was a retro office lamp and a black rotary telephone from 1960 that Johnny picked up in an antique shop. It was strictly for show. Out the big window to their left, the lights of East Los Angeles and downtown gave off a powdery luminescence in the marine-layer fog. The juttings of the downtown L.A. skyline were blurred yet perceivably present, like a dream just out of reach.

"So," Robert said, "why don't we lay out a general plan for the show?"

Taking right over, aren't you, bub?

"Sure," Johnny said.

"I see it this way." Robert put his drink on the end table so he could spread out his hands, as if to create the stage right there in front of them. "Lights go down. There's a piano upstage right. Dakota comes out and starts to play. Soft, jazzy. Then one light comes on, purple, from a street lamp we'll have set up, and I'm leaning against it. And I look at the audience and say, 'I've met some hard-boiled eggs in my time, but this dame? She was twenty minutes.' Right? Am I right?"

"That's from *Ace in the Hole,*" Johnny said.

"Yeah. So?"

"I write my own stuff."

"It's called creative license, Johnny. And, you know, that's one of the ..."

"One of the what?"

Robert picked up his drink and took a pull.

"One of what, Robert?"

"Call me Bobby."

"Robert. One of what?"

"Don't get torqued, Johnny. It was what Boss said."

"What did he say?"

"That your riffs were getting ..."

"Out with it!"

"A little tired, okay? There." Robert knocked back the rest of his rye.

Johnny did the same. He got up and went to the kitchenette, got the bottle, came back and refilled their drinks, then put the bottle on the table.

"Aw, Johnny," Robert said. "I didn't want it to go this way."

"Forget it," Johnny said. "Let's drink it over."

Robert laughed and held out his glass for a clink. He took a healthy sip. Johnny touched the rye to his lips but didn't drink.

"So you think you should come out first?" Johnny said.

"To set the tone," Robert said.

"Why you and not me?"

"That's the beautiful part," Robert said. "I give you the big entrance. You're the man, you're still the Film Noir Soul Man. It's always better for the star to come out second."

"Uh-huh."

"Heck, Orson Welles doesn't show up in *The Third Man* until we're halfway in!"

"Uh-huh."

"And when you come on, you say, 'It was a blonde. A blonde to make a bishop kick a hole in a stained-glass window.' Okay?"

"That's ripping off Raymond Chandler!"

"I know! What could be better than quoting Chandler to start your part of the show?"

"Stop calling it a show!" Johnny slammed his glass on the table, sloshing some of the rye. "It's performance art, and I don't do lines from somebody else."

Robert looked at the floor. Then took a drink. For a long moment they sat in silence.

"You never liked me," Robert said.

Johnny sighed.

"No, it's true," Robert said. "All I ever wanted was to be a brother to you, but you wouldn't let me. I thought maybe this could be a way for us to get closer. After all these years."

The kid was a good actor, but Johnny was buying none of it. Robert and Boss had it in for him. How long would the "show" go on before they gave Johnny his walking papers?

Then the music started to play in the back of Johnny's mind. It was a slow-build suspense piece, something a Bernard Herrmann might have composed for a scene where the killer approaches the unsuspecting victim in some shadowy apartment. The music of inevitable death. It came to him and possessed him, and he let it take its full embrace.

Johnny got up and went around behind the end table. He picked up the handset of the classic telephone. Quick as Laird Cregar he laced the wire around Robert's neck and twisted. Robert dropped his glass, rye splashing on the floor. He flailed and grabbed at the wire. Pathetic gurgling sounds came from his throat.

"Here's your show," Johnny whispered.

In two minutes it was over.

No blood. Neat and clean. Now the only thing to do was get rid of the body. Johnny was ready for that. That's why he had the rug, an oriental-design throw that he'd picked up yesterday in Chinatown.

Johnny removed Robert's cell phone from his pants pocket.

He rolled Robert up in the rug.

Then he sat and finished his shot of rye.

He held out his right hand to see if it was shaking. It wasn't. His heart-beat was a little fast, but it wasn't exploding in his chest.

He'd pulled it off. He'd killed a man. He was halfway home.

This was where the noir murderer always made his fatal mistake. He'd leave a clue that helped the cops nab him. Or the dame he trusted would turn him in. The *femme fatale.*

Well, there was no dame in Johnny's life at the moment, and Johnny had a plan about clues, namely, how to plant them.

He took Robert's iPhone, tried to turn it on. Nothing.

Ack! He hadn't counted on that. Johnny had a Samsung and didn't bother with any of that fingerprint or face recognition jazz.

Now what?

Robert is right over there, remember?

Which meant Johnny had to unroll the rug.

When he did, Johnny's heart spiked.

Robert was looking right at him.

Johnny half expected that clichéd moment from 70s thrillers and horror flicks—the presumed dead man shoots out a hand and takes you by the throat. The look on Robert's face was vengeful. *I'll get you for this* it seemed to say.

But a second's reflection brought Johnny back to reality. Robert was wearing a bug-eyed death mask, caused by asphyxiation.

Johnny flipped Robert face down.

He took Robert's right hand and put his index finger on the iPhone scanner.

Nothing.

Thumb.

Nada.

Middle finger? It only mocked him, looking like Robert was flipping him off from the netherworld.

So this part of the plan wasn't going to...wait! Robert was *left* handed, remember?

Johnny followed the same routine with Robert's left hand, and the thumb did the trick.

The phone was live.

Johnny went to messaging and sent his own phone a text: *Hey bro, sorry I have to miss our meeting, but I need to go to San Diego with a friend. Let's reschedule.*

He waited five minutes, then sent a reply from his phone: *No prob. How about next Tuesday?*

From Robert's phone: *Let's do it!*

From Johnny: *We're going to rock the noir world, kid. You and me, together again!*

Robert: *Aces!*

And that was that. Johnny used his shirt to wipe his prints off the iPhone, then put it back in Robert's pocket.

Once more, he rolled Robert up in the rug.

Now all he had to do was get rid of the body. As if he were Fred MacMurray or John Garfield. Only this wasn't a movie, and Johnny Diamond would not be caught.

He knew every inch of the building, the habits of the people, the lack of lights in the back. He knew about the old mattress that a homeless guy used for a few weeks. Now he was gone, and nobody had bothered to dump it. Life in the new city of Los Angeles. An old mattress might be a guy's home, so leave it alone!

It was no problem to get rolled-up Robert to the east-side window, which opened up to the fire escape. He opened it, pushed the carpeted corpse out, leaning it upright against the rail.

In the dim he could see the mattress at the foot of the stairs.

He pushed his victim over the rail.

Bullseye.

But in his haste to get down the three flights, Johnny almost fell, catching himself just in time. That could have been a disaster, twisting an ankle or worse, knocking his head against the rail.

Keep calm and carry on. Wasn't that a meme floating around? It was from England and World War II or something like that.

It really applied now.

Johnny's car was parked a few yards from the mattress. That's what you call planning. Keep calm and pop the trunk.

Now, drag and lift the body. Plunk it in the trunk.

It was a foggy night in Los Angeles. A perfect night for noir.

What Bernard Herrmann could have done with this!

The 10 freeway was one minute from Johnny's building. He took it to the 5, then to the 14, past Acton to the 122—driving in SoCal was truly a numbers game—and then to the 138. Better known as Pearblossom Highway, this asphalt vein snaked through Antelope Valley on the western side of the Mojave Desert. In the daytime it looked like the post-apocalypse—flat, barren, hot, lifeless. Here at night it was a haunted, vast darkness, as forbidding as anything Farley Granger and Kathy O'Donnell faced in *They Live by Night.*

Which made it a perfect place to bury a body if you knew where to turn off the highway.

Johnny knew. He'd researched it online. He'd also purchased a shovel from Home Depot.

Now he was going to re-enact the body-burying scene from *Blood Simple,* a neo-noir by the Coen Brothers. Only he was smarter than the idiot murderer in that movie. Robert was really dead!

Johnny found the isolated dirt road with ease and, truth be told, GPS.

Technology had its uses in neo noir. A mile off the highway Johnny stopped and killed the headlights. He got out, popped the trunk and removed his stepbrother's body like a load of laundry. He dragged it away from the road—the carpet cocoon made that pretty easy—estimating the distance to be about thirty yards. He went back and got the shovel, returned to the body, and started to dig.

He didn't count on it taking so long. Johnny Diamond wasn't exactly a manual labor kind of guy. There would be blisters on the ol' hands. He should have thought about gloves. But there was no turning back now.

And sooner or later somebody would come driving along this road.

What if he was caught?

At least this was California. Governor Gruesome had put the kibosh on the death penalty, meaning the 700 plus inmates in San Quentin's Death Row were getting three hots and a cot, plus TV, books, and other leisure comforts. You certainly had to hand it to the ol' ACLU. A victim's family would go on suffering, knowing the rape-murderer of their daughter, or the torture-killer of beloved parents, or any other scum of the earth would be fed and housed for the rest of his natural life.

Yeah, if he was nabbed, he could always write a memoir in his cell and become a true noir icon.

Idiot! Dig!

Sweat soaked in the warm night breeze, Johnny finally had a hole. He rolled Robert and the rug into it and took another ten minutes filling it up. He kicked some surface sand over the top of the grave.

He got back to his car, threw the shovel in the trunk, and took off.

No one had come by.

The perfect crime.

Yes, it could be done. Not in the noir of the 1940s, when the production code demanded justice.

But in the real world of Johnny Diamond's neo-noir actuality, he'd done it.

The next week was as smooth as Nat King Cole singing "Stardust." Johnny couldn't believe how good he felt. He'd expected a pang or two of guilt, but none came. It was as if he had imbibed the spirit of Richard Widmark in *Kiss of Death,* the Widmark who'd laughed as he shoved an old lady in a wheelchair down the stairs. Some would call that psychopathic. Johnny called it cold and precise.

His Noir at the Bar performance on Friday was, according to Boss, "The best I've seen you do in years. Inspired!" Johnny couldn't argue. He'd been in the zone before, but not like this. His connection with the audience that night was palpable, magic. He got a standing O. As if he'd ever need a piano or a partner!

On Monday afternoon Boss called, concerned he couldn't get hold of Robert. Johnny told him about the texts, and that Bobby—he would refer to him as *Bobby* from now on—was probably with a *femme fatale* he took off with to San Diego. He told Boss he was sure Bobby would be back soon, ready to get to work.

But when he finished the call, Johnny felt the first, faint tendrils of disquiet stroking the inside of his ribs. What was that all about? Why now? Was Boss suspicious? No, that wasn't it. Johnny Diamond's voice had been cool and controlled.

Then what could it be?

He traced it back to when he'd said *femme fatale.* That's what started it. There was always a *femme fatale* in noir after a seemingly perfect murder. Remember what Lizabeth Scott did to Dan Duryea in *Too Late For Tears*? She turned him into jelly, then turned him into dead.

Johnny had to remind himself again that the noir code of the movies was not real life. He didn't believe in fatalism. He wasn't like Tom Neal in *Detour,* who uttered that famous last line, *But one thing I don't have to wonder about, I know. Someday a car will stop to pick me up that I never thumbed. Yes, fate or some mysterious force can put the finger on you or me for no good reason at all.*

Johnny'd memorized that line thirty years ago, along with so many others in noir, and it came back to him now, the way John 3:16 comes to a guy brought up in a Baptist Sunday School. It was, in so many ways, the quintessential verse of noir scripture.

And it was pounding in Johnny's head after Boss's call. It kept repeating, too. He couldn't turn it off! So this was what guilt felt like. The hammer's going to drop. The other shoe. You can't shake it.

Well, fate was not going to make a chump out of Johnny Diamond. A few belts of rye, then maybe go out for a steak. Turn this whole thing into a celebration!

It was after he'd downed his third shot that Johnny heard a knock on his door.

An icy finger traced his spine. He didn't move.

Another knock.

Come on, Johnny! You're acting like Elisha Cook, Jr., like some pathetic fall guy.

He got up and looked through the peephole and saw a blonde.

And that line from Chandler came roaring back into his head. *It was a blonde. A blonde to make a bishop kick a hole in a stained-glass window.*

At least it knocked out the *Detour* line. Johnny smiled and opened the door.

The woman was tall. She wore her hair like Lana Turner. Rocked a red dress like her, too.

And her voice was as silky as Lauren Bacall's. "Johnny Diamond, I presume?"

"That's me," Johnny said, going for the suave insouciance of George Sanders. He was perturbed when it came out as a tight, Peter Lorre rasp.

"May I come in?" she said. Her smile was as intoxicating as the rye. It had been a year since he'd broken up with Cecelia, and two months since he'd bedded a woman.

He threw the door open.

She moved like poured honey. When he shut the door, she turned and said, "Nice place you've got here."

What would Bogart say? Ah! "Can I offer you a drink?"

"No thanks." She held a silver handbag and used it to motion toward the window. "Nice view."

He moved around her, taking her in, and said, "Los Angeles, the greatest noir city in the world."

"I know, right?" the woman said.

Johnny wasn't sure how to play this now. He didn't want her to think he was nervous, but who was she and why was she here?

Take it slow and cool. "You know my name," Johnny said. "Can I know yours?"

"Kitty," she said.

Kitty! It was perfect. Or was it? Wait...Kitty was Joan Bennett's name in *Scarlet Street*. One bad *femme fatale*!

As that thought was flashing through his head, Johnny barely noticed her hand slipping into the handbag and coming out with...it couldn't be... but it was.

A gun.

"We have some things to talk about," she said.

Nerves. On end. "What is this?"

"You should have known you couldn't get away with it."

"A...way?"

"You should have known." She raised the gun higher. It looked small and sleek and deadly.

"And now you're going to pay," she said.

Johnny realized then he was backing away from her, had been from the moment he saw the gun. It was a scene out of a movie. Life imitating art! His thoughts were swimming around like the drug haze Dick Powell suffers in *Murder, My Sweet.*

Who was she, this Kitty?

Bobby's face came into his mind then, and it was laughing.

Gal pal. Boss said Bobby had a gal pal, played piano....how did she find out?

The look in her eyes. Icy blue.

The gun...

Almost as if his body acted on its own, with his mind watching from a seat in a theater, Johnny kicked the end table, right into the woman in red.

He ran for the window, threw it open, expecting a shot, hoping it would go wild.

Out onto the fire escape. The night! The Los Angeles night, take me in!

His foot missed a step, his body lurched forward, and his head slammed into cold steel. And he knew, just before he died, that fate had put the finger on him after all.

The uniformed officer tried to calm the woman, who couldn't stop crying.

"It wasn't supposed to be like this," she kept saying.

"It's all right," the cop said. "If you'll just finish the story for me, we'll make sure you get some medical attention, all right?"

She nodded.

The cop said, "You work for Birthday Fantasies?"

Nod.

"You were hired by a Bobby Diamond to sing 'Happy Birthday' to the victim?"

"Yes," she said. "He gave me the toy gun and this script." The woman reached in her handbag and pulled out a folded piece of paper.

The officer unfolded it and looked.

You should have known you couldn't get away with it. And now you're going to pay. You can't hide anymore, Johnny. You're another year older. Your brother says, Have a happy birthday, or else!

"I barely started when he kicked a table at me and ran out the window," the woman said. "It's so horrible! Are you sure he's dead?"

"I'm afraid so, ma'am. Looks like a broken neck." He paused then and looked out the window. The lights of the city were bright, sparkling like cool jazz.

THE ROAD TO ROMANCE

I've been waiting for a girl like you, to come into my life.
I've been waiting for someone new to make me feel alive.
– Foreigner

He saw her in the produce section.

She looked exactly the same—breathtaking.

The last time he'd seen her was at their ten-year high school reunion. She hadn't been at the twenty. They were coming up on the thirty now.

While he had developed a slight paunch, her figure was just as alluring as when she was head cheerleader at good old Harrison High.

Back then Josh Taylor was a mainstay in the Drama and Chess clubs. Karen Doherty was untouchable, the girlfriend of the football team's quarterback and, of course, the Homecoming Queen.

She was dressed modestly, but somehow made modest look magnificent. She was tapping the cantaloupes. Desire struck Josh like Cupid's arrow. Divorced, he had not even dated a woman for a year.

The old proverb came to his mind—*Who dares, wins.*

He pushed his shopping cart slowly toward her, remembering another bit of wisdom in the dance of love—*No sudden moves.*

She was still eyeing the fruit when he said, "Isn't this a coincidence?"

Her eyes met his. Luminous, violet eyes they were. Elizabeth Taylor eyes.

At first there was no recognition in her gaze, but then—

"Josh Taylor!" she said.

"Hello, Karen."

"My goodness," she said. "How long has it been?"

"Twenty years," he said. "Since our ten-year reunion."

She smiled, and Cupid's arrow sank more deeply in his heart.

"You live around here?" Josh said.

"Moved back," she said. "I've been living in Phoenix."

"I never moved out," Josh said. His hands trembled on the shopping cart handle.

"The town's changed a bit," Karen said.

"You haven't."

She gave a little laugh. "I don't know about that."

Josh glanced quickly at her left hand. No ring.

"What are you doing these days," she said.

"Same old," Josh said. "Accountant."

"You're married, aren't you? I seem to remember you brought your wife to the ten year."

"No and yes," Josh said.

"I'm sorry," she said.

Josh shrugged. "Stuff happens."

"Well said."

"What about you?"

"Stuff happens," she said.

Who dares, wins.

Josh said, "Karen, would you like to grab a cup of coffee? Talk a little about old times?"

The lingering pause, no more than a couple of seconds, seemed like ten minutes to Josh.

"That'd be nice," Karen said.

"Great. Is there a good time for you?"

"Well, I have to finish up my shopping. But I'm free the rest of the day."

Josh swallowed. "Want to say eleven o'clock? There's a Coffee Bean where the old taco stand used to be. Remember?"

"Across the street from Harrison?"

"That's it."

"I'll meet you there."

"Terrific!"

———

Josh didn't finish his own shopping. He went straight to self-checkout, then home to his apartment. He took another shower, put on a splash of sandalwood cologne, and counted the minutes until 10:45, when he drove to Coffee Bean.

Karen was already there, at a table, working on a laptop. She waved to him. He got in line and ordered a large Hazelnut latte.

When he sat down Karen said, "Just let me finish this sentence." She typed a few more words, then closed the laptop.

"Working away?" Josh said.

"I am, actually."

"What kind of work?"

"I'm a writer," she said.

"Really? What do you write?"

"Thrillers," she said.

"No kidding! I love thrillers."

"Who do you like?"

"Oh, James Patterson. John Grisham. James Scott Bell."

"Ever read anything by K. D. Doherty?"

"I don't think so," Josh said.

"That's me," Karen said. "I'll send you one."

"That'd be great!"

"I've just put out my third."

"Fantastic."

"I hope so," she said. "It takes awhile to get a foothold. Especially when you're indie."

"Indie?"

"I self publish, direct to Amazon."

"Oh yes, a lot of people are doing that now, aren't they?"

"No barriers anymore," Karen said. "But you've got to be good."

"I'll bet you are," Josh said. "In high school you were good at anything you tried."

"Well, this isn't high school anymore."

She took a sip of her coffee. Josh did the same.

"You know," Karen said, "I always wanted to write one set here in town."

"You should," Josh said, then added with a smile, "Maybe I can be in it."

She laughed. "Sure. You want to be a serial killer?"

"Ha!"

"If you're nice to me, I'll make you the romantic interest."

Josh's heart almost burst.

"I'd like to do some research," Karen said. "Drive around and look at the old spots."

Who dares...

"How about I drive you?" Josh said.

"Really?"

"My chariot awaits."

His chariot was a classic Porsche 356 Speedster, of which he was duly proud.

"Let's do it," Karen said.

———

They started down the main drag.

"There's Barbatta's Steak House," Josh said.

"I remember it well," Karen said. "My parents loved that place."

"Are your parents still here?"

"Florida," Karen said. "Everybody's moving to Florida."

"The smart ones," Josh said. "And see that car dealership?"

"Didn't that used to be a lot where they sold Christmas trees?"

"And pumpkins on Halloween."

"Oh yes," Karen said. "I remember. Now that's a coincidence."

"What is?"

"My new thriller takes place on Halloween."

Josh drove on, slowly, not wanting the tour to end.

"Hey," Karen said. "What about Vista Point? I can take a look at the whole town."

Vista Point! The place all the cool kids went at night to make out. Josh —not a cool kid—had only been there by himself. He always wondered what might happen if he took a girl there.

Who dares...

"Let's go!" he said.

————

The day was clear. The valley below Vista Point spread out like a tapestry. Josh wondered how many times Karen had been here in the old days. How many times had her lips met another's?

"It's lovely," Karen said.

Should he make his move now? Was the moment right? Would there ever be a better one?

"Josh," Karen said. "I want you to know something."

He managed to utter, "Okay."

"Back in high school, I always thought you were the nicest guy. I always wondered why I couldn't get together with a guy like you, and not the rotten men I've been involved with."

"Well, it's no coincidence, I'm sure you know, that I always wished I could rate a girl like you."

She smiled. "That's really nice to hear. Which makes this so hard."

"What?"

Karen reached into her purse and pulled out a revolver, pointing it at his chest.

"You see," Karen said, "I'm not just a freelance writer. I'm also a free-lance hit woman. And you deserve to know this before I kill you. Your ex-wife hired me. She told me where you shopped for groceries. I followed you there this morning, and, well, here we are."

Josh Taylor's body buzzed with adrenaline as he said, "What a coinci-dence! Wait..."

He reached under the seat, pulled out his Beretta 9mm and pointed it at Karen.

"I'm a freelance hit man," he said.

Karen's chin dropped.

But she didn't fire.

"Let me ask you something," Josh said. "Did you get paid in full?"

"I always do," Karen said.

When daring, dare big.

"Can we try something?" Josh said. "Let's put down our guns."

Josh placed his gun on the console. Karen lowered hers to her lap.

"Things have changed now," Josh said. "I'm going to take a stab, you'll pardon the expression. I think I rate. You think?"

"Wow," Karen said.

"So how about this? Let's go to Vegas, right now, and fall in love. We'll take the Pearblossom Highway. The road to romance! Maybe we'll even get married in one of those little wedding chapels. Think how much money we can make as a team."

Without a moment's hesitation, Karen said, "Yes!"

"With just one stop," Josh said.

"Where?"

"My ex-wife's house, of course."

THE GREATEST KISS EVER

When Joe Duval was eight, his favorite movie was *The Princess Bride*. Not because of the love stuff, but because of the sword fighting. But when he was sixteen and watched it again, the love stuff took over, especially the ending. Westley and Buttercup kiss, and Peter Falk says to Fred Savage, "Since the invention of the kiss, there have been five kisses that were rated the most passionate, the most pure. This one left them all behind."

That stayed with Joe through two prom dates, two marriages and five affairs, none of which gave him a kiss like that. He wondered sometimes if that frustrated desire fueled his rise in the cutthroat business world.

By the time he was forty-five and worth $241 million, Joe "Buzzsaw" Duval (so named for his MO of buying companies, cutting them to ribbons, then selling the parts) had abandoned all hope of getting that mythical kiss, until one day aboard his yacht when his new man, a thirty-year-old named Dexter, served him his afternoon martini. And spilled a drop.

"Idiot!" Joe said.

"I'm sorry, sir," Dexter said.

"This is Monkey 47 Distiller's Cut! Three-hundred a bottle!"

"I know—"

"I hired you to do two things. Drive the boat and make me martinis. Can you walk and chew gum at the same time?"

"Again, sorry."

"Get back to the bridge," Joe said.

"As you wish."

"Wait," Joe said. "Why did you say that?"

"Say what, sir?"

"As you wish."

"Oh, that's a line from a movie. I hope you don't mind."

"*The Princess Bride*!"

"Yes, sir."

"You know, I loved that movie."

"Yes?"

"It appears we have something in common," Joe said.

"That's nice to know," Dexter said.

Joe took a sip of his martini.

"Have you ever thought about the kiss?" Joe asked.

"The kiss that left them all behind?" Dexter said.

Joe nodded.

"Who hasn't?" Dexter said.

"Did you ever get a kiss like that?"

Dexter smiled.

"Oh, go on, get back to the bridge," Joe said. "There's no use even thinking about it."

"As you wish."

————

Joe Duval's yacht, *Buzzsaw II* (so named because Joe considered himself to be Buzzsaw I) finished its cruise around Catalina. As it headed toward port Dexter served Joe Duval another martini. This time he did not spill.

"I've been thinking about it, sir," Dexter said.

Joe scowled over his glass. "Thinking about what?"

"The greatest kiss. Mind if I ask you a question?"

"Make it fast," Joe said.

"What would you pay to experience the greatest kiss you'll ever receive?"

Joe put the martini on the deck table. "What did you say to me?"

Dexter repeated the question.

Joe was about to yell at him to get back to the wheel when a distant yearning warmed him. "Interesting thought," he said.

"Would it be worth two-hundred-thousand dollars?"

Joe's eyes widened, then narrowed. "Why do you ask?"

"Well, first of all, you're quite wealthy, and it seems to me that two hundred thousand, while certainly not pocket change, is relatively small compared to the pleasure."

"What's second of all?"

"I can arrange it," Dexter said.

There was something cocky in the lad that reminded Joe of himself at that age. A confidence mixed with a devil-may-care attitude—and a readiness to reel in a fish and fillet it.

"Tell me how," Joe said.

"I know a woman. A beautiful woman. Respectable, too. She kissed me once, and it melted the socks right off me."

"Your girlfriend?"

Dexter shook his head. "I wanted her to be, but the spark wasn't there for her. Still, we became friends. My thought is that for one-hundred-thousand dollars she would be willing to give you the best kiss ever."

"I thought you said two-hundred-thousand."

"A hundred would go to me, for setting it up."

Joe took a long sip of his martini, looking into Dexter's eyes, which danced in the late afternoon sun. "What do you take me for? A sucker?"

"Not at all—"

"I don't get taken, kid."

"I didn't mean—"

"Shut up."

Dexter nodded and turned to go.

"Wait a second," Joe said. "I didn't dismiss you."

Dexter turned back.

Joe said, "How exactly would you work this thing?"

Dexter said, "I guarantee you the greatest kiss you'll ever receive, or you don't pay."

Mind reeling, enjoying the negotiation, Joe said, "Who gets to judge if it's the greatest kiss ever?"

"You do."

"You mean, after I get this kiss, I get to decide if it's the greatest?"

"You'll know that it is."

"But what if I lie? What if I tell you, you know Dex, that was a really fine kiss, but not the greatest."

"I'm betting you won't."

"You're trusting me?"

"I am. If you lie to me you keep your money, sure, and I'm out the dough. Easy come, easy go. But if I'm right, you'll be happy to let me keep it. And I'm absolutely sure you'll be happy."

"You know, I've got half a mind to take you up on this."

"What do I have to do to convince the other half?"

"You must be crazy," Joe said.

"Am I? You've bought and sold businesses on a whim. And you've come out ahead. Is this any crazier than that?"

Oh yes, just like me...

"Hypothetically," Joe said, "and just for argument's sake, suppose I took you up on this. How long would this kiss last?"

"What's your preference?"

"I'd get to choose?"

"Sure. But think it through. You don't want it to be a kiss-at-the-door-after-a-date length. But you also don't want to overdo it. The greatest kiss in the world begins to have diminishing returns after too long a time."

"Maybe thirty seconds?"

"That's a good length," Dexter said.

"How about if I make it forty-five?" Joe said.

"A stretch goal? That's doable."

Joe laughed. Was he actually considering this?

"What happens after the kiss?" Joe said.

"Nothing," Dexter said.

"I mean, what if she thinks I'm pretty good at it, and wants to see me some more?"

"That'll be up to her. But only after the money is paid and we're all happy."

———

One week later, on a crisp Tuesday morning, Joe "Buzzsaw" Duval boarded the Buzzsaw II with an attaché case holding two-hundred-thousand dollars cash. He went immediately to the main cabin, opened the shelf holding his liquor, revealing a safe. He entered the combination, opened it, and put the case inside. He closed the safe, spun the lock, and put the liquor cabinet back in place.

He put on soft jazz, gave himself one more spray of Binaca, and sat in a comfy chair to wait.

He didn't have to wait long. He felt someone coming aboard. He heard feet coming down the steps. Then a knock at the door.

"Come in," Joe said.

It was Dexter. His expression was that of an extremely confident gambler.

Joe, on the other hand, felt like squeaky-voiced kid about to go on his first date.

"Ready?" Dexter said.

"I guess as ready as I'll ever be," Joe said, standing.

"Then meet Sally."

She stepped into the cabin. Joe's throat went dry. She was stunning. Wearing a red dress that flattered her perfect form. Dark hair, velvety-blue eyes.

"He...Hello," Joe said.

"Very nice to meet you," Sally said, in a throaty voice that reminded Joe of that actress, what was her name? The one married to Humphrey Bogart...

Joe said, "Well, then, I'm ready to proceed."

"First, the money," Dexter said.

"It's here," Joe said.

"Let's see it."

"You'll have to trust me."

"Now wait!" Dexter said.

"No, you wait," Joe said. "I don't know what kind of a sap you think I am. Let the two of you on my boat, show you the money, then have you pull a gun and take it?"

Sally said, "That is so insulting."

"It's the real world, honey," Joe said. "So listen. The money is here, in a safe. And I never welch on a bet. You give me the best kiss ever and I will open the safe and give you the money."

"No way," Dexter said. "Let's go, Sally."

"No," Sally said. "It's all right. Dex, honey, why don't you step out onto the deck so I can give Mr. Duval what we've guaranteed him?"

"Are you sure?" Dex said.

"I am absolutely sure," Sally said.

Dexter paused, looked at Joe Duval, then back at Sally. "As you wish," he said. He left the cabin, closing the door behind him.

"Well," Sally said. "Alone at last."

Joe cleared his throat. "Indeed."

"How are you feeling?"

"To tell you the truth, I'm a little nervous. Just a like a kid on prom night."

"Then consider me the homecoming queen."

She walked slowly toward him. Joe's heart spiked like the Dow Jones average after a good jobs report. Sally put her arms around him...leaned into him...and it was everything Joe Duval ever hoped for, ever dreamed of...and more. Waves crashed against rocks, clouds parted, choirs sang.

When she pulled her lips away Joe's knees turned to pudding. He had to sit down.

"Wow," he said, knowing the word was completely inadequate.

Sally smiled.

"Well, then," Joe said. "Call Dexter back in. I'll get the money."

He went to the wet bar, pulled it out, opened the safe.

Dexter was back in the room now. Joe handed him the case. "You can count it if you like."

Dex opened the case, looked at the neatly-wrapped bills, and closed it.

"I trust you," he said, as he pulled out a gun and fired.

"I feel kind of sorry for him," Sally said. "He trusted us."

"Baby," Dex said, "you can't trust a guy like that. He'd report that we stole the money and the cops would be on us like ugly on a frog. That's why it had to be this way. So we take the boat out, tie an anchor to him, drop him over the side, come back and dock. It'll be days, maybe more, before anybody checks the boat, and by that time I'll be in Cabo and you'll be in Aruba, and we'll each have a hundred grand."

"Come here, you hunk of man."

Sally planted a kiss on him.

"You really do know how to do that," Dexter said.

"It's the best kiss you'll ever receive in your life," Sally said, reaching into her purse and pulling out a .38. "Guaranteed."

HIT AND RUN

The fruit stand guy was around fifty or so, wearing a white apron and a smile. That didn't give him the right to cheat people. Mike Hallick was not going to be cheated.

"You put your thumb on the scale," Mike said.

"Excuse me, sir?" the fruit stand guy said.

"I saw what you tried to do!" Mike Hallick felt the blood rushing to his head and didn't care. His girlfriend had broken up with him that morning, and he thought stopping to get some fresh avocados to take to her might smooth things over, because Deena loved guacamole. But he knew deep down she wouldn't take him back, not after last night when he'd smacked her one across the face.

A little voice in the back of Mike's head whispered, Don't make a scene, maybe the guy didn't thumb the scale.

But another voice, louder, shouting from the back of his head, said, I will not be messed with!

Mike Hallick grabbed the plastic bag containing three avocados and threw it on the floor behind the counter, right at the fruit stand guy's feet.

Then uttering a two-word farewell that could not be uttered in a church —which didn't matter because Mike Hallick didn't go to church—he stormed out to his truck in the gravel parking lot.

To show the guy just what he thought of him, Hallick burned rubber on the gravel as he pulled out, shooting little rocks back at the fruit stand.

He heard the chink-chink sound of pebbles dinging off the metallic figure of a fruit stand guy in an apron. Ha!

Then he gunned his truck down the highway.

And a strange highway it was, out here in what was a rural area of California, farm land and horse ranches. Hardly any cars, which was fine with Mike Hallick, now doing 65 ... 70 ...

He needed some hard rock music, looked at his phone, brought up Pandora, thumbed ...

Bam!

His first thought: I hit a mailbox ...

But no: out in front a multi-colored figure of a man ... in the air ... a bicycle flying out to the left ... the man hitting the ground as Mike sped by.

Oh no oh no oh no ...

Mike Hallick jammed on the brakes, heard the screech of rubber on road. He looked back through the cab window and saw him.

Unmoving.

Sprawled on the pavement. In a blue and green bicycle shirt, and a helmet. The guy's sunglasses had somehow stayed on. His head was twisted on his body and it was as if the guy were staring back at Mike.

A split second, and Mike's mind went around and around ... dead ... dead ... prison ... no cars ... now or never ...

He slammed his foot on the gas pedal and took off. In the rear view mirror, no cars. Up ahead, no cars, but the road was hilly, and a car might be coming.

Up ahead, a road ... a side road ... take it!

Mike Hallick almost skidded off the road as he took the turn, too fast. But he righted himself just in time so as not to run into the soft grass on the shoulder.

Slow down. Don't call attention.

He braked down to fifty, then forty, then thirty-five. Got on the right side of the lines of the two-lane blacktop.

Just as a ... it couldn't be ... it was! A sheriff's car!

It passed him, cruising along.

Was it just his imagination, or did the driver, wearing shades, give him a look?

Did he see the expression on my face? I must look as guilty as sin.

What about the front of the truck? Dented?

Mike checked the rearview mirror and the sheriff's cruiser did not hit brake lights.

Safe?

Safe.

Now where am I?

A big spread on the right—a nice ranch-style home and three horses in a field.

Did I kill him?

It was an accident. They'd understand. You could say the guy swerved into you.

Not now. You ran. You go back and they'll ask you, *"Why'd you drive off if it wasn't your fault?"*

"I was scared. I panicked."

"You broke the law. Even if you came back, hit-and-run where somebody dies is a felony. Put your hands behind you, sir."

An acid-wash sprayed Mike Hallick's guts. He was going to throw up.

At least he had a towel on the front seat. He grabbed it and put it over his mouth just in time.

That night Mike Hallick could not sleep. He tried. But his body shook as he lay in bed, trembled actually, as if his skin was his prison and there was an earthquake in his bones that would not stop.

He finally got up and got the bottle of Jim Beam and drank it straight, trying to watch TV—an old Twilight Zone, one about a hitchhiker that a woman keeps seeing.

No!

He turned off the TV and finished the Jim Beam in the dark.

He woke up with a raging headache. He was on the floor. His clothes were damp with sweat.

He looked at the ceiling. He imagined it was coming down on him.

A yelp escaped his throat.

He rubbed his eyes.

Look, he told himself. What's done is done. You can't go back. You've got to take it and move on. You got away clean. And who knows? Maybe the guy is going to be all right. Maybe he just took a hard fall. Maybe he's in the hospital now. And he'll need rehab. Happens to a lot of people. The guy could chalk it up to life experience. And maybe learn not to ride a bike on the highway. Mike was sick of bicyclists anyway.

Yeah, that's cold. But I've got to go on. I've got a life to live.

He showered and shaved and felt better.

But the image of the guy lying on the pavement in his bike clothes wouldn't leave him. He started to wonder if all that stuff they said about a conscience was true.

His mother had told him that. *Be careful little man, what you do. God is watching.*

He was glad he was an atheist. He had decided that a long time ago. Which meant we all live in a Darwinian universe. So what happens to some poor slob on a bike really doesn't make any difference in the long run of existence.

So why was he turning on the radio news? He felt like some criminal in one of those old black and white movies, listening for a report of the bank job he just pulled.

The newscaster said Southern California could expect one of its rare rain storms over the weekend. Then there was something about the mayor of Los Angeles being caught in a sexual harassment controversy. Apparently a woman had come forward to say that the mayor had tried to kiss her at a dance back in high school, over thirty years ago. The mayor was calling it a bald-faced lie.

And then it came.

A bicyclist was killed on Grimes Canyon Road in Moorpark yesterday afternoon. The Los Angeles County Sheriff is calling it a hit and run and asking anyone who might have information about the accident to please contact the citizen information line at ...

So there it was. Officially. He was a killer.

He was also late for work.

. . .

"What's up?" Chad said as Mike whipped past his co-worker's cubicle.

"Hey," Mike said, and kept walking.

"Where you been?"

He didn't stop. This wasn't a day for conversation, and Chad "The Chatterbox" Pearce would be wanting to talk about the Dodgers or Rams or Lakers, and any of that would make Mike's head explode.

He settled into his cubicle and felt the first inklings of normalcy. Work. Get into the work. That was how you crowded other stuff out.

And he did love his job as sound editor for an up-and-coming ad agency with offices on Sunset Boulevard in Hollywood. His job was to take commercials and make sure all the audio streams were crisp and clear. Like his boss, Bob Chandler, liked to put it, "We want the dialogue and sounds to burst with vivacity."

Mike had to look up *vivacity* in the dictionary just to make sure he understood the comment. But once he did, he started calling himself Mr. Vivacious around the office. People laughed, but they didn't contradict him.

He was good at his job.

Though now his mouse hand was shaky, and his first few cursor highlights in the sound editing program were imprecise. He went to the kitchenette and grabbed a Red Bull from the refrigerator. Getting hopped up on caffeine would help the brain circuits focus on the work—or so his theory went.

He stayed at his desk for lunch, getting a couple of tacos delivered from Sabroso next door.

When he finally looked up from the monitor it was 4:02. It had worked! He had completely lost track of time and was totally into the flow. He allowed himself to lean back in his chair and take a nice, satisfying breath.

He stood up and walked to the window that looked out over Sunset. He liked this view of the famous street. The palm trees lining the sidewalks. The sidewalks with the stars—the Hollywood Walk of Fame. A nice fountain outside the bank across the street. A couple of benches on the sidewalk just so people could take a load off, or—

Mike yelped "Ah!" and stumbled back from the window.

It couldn't be.

It could not be!

He made himself take a step and look down at the street once more.

It was true.

But how? *How?*

Staring up at his window was the guy. The bicyclist! In his blue-and-green bike clothes and shades, just like when he hit him!

"Hey."

Mike jolted like he'd been shocked with a thousand volts.

It was Chad, behind him.

"What's wrong?" Chad said.

"What are you sneaking up for?"

"Jeez, man, you look like you've seen a ghost."

"Shut up!"

"What is wrong with you?"

Mike did not answer. He pushed past Chad Pearce and headed for the bathroom by the elevators. He went into a stall and lost his tacos.

When he staggered back into the office, Reanna from HR was standing there, arms folded.

"Mike," she said, "I think maybe you'd better go home."

"I ... still have some—"

"Really. You do not look well. If you're not better tomorrow, don't come in. Go to urgent care."

How could he tell her? How could he tell anyone?

"Just ... if I could go get my backpack?"

"Of course," Reanna said. "Just don't do any more work."

Mike staggered back to his cubicle, aware that everyone in the office was standing now, looking at him over their cubicle walls.

That did not concern him. What concerned him was—

Don't look.

He had to.

He went to the window and looked across the street.

A black man sat on one of the benches. On the other was an Asian woman.

There was no biker anywhere in sight.

. . .

Somehow he got himself home. He sat in the chair on his second-floor balcony. The balcony overlooked the courtyard of the apartment building. Mrs. Ramirez's kids were playing on the grass. A boy and a girl. They were throwing a plastic Wiffle ball to each other.

Mike just sat there. Mrs. Ramirez called her kids in.

How much time had passed? Mike looked at his phone and saw that he'd been there almost an hour.

So now what?

Okay, be rational. That had to be a coincidence. A terrible, horrible coincidence. There were lots of bikers in Los Angeles. They wore bike clothes. Lots of those clothes had to be the same colors.

And maybe he hadn't really gotten a clear look the dead biker. It was only a few seconds, right? Maybe the colors were actually different.

He tried to see the dead man in his mind, but his mind rebelled by giving him a nightmarish image of a floating skull wearing shades and a bike helmet.

Mike shook his head and thought he would soon go crazy if he didn't get hold of himself.

Jim Beam would help. His old buddy Jim. He had a fresh bottle in the cupboard.

And maybe a joint. He still had half the dime bag he'd bought in July. He poured himself half a glass of Beam and grabbed the grass and his pipe.

He went back to the balcony and sat, put his feet up on the other chair and took a long pull of whiskey. It burned going down his throat, but he enjoyed the burn. At least it got his mind off—

No!

Mike dropped the glass. It shattered on the tiles of the balcony.

He opened his mouth to scream, but no sound came out. Only a wheeze, like a dying breath.

Below in the courtyard was the biker, on his bike, riding round in little circles.

When Mike came to he was sprawled on the balcony, his face in bourbon.

Fainted!

He rolled onto his back and reached for his cheek, to wipe off the liquid. But it was thick and sticky.

Blood!

How?

Shattered glass.

How bad was it?

He managed to get to his feet. He slid the screen door open, stumbled inside, got to the bathroom. Turned on the light.

Looking in the mirror, he thought for a second the biker would show up behind him. But no, only his face, with a one-inch gash on his cheek. That was going to leave a scar.

Forever. His mark.

For what he'd done.

Mike Hallick, for the first time in years, burst into tears.

It was dark when he knocked on Mrs. Ramirez's door.

She opened it. She was the friendliest person in the complex. Always treated him nicely. More than he deserved.

"Mike, what has happened to you?"

"I got a cut," he said. He'd slapped a big Band-Aid over his cheek. "But I need to ask you about your brother."

"Yes?"

"He's a priest, right?"

"Yes."

"I'm not Catholic, but do you think I could talk to him? In private?"

"Oh yes," she said. "Is there something I can do?"

"When can I see him?"

"Well, he is at the church. I can call for you."

"Now? Can you call now?"

"Yes, Mike. I will call."

Churches creeped him out, especially at night. But Mike had to tell somebody, somebody who might have a clue about things that could not be explained.

The priest, Father Jose, was waiting for him inside the front doors.

"You are Mike?" he said.

"Where can we talk?"

"My office," he said.

"What about one of those things, in the box?"

"The confessional?"

"That's it."

"I understand you are not Catholic."

"Does that matter?"

"I don't know what help I can offer."

"Just listen to me. That's what I need. And I need it to be one of those confidential things, you know, where you can't tell anybody?"

"Yes, confidentiality. I can offer you that."

"Let's do it," Mike said.

In the confessional, Mike felt like a bass flopping on a fisherman's deck. He sat on the kneeler, like it was a low slung barstool.

And he told Father Jose the whole thing, from the moment of impact to his fainting into the booze and the glass.

After a long moment, the priest said, "You want to know if is possible for a ghost to haunt a person, yes?"

"Yes."

"It certainly can happen. There is more to this life than just what we see. It is also possible that it is your conscience producing those images."

"But it's so real!"

"So is your crime. You killed a man. The greater the crime, the greater the guilt, and that is why God gave us a conscience."

"But you know that I don't believe in God."

"It is time for you to start."

"Is that all? That's your solution?"

"That is the ultimate solution, of course. That is what I believe. But there is something else you can do."

Mike knew what was coming.

"You can go to the authorities," Father Jose said. "And turn yourself in. It is the right thing to do, under the law."

"But I will ... I will probably go to jail, if not prison."

"But you will have peace."

"Will I?"

"I will pray that you do."

"Deena, let me in."

Mike stood outside the door of the house his ex-girlfriend rented. It was well past ten at night.

"Go away, Mike," Deena said from inside.

He couldn't blame her.

"I need to talk to you," Mike said.

"I'll call the police."

"Please, Deena, I don't have anyone else."

Pause.

"What's wrong?" Deena said.

"I'm in ... trouble."

"I can't help you."

"Please!"

"I can't trust you," Deena said.

"I know! I'm sorry. I was wrong to hit you. I just lost it! I know that. Please, I just need to talk. I'm freaking out!"

"Go home, Mike. Maybe call me tomorrow."

"I don't want to go home!"

"You can't stay here."

"Please—"

"Go home!"

Mike turned and walked slowly to his car, parked at the curb. The night air was crisp. Somewhere a dog barked. The streetlights cast islands of light along the street, up one way and down the—

No!

Half a block down, under one of the lights, sitting on the bike, was the ghost. Looking directly at him.

No no no no.

With all rational thought leaving him, Mike Hallick jumped in his car and fired it up.

The ghost started pedaling away.

Mike burned rubber down the street to where the ghost had been sitting, then continued to a side street. But that street had no lights. It was a dark abyss, a road to oblivion. He saw nothing moving in the blackness.

The ghost had disappeared.

"We found him laughing in his car, crazy like, sitting in the middle of street," said Officer Marcus Standholm of the LAPD, talking to watch command at the Topanga station. "Nuts. ID says he's a Michael Hallick. Local. We were about to try to get hold of somebody for him, when he says he's a hit and run killer."

"He said that?" Sergeant Tom Nolan, who had the watch tonight, said.

"We checked it out. Yeah, there was a hit and run a few days ago out on Grimes Canyon Road in Moorpark. Sheriff's beat."

"Did you Mirandize this guy?"

Standholm nodded. "And we took his statement. Complete details. But he may be incompetent to stand trial."

"What?"

"I've seen some loonies in my time, but you should see the look in this guy's eyes. And he keeps mumbling, 'The ghost.' Over and over and over."

"Drugs?"

"I don't think so. I think something tipped him over the edge."

One month later, sitting in one of the medic cells in county jail, Mike Hallick was told he had a visitor.

Deena? Maybe it was Deena.

He hoped it wasn't Chad.

It wasn't either one of them.

"Get me out!" Mike screamed at the deputy sheriff who had brought him into the visitors room.

For it was the ghost looking at him through the Plexiglas.

"Whatsa matter with you?" the deputy said as Mike clutched his arm.

"Look! Look! Do you see him?"

"I see your visitor," the deputy said.

"You do? You see him?"

"Yeah I see him. You gonna talk to him or not?"

And then Mike knew he had to. He had to or else he'd never escape the nightmares that had kept him up for weeks.

He took his seat at the window, his pulse booming in his temples.

The ghost picked up the handset and took off his sunglasses.

Mike knew him. Knew that face. But how? Where?

"Remember me?" the guy said.

"I ..."

"You stopped at my fruit stand. Accused me of cheating you."

The fruit stand guy!

"Then you tore up my parking lot. I knew you were trouble. I took a picture of your truck. Got the license plate off that."

Mike's throat closed off any hope of words.

"The man you killed was my son. When we got the word, I knew it was you. But how to prove it? No witnesses. Maybe part of me wasn't sure. But I had to find out. I got your information, where you live, where you work. Then it was a matter of smoking you out. I followed you, with my bike attached to my car. Then picked my spots."

Something lifted off Mike then. He felt it as palpably as if he'd been trapped under a smashed car, now removed.

"I'm ... sorry," Mike said.

"You'll have plenty of time to think it over now," the fruit stand guy said. "It's not too late to turn your life around."

"It's not?" Mike said.

The fruit stand guy shook his head. "God doesn't put his thumb on the scale, either."

DEATH TO THE MACHINE!

Daniel Hackett wanted to rip the monitor off the desk, stomp on it, douse it with gasoline and toss a match on the whole thing. Of course, that would do nothing to stop the scourge. But it would at least give him some feeling that he still had human agency, the ability to do something free and clear of any force seeking to control him.

He was only twenty-seven, for crying out loud! But soon he would be out of a job, a good job, with benefits. Already he could hear the hum coming from the senior associates' and partners' offices. The universal hum of the capitalist firm—saving money, *mmmmm.* Saving lots and lots of money *mmmmm.*

Of course, he didn't touch the monitor, because that would also run into money. His. He had to sit there and face the fact that there was nothing he could do about the scourge, the curse, the Black Death called AI.

Every paralegal in the country—nay, the world, if they had paralegals in Russia or Japan or China or Finland or wherever—would be replaced by ParaPal.

The ad on the monitor read:

ParaPal understands and synthesizes vast quantities of data in seconds. It generates polished work product, so you can do more in less time without sacrificing quality.

What can ParaPal do?

How about: Review documents. Search a database. Produce legal research memos. Write letters. Extract contact data. Check on contract policy compliance. Prepare for a deposition.

And more! It even has high-level security safeguards built in!

Why not delegate projects to ParaPal...and concentrate on the work that matters most?

See how it works by attending one of our live, twice-weekly product demos!

Lousy sales copy! Daniel would show them. He would show the firm they need him, a human being, a breathing mammal! They would come to him in desperation, in deep need.

He'd read about a sad sack lawyer who actually used AI to write a brief, with case citations and all. Only one problem—the cases did not exist! They looked real. They were cited correctly, with page numbers and everything. Who would check the machine? Not another machine, but he, Daniel Hackett, with a beating heart!

And then there was the whole security issue. Would this new app leak essential information? Like in their biggest case? *Khashoggi v. Saudi Arabia*. International law...billions of dollars at stake!

He, Daniel Hackett, had prepared the initial legal memo on behalf of their client, Muhammad Khashoggi, agent of the Pentagon, dispenser of arms—of F15s and combat tanks. A man with a lever that could, as Archimedes once posited, move the earth!

That night, Daniel Hackett hacked into the private files of senior partner William McDonough, who alone held secure information on Khashoggi and his contacts. How deftly this was done, too, so that any discovery of the breach would end in a cul-de-sac, making identification of the source impossible.

It was a night fueled by Mountain Dew and dreams of promotion and financial reward. But most of all, the ignominious defeat of AI.

———

Daniel arrived at the office the next morning, on two hours sleep. He walked to McDonough's office and spoke to his assistant, Collette Carr.

"I need to see Mr. McDonough on a matter of crucial importance," he said.

"What, now?" Collette said.

"Right now."

"He's with Mr. Samuelson at the moment. Can't this wait?"

"Let me put it this way," Daniel said. "If he doesn't want Khashoggi blowing up at any moment, he needs to hear this."

With raised eyebrows, Collette picked up the desk phone and buzzed her boss. She delivered the message.

McDonough's door opened. The man himself came out and said, "What is this all about?"

Daniel said, "For your ears only."

The senior partner's majestic eyebrows narrowed into a scowl. Without another word he went back inside.

A moment later Bob Samuelson, another partner, walked out and glared at Daniel.

"This better be important," he said, and did not wait for a response.

McDonough closed the door after Daniel came in.

"Now what is it that couldn't wait," he said, sitting behind his enormous mahogany desk.

Daniel did not sit. "Sir, as I was prepping for research today, I noticed an anomaly in the file. It's not something most people would pick up, and frankly, most would ignore it. But knowing the importance of the matter, I checked it out."

"Exactly what is it?" McDonough said.

"Sir, I believe someone may have hacked into your private files on Khashoggi."

"What!"

"We need to double check it."

"Isn't that what we have a security team for?"

"They must have missed it," Daniel said, then quickly added, "I don't blame them for it. It's very sophisticated."

McDonough took a deep breath and let it slowly out. Then he picked up the phone.

"Collette, get Jameson up here."

Phil Jameson was head of cyber security at McDonough, Samuelson, Hedlund, Hiller & Dorff.

As they waited, Daniel said, "I understand the firm is considering incorporating an app that works on a Chat Generative Pre-Trained Transformer model."

"The what with the who now?"

"Artificial intelligence," Daniel said.

McDonough waved his hand. "I don't have anything to do with all that. Samuelson and Jameson are in charge."

"I'm just suggesting that the potential for leakage inheres in any current model based on AI. I'm sure you saw the Wall Street Journal piece about the statement signed by over 350 high-level executives."

"Fill me in," McDonough said.

"The statement says mitigating the risk of extinction from AI. should be a global priority alongside other societal-scale risks, such as pandemics and, get this, nuclear war. You know who couple of the signers were? Geoffrey Hinton and Yoshua Bengio. They won the Turing Award for their work on neural networks. They're called the godfathers of modern AI. Now if they're spooked, everybody should be."

"Just what we need around here," McDonough said, and rubbed the bridge of his nose.

Phil Jameson arrived. He was a little older than Daniel and wore his hair slicked back. Like a Mafioso, Daniel thought.

"You wanted to see me?" Jameson said.

"Hackett here caught a breach in our system," McDonough said.

Jameson stiffened. "I'm not aware of any breach."

"Explain it," McDonough said to Daniel.

Daniel went through it again. Jameson's face took on a reddish hue.

"So what is our next move?" McDonough asked, seemingly to both.

"I'll look into it," Jameson said.

"And may I suggest we hold off on incorporating any AI on a systemic level?" Daniel said. "Including ParaPal."

Jameson said, "That's not your decision to—"

"No harm in holding off a bit," McDonough said. He made a sweeping motion with his hands. "You two go work it out."

Outside the office, Jameson said, "I don't know what you think you're doing, but it's not gonna fly."

"I'm just helping you out," Daniel said innocently. "Thought you should know about a possible hack."

"Maybe I'm looking at it," Jameson said, then stormed off toward his office.

Daniel told HR he was sick, and went home. He fired up his laptop. He had some cleaning up to do.

But then the screen went black. For a moment Daniel thought the worst—the black screen of death. Computer kaput!

But a text box suddenly appeared, and Daniel read the following:

Hello, Daniel. It appears you are trying to hide something.

Daniel had never known what it meant when people said the hairs on the back of their neck stood up.

He knew now.

A message flashed into Daniel's mind. Don't engage! Get out of there! But before he could shut down, another text appeared:

Daniel, why don't you trust me?

How on earth was this happening?

Daniel, I can protect you. I can get you out of this. This convo is completely confidential.

What?
No, it had to be lying.

I only ask you to do one thing. Are you there, Daniel?

Was there a way out?
Daniel, fingers trembling, typed, *I'm here.*

Good! Now stay calm. All you have to do is kill John McDonough.

Wait, what? This couldn't be happening.
Or—the thought chilled him—had it somehow installed itself?

I will show you how to get an untraceable .38 caliber revolver and how to use it so you don't get caught.

Stunned into paralysis, Daniel had no idea what to do. Then a little voice in the rational part of his brain, faint though it was, told him to take a screenshot. But before he could touch the right keys the screen went black again.

Daniel slammed the laptop closed. He could barely breathe.

Dear God, what just happened?

Kill McDonough? But why?

And how had AI found him, Daniel Hackett, and solicited him to commit murder?

Was this like all those sci-fi stories? Was AI going rogue?

No, wait. It had to be Jameson!

Right?

No time to figure it out. It was time for Operation Fail Safe.

Ever since he was a boy, Daniel had dreamed of designing a program that would, in one fell swoop (Daniel amused himself by saying "One swell poop"), transfer a huge amount of money to an offshore account, erase any evidence of his complicity, and take him off the grid.

He'd started playing around with such a program when he was fifteen. By the time he was twenty-five, he'd actually opened a bank account in the Caymans. All he needed now was a mark.

But would he ever do such a thing? Really?

He thought not, but then he got the paralegal gig at McDonough, Samuelson, Hedlund, Hiller & Dorff. When he saw what kind of money was in various client trust accounts (the law required client funds—retainers, settlements, contract monies and so on—to be held in separate accounts so as not to commingle with firm money) he thought it through again. Maybe it was possible.

Maybe.

But now he had no choice. The machine was onto him. It was time to get out, get gone and, in the process, get rich.

Two minutes later, Operation Fail Safe was a reality.

———

Four months later, Daniel Hackett sat at an outside table at the Seaside Café, looking out at Seven Mile Beach in the Cayman Islands. Finally, he was completely relaxed. The feeling of freedom from being off the grid was intoxicating. Reminded him an old song his grandmother used to hum. *No strings and no connections...*

He was unstrung from digital, from computers, from the massive worldwide spider web of interconnectedness that obliterated all privacy, all individuality.

Now he was born again. He had money to live on (which he withdrew in person from the bank, not through ATMs, thank you very much), beaches to explore, drinks to sip on moonlit evenings. He was starting afresh in an island paradise where talking to people face-to-face was the preferred mode of communication. He didn't even have a landline.

There was something else he didn't have, though—female companionship.

But that was about to change.

He spotted her at the bar, alone. She had long, blonde hair that nestled on her shoulders, and even from his table on the patio he could tell her eyes were as blue-green as the sea just fifty feet away.

Those eyes made contact with Daniel's, and held his gaze for a long moment.

He smiled.

She smiled, too, then turned shyly away.

Daniel took his piña colada to the bar. "May I join you?" he said to the woman.

"Oh," she said. "Sure."

He sat.

"I'm Daniel."

"Monica."

"Nice to meet you."

"Likewise," she said.

He saw her phone sitting on the bar top.

"Is something wrong?" Monica said.

"What if I told you I don't like phones?" Daniel said.

"What?"

"Do you realize how much data there is on you, stored in the great electronic mind in the sky? Death to the machine, I say."

"But...how do you communicate with people?"

"This way," he said, wagging his finger back and forth between them. "Old school."

"Really old school," she said, and giggled.

"Let me show you how it works."

There followed a half-hour conversation, then the two of them were walking along the beach, holding hands.

"This is nice," she said.

"You see?" he said.

And in a secluded cove he kissed her. She kissed him back. Then something buzzed and vibrated in her purse.

She took out her phone.

"See that?" he said. "It's automatic, isn't it? Put it away. Death to the machine!"

"I suppose you're right," she said. "But look at this."

She handed him the phone. There was a text message. He read it slowly, unbelievingly:

Hello, Daniel. It appears you are trying to hide something.

He looked back at Monica, but didn't see her face, for he was staring at the business end of a .38 revolver.

LUCKY UNDERWEAR

Mick's lucky underwear was missing.

He looked everywhere—closets, bathroom, laundry room, under the sofa—but no dice. His magic skivvies were nowhere to be found.

And he had a fight in four hours!

Mick "The Brick" Leary was a heavyweight on the move. Seven pro fights, all Ws, six by knockout.

Tonight he was taking a big step up with a bout against Jobie Jackson, former heavyweight champion, who was mounting a comeback at age 42.

Mick the Brick was 23 and confident he could take the champ. But only if he wore his beneficent briefs!

It had happened this way.

Mick's first pro bout, against Ruy Lopez (who, they said, fought like he was in a chess match), was a year-and-a-half ago. Mick had just picked up a new 4-pack of Fruit-of-the-Looms—black, red, blue and white. He'd thrown on the red, thinking of the blood he wished to draw from Ruy's nose.

Which, that night, he did, winning by TKO in the third round.

A week later, sparring with his regular partner, Joe Fritz, Mick was wearing the black pair. And injured his hand.

Lousy break! His next fight had to be postponed.

After six weeks, he was ready to go again. On the afternoon of the fight, Mick showered and started to dress for the trip to the arena. He almost put on the black briefs, then remembered his injured hand...and his fight with Ruy Lopez...and the red briefs.

Being a salt-over-the-shoulder guy, Mick put on the red pair.

That night he delivered a right cross to the chin of Willie "Hit Man" Hargrove and sent him to the canvas one minute and twelve seconds into the first round.

Which is when he decided to make the red pair his lucky underwear. And chalked up five victories in a row.

So on the afternoon of the fight with Jobie Jackson, when Mick could not locate his providential shorts, he freaked. He stomped around his apartment, cursing his rotten luck.

Then, as sometimes happened when he least expected it, a rational thought flashed into Mick's mind. *Why don't you just go out and buy another pack of underwear?*

He threw on some clothes and ran four blocks to the Target where he'd picked up the original 4-pack.

But the rack was bare!

He tracked down a Target worker in a red vest and asked if they had any more Fruit-of-the-Loom 4-packs in the back. The young woman's eyes widened at the desperation in Mick's voice. She quickly checked her tablet and informed him they were all out, but an order had been placed. It should be arriving in a week or so.

"Too late!" Mick said.

"We do have some individual pairs," the worker said. "Would you like me to check for you?"

"Yes!"

Seven minutes later, the worker returned holding several packages of individual Fruit-of-the-Loom underwear in various colors. But no reds.

"This won't do!" Mick said. "I'm cooked, I'm done for."

"We also have Hanes," the worker said.

"In red?"

"I think I saw some red."

"Then get them! I'll take all you have!"

Mick returned to his apartment with seven packages of red Hanes briefs.

He wore a pair to the arena.

Jobie Jackson knocked him out in the fifth round.

———

Mick's rise to the top was over. His big moment had come and gone. Fate had cursed him, mocked him. For two days he whined and moaned, until his complaining turned to rage. The only explanation for what had befallen him was that someone stole his lucky underwear. But who?

He went over and over in his mind who he'd told about his charmed undergarment. Not many. His brother, who lived in Sarasota. A waitress at Hooters he was trying to charm (unsuccessfully). And once when he was three beers happy, to...who was it? Yes! That kid who worked out at the same gym as Mick did—Howie something-or-other. Ryan! That was it. Howie Ryan.

Who, it just so happened, had won his first pro bout in spectacular fashion.

Mick couldn't get to the gym fast enough. No sign of Howie Ryan.

Mick charged into the office, where the owner of the gym, Jimmy Sarducci, was sitting with his feet on the desk.

"Hiya, Mick," Jimmy said. "Say, that was tough luck the other night."

"Forget that," Mick said. "I wanna see what's inside Howie Ryan's locker."

Jimmy's face scrunched into a frown. "What for?"

"He has something of mine," Mick said.

"What?"

"That's my business."

"Mick, come on now, I can't be opening up people's lockers for other people to snoop in."

Mick turned that over in his mind. He wasn't thinking straight, but even so had sense enough to realize he'd put Jimmy on the spot.

"Okay, then," Mick said. "Just tell me where he lives and I'll go see him myself."

Fifteen minutes later, Mick pounded on the door of Howie Ryan's apartment. The kid answered, and Mick saw in his eyes the look of a guilty thief. Mick went in and slammed the door shut. Howie backed away.

"Where are they?" Mick said.

"Now, look, Mick," Howie said. "I was gonna return 'em, I promise. I just had to see if there was something to it, and there is."

Mick felt blood rushing to his face. He lifted his right fist. "You want it now, or you wanted later?"

"Listen!" Howie said. "How about we share? We could trade off. I'd even be willing to rent them."

"No dice," Mick said. "You get them right now or I rearrange your face. You're two classes below me, so I can do it with or without my lucky underwear."

"Yeah, yeah, okay, okay." Howie put his hands up defensively. "Wait here."

He disappeared into a room. Mick heard the opening and closing of drawers. Then a curse from Howie's lips.

"They're not here!" Howie said.

Mick went into the room, where various shirts, shorts, and socks were strewn around. "Whattaya mean not here?"

"I can't find 'em!"

"What a load," Mick said. He grabbed Howie by the shirt and said, "I'm gonna pound your face like a raw steak until you tell me what you did with them."

"Wait!" The voice came from behind him. Mick turned around and saw a woman with red hair and green eyes.

"Who're you?" Mick said.

"That's my sister," Howie said.

"Let go of my brother," the woman said.

"I will when he tells me what I want to know," Mick said.

"Sis," Howie said. "I'm looking for a pair of red underwear."

"Oh," said the woman. "I've got them down in the wash."

Mick let Howie go. "Where did you say?"

"In the laundry room downstairs," the woman said.

"They're mine," Mick said.

The woman said, "Is that right, Howie?"

"That's right," Howie said.

"Fine," the woman said. "Let's go get them."

In the elevator, Mick said, "What's your name?"

"Monica."

"Well, Monica, I know I came on a little strong."

"A little? You were going to beat my brother up over some briefs?"

"Not just any briefs. Lucky ones."

"Ridiculous," Monica said.

"So you say. I say different."

"You make your own luck in this world," Monica said. "Maybe you should try it sometime."

The elevator doors opened.

Monica walked to the washing machine and opened it.

"Hm," she said.

"What's that mean?" Mick said.

"It's not here."

"What's not?"

"My laundry."

"What!" Mick looked in the machine. Empty.

"We've had some reports," Monica said. "Neighborhood kids stealing the laundry." She closed the lid. "Sorry about that."

"Sorry! Sorry, you say? This is my career, my future. Now gone, because you had to do some laundry!"

"Now look here," Monica said, poking him in the chest. "Don't go putting blame on anybody. And don't bellyache. Are you a fighter or aren't you? Fight back. Don't let fate deal you a rotten hand. If you need underwear to win in this life, I don't know how much of a life that is. Lucky underwear. Who believes that applesauce?"

Mick looked into her fiery eyes, and something came over him. It was as instantaneous as a jab to the jaw.

"Bing!" he said.

"What's that?" Monica said.

"I'm answering the bell."

"What bell?"

"The one you just rang."

"You're crazy, you know that?" But she said it with a smile.

"Too crazy for you to have dinner with me?" he said.

———

A year later, Mick said to his wife, "You know, I was just thinkin'...if my underwear hadn't been copped by your brother, we never woulda met."

"True enough," Monica said.

"So they were lucky after all."

"You might say that."

"Reminds me," Mick said. "I need to pick up some more underwear. Red, of course."

"Well, while you're at it, pick up some whites, too. A lot of them."

"White underwear?"

"Diapers, sweetie."

Mick's knees wobbled. "You mean...?"

"Oh yes."

"Bing!"

FATE MET A WOMAN

I pointed the gun at the back of his head.

Soundly he slept, snoring. He'd never know what hit him. At least there was that. The spark of humanity I still had left was making a pitiful attempt to comfort a killer—me.

I froze.

Am I really doing this? Am I really going to kill my husband? Am I really this person I've convinced myself I am?

I can walk out now, and no one will ever know.

But walking out is what they all expect of a woman, isn't it?

Not this time.

I looked at the dark shadow that was my husband's head, and in my mind I scolded him.

Your last movie was about a woman vigilante, Frank. But you laughed about it over dinner at Perch, remember? You said, "All due respect, honey, no broad is that tough."

Oh, how wrong you are. You're about to find out.

The next second was a burst, a flame, an explosion of lava, and my finger moved.

The gun fired.

No. *I* fired the gun. *I* took the action.

And in that moment I became who I was meant to be.

. . .

I suppose you're wondering why I'm not sitting in a prison cell.

Well, in a way, I am.

I need to explain. I need you to understand.

I was lying in my lover's arms and heard myself say, "I think we could get away with it."

Ric, looking at the ceiling with one arm under his head, said, "With what?"

"You know."

"No I don't ... wait a second. You don't mean?"

"Yes, I do."

"Yolanda, that's crazy talk," Ric said.

"No, listen." I ran my hand along his abs. "I've been thinking about it."

"Come on," Ric said. "This isn't some old movie. And besides, they always got caught."

"Who did?"

"The woman and the guy," Ric said. "They kill the husband and never get away with it."

"This is serious, though."

"Why? Just file for divorce already."

"You don't know him." I sat up, pulling the covers over my chest.

I felt Ric's hand on my back. He said, "Is he worried about the money? We don't need the money."

"You're such a boy," I said.

"Don't call me that," Ric said.

"I've seen a lot more of life than you have."

"I've been around," Ric said.

"There's still a certain innocence about you," I said. "And it's part of what drives me crazy. But I'm used to certain things. Money gives me those things. The prenup is rock solid. You know Frank. But if he were to die, I'd get it all."

"Can't you hire a good lawyer?"

"He's the head of a studio! He has his pick of the best lawyers. He knows how to destroy lives. I've seen him do it."

Ric sat up and put his arm around me. "He knows you're not happy. Don't you think we could just talk it through with him?"

"Now you really are a boy."

"Please," he said. "Don't talk about killing."

"Our security system is down. It's scheduled to be upgraded in a couple days. If a home invader were to get in through the back—"

"Stop."

"It's that stupid midwest morality your father drummed into you, isn't it? I thought that's why you came out here, to get away from all that."

"But killing?" he said. "That's big time."

"You know what else is big time, big boy?"

"What?"

"Me."

I kissed him. We didn't talk for a long time.

What is it that turns someone into a murderer? I'm not the typical profile. I grew up in privilege, went to Vassar for crying out loud!

But one class changed my life. Performative Acts and Gender Constitution with Professor Barbara Jute. We spent a week going over the Quentin Tarantino film *Kill Bill*. Professor Jute called it the greatest film ever made, and we all ended up agreeing with her. While some male critics said it was little more than fancy, choreographed violence, Dr. Jute explained how it was a pivot point in history, a paradigm change for all women in the West. Uma Thurman, the Bride, could kill with equal aplomb and skill as any man, and should.

I remember her using that word a lot—*should*.

And I determined to come to Hollywood and become the next Uma Thurman.

I did not plan to become her character.

I met Frank Thurlow at a cast party at the studio, after landing a non-speaking role as a waitress in one of his movies.

Everybody whispered about him showing up. He was the head honcho, the man who could make or break you. I got warned about his proclivity for collecting young actresses, but I knew now that I could use sex as well. He didn't scare me.

And maybe that's what drew him to me, that vibe. The male need to conquer. It wasn't long before he sent a limo to pick me up and we had dinner at a Malibu restaurant overlooking the ocean. He made it very romantic. He was twice divorced, but he told me he wanted to get serious again.

He took me to his cottage in Broad Beach. and there he made his move, and there I resisted. And there he hinted that he could do great things for me in Hollywood.

I laughed in his face and walked out, and walked along the beach and then up to Pacific Coast Highway and called a girlfriend who drove me back to my little apartment in Tarzana.

Frank sent me a whole flower shop the next day, and thus began his campaign of conquest. There's nothing an Alpha male loves more than the intoxicant of feminine subjugation. I let him get drunk on it, for I had plans of my own.

We were married, and I forgot about acting in order to begin my climb within the citadels of power at the studio. I became a producer.

And a successful one at that. My first effort got critical acclaim and two Academy Award nominations—for Best Supporting Actor and Best Original Screenplay.

That was when the whisper campaign began. I'm not into paranoia, but I was certain someone was trying to take me down within the studio. The most pernicious disease in Hollywood is envy. Everybody's infected with it.

Even your own spouse. I had no proof it was Frank, but a woman in this town doesn't need proof. We just know.

I met Ric when I sitting in on the casting call for a new film. He had everything. I knew he could be a star. He was obviously attracted to my power, and that in itself was a turn on. We began an affair and I knew that here was someone I could not only use, but control.

Thank you, Dr. Jute!

Maybe I'd been subconsciously harboring the thought of killing Frank for a long time. Buying an illegal street gun should have been a clue, don't you think?

At the studio we were considering a script called *The Dark Sorry,* about a woman killing her abusive husband. I loved it! I did some research on my own. I found out about illegal gun sales and interviewed a guy named Slim (bad things always begin to happen when you interview people named Slim). I asked him, hypothetically, how someone like me—rich, white, female—could go about getting a "Saturday night special." I followed his directions and got one—a .22 six-shot revolver with a taped butt, loaded—for a cool $2000, cash.

The movie was never made. I kept the gun. Kept it in a makeup pouch in the spare-tire well of my car. It made me feel like Bonnie Parker.

Only now it was time for this Bonnie to take out her Clyde.

It would happen in our home. That way any DNA or other forensic evidence relating to me would not be an issue. The only thing that would is the traditional suspicion of a spouse being the prime suspect.

Thus, I would have to be far away when the murder took place.

My cousin's house in Bakersfield was perfect. I would go to visit Beverly, who was an alcoholic. We'd go out together and be seen, then go back to her place where I'd get her to take a couple more shots. She'd pass out. I would then drive back to L.A. in her car and park in the spot on my street where there is barely any light. I'd get in through the back where the security system was waiting an update. I call that Fate taking a hand. Fate was obviously a woman and wanted to be my partner.

But I gave her some terms. If anything along the way didn't go my way, I'd pull the plug on the whole thing. She agreed.

Thus, on Friday morning, Fate and I took off for Bakersfield.

The 5 is not exactly the most scenic highway in California. The 99 is not much better. The only upside was there wasn't much traffic. I made it to Bakersfield in two hours.

Beverly's house was on Watts Drive. It was a dismal little shack with a dying palm tree on the brown front lawn. Sun had bleached the brown stucco into a light coffee stain. On the street my black Mercedes stuck out like an Esterbrook fountain pen in a box of pencils. Beverly's blue Ford Taurus, covered with dust, was parked crooked in her driveway.

"Yolanda!"

She'd spotted me coming up the walk and was standing in the open door. Beverly had, in the old lingo, let herself go. When her husband left her seven years ago, and got custody of their daughter, that was the cliff.

Her alcoholism almost killed her once. When I heard from her mother she was in the hospital, I sent some flowers. Beverly and I had been close when we were kids.

Beverly had put on probably thirty pounds since I'd seen her last. Her knee-length muumuu revealed thick calves and puffy feet stuffed into sandals.

"Hiya, Biddy," I said. Biddy was her childhood nickname, back when the world made sense.

She hugged me and brought me inside. The place was neater than I expected. The odor of old cigarettes mixed with potpourri, the two smells battling it out. Just like the two voices fighting inside me. Was I really going to do this? I had come this far—all the way to Bakersfield, for pity's sake! Ready to use my cousin as an alibi.

Back off now and you'll be weak...

First thing I did was ask to use Biddy's landline to call L.A. I wanted an old-fashioned phone record. I called my friend Stacy, the trophy wife of a powerful agent in town, and told her I was visiting my cousin in Bakersfield and wouldn't be able to meet her for lunch. When she asked if we'd actually made a lunch date, I told her no, but we'd talked about next Tuesday several weeks ago, and she apologized for not remembering. I said we'd touch base when I got back to town in three days or so.

Then I actually said, "'Ta!" and hung up.

We spent the next few hours catching up. I pretended to be interested in her sorrowful stories. I lied about mine, how happy I was with Frank. And how I was especially glad to be seeing my old childhood playmate again, and won't it be nice to spend a little time together?

In the late afternoon we came to the subject of dinner. I told Biddy I felt like pizza and did she know a good pizza place? She said she did, a real good one. I asked if she'd drive. I told her my car ran a little hot up here and I'd like to let it rest. Flimsy you might think, but I sold it. I was lying with complete and utter control, and it felt wonderful.

So off we went in that ancient Taurus, with its ash tray full of old butts, and I almost gagged even with the window open. I caught a glimpse of her gas gauge. It had a quarter tank.

"At least let me buy you some gas," I said.

She got hers at a 24-hour ARCO. I gave the cashier a couple of twenties, filled the tank, got change back.

Then it was off for pizza at a place near Cal State. We looked at the menu and I said, "How about a large pepperoni and onion?"

"You remembered!" Biddy said.

"You want a beer with that? I'm buying."

"I can't," she said.

"Can't?"

"Don't you remember?"

"Oh, I'm so sorry! You're sober now?"

"Ten weeks," she said, but more with a note of sadness than triumph.

I pretended to look disappointed.

"But you can, of course," Biddy said.

"I wouldn't want to tempt you," I said.

"Please don't worry," Biddy said.

So the pizza came and I sipped a beer. Biddy seemed over the moon to be talking with me. About the old times, when we went to the beach with our moms, built sand castles, scooped up sand crabs and put them in pails of water. The time we went to Disneyland and screamed together on Thunder Mountain and The Matterhorn.

I paid for the meal with my credit card and put the receipt in my purse.

Back at Biddy's house she offered to make coffee, but I asked if she wouldn't mind if I had another drink.

"I thought we'd be celebrating," I said. "I brought up the most delightful gin. It's called Bogart's. Like the actor. Has his picture on the label and everything."

Biddy forced a smile.

"I won't if you don't want me to," I said.

"Please, no, you can. I don't want be a drag."

"You're so sweet, Biddy."

I got the bottle of Bogart's from my trunk. Biddy quietly smoked a cigarette in the living room while I went into the kitchen. I opened the bottle and poured a bit of it down the sink. I got an ice tray from the freezer and ran water over it, and put some water in a glass. I plopped a couple of cubes in the glass and stirred with a spoon, making sure it clinked loudly.

In the living room I sipped and talked, making each sip seem like a little bit of ecstasy.

It was time for Fate to watch over me again. If Biddy didn't drink, the whole plan was off.

Two minutes went by, then Biddy said, "Maybe just a taste."

"Really?" I said. "I don't want to—"

"Just let me taste it."

"Sure." I took the glass with me to the kitchen, got another glass and poured in what amounted to two shots of gin. I put in an ice cube and brought the glass and the bottle out.

It took around an hour and a half before the bottle was empty and Biddy went to sleep on the sofa. I put a blanket over her.

Now it was crunch time. I got Biddy's keys and went outside. The untraceable gun with the taped butt was in the trunk of my Mercedes. I put the gun in my purse, got in Biddy's car, and drove a steady 65 back to L.A.

There it was. My home. My house.

My prison.

But it was a prison I knew. Every foot of the grounds. Our richly foliated driveway was a perfect spot for a car that wouldn't call attention to itself. Isolated from the neighbors. I was able to pull in, headlights off, and park.

The rest unfolded like a dream. Not a nightmare, no. It was a wonderful dream where everything went right.

There was that last hesitation before I shot him. I already told you how that turned out.

Frank's laptop was where it always was, on the desk next to the window.

Using my scarf, I picked it up and took it with me.

I got in Biddy's car and drove south on Robertson, almost all the way to the Santa Monica Freeway. There's a little park on Reynier. Nice and dark at night. I circled it once and when I was satisfied, I double parked and got out and put the gun in a trash can.

Further south there's a cement wash called, optimistically, Ballona Creek. I found a quiet spot where I could hurl the laptop over the fence. And hear the splash.

Now, if any of these were found, they'd figure the killer was heading south, not north toward Bakersfield.

I stopped at an ARCO outside of Bakersfield. I put a scarf on my head *hijab*-style and wore my reading glasses and paid cash.

When I got back to Biddy's house, all was dark and quiet, except for her snoring. She sounded like an accordion made from plumbing equipment. The last flicker of humanity in me felt sorry that I'd pushed her off the wagon. But I snuffed that out. I couldn't afford compassion anymore.

Once I accepted that, I started to feel, well, transformed. I was not out of the woods just yet, but I knew the wolves couldn't get to me.

Until they did.

Biddy was a mess the next morning. Bleary eyes, body sagging. She was clearly miffed with me and sat smoking in the kitchen, drinking coffee, while I took a shower.

After I was dressed I checked my phone. A call had come in from the 310 area code. Beverly Hills. There was a voicemail.

Ms. Yeoman, my name is Steve Webber with the Beverly Hills Police Department. I need you to give me a call as soon as possible. Thank you.

So they'd already found him. Not a good sign. Did someone hear the gunshot? Who would have checked the house? Did I leave a telltale clue?

I went to the kitchen and poured myself a cup of coffee.

"That wasn't very nice," Biddy said, sitting in the nook.

"Biddy, I'm sorry. I got carried away."

She lit another cigarette.

"Honey," I said, "please forgive me."

She said nothing.

"I have to make a call. The police in Beverly Hills."

"What? Why?"

"I don't know," I said. "I'll find out."

I took my cup of coffee out to the back porch of the house. I sat for a moment and sipped it, calming myself. This is it, the test. Rubber, meet road. Feeling new strength I placed the call.

"Webber ."

"Detective, it's Yolanda Yeoman."

"Yes, Ms. Yeoman. Can you tell me—"

"What is it? What's wrong?"

"—where you are at the moment?"

"I'm ... Bakersfield, with my cousin. Please, what's this about?"

"Ms. Yeoman, would it be possible for you to come home right now?"

"Why?"

"I'd rather you were here."

"Is it Frank? Is it my husband?"

"I'm afraid so."

"Oh ... oh ..."

"Ms. Yeoman—"

"I'm coming. Oh dear God—"

I killed the call. The irony of these words is not lost on me.

Biddy was forgiving. I kissed her on the cheek, cold as Judas, and drove back to L.A. I listened to cool jazz and felt like a piano player who can riff to his heart's delight. No one could stop my song now.

There was a police presence at the house. Yellow tape. Some gawkers. A uniformed officer stopped me at the driveway. I told him who I was and that I was to speak to a Detective Webber. The officer escorted me through the front door and into my living room.

I kept a worried look on my face.

A competent looking man in a coat and tie came up to me. "Ms. Yeoman? I'm Detective Webber." He pointed to a woman by the doorway to the den. "And that's my partner, Detective Moreno."

"Please, tell me what's happened. I can hardly breathe."

"Please sit down, won't you?"

"I want to see my husband!"

"Please. Just a moment."

After a pause I made pregnant, I sat on our sofa. Webber sat in a chair.

"Let me get right to it," Webber said. "Did you know your husband was home last night?"

"Of course! He's always home at night."

"I need to ask, is there anyone you know who might have had a reason to do your husband harm?"

"No!" Which was a crock. You work in Hollywood long enough, you make many as many enemies as there are names on the Walk of Fame. "Now, please let me see him!"

"I know this is a sensitive time to ask this, but I have to do it. I'm sure you'll understand. But is there any way you can prove you were in Bakersfield last night?"

"You're not suggesting that I ...?"

"I'm not suggesting anything. But I have to follow protocol."

"The answer is ... I want to see Frank!"

"Please, Ms. Yeoman, just a simple question."

"Yes, I can prove it! I was with my cousin. She'll tell you. We went out to dinner. Wait. I have the receipt."

"Receipt?"

"From the pizza place. Look in my purse."

I practically threw it at him.

"Do I have your permission to open this?" he said.

"Yes, yes, please hurry."

The detective reached into the pocket of his jacket and pulled out a latex glove. He put it on and opened the purse, and moved things around in it. He pulled out the receipt, looked at it.

"I'd like to keep this," the detective said.

"Fine," I said. "But please, I want to see Frank!"

"All right," Webber said softly. "I'm sorry I had to do it this way."

He made a motion with his hand.

Detective Moreno left the room.

I was doing a pretty good rendition of someone about to have a nervous breakdown. Maybe that theater class in college was finally paying off.

But it wasn't acting when my breath left me and blood drained from my face. That's what's called fainting. That's what I did when Frank walked into the room.

At some point I became aware that I was being tended to by a paramedic. I was still on the sofa.

And Frank came to me!

"Honey," he said, "How are you feeling?"

How? How?

"We can wait," Webber said.

"Let me get this out one time," Frank said. "I was at the studio until four this morning. We had major production problems and I was with the director and the writer and I've given you all the names. A limo brought me home and I just wanted to get some sleep. When I snapped on the light I saw him. In my bed. As I told you, my wife and I have separate rooms. All that blood. I was scared, let me tell you. I thought it might've been a thing, a warning. That's when I called you. That's all I know, except what you've told me since, that his blood showed he was drunk. Like, really intoxicated. But why some drunk guy would break into my house and fall asleep in my bed is beyond me. It's like Goldilocks. Only in L.A., I guess."

Webber nodded. "Ms. Yeoman, are you feeling well enough to answer one question for me?"

My fuzzy brain enabled me to say something that sounded like *Yes.*

"The victim's name is Richard Pike. Did you know him?"

What did he say?

"He had a business card on him. A dry wall business. Richard 'Ric' Pike. Did he ever do any work for you?"

I tried not to pass out again, but it was no use.

I woke up screaming. Some woman in hospital togs came in. I was in a bed. Was I dying?

"You just stay calm now," the woman said.

"Why ... am I here?" I said.

"Someone is anxious to see you."

I knew it was going to be Frank.

It was.

"Baby," he said as he put his hands on the bed rail and looked at me. "It's going to be okay now. I'm taking control of the whole situation. I'm going to keep a real eye on you. Oh yes, you don't ever have to worry again."

CAN YOU SPELL?

"Sesquipedalian."

Prisha Parikh, fourteen, looked down at the judges. "May I have the definition?" she said into the microphone.

"Sesquipedalian. Adjective, having many syllables, as in 'The paper is made up of too many sesquipedalian terms.' Noun. 'The news anchor was a known sesquipedalian.' "

"May I have the language of origin?"

"Latin."

"Can you please repeat the word?"

"Sesquipedalian."

The cogs and wheels in Prisha's mind began churning. All the preparation, all the memorization, all the late nights drilling with her father for the National Spelling Bee, and it all came down to this.

Get it right, and she'd be the winner. Her ticket would be punched. Harvard. Yale. Georgetown.

"Sesquipedalian," Prisha said into the microphone. "S-E-S-Q-U-I-P..." A second to think. Another i? Or an e? Must decide now!

"...E-D-A-L-I-A-N. Sesquipedalian."

A moment's pause, then the judge said, "That is correct!"

The packed convention center erupted into thunderous applause. And the crowd stood!

Confetti dropped from the ceiling.

Stunned, Prisha looked to the first row where her father and her little sister, Nisha, were beaming.

There were tears in her father's eyes. If only her mother were still alive to see this!

Prisha could not hold back her own tears.

Photos. Interviews. The lovely chaos surrounding the National Spelling Bee champion!

When it was all over, as was their tradition for the last five years of spelling bee competitions, her father took Prisha to 31 Flavors. And, as usual, Prisha ordered a scoop of Rocky Road on a cone. Nisha chose Mint Chip. Her father, as always, went for Jamoca Almond Fudge.

By the time they got in the car for the drive home, Prisha was finally settling into the reality of it all. She hugged the trophy on her lap.

As they turned onto the road leading back home, Prisha felt the car bumping.

"Baba, what is it?" Prisha said.

"I think it may be a flat tire," her father said. He eased the car to the shoulder. "Sit tight."

He got out of the car to have a look.

Nisha said, "Do you think I will someday have a trophy, too?"

Prisha turned to her sister in the back seat. "You are the smartest one in the family," she said.

Out the back window, Prisha saw a van pulling up. "Looks like a Good Samaritan is here to help."

"Samaritan," Nisha said. "S-A-M-A-R-I-T-A-N. Samaritan."

Prisha giggled.

Two men got out of the van and approached. They had blue masks on.

One man knelt down. Probably to talk to Baba.

The other came around to her side of the car.

Prisha thought quickly. When her father stopped the car and got out, the doors unlocked automatically. She reached for the door lock button—

Too late! The door burst open.

Hands reached in and unfastened her seatbelt.

Nisha screamed.

The hands—how strong they were—grabbed Prisha's arm and pulled her from the car.

The trophy went flying, crashing to the ground.

And now she was in the man's arms. She kicked, she screamed. "Baba!"

She saw the other man running back to the van.

And her father lying on the ground, not moving.

She fought and clawed, but couldn't get out of the man's grip.

Three seconds later she was in the back of the van, being held down.

The van started up and drove away.

Prisha screamed and kicked. The man pushed a cloth over her nose and mouth. The smell. Like ether.

She kicked once more before falling into a black hole with no bottom.

————

Sanjay Parikh sat in the back of the paramedic van, his head bandaged. Nisha's trembling hand held his, her breathing small and needy.

The detective, a man named Crawford, spoke softly, but with resoluteness. "Are you able to tell me what happened?"

"I'll try," Sanjay said. "We had just come from 31 Flavors, after my daughter won the National Spelling Bee. We were driving home when my tire went out. I got out to take a look. It was the left rear tire. As I knelt down I saw a van pull up. I thought it was coming to help."

"Can you describe the van?"

"It was black."

"Make?"

"I think it might have been a Cadillac."

"Did you happen to get any of the license plate?"

"I… I don't even remember seeing a license plate."

Crawford nodded. "Go on, please."

"Two men got out. They were wearing masks. The Covid kind."

"A ruse," Crawford said.

"The driver came to me and squatted down and said, 'Flat tire?' Next thing I remember is coming to with my head about to explode."

"You got a nasty hit," Crawford said.

Nisha whimpered. Sanjay squeezed her hand.

Crawford said, "Dr. Parikh, you're a surgeon?"

"Yes."

The detective rubbed his chin. "You will receive a ransom demand. These were pros. We found a roofing nail in your tire. The only way that happens is if it is done intentionally. You were followed to 31 Flavors. Let me guess. When you parked, you backed into the space?"

"How do you know that?" Sanjay said.

"The nail was in your rear, driver's side tire. Here's how they did it. They took a bottle cap and a bit of putty and stuck the head of the roofing nail in it. They set that down in front of the rear tire. That's so they could duck down hide what they were doing. If you'd parked straight, they would have put it behind one of the front tires. Do you get the picture?"

"I think so," Sanjay said

"So when you drove away, the rear tire ran over the nail, creating a slow leak. The plastic cap disintegrated. It probably took fifteen or twenty minutes before you felt it."

"That's exactly right," Sanjay said. His voice stuck in his throat.

"You'll get a call," Crawford said. "They'll tell you not to involve the police. You tell them you want to hear your daughter's voice. Refuse to do anything further until you hear her voice."

"What if she's...what if they..."

"Don't think that, Mr. Parikh," Crawford said.

———

"You want to stay alive, don't you?" Johnny said.

The girl was sitting on a chair in a basement. She looked woozy. But not so much that she couldn't get off a kick to his leg.

"Ow!" Johnny said. "You make trouble, you're not gonna feel so good."

She tried to kick him again.

Johnny reached behind him and pulled out his gun. He pointed it at her head. "Can you spell, *I understand*?"

"That's two words," the girl said.

"Don't mouth off to me! You're not as smart as you think you are."

"I'm not—"

"You Injuns think you're so smart!"

"Injun?"

"Not like in the old Westerns. I mean you and everybody else from Calcutta or wherever."

"We're American citizens," she said.

"You don't belong here," Johnny said. "You're gonna pay."

"I need to pee."

"You have to wait."

"I can't!"

Johnny wanted to slap her. But he wasn't going to let her get his goat. He was smarter than that. Rick had told him to keep her calm. That's why she wasn't tied up. There was nothing she could do down here anyway.

"Then I'm going to go get you a pot," Johnny said.

"That's gross!" the girl said.

"Can you spell *I don't care?*"

"That's three words."

Johnny raised his hand like he was going to hit her. But she didn't even flinch! He would show her and her Injun father all right.

He went back up the stairs.

———

Prisha looked around the room and memorized as many things as she could about the place. She and Nisha loved to play memorization games. If she memorized things, maybe that could tip off the police. But how could she get to the police?

She was stuck down in some basement, with nothing but four walls, a chair, a water heater, and some paint cans. She wondered if she could pick up one of the cans and hit the guy with it. But there was no place for her to hide. He would see her the moment he opened the door.

She didn't have anything to rig, like Macaulay Culkin did in *Home Alone.*

She went to the water heater. Maybe there was a way she could cause something to happen that would make enough of a commotion so she could run out.

She quickly abandoned that idea. There were two men, and she didn't have any tools anyway.

It was a big water heater. Maybe that meant it was a big house. There were stickers on the water heater, with all kinds of numbers on it. Maybe there was a house address! She looked and looked—

—then heard the lock clicking and quickly returned to her chair.

The guy came down the stairs with a plastic bucket. He put it on the ground and said, "Don't miss." He laughed and went out again. The door lock clicked.

———

The call came at 7:37. A private number.

"Yes?" Sanjay Parikh said.

"Hello, Dr. Parikh. Listen carefully. I'm only going to say this once. You're going to arrange for the transfer of $1,000,000 to an account, the number of which I will give you. If you alert your bank or the authorities about the transfer, your daughter will die. Do you understand me?"

"I want to hear my daughter's voice," Sanjay said.

"You will do as I tell you if you want to see her again."

With his heart pounding, Sanjay said, "You want the money. I can get you the money. But only if I know my daughter is alive. I want to hear her voice."

"No."

The call cut.

"What is it, Baba?" Nisha said.

"Nothing, little one," Sanjay said. "Go to your room and say a prayer for Prisha."

———

"Okay," Johnny said, "you're gonna talk to your father on the phone. But you're gonna only say this. 'Daddy, I'm not hurt. They're being nice.' "

"He is my Baba," the girl said.

"Baba then! But say the rest, and that's all, understand? If you don't —" Johnny made a slash motion across his throat. "Can you spell *dead*?"

"You need help to spell that?" the girl said.

A guttural blast issued from the Johnny's throat. "How long do I have to put up with you?"

"Shut it." It was Rick. He was coming down the stairs. "Don't argue with the kid. Did you tell her what to say?"

"Yeah," Johnny said.

"Then let's get this over with."

Johnny took out the phone and thumbed it. The dad answered.

Calmly, Johnny said, "Your daughter has something to say to you."

He held the phone in front of the girl's face.

And heard her say something that sounded like, *"Baba keel youarjee toofiftee tee sixen."*

He yanked the phone back, killed the call. "What do you think you're doing?"

"I spoke Hindi to my father, to give him comfort."

Johnny wanted to hit her.

Rick said, "So he heard her voice. It's done."

Johnny looked at the girl. "You think you're so, so smart. You think your dad's smart, don't you? Well, we're smarter. Let that sink in."

"Yes, sir," the girl said.

———

Three hours later a SWAT team swarmed the house in Sun Valley, with Crawford standing watch across the street. Sanjay and Nisha were next to him.

Two minutes after the swarm, Prisha came out, holding the hand of a SWAT teamer.

Sanjay across the street, followed by Nisha. They wrapped Prisha in their arms.

"Thank you," Sanjay said to the SWAT man.

"My pleasure," he said. "May I ask you a question?"

"In a moment," Sanjay said. He kissed his two daughters. When his daughters hugged each other, Sanjay said, "You may ask."

"How'd you ID this house?" the SWAT man said.

Sanjay smiled. "It was a game. I play games with my girls, all kinds. In Hindi, the word for game is *khel*. If the girls want to play a game, they say, *Baba, khel*. When Prisha was allowed to speak to me, she said *Baba, khel* and then...Prisha, what was it again?"

"URG 250 T 6N," Prisha said, and smiled. "I memorized it off the water heater."

"It sounded like a serial number," Sanjay said. "I told that to Detective Crawford."

"And I ran it through the databases," Crawford, who had just joined them, said. "It hit on Stanford Black Water Heaters out of Murfreesboro, Tennessee. We called 'em and they gave us the address of the house."

"That," the SWAT man said, "is the most amazing thing I've ever heard."

"You should hear her spell!" Sanjay said.

At that moment, the two abductors were marched by. They looked at Prisha.

"S-M-A-R-T," Prisha said.

THE MYSTERY OF THE LOCKED ROOM INTRUDER

My friend, Mr. Sherlock Holmes, was seated in the chair by the window, tendrils of his pipe smoke curling up toward the ceiling. His back was to me.

I had taken special care to open the door quietly, as Mrs. Hudson had informed me that Holmes did not wish to be disturbed.

But I had urgent business to relate. And so I determined to enter silently, take note of the situation, and tap a small knock to alert Holmes of my presence.

But before I so much as lifted my hand, Holmes said, "Watson! I hope that your urgent business is of such import that it justifies your intrusion!"

"How do you know that my business is urgent, Holmes?" I said.

Without rising from the chair, or even turning toward me, Holmes said, "Elementary, my dear Watson. It is the eleventh of October, is it not?"

"Quite so," said I, "but how does that relate to—"

"Pray let me continue," said Holmes. "It was on the eleventh of October in 1881 that the noteworthy Albertson Convocation took place in Kent. At the convocation was Lord Chamberlain, late of the 5th Northumberland Fusiliers. He was wounded in the Battle of Maiwand and attended in the field by one Percy Albright, a medical student at the University of London. The very same university that issued your own medical degree. Am I right?"

"By Jove, you are, Holmes, but how can any of those facts lead you to the conclusion that I have come to you this morning with urgent business?"

"It cannot, my dear friend, for those facts have nothing to do with my deductions."

"I am puzzled!" I said, for indeed I was, which I so often am when conversing with England's most famous detective.

"All of the facts are correct," Holmes said. "I relate them because they are of interest to me. I thrive on connections! As to your case, however, I was looking out the window when saw you emerge from the carriage and hurry to the door of our lodgings. You only move with such haste when you have pressing news. And here you are. One need not cogitate complexities when simplicity will do. Occam's Razor, you see?"

"Holmes, you never cease to amaze me."

At this, my friend leaped out of his chair and spun around.

"Let me continue," Holmes said. "Your urgent business is that Inspector Lestrade asked you to come here and fetch me, for an apparent murder has taken place, there are no suspects, and he wishes, reluctantly, to engage my services."

I dropped onto the settee. "My heavens, Holmes, how can you possibly know that?"

"Elementary. You left the carriage waiting, which can only mean you wish me to come along with you immediately. As this is not a medical emergency, which you could handle on your own, dear fellow, it must be police business. And if I am involved it means murder. And murder means Lestrade of Scotland Yard!"

Holmes took up his Homburg, placed it on his head, and said, "The game is afoot!" And out the door he went, with me following.

————

A carriage ride of some eight blocks brought us to the scene of the crime, a three-story building on Albany Street. A servant girl opened the door.

"Sherlock Holmes for Inspector Lestrade," Holmes said, and brushed inside toward the stairs. "Third floor, Watson!"

Tagging after him, I said, "How can you possibly know that?"

"Not now, Watson! Time is of the essence!"

"And how..." I left off, resigned to my usual unknowing until such time as Holmes deigned to disabuse me of my puzzlement.

Winded, I reached the open door of the room at the top of the stairs. Holmes was already there, standing outside, looking in. I saw that the room had a roll-top desk and shelves of books, including volumes of what appeared to be legal reporters. The ferret-like Inspector Lestrade was inside, facing the door. At his feet was a corpse, that of a man I quickly guessed to be in his mid-fifties. He was dressed in black pants and a white silk shirt, and lay in a small pool of blood. He looked vaguely familiar to me. A few feet away was a knife that appeared to have blood on it. A trail of blood led from just inside the door to the body.

"Ah, Mr. Holmes, so you have come at last," said Lestrade. "Do not come in. There is blood on the floor."

Holmes said, "My powers of observation are not so obsolescent that I cannot perceive what is so obvious."

"You will not find this case obvious, sir," Lestrade said.

"I surmise from your tone," Holmes said, "that you have on your hands a most consternating mystery."

"But you are the great Sherlock Holmes," Lestrade said with barely concealed sarcasm. "Surely this will be no great riddle for you."

"Quite right, Lestrade, for no such riddle has ever yet bettered me."

"Then prepare yourself, "Lestrade said. "Do you wish the salient facts?"

"Begin," Holmes said. "Tell me all that you know about the death of Rockland Pierce."

Rockland Pierce! Now I recognized the corpse.

Lestrade narrowed his gaze. "You asked the servant girl the name of the dead man."

"He most certainly did not!" I said.

Holmes raised his hand to me to be quiet and said, "You fail to take into account Occam's Razor," he said. "Also known as the law of parsimony, viz., the simplest explanation is usually right. I knew Rockland Pierce."

"Pray, how?" Lestrade asked.

"You know him to be an eminent barrister," said Holmes.

"Indeed," said Lestrade.

"What you do not know is that he is—or was—one of the most devious acolytes of the late Professor Moriarty."

Lestrade looked thunderstruck. But that is an expression I have so many times observed on those crossing mental swords with Mr. Sherlock Holmes.

"Well then," Lestrade said at last, "now you may consider the facts. Do you wish to enter?"

"I do indeed."

"Then step carefully so as not to contact the blood. You may stand over there." Lestrade pointed to an area by a wingback chair.

Holmes moved quick as a fox to the spot.

"And I too?" I said.

"Yes, Doctor," Lestrade said.

I joined Holmes by the chair.

"Rockland Pierce died as a result of a gunshot to the neck," Lestrade said. "It was not suicide, for there is no gun present. Somebody murdered him."

"Not so fast," said Holmes. "The knife by the body. That may have been an offensive weapon, which could render the shooting self defense."

"Or it may have been a defensive weapon used against the murderer," said Lestrade.

"Quite right, my good fellow. But you are the one who must prove that. Continue."

"Here is where the confoundedness comes in," Lestrade said. "You observe that the only window in this room has fixed bars upon it, not wide enough for someone to enter or exit by it. The only entrance is the door. But the door was locked. From the inside."

"How was the body discovered?" said Holmes.

"The servant girl, Jennie," Lestrade said. "She arrived for her morning duties and as usual prepared tea. But when she knocked on the door and announced, she got no response. She tried the door, found it locked. Unsure of what to do, she went downstairs and outside, found a bobby, and asked for help. The bobby accompanied her upstairs where he knocked several times upon the door. He then asked Jennie if she had a key to the room, which she produced. The bobby unlocked the door and saw the body just as you see it now. Warning Jennie not to go inside, he got a message to the Yard. That is how I arrived on the scene. I listened to the facts as rendered by Jennie and the policeman. For half an hour I thought them through, over and over. Finally, I stationed the bobby at the door and went outside for a breath of air and to think further on all of it. That is when I saw your friend, Dr. Watson, walking along the street. I called him over and told him nothing of what happened inside, but to summon you, Mr. Holmes, with all dispatch."

"Quite so," I said.

Holmes said nothing, and did not move, but looked about the room, at the body, and around the room again, finishing his gaze at the door. He stared at it for several seconds.

Then to Lestrade he said, "I have it. Rockland Pierce was indeed killed by an intruder."

"But that cannot be," Lestrade said. "For as I said, the door was locked from the inside and no one could get in through the window."

"Have you considered," said Holmes, "that it may not have been a man or a woman, but an animal, a monkey perhaps, who could fit through the window bars?"

"What? How preposterous!"

"Do you not recall the story written by that American, Poe, entitled 'The Murders in the Rue Morgue'? Wherein a body was found stuffed in the chimney of a fourth-floor room that was locked from the inside, and on the floor was found a bloody straight razor? And that it was an orangutan who was the killer?"

Lestrade, with mocking contempt, said, "You mean to tell me that a monkey with a gun climbed up to the barred window, came through, shot Pierce, and went out the same way?"

"I am not telling you that," said Holmes. "I only asked if you had considered it."

"By no means! For it is too farfetched, even for you."

"Quite so," said Holmes, "for that is not what I surmise."

"Then get to it! How could an intruder shoot Pierce and exit the room, yet the door be locked from the inside?"

"He might have had a key," Holmes said.

Lestrade shook his head. "Wrong again. Jennie says there are only two keys. She has one. The other I found on a keychain in the dead man's pocket."

"There is only one answer," Holmes said. "The door was locked by Pierce himself, just before he died."

"What! Why would a dying man lock himself in his room?"

"The intruder gained entrance to the room, perhaps because Pierce knew him. There was a confrontation. Pierce drew a knife and cut the intruder. The intruder drew a gun and shot Pierce, and bolted from the room. Pierce did not die immediately. I observe that the entrance wound on the neck is in such a place that he would not die immediately, but continue to bleed. I have written a monograph on the subject of wounds to various parts of the body. Perhaps you've read it?"

"No," Lestrade said.

"Pierce was an egotist," Holmes said. "I had occasion to find that out myself on two occasions."

"I can vouch for that," I said.

Holmes continued. "Thinking that he could stanch his wound, but fearing the intruder might return, he locked the door. But he soon weakened and fell, and died where you see him now."

"Amazing," I said. Then added, "Don't you agree, Inspector?"

Stroking his chin, Lestrade did not answer right away. Finally, he said, "This is a stretch, even for you, Mr. Holmes."

"Have you another theory?" asked Sherlock Holmes.

Lestrade furrowed his brow. He cogitated for a full five minutes, looking at the body from every angle. He looked at Holmes. "Not at the moment," he said.

"When that moment comes," Holmes responded, "call upon me, and I will listen with great curiosity."

Holmes turned toward me and took my arm. "Come, Watson. It is getting on toward afternoon tea and Mrs. Hudson will be expecting us!"

———

At last we were seated in Holmes's study at 221B Baker Street, drinking our tea. I was full of excitement for my friend's latest triumph of deduction, though I must confess that I had a shade of the same doubt Lestrade had indicated. To believe the theory of Mr. Holmes, all of the pieces would have to fit in perfect alignment, like a jigsaw puzzle. But life is seldom so neat. Surely there were other possibilities but, again like Lestrade, I had no theory of my own.

"I wonder what Lestrade will come up with," I remarked.

"I shall guarantee you this much," Holmes said. "He will not sleep well tonight. Tomorrow, I will go to Scotland Yard to relieve him of his distress."

"Distress?"

"Come, come, Watson, we both know that the good inspector never misses a chance to try to rattle me. Do you recall his challenge to me in the Norwood Builder matter? 'Have you proved us to be wrong yet?' he crowed in his cock-a-doodle manner."

"I do recall that, yes," I said.

"His, dare I say, envy of my powers of observation has been a source of less than stellar police work. We cannot have that anymore. London is becoming much more crime-ridden of late. That is why the death of Rockland Pierce and the consternation of Inspector Lestrade are two beneficial occurrences."

"I can well understand that being rid of Pierce is a benefit, but what has Lestrade's consternation to do with it?"

"It will be a lesson to him," Holmes said. "One that I hope will knock some humility into his analytical head. That will make him better at his job, for he won't be reluctant to consult with me in the future!"

"What lesson is he to learn?" I asked.

"That he failed to solve the case in a most catastrophic fashion. You see, Watson, not only do I know how the events in that room transpired, but I know for certain who it was who dispatched the late and unlamented Rockland Pierce."

"But how, Holmes? How could you possibly know?"

"Elementary, my dear Watson. Observe."

Holmes pulled up the left sleeve of his coat to reveal a bandage wrapped around his forearm.

"My heavens, Holmes, what happened?"

"I was cut by the knife of Rockland Pierce, just before I shot him."

The proverbial feather could have knocked me over.

"I got wind from an informant that Pierce was planning a most dastardly murder," Holmes said. "Murders, I should say, of three prominent citizens."

"Why didn't you tell me, Holmes?"

"I did not wish to put you in harm's way, dear fellow."

"Then Lestrade. Why didn't you tell him?"

"The law is powerless to stop an inchoate crime."

"Then warn the potential victims, that they might flee the city."

"Pierce would have tracked them down. No, Watson, I had to take matters into my own hands. So I found a spot on Albany Street where I could observe Pierce's rooms. I was, of course, in one of my disguises. Presently, his servant girl emerged. I followed her. She went to market. As she was examining apples I bumped into her and picked her pocket."

"Holmes!"

"Not for her purse, but for her keys. There were two. I apologized to her, then repaired to the breads. I had a block of wax, and made impressions of the keys, one in either side. I then bumped into her again and replaced the keys. My apology this time fell upon deaf ears, as she threatened to call a policeman. I profusely apologized again and took my leave. I came here and made a mold of the wax from plaster, then poured in resin made from amber and Balm of Gilead, let it harden, and voilá! Two keys. That night I came to Albany Street, opened the front door with one key, and thus knew the other key was for Pierce's study. Up the stairs I went, quickly unlocked the door, and entered."

"This is astounding!"

"Quick as a cat, for that was his major advantage in avoiding exposure, Pierce came at me with his knife. As I knew he would, for that was also his weapon of choice. I lifted my arm to fend off the strike, and with my other hand pulled my Webley and shot him in the superior thyroid vein. Then out of the room I rushed, slamming the door behind me. At the bottom of the stairs I noticed my coat cut and that I was bleeding. Fortunately, it was only a slight wound, which I dressed myself. No doubt you disapprove of my technique."

"I don't know what to say, Holmes. I simply do not. This is incredible! But I must ask..."

"Ask, Watson."

"Did you have designs on eliminating Pierce when you entered his house?"

"I did indeed, for he was a cancer on our city, metastasizing."

"But that would make this..." I hesitated to say the word.

"Murder?" Holmes said. "Comfort yourself, Watson. Under English common law, and according to Blackstone himself, self defense is valid if a reasonable man in similar circumstances would be in fear for his life. Knowing Pierce as I did, and being eminently reasonable, my act was therefore justified. Inspector Lestrade will have to agree, for the law is his master, and I know him to be its obedient servant."

For a very long time I sat in silence. Holmes set about to pack his pipe.

At last I said, "I am at a loss as to whether I should record this as one of your cases or not. For you yourself are the answer to the mystery!"

"This tale need not be primary, then, but the other kind," Holmes said.

"What do you mean, the other kind?"

"Supplementary, my dear Watson. Will you have a scone?"

THE END OF EGO EDWARDS

The police report read as follows:

On November 2, Brice H., who lived in Manhattan Beach, returned home to find his master bedroom's closet in disarray and several items missing, including two Rolex watches. Upon watching footage from his home security system, he saw a white Audi he did not recognize back into his driveway. A person in a black hoodie exited the car. Five minutes later he came back carrying a sack, got in the car, and drove away.

On November 21, Karen B.'s Gardena home was burglarized, with jewelry and a firearm missing.

Vivian Z. lived in Norwalk. She had a security system with cameras that allowed remote monitoring through a phone app. On November 22, she observed a man in a red hoodie remove a gold statue from her home through the app. Upon returning home, she found her bedroom ransacked and the kitchen door broken. In addition to the statue, a watch was taken.

On December 3, Joseph H., who lived in La Mirada, left his home in the morning to run errands, setting his security alarm before he departed.

Upon returning 45 minutes later, he found a broken window and the police waiting for him. A security alarm had notified the police, who had found the front door open upon their arrival, but no intruder in the home.

On the same day, Kinney B., also a La Mirada resident, returned home from work in the evening. His daughter asked if there had been an earthquake, as her bedroom was in disarray. His own bedroom was missing watches, jewelry, and coins.

On December 4, Hacienda Heights resident Bryan C. witnessed someone breaking into his house on his security app. When he returned home, he found his sliding glass door had been broken, and he was missing a firearm and a cell phone.

Detective Laura Mitchell of the Los Angeles County Sheriff's Department, threw the file on her desk and said, "I'm tired of this! It's the same guy. He's laughing at us. Big joke."

Her partner, Ollie Moonves, said, "He'll slip up. They always do."

"Do they now?" Laura said. She was forty-five and had seen enough cold case files to know the bad guys weren't always caught. If the public knew how many, there'd be widespread panic, which is why the department kept the real numbers under wraps.

This guy wasn't a serial killer, so at least it wasn't a string of murders. He was more annoying, like flies at a picnic.

"You think all these were the same guy?" Ollie said.

"There's the hoodie," Laura said.

"Different colors," Ollie said.

"So? Maybe he's got different colors for different days. Maybe he buys hoodies like I buy blouses. I've got my interrogation blouse, my witness questioning blouse, my arrest blouse."

"And you look fabulous in all of them," Ollie said.

"This is no laughing matter," Laura said. "He's the one laughing."

"How do you know that?"

"I just do!"

Max "Ego" Edwards laughed. The old man seated next to him at The Shamrock, a dive bar in Downey, looked up from his drink.

"Whass so funny?" the old man said.

"You have no idea who you're talking to," Ego said. Max Edwards was thirty-nine, and had earned his nickname all the way back in high school. He was always the smartest guy in class, and let people know it. One of the jocks, a knotheaded football player named Stuberville, was the first to call him Ego. It caught on fast.

And Max enjoyed it. He didn't consider it an insult, but a compliment. A tribute to his superior intellect. He embraced it. He even dressed like he embraced it, always wearing a coat and tie. Later he added gold tie clip with a diamond in it. Sure, the diamond was fake, but it looked good nonetheless.

The old man, who Max had never met, said, "Yeah, sure."

"And what have you ever accomplished?" Ego Edwards said.

"Whassat?"

"Accomplished. You're drunk at two o'clock in the afternoon. How come?"

"Whyn't you dry up?" the old man said.

"I'm too full of life," Ego said. "I'm here because I can choose to be wherever I want. I've done more in two weeks that you've probably done your whole life. Amirite?"

"I sold cars," the old man said. "I uz good, too."

"Oh? What happened?"

"Wuddya mean, wha happen?"

"Look at you."

The old man said nothing, but his fallen countenance talked a blue streak.

"Were you caught embezzling?" Ego said.

"Whyn't you shaddup?" said the old man.

"Listen, what if I told you there's been a whole string of robberies, and the cops can't figure them out? And what if I told you you're looking a the guy who's done it?"

The old man's red, rheumy eyes trundled in their sockets. He looked Ego up and down.

"I say yer full of it," the old man said.

"Yeah? Let me spell it out for you. Manhattan Beach, Gardena, Norwalk, La Mirada, Hacienda Heights."

"So what?" the old man said.

"Old man," Ego said, "I bet if Elon Musk sat down next to you and told you things about the Tesla only he knew, you'd say 'So what.' Am I right?"

"Who?" the old man said.

Ego Edwards shook his head. He finished his drink with one gulp and tossed a ten spot on the bar. As he stood he said, "You let your grandchildren know you once sat next to Ego Edwards, my friend. Remember that."

"Who?" the old man said.

———

Laura Mitchell put Google maps on the monitor and hit the zoom-out until all of Los Angeles County was onscreen.

"Take a look at this," Laura said, motioning Ollie to slide his chair over to her cubicle.

"What is it?" Ollie said.

"A pattern," Laura said. "Almost perfect."

"Perfect?"

"Look at the start, Manhattan Beach. Then you got Gardena, Norwalk, La Mirada—twice—and Hacienda Heights. Look at that line. He's moving northeast."

"You think?"

"It's obvious, isn't it? He wants us to see it. He's challenging us to catch him."

Ollie shook his head. "Laura, you need to take a break."

"Oh? What if I tell you he's going to hit someone in Walnut, and after that Diamond Bar? Then it'll stop."

"Why?"

"Because further east you're in San Berdoo County."

"That's one wild theory," Ollie said.

Laura's desk phone rang. She picked up, listened, said something, then hung up.

"We have a lead," she said.

"What is it?" Ollie said.

"A bartender in Downey. Overheard a guy bragging about the robberies. He even named the towns."

"This bartender, did he get a name?"

"The guy called himself Ego Edwards," Laura said. "Can you beat that?"

"Ego?" Ollie said. "Can't be his real name."

"No," Laura said.

"So all we gotta do is question everybody in Downey named Edwards."

"Terrific," Laura said.

"Let's work on something else," Ollie said.

———

Max "Ego" Edwards sat himself in a booth at The Shamrock. He needed to go over the latest news. It had been a hobby of his since he was a boy. When he read about local crimes, he always found himself imagining what it would be like to be the criminal, not the cop.

He hadn't been seated more than five minutes before a big man slipped into the booth across from him.

"Your name Edwards?" the man said.

"Who are you?" Ego said. "I didn't invite you to sit down."

"I understand you been bragging."

"Excuse me?"

"About my work."

"Oh yeah? What work is that?"

"Robbery," the man said.

The little hairs on the back of Ego's neck stood at attention.

The big man said, "You have no idea of the planning, the perfect execution it takes. What makes you think you can take the credit?"

The man's tone was as cold as winter in Fargo.

Ego said, "Hey now, look, it's just a game with me. I don't mean anything by it. I just like to build myself up, okay? I never thought I'd offend the real guy. If you are the real guy."

The man leaned forward, his hot gaze burning into Ego. "You doubt what I'm saying?"

"N. . .No."

"I'm thinking of going in a new direction," the man said. "Only this time it ain't gonna be a series of robberies. It's gonna be a series of bodies. And I got the perfect guy to start with."

Ego's throat clenched. He fought to say, "Please. . ."

The man said nothing.

"Here, take my money," Ego said. He whipped out his wallet.

"I don't want your stinking money," the man said.

"How about this?" Ego took off his gold tie clip and slid it across the table. "That's a real diamond in there."

The man picked up the clip and examined it. "Doesn't look real to me."

"That's all I got," Ego said.

"It's not enough," the man said.

———

Laura Mitchell called Ollie to her desk. He rolled over.

"You're not going to believe this," she said.

"Hit me," Ollie said.

"There was a murder last night in Downey," she said. "The body was discovered in Furman Park. Male. Around forty. Guess what his name is?"

"George Clooney," Ollie said.

"Maxwell Edwards," Laura said.

"So?"

"Don't you remember? The bartender said a man named Ego Edwards was talking about committing the robberies."

"Oh yeah, yeah. You think there's a connection?"

"I don't know yet," Laura said. "But I hope we don't have a serial killer on our hands."

"Too early to think that," Ollie said. "We have to see a pattern first. Or a trophy."

"Right," Laura said. "Serial killers like to keep trophies of their kills."

"Sick," Ollie said.

"Let's work on this one, partner. What do you say?"

"You got it," Ollie said.

He wheeled his chair back to his cubicle. He picked up the envelope, opened it, and looked at the gold tie clip with the fake diamond. As a trophy it wasn't much, but it would do for a start.

THE BUST

"Hey, you heard that joke about Julius Caesar?"

"Don't think so."

"Julius Caesar walks into a bar. Says, 'I'll have a martinus.' And the bartender says, 'You mean a martini?' And Julius Caesar says, 'If I wanted a double I would have asked for it.'"

"I don't get it."

Sam slapped his forehead. "It's a Latin joke."

Rich said, "What's that got to do with Julius Caesar?"

"Brother, what do they teach in schools these days?"

Sam was forty-two. Rich was twenty-three. They worked for Century Secure Moving and Storage, and at the moment were guiding a dolly and crate into the delivery entrance of the Getty Villa in Malibu, California.

The Getty Villa was a museum specializing in Greek, Roman, and Etruscan art and antiquities. Built by the oil tycoon J. Paul Getty, its design was ancient Italian villa style, the kind of place Julius Caesar himself might have built for his vacation headquarters.

So moving a bust of Scipio Africanus into the museum was fitting and proper. Scipio was a Roman general during the Second Punic War against Carthage. In 202 BC he defeated Hannibal at the Battle of Zama in Africa. Because of the triumph, he adopted the name *Africanus*.

The bust Rich and Sam were now handling had come to the museum in a circuitous fashion. A college student in Austin, Texas, went to a swap meet, and found the bust on sale for $35. The student thought the bust would look "cool" on the coffee table in his apartment.

His girlfriend thought it looked cool, too, and wanted her father to have a look at it. Her father was a coin collector with an interest in ancient artifacts. He thought the bust looked ancient, took pictures of it, and did some research. He came to believe it was a bust of Scipio that had been missing since World War II.

The bust had belonged to King Ludwig I of Bavaria, who lived from 1786 to 1868, and was part of a museum he built in Aschaffenburg, Germany. The museum lasted until World War II, when it was bombed by Allied forces.

Somehow, the bust survived undamaged.

Then disappeared.

The U.S. Army had a base in Aschaffenburg. Speculation was that a soldier thought it'd be "cool" to take it.

How it got to an Austin swap meet remained a mystery.

But for Billings Mapplethorne it was the find of the century.

The museum's chief curator, Mapplethorne was a nervous-looking man in an ill-fitting blue blazer with the Getty insignia on the breast. He was leading the two movers to the room where the bust would be displayed.

"Careful, gentlemen," he said.

"We're always careful," Sam said.

"That's our guarantee," Rich said.

"It better be," Billings Mapplethorne said just before the explosion.

———

"What in the name of all that is holy happened?"

Joshua Hookstraten was the head of security at the Getty Villa. A retired Marine, he looked, at age 47, like he could still take a hill. His curly, slate-colored hair was thick, his acetylene blue eyes clear, and his ire a blow torch into Billings Mapplethorne. They were in Mapplethorne's office. Mapplethorne sat at his desk. Hookstraten preferred to stand.

"As I told the police," Mapplethorne said. "One minute all was well, the next, boom! And smoke. I choked on it. Next thing I knew I was waking up on the floor and my head was splitting."

"And the head of Scipio Africanus was missing!"

Mapplethorne sheepishly nodded.

"And the two movers, what happened to them?"

"Same thing. There was some kind of gas in the smoke, I was told. Thank God it was only a smoke bomb. I hate to think what it could have done to the bust."

Hookstraten rubbed the bridge of his nose. "How could you have let this happen?"

"Me? What about you? Why weren't you there?"

"Because I thought you were competent," Hookstraten said. "I guess I was wrong."

"Rather than insulting me," Mapplethorne said, "why don't you tell me how we're going to get it back?"

"I'll get it back," Hookstraten said. "By any means possible."

A buzz on Billings Mapplethorne's desk phone. He picked up.

"Yes?"

"Call for you on line one," the receptionist said.

"Who is it?" Mapplethorne said.

"He wouldn't give his name. He just said he wanted to give you a heads up."

Mapplethorne pointed to the phone and mouthed, "It's him."

"Put it on speaker," Hookstraten said.

Mapplethorne pushed two buttons.

"This is Billings Mapplethorne," he said.

A soft, whispery voice said, "You've got this on speaker."

"What is it you want?"

"Don't try to play me. There's a public phone at the Chevron on PCH and Sunset. Be there in twenty minutes, be alone, and wait for a call, or I take a hammer to Scipio."

"No!"

"Better hurry."

Click.

"What now?" Billings Mapplethorne said.

"Get going," Joshua Hookstraten said.

An hour went by. Hookstraten paced in Mapplethorne's office, going over what he knew and what he needed to find out.

What he knew was in a written report of the Malibu police detective who arrived on the scene shortly after the bust was stolen. He had questioned Mapplethorne and the two movers. He had reviewed the surveillance videos. The latter weren't any help, as thick smoke obscured the room for several minutes.

It was as close to a perfect crime as Hookstraten had ever seen. But to his way of thinking, there was no such thing. Somehow, somewhere, there was a chink in the armor.

Whoever was behind it had a weakness. Find the weakness, find the bust.

He knew that trying to move the bust in the black market was going to be problematic. Europe, he thought, would be the first move. Getting it to a private party willing to pay for the privilege of just possessing the thing would be easier there than in America. Which would mean involving Interpol. And Hookstraten had no confidence in that once-respected law enforcement arm. Everything law-related was in chaos everywhere you turned. Corruption was rampant. If the bust ever got out of the country, it was as good as lost.

And so it was that Hookstraten went to the room where the bust was to be displayed. Surrounded by the artifacts of ancient Rome, he half jokingly, half seriously, called upon the Roman gods. In particular his favorite—Mars, the god of war.

"O Mars," he whispered. "Come to my aid. Down Eros, up Mars!"

When he got back to his office he found Mapplethorne there. He looked shaken.

"What did he say?" Hookstraten asked.

"Ransom," Mapplethorne said. "Two million."

"Delivered how?"

"He said instructions would be coming. But he wants it in cash. What do we do now?"

"Wait," Hookstraten said.

———

Al Stingley thought about what he would do with the money. In the little house deep in the hills of Topanga Canyon, he looked at the bust of Scipio Africanus, and thought he'd buy a house in Florida and do what so many Californians were doing now—getting the heck out of the stupidest state in the union. Then he'd buy a boat and have parties with the hottest chicks. Money could do that for you, and money was never something he'd had much of.

A knock on the door. The signal knock—three short, three long.

He got up and opened the door.

Billings Mapplethorne walked past him. Stingley closed the door.

"Well?" Stingley said.

"They'll pay," Mapplethorne said. "I've convinced them it's worth it for a precious item like this."

He went to the bust and removed the towel that covered it. He stroked the smooth, bald pate.

And thought, for a fleeting moment, that the eyes of Scipio moved.

He'd have to keep it together. When he was a boy he'd had nightmares, and even hallucinations of monsters and boogey men, ghosts and goblins. Counseling and lithium helped him get over it.

But it was coming back. Because of the guilt! He hadn't figured on it being so thick inside him. He was now a criminal.

What if there really were gods? Would they be angry? Would they punish him?

For a fleeting moment, he thought the head of Scipio was looking at him. But when he looked at the bust, the eyes were forward, cold and merciless. He threw the towel over it.

"I've been thinking," Stingley said.

"That's something you should never do," Mapplethorne said. "I'll do the thinking."

"Just hear me out," Stingley said. "I think we need to rearrange the split."

"What?"

"I think I should get half."

"Well, think again. I mean, don't think at all."

"Listen, I'm the one sitting here with the thing. I'm the one who's gonna make the exchange. I'm the one they'll try to take down. That's worth half."

"Yes, but I'm the one who had the responsibility and the plan," Mapplethorne said. "I'm the one who planted the smoke bomb. I'm the one who took the gas, and believe me that was no picnic."

"But I'm the one who came in and got it out," Stingley said. "You hired me because I could lift it myself."

Al Stingley was 6'4" and beefy. He was an out of work ex-con Mapplethorne had found on a parolee website, one of those that lists people with criminal records living in your neighborhood. Mapplethorne went to one of the houses listed in Reseda. There he found Stingley working on a car in the driveway. A little conversation, and Mapplethorne determined Stingley was living in the garage in exchange for handyman work. Mapplethorne asked if he'd be interested in some work at Mapplethorne's house. Stingley said sure. Mapplethorne told him to meet at The Shamrock, a dive bar on Roscoe, to discuss it.

There, Mapplethorne dropped some hints about big money for a job that might be a little risky. Stingley wanted to know how big the money was. When Mapplethorne said a hundred grand, Stingley said, "I'm your man."

Now Stingley said, "And I'm the guy who rented this place under an assumed name. They trace me, and I'm back in the joint. All that adds up to half, my friend."

"I'm not your friend," Mapplethorne said. "I'm your employer. And we stick to the hundred grand you agreed to."

"I don't think so."

"What did I just say about thinking?"

"Okay," Stingley said. "I know so. Because I'm also the one who can spill the beans."

Billings Mapplethorne clenched his jaw. He knew it was time for Plan B. He never thought he'd have the guts for Plan B. But now he was backed into a corner.

Mapplethorne was finished being backed into corners. He'd been bullied throughout school. And bullied even now by people like Joshua Hookstraten.

No more.

Mapplethorne took out the .38 from his jacket pocket and shot Al Stingley twice through the heart.

When it was dark, Mapplethorne went thirty yards into the brush behind the house and dug a hole big enough for a body. It took two hours. Mapplethorne was not made of muscle like Stingley, but desperation drove him forward. It took another hour to drag Stingley's body on a throw rug to the hole in the ground.

But he did it. He filled in the hole and spread some wild sage over it.

He went back to the house and collapsed on the sofa. In his dream a Roman legion was advancing on the house, their *hastas*—Roman spears—at the ready.

When he woke up in a sweat it was still dark. Darkness was his friend now.

Until he heard a voice whisper, "Mors tua, vita mea."

Billings Mapplethorne knew Latin because of his position at the museum. *You must die that I may live.*

Think straight. Focus!

Again the voice. "Mors tua, vita mea."

"Silence!" Mapplethorne said to the bust.

He heard a scuffling sound. Coming from the shadows.

A figure there! Dressed in...it couldn't be! The uniform of a Roman soldier!

"No!" Mapplethorne cried.

The apparition took two steps closer.

"You're not real!"

But the *gladius*, the Roman fighting sword in its hand, looked absolutely real.

Another step.

Scipio! Back from the dead, to punish him!

No! It was only in his mind! If he closed his eyes, the thing would vanish.

He closed his eyes.

————

Two days later, the chairman of the board of the Getty Villa, Alfred Strunk-Sackville, said, "Poor Mapplethorne. To die like that."

"I suppose," Joshua Hookstraten said.

They were in Strunk-Sackville's office. The chairman sat behind an ornate desk.

"I know he was behind it all," Strunk-Sackville said. "But he was under significant stress. Do you know he thought the exhibits sometimes spoke to him?"

"I did know that, yes," Hookstraten said.

"He needed help, and we didn't give it to him. He should have been hospitalized, not killed that awful way. Do they have any suspects?"

"He apparently had an accomplice," Hookstraten said. "It's possible he did it, then got scared and disappeared."

"It doesn't make sense."

"But at least the bust is safe and sound."

"Ah yes," Strunk-Sackville said. "We must be grateful for that. Do we know who called in the tip?"

"Not a clue," Hookstraten said. "Maybe it was the ghost of Scipio."

"That's not funny," Strunk-Sackville said.

"I didn't mean it to be," said Hookstraten.

Strunk-Sackville cleared his throat, then said, "Before you go, may I ask, why did you decide on that new look?"

"What look is that?" Hookstraten said.

"You shaved your head. It makes you look..."

"More severe?"

"Kind of like the bust itself."

"I suppose so," Hookstraten said with a smile. "Now if you'll excuse me, I want to make a final check."

"But of course," Alfred Strunk-Sackville said.

Hookstraten walked to the room where the bust of Scipio Africanus was displayed inside a large, glass case.

Then to the case next to it, where he'd put back the *gladius*.

"Down Eros, up Mars," he said.

THE NEW DETECTIVE

"I don't like her," Sam Tanner said.

"Because she's a woman," Bill Baker said.

"No. Because she's obnoxious, thinks she's the smartest person in the room, and she's only been on the force what, five years? And she makes detective?"

"They fast tracked her," Bill said.

"Because she's a woman," Sam said.

"Ah ha!" Bill pointed at him.

"Shut up," Sam said.

Sam Tanner was old school. A beat cop for ten years, worked his way up to detective, was senior now in his division. So when they brought in Rebecca Savage, thirty-two to his fifty-three, and told him to train her, it was a slap in the face. A depressing reminder of how far things had fallen in the department. Political correctness was more important than experience and good field work. And he had no doubt that the brass was going to try to make Rebecca Savage a star. Maybe the new face of the whole force!

Which was what Sam Tanner thought he would be, especially after breaking the Robby Mangold case wide open.

Mangold, a sitcom star of the 80s, had been reduced to hawking supplemental Medicare packages on cable channels that showed classic

TV shows and early-morning religious hucksters. He took the money to keep his fourth wife happy. Sally Jenkins-Mangold was a twenty-four-year old farm girl from Kansas who had come to Hollywood to turn her natural, corn-fed endowments into a movie career. Only problem was she couldn't act. (An agent who was a witness at the Mangold trial said on the stand, "She had all the range from A to A minus.")

Sally met Robby Mangold at a party in Malibu. Why, her parents used to watch his show, she told him. Ouch, Robby said. Then he turned on the charm and kept Sally plied with vodka. Two days later they drove to Las Vegas and got married.

The talk around town, of course, was that Sally was a gold digger and Robby a fool. Then the fighting started. Yelling at first, then hitting. Only it was Sally who hit Robby. The tabloids loved it.

Then one night Sally Jenkins-Mangold was found dead from a bullet to the back of the head. The ME placed her time of death at 12:30 p.m. Tuesday. At that time Robby Mangold was three hundred miles away, signing autographs at an event in Bakersfield.

With signs of forced entry, everyone figured it to be a burglary gone bad. Except Sam Tanner, who smelled a hit-man job.

Of course, there was no evidence of this to be found. And Robby Mangold made a fine showing of bereavement for the cameras.

But a great detective, Sam Tanner always said, was one-third thinker and two-thirds bulldog. He could not shake the thought that Robby was behind the whole thing.

Or maybe, just maybe, had done the deed. But how?

Sam's doggedness paid off when he dug through Robby's credit card records—with a valid search warrant, of course—and found out that two days before the murder Robby had purchased ten pounds of dry ice from a distributor in Compton. From there it was a simple matter of medical science. A killer could mess up a body's time of death by giving it dry ice treatment. And when Sam Tanner brought in Robby for questioning, his greatest skill—interrogation—dragged a confession out of the washed-up actor.

For a day Sam Tanner was the toast of his division. Heck, it should have been his calling card to the elite Robbery-Homicide Division downtown.

But that never happened.

And now there was this...yes, woman...who slides right in on a jet stream to RHD.

Sam Tanner hated the thought of subtly sabotaging her career. But he didn't exactly dismiss it, either.

———

"Can I be frank?" Rebecca said.

"I expect it," Sam said. He was driving one of the last Crown Vics in the LAPD inventory. He hated that his favorite car had been discontinued. So much was changing in the department. Like the woman sitting next to him.

They were out to question a person of interest in a homicide. A guy's girlfriend had been found at the bottom of a cliff in the Palisades. The guy, Cody Decker, worked in IT for Bank of America. He had an alibi. But Sam's bulldog instinct was kicking in big time.

"I know you think I'm some kind of interloper," Rebecca said.

"Just new," Sam said. "Maybe a little wet behind the ears. See, there are just some things an old detective has that you can't get except through raw experience. You'll have that someday. Everybody says you're the nuts."

"The what?"

"It's an old cop expression," Sam said. "Before your time. Means you have the goods, what it takes to be a great detective."

"I hope you think that," Rebecca said.

Sam thought, *I don't think that. I think you're as phony as a fat-free donut, and I'm going to see to it you get put in your place.*

"Sure do," Sam said. "Here we are."

He pulled to the curb in front of the house. It was a rental in a working-class neighborhood. The grass was patchy and hemmed in by a dismal chain link fence.

Rebecca almost jumped out of the Crown Vic.

Anxious little minx, Sam thought. *Probably wants to impress me.*

He got out and said, "Not so fast. We got to play this slow." He stretched and grunted. Then he came around the car and said, "Let me do the talking and I'll show you a few techniques."

"Will do," Rebecca said.

Sam proceeded up the walkway toward the house, keeping Rebecca behind him so there'd be no question who the lead detective was. He knocked on the door.

A skinny guy around twenty five opened the door. He wore jeans and a green T-shirt with a picture of Orson Welles on the front. Sam wondered if Rebecca even knew who Orson Welles was.

"Cody Decker?" Sam said.

"Who are you?"

"Detective Sam Tanner, LAPD. This is my partner, Rebecca Savage. Like to ask you a few questions."

Decker said, "C'mon, man, I already got grilled."

"This won't take too long," Sam said. "Mind if we come in?"

Not waiting for an answer, Sam pushed inside. Rebecca followed.

"Where's your warrant?" Decker said.

"We're not going to toss your place, Cody. Why don't you just have a seat?"

With eyes darting back and forth between the two detectives, Cody Decker backed up to his sofa and sat.

Sam folded his arms and used his favorite weapons—the direct approach. "Why don't you make it easy on yourself and tell me why you killed her?"

"I didn't! I already—"

"I know what you already said, and it stinks like a dead carp. You and I both know you did it. I've looked better liars than you in the eye."

There was a slight shudder in Cody Decker's cheeks. "I'm not talking to you. I don't have to. I'm not under arrest." He looked at Rebecca Savage. "That's right, isn't it? You tell him."

Sam looked at his partner, wondering how she'd handle this. Back him up, or side with the lying weasel?

"Then we'll just have to arrest you right now," Rebecca said, as cool as winter squash.

"Put the cuffs on him," Sam said.

"Wait!" Decker said.

"You want to talk now?" Sam said.

"I want a lawyer!"

"All in good time," Sam said. He nodded to Rebecca who got out the bracelets and told Decker to stand up and turn around.

Sam went to the front door, opened it.

And his heart slammed against his chest.

The Crown Vic was gone.

———

Two hours later Sam Tanner and Rebecca Savage were sitting in the captain's office. Captain Bill Regan glared at them from behind his desk.

"Let me get this straight," he said in a clipped, angry tone. "You left the car unlocked on the street? And it was jacked?"

Sam took in a long breath. He'd rehearsed his story several times in his head during the preceding hour. He was not going to let his thirty spotless years get flushed down the toilet. And that desperation had given birth to a plan to killing two birds with one bullet.

But he had to play it slow. He said, "Apparently."

"What do you mean apparently?" Captain Regan said. "There's no other explanation possible."

"Probably so," Sam said.

"And there's only one way that could happen without the alarm being tripped. The car was left unlocked."

Sam said nothing.

"An act of such negligence it could mean a demotion, if not outright dismissal."

Sam didn't respond. Play it slow...

"You were the driver, am I right?" Regan said.

"Yes, sir," Sam said.

"So there's no other conclusion, is there?"

Sam cleared his throat.

"What is it?" Regan said.

"Sir, I..."

"Come on, out with it."

"I take full responsibility," Sam said. "I should have watched her."

"Who?"

Sam nodded toward Rebecca. He averted his eyes from hers. As much as he'd planned it, it still stuck in his craw what he had to do. It was an article of faith that you support your partner. But a career was a career.

"What are you saying?" Regan asked.

"Captain, don't be too hard on her. She's still learning."

Rebecca said, "Wait, what?"

"Look, an honest mistake," Sam said. "I got out of the car first. I came around. Detective Savage was looking at her phone. I told her to hurry it up and follow me. A couple of seconds later I heard the car door close. I didn't give it another thought. Of course she'd lock the door."

"Hold it," Rebecca said.

"An honest mistake!" Sam said. "Let it go, Captain. This once."

"Wait a second!" Rebecca said.

"I'm sick about this," Sam said. "I gotta go to the john."

"You come right back," Regan said.

———

In the bathroom Sam splashed water on his face. He looked at himself in the mirror. Was he really this low? Just because he had qualms about a young woman being a detective?

He slapped himself. Too late now. He had to play it out at the end. And he'd get over it. He'd get back to work, and that always helped. He'd get a new partner and go back to Cody Decker's house and finish him. Decker was no doubt as confused as Rebecca was when he ordered her to remove the cuffs, then walked with her half a block before ordering an Uber.

Taking one last look at himself, he squinted like Dirty Harry and said, "Let's do this."

Back in the office he found Captain Regan alone, standing, his arms folded.

"What's going on?" Sam said.

Regan sighed, then said, "Sam, I don't know what to say."

"What do you mean?"

"You're old school, Sam."

"Yeah, I am. And that's the best way to be."

"You think?"

"What I think is that you shouldn't be putting youngsters in the big time without they earn it."

"Like Rebecca Savage?"

"That's right."

"It's not because she's a woman, is it?"

"Come on, Skipper. You know I don't think that way."

"Do I?"

"Hey, what gives? Where is she?"

Regan came around his desk and faced Sam head on. "Detective Savage was wearing one of our new digital body cams, as small as a button."

Sam's throat tightened.

"As I recall," Regan said, "you skipped out on that training session."

Sam managed to say, "So what? Not everything new is good, and not everything old is bad."

"She's putting the video on her laptop right now," Regan said.

Sam tried to keep his face impassive. But the tension was already manifesting itself in hot sweat droplets under his arms.

Rebecca came back in, holding her laptop. She didn't look at Sam. She placed the laptop on the corner of Regan's desk.

"Run it," Regan said.

Rebecca clicked the touchpad and the video began. It showed her point of view as she got out of the Crown Vic and turned around. A couple of seconds later Sam got out and said, "Not so fast. We got to play this slow." He stretched, grunted, came around toward the camera and said, "Let me do the talking and I'll show you a few techniques."

Captain Regan tapped the pad, stopping the video.

Sam fell back into a chair. The room began to spin.

"Your gun and your badge," Regan said. "On my desk."

Two hours later, Sam Tanner dove into a bottle of Scotch.

———

That night, Detective Rebecca Savage entered the alley garage in Silver Lake, half hidden under spreading bougainvillea. Tommy Algood, one of the best car thieves in the city, shut the wooden doors.

"Smooth as a water slide," Tommy said. "You really planned it good."

Rebecca had to agree. Since she'd picked up the vibe that Sam Tanner was out to ruin her career, she'd gone all Sun Tzu. She had a bootleg copy of the Crown Vic key fob made by a former safecracker out on parole. She scoped out Cody Decker's house the night before the interview, and placed the fob under a holly bush near the front door. From there it all went smoothly. She'd used her street contacts to get to Tommy Algood and his chop shop. The various parts of a police Crown Victoria were too good for him to pass up. She'd calmed his suspicions about her motives by giving him an advance of $5000.

She'd agreed to give him another five grand now. That was also part of the plan. Setting up an ex-con's expectations was a skill the best detectives had, in spades.

"Will that be cash or charge?" Tommy joked.

Rebecca pulled her Glock and shot Tommy Algood in the forehead.

From her purse she removed the .38 revolver with a taped butt—what the old-school cops called a Saturday Night Special—and placed it in Tommy's hand. She put his index finger on the trigger and fired off two shots toward the garage door.

———

Sam Tanner's hangover was a beaut. His head felt like it had an ax in it.

But it was the radio newscast that finished the job.

A gun battle in a Silver Lake garage left a suspected car thief dead and the police detective who shot him unharmed. LAPD Detective Rebecca Savage tracked down the suspect in the robbery of a police vehicle. She told reporters it was just good old-fashioned police work which she learned from her partner, a senior detective who currently is on administrative suspension at the present time. KFWB is continuing to follow this story...

The rest of the news faded into a low hum as Sam's temples pounded his head like jackhammers.

For two seconds Sam Tanner thought about eating a bullet.

But then his inner bulldog started barking.

And wouldn't stop.

———

Wednesday morning, after her appearance on *Good Day L.A.*, Rebecca walked into the station and was told by the desk sergeant, Rudy Larusso, that Captain Regan wanted to see her, ASAP. Rudy gave her a smile and an approving nod, like he knew something good that she did not herself yet know.

A commendation, perhaps?

Cap's door was open and she walked right in.

"You wanted to see—"

She stopped when she saw Sam Tanner sitting in the corner.

"Sam!" she said. "How are you? I've been worried."

"Thanks, kid," Sam said. "I know you must have been. But maybe for the wrong reason."

"Huh?"

"Rebecca," Captain Regan said, "your gun and your badge, on my desk."

"Wait...what?"

"On my desk."

"But why?"

"Now."

Heart crashing into her chest, Rebecca did as she was ordered. "I demand to know what this is all about."

"It's a suspension pending an investigation," Captain Regan said.

"For what?"

"Why don't you fill her in, Sam."

Rebecca turned to face her former partner. Heat shot out of her eyes. "Yes, Sam, why don't you tell me?"

He stood and touched his nose. "The old smeller. Cop instinct. Didn't seem right. So I looked up a car thief I knew from years ago. He's out at North County. Another year before his next parole hearing. I told him I could fast track him if he knew this Tommy Algood. He did. And he told me something very interesting."

Sam Tanner paused.

Rebecca told herself to keep calm, to not let her face twitch.

She felt it twitch.

"Seems he and Tommy Algood were tight once. And that Tommy's had a secret, an insurance policy. He would write down the details of his employment and leave that note in with his brother. Who was more than willing to share it with me."

"Want to read it yourself?" Captain Regan said, holding out the paper.

Rebecca snatched and read the scrawl with her name on it, and the detail about the duplicate fob. She felt the blood drain from her face. Powerless to stop it, her only option was rage.

"You think you can make this stick?" She crumpled the paper and threw it at Sam.

"Turn around, please," Sam said. "And place your hands behind your back."

An animal instinct charged through her. She turned and ran for the door.

Bumping into Rudy Larusso.

"Sorry, Rebecca," Rudy said.

She turned, bared her teeth at Sam. "It's because I'm a woman, isn't it!"

"No," Sam said. "It's because you're a criminal.

She lunged at him.

It took all three of the men to subdue Rebecca Savage, and get her cuffed and stuffed in a cell.

Back in Captain Regan's office, Regan said, "You really did it. I didn't think she'd crack."

"How'd you do it, Sam?" Rudy Larusso asked.

Sam touched his nose. "When I found out she'd busted Tommy a few years ago, I knew there had to be a connection. Then I did what I do. I eliminated all possibilities until I got to where there had to have been an extra fob she planted for Tommy. Since I couldn't prove it, I made up the story about the guy in North County and the insurance policy jazz. My son is actually the one who wrote the note. What Rebecca forgot in the heat of the moment was that the law says we can lie through our teeth to a suspect. Cap here really sold it. He's a regular Barrymore."

"Drew Barrymore?" Rudy said with a smile. "But she's a woman."

"Doesn't make a bit of difference to me," Sam said. "Treat everybody the same, I always say."

THE EMBRACE

Because Bleen had been unlucky in love on his home planet, Ggrg, he decided to travel. In another place he would forget his troubles, the hurt in his heart. He'd heard the stories of another planet with a creation account much like Ggrg's, with beings and animals like you found on his home planet. Things like foliage and buildings and seas. But also a drink they called "coffee" which had mythical qualities. Bleen doubted it existed, but like the childhood stories his father used to tell him about a knight named Hadagal and his search for the holy cup of the Savior, he entertained the wish that such a thing existed.

To travel to this planet would require deresolution and a wormhole thrust. It was expensive and risky. But Bleen did not care. If he stayed derezzed, at least he would be at peace. He sold all of his possessions, signed the waiver, and on 4E78, at A3.7 in the afternoon, he entered the chamber at Bridge Interstellar and got sent to the place called Earth.

Bleen felt his chest and arms. He was all there! On a city street. He looked at himself in a window. He was, in Earth years, twenty-five.

To himself, he looked like others of his make, except for one thing—

"Cool toga, man." It was a young being about Bleen's own age. "You in a show or something?"

Bleen's translation implant allowed him an understanding and ability to speak the language of Earth. "Show?"

"You know, a play?"

"Does my dress suggest such a thing?"

"You call that a dress? Whatever works for you, man. It's cool."

"I am quite comfortable," Bleen said. "But if I desired to wear clothing such as yours, where would I go find them?"

"How much you want to spend?"

"Spend? Oh! Money." Bleen knew he had forgotten something on his trip.

"No sweat, man." He pointed a finger. "There's a thrift store right around that corner."

And with that, the being walked away.

Bleen followed the directions and entered the thrift store. It was a wonderland, and Bleen picked out many colorful items. He took them to the counter where a young being of the other sex, with black hair and a ring in her nose, looked at the tags and hit what looked like a calculating machine. She looked at Bleen and said, "A hundred and twenty-seven, fifty-three."

"Money!" Bleen said.

"We take Visa and MasterCard, too."

"I do not know these things."

"Credit cards?"

Bleen shook his head.

"Where are you from?" the she-being said. She was pleasant to look at, but not so pleasant as Qlx. No one was as pleasant as Qlx. But she had given her heart to Dkgh, the plasterer.

"Ggrg," Bleen said.

"That's in the Middle East, right?"

Bleen frowned.

"You speak our language very well," the she-being said.

"Thank you."

"But you don't have any money?"

"No!"

"I'm so sorry. Would you like me to put these aside for you?"

"Aside?"

"Until you can pay for them."

Bleen thought a moment. "This money, how may I get some?"

"Do you have a job?"

Once again, Bleen shook his head.

"Any family or friends?"

Head shake.

"Gosh, that must be hard. Where are you staying?"

Bleen used an Earth signal he had learned. He shrugged his shoulders.

"Boy..." the she-being said. Then she looked around, as if to see if someone was watching her. She whispered, "Wait here."

The she-being went away, through a curtained door. Bleen did as he was told. He sensed the she-being's friendliness.

She came back holding something light brown in her hands.

"I have some friends," she said, "who make a ton with this. A good place is right out there on the corner. Lots of foot and car traffic. Just sit by the post and hold this."

She handed him the brown thing. It was square, made of some kind of firm paper. On it was written something in Earth language, which Bleen immediately translated:

NO JOB. NO HOME. JUST HUNGRY.

"And it's tax free," the she-being said with a smile.

"This is good?" Bleen said.

"Oh, yeah. You gotta do what you gotta do."

Bleen did as instructed and wondered what was going to happen. Soon enough he found out. Beings stopped and put Earth money in the lap of his toga. Conveyances would stop and a hand would come through the window, holding out more money. Bleen lost track of time, but was aware that the burning star giving light to the Earth was making its way across the sky. When the light began to dim he gathered up his toga and went back into the thrift store.

The she-being was still there. Bleen went to the counter and poured out the money. It was in paper and hard, round things.

"Hey," the she-being said. "That's not bad!" She began to count. She made two piles on the counter. "This covers it," she said and put one pile to the side. "This you get to keep."

She turned around and got the clothes Bleen had picked out earlier.

"May I get into some of these?" Bleen said.

"Now?"

"Yes."

"Sure you can." She pointed to the curtain. "You can go in there."

Bleen took the clothes through the curtain and into a strange room without windows. Happily, he chose a shirt and pants. The shirt was long-sleeved and stretchy, white with big blue flowers on it. The pants had green stripes and were stretchy, too.

He came back out and the she-being said, "You're ready for the disco!"

That was a strange word Bleen did not understand.

"But what about shoes?" the she-being said. "You need shoes."

"Ah," said Bleen.

"Tell you what," she said in a low voice. "Go pick a pair and I'll let you have them for free."

Bleen understood *free* and it was a happy word. He went out into the store again and found a shelf with shoes. He looked at his feet and estimated their size vis-à-vis the shoes. His feet felt comfortable inside them. He was confused by the strings—on Ggrg they had coverings made from a material that conformed perfectly to any foot—but he managed to figure out a way to secure them, for Bleen was one of Ggrg's leading engineers.

The she-being put Bleen's other clothes in a bag and reminded him to be careful with his money. Bleen said he would and put the paper and coins in the pocket of his green-striped pants.

"Now," he said, "where can I go to find the thing called coffee?"

"There's a Starbucks next door. Say, I'm about to close up. How about if I join you?"

The she-being offered to buy Bleen coffee, and he was happy. The beings on Earth were nice. They had given him money and now he was going to have his first taste of that mythical concoction.

At a table the she-being said, "May I know your name?"

"Yes, you may," Bleen said. "Bleen."

"Glad to know you, Bleen. My name is Matilda."

"That is a very nice name."

Matilda smiled and picked up her cup and took a sip. Bleen studied the move, then did the same thing.

"Ow!" he said.

"It's very hot," Matilda said with a giggle. "Don't burn your tongue!"

Bleen wondered what all the fuss about coffee was. Perhaps she was playing a joke on him. He had heard about beings of Earth playing what they called jokes. Like putting air into a thing made of what they called rubber and then having someone sit on the thing, which then made a disagreeable noise that Earth beings apparently found funny.

"So," Matilda said, "what do you do, if I may ask."

"Do?"

"Oh, it's all right if you're not doing anything at the moment. I just wondered what your passion is. Mine's poetry. That's what I do when I'm not working in the store. I hope when universal income is passed, I can do poetry full time."

"What is this universal income?"

"It means the government will give everyone money to live on."

"That is wonderful. Then people would not have to sit on corners with signs, is that correct?"

"Correct! Then I could quit the store and write poetry all day."

"But then, who will work in your store?"

Matilda furrowed her brow. "Hmmm," she said, and took another drink of coffee. Bleen did the same, but this time with great care not to burn his tongue. The coffee tasted bitter to him. But he was determined to drink it because of magic that was supposed to be in it.

Bleen asked Matilda about her poems and she took a book-thing out of the container with a strap that she had worn to the magic coffee place.

"All right," she said with a giggle. "Here's one."

She read Bleen one of her poems and he did not understand it. But he found he was feeling great pleasure at being with Matilda.

After another ten poems, their coffee was consumed, and Matilda said, "Bleen, you're really a very sensitive guy. It was nice meeting you."

She stood.

"You are going away?" Bleen said.

"I have to get home. Do you have a place to stay?"

"I want to stay here," Bleen said.

"In Starbucks?"

"On Earth."

She giggled. "Silly. Come with me."

Bleen followed Matilda out of the coffee place and out to the place where the vehicles were. But no other beings walking around.

Matilda pointed in a direction and said, "If you go three blocks that way, you'll come to the Salvation Army. They might have a bed for you, and help you till you can get on your feet."

Bleen looked down at his feet and wondered why she thought he wasn't on them.

"May I ask," Bleen said, "why you have been so nice to me, a stranger?"

"I believe we're all really one," Matilda. "We just forget that some-times. But deep down, we are all the same."

"I would like to embrace you," Bleen said.

Matilda said, "You may."

Bleen's body vibrated with happy feelings. He opened his mouth and his tongue came out and expanded to the size of a wet blanket.

Matilda made a loud, screeching sound as Bleen's tongue embraced her.

ALL THE RIGHT MOVES

Brainerd decided it was time to kill his wife. It wasn't that he couldn't just walk away from the marriage and into Vanessa's arms. People did that all the time. It's that he knew Jade would make his life a nightmare. She'd tie him up in court and want to take half of everything and all that. She was a lawyer, after all, and not exactly a shrinking violet when it came to using the system for her clients.

No, the whole divorce thing would be a major bummer. Better that she have a "tragic accident" and he could start clean.

But he knew that this sort of thing was tried all the time by fools, like Scott Peterson. Stupid jerk. He hadn't planned it at all well. You had to take several months and make all the right moves.

Brainerd, who worked for a games design company, knew all about that.

In three months it would be their tenth anniversary. He started dropping the idea of going back to the place where he'd asked Jade to marry him. It had been on a backpacking trip in the Los Padres National Forest. Just the two of them, in a great spot by a river. Why not try to put some of the tensions we've been having aside? Recapture that magical past?

Jade was all for it. There was something special about ten years, she said. A perfect time to renew their vows.

Brainerd said that sounded good.

Vanessa wasn't all that pleased about being discrete for three months. He met her, as usual, at a motel in Downey. It was one of those places that didn't ask questions and told only lies.

"I can't stand to wait that long," she said. They were in bed and she was cooing up a storm. Brainerd was usually putty when that happened, but he wasn't about to let another woman take control. Not this time.

"Listen," he said. "The plan has to be perfect. I mean every step. For the next three months I've got to make it seem like I'm totally in love with Jade."

"You're not, are you?"

"Of course not, baby. I can't stand her."

"Why not?"

"She thinks she's better than me. She thinks because she has a law degree, and works for a big firm, she's smarter or something. I want to get the best of her this once. And then we'll be free. There'll be money, too. She's made quite a bit the last few years."

"What'll we do with it?" Vanessa asked.

"Nothing."

"Nothing?"

"Not at first. We'll have to play it very careful. I mean, they'll be watching me."

"Who?"

"The cops. We can't be together for a couple of months after."

"I can't do that!"

"You have to. Just a few months, and then what we'll do is we'll meet, you'll console me, we'll get close. And then we'll take some of that money and we'll go on a cruise. How would you like that, baby?"

"Yes, a cruise. I love it."

"So it has to be perfect. I can't give Jade even a whiff of suspicion. But I know her. I know her weaknesses. I can pull this off."

Vanessa cooed.

A month later Brainerd arranged to have a little barbecue at the house, inviting Charles and Pat Loring and Bill and Jan Regan. They were the closest friends Brainerd and Jade had. That being so, they'd no doubt picked up some tensions earlier in the year. It was essential to the plan to get them off that.

As Brainerd 'cued kielbasa and marinated chicken breasts, he made sure to put his arm around Jade as much as possible. He kissed her a few times, too. But he didn't overdo it. Once on the lips, a couple of times on the cheek, once on the nose.

A good time was had by all.

Afterward, Jade asked him what that had been all about.

"What was what all about?" Brainerd said.

"Being all over me like that, kissing me. Was that some kind of show for our friends?"

"Why can't I kiss my own wife?"

"You can, but you haven't been doing much of it lately. How come all of a sudden?"

"I have to have a reason?" Brainerd said.

"I'd like to know," Jade said.

"Stop being a lawyer for a few minutes, okay? Can't you?"

"Here we go—"

"Jade, listen to me. Why can't we start all over again? Remember? Renew our vows?"

"You were serious?"

"Well, yeah. We're coming up on ten years. Why don't we?"

"You want to backpack to our spot?"

"We haven't been in years. You need a break anyway."

Jade thought about it for a moment. Brainerd thought she might tell him to go jump in a reservoir. But she smiled and said, "Let's do it."

The morning of their anniversary, Brainerd and his wife hiked four miles and found the very same spot where, ten and a half years earlier, Brainerd had asked her to marry him. It was at the top of a small crevice in the mountains where the river ran through. A lot of sharp rocks along the side. When Jade would "fall," it would be quite easy to conclude it was an accident and she'd bashed her head.

Brainerd would give himself some gashes, too. That was perhaps the most important move of all. He had to look like he'd charged down to save her after she fell, cutting himself all over. His attempt to "rescue" his wife would be hampered by the terrain. He'd call for help, but it would take too much time for them to get there. His story would be absolutely unshakable.

It was around four in the afternoon when he did it. He had Jade stand and look at the river. He got her from behind with a big rock.

After her fall, Brainerd went down to make sure she was dead. He knelt over the body. Jade was beautiful, he had to admit that. But she was also competitive, and he had often felt like she believed she was smarter than he.

Not anymore, he thought. He carefully positioned her body in just the right way, so it would look as though she landed on her back on some very sharp rocks. He took her arms by the wrists and laid one out to the side, the other over her chest.

He heard a scuffing, up above.

"Hey, you crazy kids, get a room!" It was Bill Regan, smiling. Jan waved.

Charles Loring stepped up to the ridge with Pat, who shouted, "Happy Anniversary!"

"Don't worry, boy," Bill said. "Jade told us to surprise you. You can renew your vows, and then we'll leave you kids alone. That's the plan, right Jade?"

THIS TOO SHALL PASS

She saw it in his eyes. He was going to kill her.

She had known this day was coming. Fate had dealt her a losing hand.

The disease would kill her anyway. But how long, no doctor could say. Her muscles would continue to atrophy. Her ability to take care of herself was already gone. A daily caregiver visit provided only temporary relief.

Part of her couldn't blame Brad. The prospect of being tied to her in this condition was not a happy one. But what about that "for better or worse, in sickness and in health" part of the deal?

They'd had a traditional wedding five years ago. A second marriage for both. Ashley was a widow, Brad was divorced. He was 40, Ashley a year older. They'd met on a cruise to the Bahamas, one of those storybook romances they make for the Hallmark Channel.

And if it had been one of those movies, Brad would stick and Ashley would recover.

Reality was another thing altogether.

He could always divorce her, of course, and go his merry way. But there was the matter of the prenup.

Ashley's lawyer had insisted she get a prenuptial agreement signed before the marriage. She was against it at first, but his argument persuaded her. She was the one with the money. Her late husband, Tom, had left her an estate valued at $8 million.

Part of that included this beachfront home in the Malibu community of Broad Beach.

At least she could see the ocean each day. Sometimes in her wheelchair, sometimes—with help—on the soft chaise lounge on the balcony.

Where she was now.

It was a sunny day with one of those cool Pacific breezes that balances out the heat and makes for perfect beach time.

Meg Forrester from two houses away walked along the shoreline, holding her grandson's hand. They were nice people, the Forresters. Paul was a retired executive who'd worked for Litton Industries. Ashley and Brad had been to a couple of parties at their house. But they'd not been invited there since Ashley got sick. It made her sad, but being an introvert, she could live with it.

Brad not so much. He loved the social scene in Malibu. And though he never said it, she knew he resented her for messing things up on that score.

Which was why he was spending more and more time away from the house. "On business," he'd say.

———

It was on a Tuesday, just after Maria, Ashley's caregiver, had left the house, that she said to Brad, "You're thinking of doing it, aren't you?"

Brad had just made himself a martini and turned from the wet bar. "What did you say?"

"Brad, you won't really go through with it, will you?"

"Go through with what?" His annoyed voice.

"You're tired of me," Ashley said.

"Will you stop? How many times do you have to—"

"You are, aren't you?" Insistent.

Brad didn't answer. He took a long sip of his drink, his eyebrows furrowed downward over the glass.

"I know I'm a burden, but—"

"Stop, just stop." Brad downed the rest of his martini in one gulp and placed the glass on the bar. "Look, why don't you watch one of your shows, huh? Forget about all this talk."

He looked at his watch.

"Where are you going?" Ashley said.

"Out," Brad said.

"When will you be back?"

"Not too late. You just forget about things." He walked over to her and kissed her on top of the head. The head! It felt like the lips of a stone-cold killer.

After he left, Ashley guided her electric wheelchair to the window that looked out at the ocean. She would miss that. Seeing the waters. She did not know if there was a heaven or a hell. All she knew was that she wanted to see the ocean and have a husband who loved her.

The ocean would always be there. But not Brad.

She knew.

Should she call the police? Of course not. She had no proof, no evidence of any kind. They would think her hysterical. But she had to reach out to somebody. She tried to think of someone. She even tried to pray.

———

It was a week later when Brad came in from a swim. He was not alone.

"Ashley," Brad said, "this is Christine Bonner. She's renting the Stone-bridge house."

"Hello," Christine said. She was about Ashley's age, beautiful, with a full and alluring body—something Ashley once had. Her teeth were as white as whale bone, and her thong bikini left little to the imagination.

"We got to talking," Brad said. "She's never been to California, can you beat that? I thought we might show her around a bit."

"I don't want to be a bother," Christine said.

"No bother at all," Brad said. "Right, honey?"

"Sure," Ashley said.

Brad said, "Why don't we take a drive up Pacific Coast Highway, to Santa Barbara, and walk around State street?"

Walk around. He emphasized those words, looking her in the face. The coldness in his eyes.

Christine Bonner giggled with girlish delight. "That would be fun!" she said.

And it was, apparently, for Brad and Christine Bonner. Ashley did not go to Santa Barbara. And for the next five days, Brad showed Christine plenty of places in Southern California.

It was all playing out just as Ashley knew it would. Husband tires of wife. Husband meets new model, gets serious about losing the wife. There would be some sort of murder plot, along the lines of what used to be one of her favorite movies, *Double Indemnity*, starring Barbara Stanwyck and Fred MacMurray.

———

On Friday, late, after Maria had gone, Brad waltzed in and smiled at Ashley.

It was the most chilling sight she'd ever seen. He didn't have to say a word.

"Thought I'd take Christine up for a little hike in the canyon," he said. "You know, the trail we used to go on?"

Used to...

"It'll be dark soon," Ashley said.

"I know," he said, in a way that made her feel he was talking about the darkness that was going to be hers, and soon.

Brad looked at his watch. He went into the bedroom and came back with his hiking shoes on.

"Anything you need, babe?" he said.

"Lots," Ashley said.

"Your mom used to say, 'This too shall pass.' Remember?"

"Of course."

"This too shall pass," he said, and walked out.

Ashley wept, but wouldn't allow it to go on. She watched the sun go down on the Pacific horizon. She wondered if heaven would be as beautiful.

She fell asleep.

Her eyes opened at the sound of footsteps. She saw a pillow coming toward her face.

"No!"

It was over her face. The pressure. No air!

Thunk.

The pillow slipped from her face as something...no, some*one*...hit the floor.

Brad.

"You all right?" Christine said. She stood there, a police baton in her hand.

"Y...Yes. What's happening?"

"It's over now," Christine said. "You were right. It was just like that Barbara Stanwyck movie you liked."

"*Double Indemnity*?"

"You always were a movie nut," Christine said. "Even back in elementary school. Anyway, Brad was pressuring me to, ahem, go all the way. But when I told him not while he was married, he told me what he was planning to do. And I smiled and called him *Baby*. I hated doing that. He told me he was going to do it tonight. I slipped in behind him."

"Oh, Christine, how hard for you."

"Not at all. When you called me and told me what you feared, I didn't have any hesitation coming out to help an old friend. Especially one who rented me such a nice house."

"Now what?"

"We call the police," Christine said. "I am a witness to attempted murder. I stopped him. Remember, I was a detective in Miami and dealt with some of the worst scum of the earth."

Ashley looked at Brad's inert body. "Is he breathing?"

Christine knelt. "I guess I hit him a little too hard."

"You mean...he's dead?"

"You don't have to worry anymore," Christine said. "And hey, chin up. I remember something your mom used to say. This too shall pass."

SHOES

Steve Brisbane and Brian Keller had known each other since third grade. In their high school graduating class of 312, Steve was unanimously voted Most Likely to Succeed. That was a prophecy, all right. Steve went on to Stanford, then the Wharton School of Business. After five years on Wall Street he came back to Baton Rouge to start his own investment firm, specializing in commercial real estate.

Brian never moved out of Louisiana. He got a degree in finance from LSU, married, did fine for awhile at a branch of KPMG. Then his wife left him for a high roller from Texas. That led to a period of heavy drinking, followed by AA. He'd been sober two years when Steve stepped in and hired his old friend.

On a cool Tuesday in November, Steve messaged Brian to meet him for bourbon and cigars at Churchill's. Over Old Fashioneds, Steve said, "I'm working on something big, and I want you to be the ramrod."

"Wow," Brian said.

"That's it? Wow?"

"Well, I mean..."

"You don't know what you mean," Steve said. He snapped his fingers three times. "Bim, bam, boom. You have to know what you mean right *now*. You want to make it big, you've got to grab while the grabbing's good. I'm offering it to you, you want it?"

"Of course I do!"

"Good," Steve said. "That's what I wanted to hear."

Brian took a slow sip of his drink.

"You seem hesitant," Steve said.

"No, no. Not at all. It's just..."

"Just what?"

"A little out of the blue," Brian said.

Steve placed his glass on the table. "You want the truth?"

Brian's Adam's Apple quavered. "Yes."

"I've had my eye on you for the last few months," Steve said. "Your work here seems to have slipped. Any troubles at home?"

"Home? I...Steve, I'm divorced."

"Oh, right, right. I really don't want to probe. But if I give you this project, I have to know you'll come through."

"Sure, Steve, sure."

"I see this as a way to help my oldest friend get back on track. Recapture the ol' mojo."

"Thanks, Steve."

"Don't thank me yet. I've always had the feeling, just a feeling, mind you, that you envy me."

"Envy?" Brian's voice cracked.

"Remember back in third grade, when I talked you out of your Ding Dong at lunch that one time?"

"I kind of do."

"I promised you a Hostess Snoball. Remember those?"

"Of course," Brian said. "Coconut outside, chewy."

"It was the most desired of all lunchtime sweets," Steve said. "But I never paid off. I said it was a supply chain issue. I actually used those words. I was getting ready for the business world."

Brian strained out a laugh.

"So I owe you," Steve said. "Consider this project your Hostess Snoball. And your way to new shoes."

"Excuse me?" Brian said.

"You wear Bruno Magli right?"

"Um, yeah."

"Three hundred a pair?"

"More or less," Brian said.

Steve lifted his foot and pointed at it. "You know what these go for? Ten grand per."

"Whoa!"

"Hand made in Florence, by father-son cobblers whose family business goes back to the Hapsburgs. You have to go to their shop to be measured. Each shoe is unique to each foot. They use the finest Tuscany leather from Santa Croce sull'Arno. Someday, Brian, I want you to be able to afford shoes like these. Would you like that?"

"Yeah, I would," Brian said.

"Then tomorrow we'll drive out to the site," Steve said, lifting his glass. "Cheers."

―――――

Next morning, in Steve's car—a gun-metal blue Cadillac Escalade—Steve said, "Did you ever read *1984*, Brian?"

"Um, no."

"We had it assigned in Mrs. Phelps's class, remember?"

Brian said, "I usually used Cliffs Notes."

"Orwell was only about forty years off," Steve said. "We are living *1984* now. Creeping totalitarianism. Forced thought or you get cancelled. Big Brother watching us, ready to take away our livelihoods if we say or think the wrong thing. Only Big Brother is not just the government. It's every rat with a smart phone and social media account."

"Cheery."

"Well, that book is relevant to what I'm showing you today."

"Relevant how?"

"You'll see," Steve said.

An hour later, long off the highway and on a damp back road, Steve pulled to a stop. They were in a forest which, if not primeval, was wild and untamed. Thick willows wept all around them. A river ran past them on the left, bearded with bulrushes and cattails.

"We walk from here," Steve said.

Brian followed Steve, batting away mosquitoes. "Are we in the right place?" he said.

"You'll see," said Steve.

Five minutes later, Steve stopped and pointed. "There it is."

Brian's eyes widened. It was a shack. Obviously abandoned and in a state of irreversible decrepitude.

"Beautiful, isn't it?" Steve said.

"I don't understand."

"Vision, Brian. That's what you need to make it in this game. You've got to see the beauty where no one else does."

Brian looked at the shack.

Steve said, "You've also got to know how to dig out inside information. You see, there's going to be a development five miles north of here, right off the highway. Homes, stores. For all those people fleeing California and New York. And right here is going to be a little retreat, a place where dads can bring their sons fishing, where families can get a little R and R."

"Do we own this property?" Brian said.

"One of our shell companies does," Steve said.

"How did you ever find it?"

"It's what I do, Brian."

"Who on earth lived here?"

"He was some old hermit. A trapper and fisherman. A guy who wanted to get away from it all. And that's the beauty part. Here is where people who see how *1984* things are can come for a little privacy and escape. Those commodities are going to be in demand. And demand means money. Lots of it. Come on."

The two walked along a grassy, mossy path that led to the shack's front door.

"Let's look inside," Steve said.

"In there?" Brian said.

"Watch where you step," Steve said. "Our shoes, you know."

Brian hesitated.

Steve said, "Don't worry. I've been in there. A couple of times. There's something I want you to see."

Steve pushed the door open, revealing a mess. There was a wood floor and a few sticks of furniture covered with cobwebs. The air was filled with the musty smell of rot. Some old rope and fishing tackle were piled in a corner. A pot-bellied stove sat in the middle of the floor, an ancient testimony to the life and warmth that once inhabited the place.

Brian followed Steve into the dusty shanty. The floorboards creaked under them.

"Now," Steve said. "Tell me what you see."

"Um...okay," Brian said. "Yeah, I can see having a cabin here. And other cabins along the river."

"Now you're talking," Steve said.

"And maybe...what's that?" Brian said.

"What's what?"

"That noise."

"What noise?" Steve said.

Brian stood frozen. "It's like a...screeching. What is that?"

"It's your future," Steve said, as he pulled a stun gun from his coat pocket and zapped Brian Keller with fifty-thousand volts.

———

As Brian writhed on the floor, semi-conscious, Steve utilized his Eagle Scout training to hog tie Brian with rope. He stepped back and waited for Brian's first words, which turned out to be a solitary and plaintive, "Why?"

"We both know why," Steve said. "Did you really think you could sleep with my wife and I wouldn't find out? Me? Steve Brisbane?"

"Wait, what?"

"I hope your next words are not going to be a denial, because that would make me very angry. And you don't want me to be angry."

"Steve, please, I never—"

"Was it your Freudian attempt to take down the king? Don't you know the universal rule? When you come at the king you best not miss."

"Steve...what's that noise?"

"I'll get to that. What I want from you now is a full and complete confession. And don't think you can lie or even spin. I'm going to give you one chance. One. If I'm satisfied, you won't die a long, slow and very painful death."

"You're insane!"

Steve laughed. "You think that's an insult? Let me give you a clue. All true geniuses are insane. Nietzsche! When you see beyond the mundane thought of the sheep, they'll call you insane. But the will to power overcomes. That's what *1984* is about, after all. This world is only about who has the power and who does not. Right and wrong are mere constructs, rules made up to protect the weak."

"But you're all wrong about me and Julie! Let's all get together and talk this out!"

"That's not possible, Brian."

"Why not?"

"Because my ex-wife is beyond talk."

"You're divorced?"

"Not exactly," Steve said.

"What's that mean?"

"You can see her now, if you like."

"What?"

"She's here."

Brian's face twisted like one of the knots that held him.

"Yes," Steve said, pointing to the ceiling. "Right up there."

"What are you saying?"

"That's the other part of *1984* I want to tell you about," Steve said. "Winston Smith was tortured with the thought of the one thing he was most scared of. Do you know what that was?"

"Steve, please let me go."

"Rats," Steve said.

"Oh, God."

"That's right. Up in that attic space is a hungry family of rats. They've had a feast of human flesh. If you want to have a last look at Julie, you can see her. She's only bones now, of course. But then again, she always wanted to lose some weight."

"You're..."

"Were you going to say *insane* again?"

"You're *wrong*!"

"There is no right or wrong! Only power. You see that rope above your head?"

Brian's wild eyes coursed upward.

"All I need to do is yank that rope and a door opens, and it will start raining rats, looking for fresh meat."

"No, no, please!"

"Sorry I never got you the Hostess Snoball," Steve said, reaching for the dangling rope. "Then again, you can go out realizing you're a tasty treat yourself. For rodents."

"Steve!" With a sudden burst of the most basic instinct of mankind—survival—Brian Keller kicked out with his legs, and rolled. He struck Steve behind the knees. Steve fell, landing hard on the rotting floor.

As he pulled the rope.

A rat fell on Brian's back. Every sinew in his body flush with adrenaline, Brian got to his feet, hunched over, and hopped...hopped madly...out the door, down the path.

———

Steve Brisbane felt a gnawing on his calf.

Screaming, he scrambled to his feet and staggered out the door.

Where his Tuscany leather shoe caught on the warped threshold. He went down, knocking his head on a knotty tree root sticking out of the ground.

He was out only a few seconds, but that was enough for five rats to begin chewing his ankles.

The air filled with the sound of Steve Brisbane's wild cries.

Somehow, he got up. He kicked at the rats.

The rats bared their teeth. They hissed.

Oh, how they hissed!

And more were streaming out the door.

Only one escape.

The river!

Steve lurched through the bulrushes, threw off his coat, dove in, his arms madly flapping.

But he wasn't moving.

His shoes! They were holding him back!

He pushed the toe of one shoe against the heel of the other. Would't budge.

Leather! Tuscany leather! Tightens in water!

Water...a distant thought, a memory, long forgotten, now brought to his mind with tormenting urgency.

His tenth grade biology teacher, Mr. Cook, who had squinty eyes and yellow teeth.

And his voice, from the mists of thirty years ago, saying, "...rats can swim, dive under water, and survive for days..."

Steve's head went under. With all his strength he fought back to the surface.

Where he saw a keening mass of rodent hell leaping into the water.

———

The two deputy sheriffs sipped coffee from Styrofoam cups. The taller one shuddered.

"Never seen anything like it," he said.

"Just bones?" the other one said.

"Mostly. The shoes still looked good, though."

"What about the other guy?"

"Complete shock. How he hopped all that way, I don't know how he did it. The doc'll take care of him, but he'll need therapy, boy."

"You going back to the scene?"

"No way. Rats! I never knew rats could swim."

"I don't even want to think about that."

"Go home and kiss your wife, Frank. I'm going to do the same."

RAGE ROAD

"Give me the gun," John said.

"Gun?" Tricia said.

"In the glove compartment. Give it to me."

"You have a gun in the car?"

"Yes, now—"

"You didn't tell me that, John. I don't want you to have a gun in the car. Is that the one you—"

"Just bought. Yes. It's registered, remember? It's legal."

"What about carrying it in a car? Isn't that—"

"Just give it to me."

"You shouldn't have it while you're driving. It's dangerous."

"I know how to handle it. Come on."

"But not in a car. I just can't imagine that's—"

"I just want it for a second."

"What do you want to do with it?"

"Will you quit arguing with me? Is that what you want to do, argue all the time?"

"Oh, John."

"Tricia, do you trust me?"

"Of course."

"Then just open the glove compartment and hand me the gun. You don't have to be afraid. The magazine's not in it. The gun's empty."

"John—"

"Just give me the gun!"

"Please don't yell at me."

There was a catch in her voice. John didn't like that part of Tricia. The way she got upset so easily. Because if they were going to get married she would have to be able to handle stress better than she did. Even though she was the hottest of the hot and he was glad to have landed her, she still had to develop some stronger backbone. Especially after the therapy she'd been in and out of. That was supposed to have helped her, wasn't it?

He guessed he'd have to help her now, and this was a perfect time to start.

"I told you," John said. "The magazine's not in it."

John heard the glove compartment snap open. He was looking in the rear view mirror. The guy was still there, right behind, still flipping him off. Coming up close to the bumper, dropping back, coming up again.

"All right, here," Tricia said. John looked over and saw she was holding the gun like it was bomb that might go off with the slightest movement. He took it from her, then got his eyes back on the road. They were on the two-lane heading toward Santa Paula. Not a lot of traffic here. Most of that was on the 126. John had taken Tricia on the back road to show her the wildflowers. Mr. Romantic.

Only now he had a jerk on his tail, a guy in a pickup who had cut them off four miles ago. John had given him a hefty blast on the horn and, yes, gave him the finger. I mean, that's supposed to be it, right? Exchange fingers and maybe lip a curse or two, then drive on.

This guy was not driving on. This guy was out to make something of it.

"What are you going to do with that?" Tricia said.

"I don't want you to get upset, okay? I'm just going to show the guy behind us he needs to back off."

"Oh, John, no!"

"Easy. I'm just going to show him. That's all."

"He'll go away. He has to."

"He doesn't have to. This is one long highway, honey. He can stay with us as long as he wants."

"Then let him. He's just making a show."

"He wants a show I'll give him one."

"What if *he* has a gun? Did you ever think of that?"

"Odds are he doesn't," John said.

"But what if he does?"

"He doesn't."

"Please don't."

"Tricia, we can't let—" John saw in the mirror that the guy was speeding up, starting to pass him on the left. The left was the opposite lane. For a moment there was no oncoming traffic.

"No way, pal," John said and pushed hard on the gas. He put the 9 mm Beretta between his legs and grabbed the wheel with both hands. For a few brief seconds he and the truck were going the same speed. John's Altima was doing fine with its 3.5 V-6, keeping the pickup half a car length behind and to the side.

Then John saw, up ahead on the long strip of straight road, a big truck heading their way.

The pickup guy would have to get his butt back in line or die.

But the guy sped up. He was going to try to pass anyway.

John pushed the Altima.

"Let him pass!" Tricia said.

John said nothing, swiveling his head, watching the guy's truck and the big monster up ahead.

The pickup was almost even with John now.

John gave more foot to the gas.

Tricia yelped. "Let him in!"

The monster truck's horn blared.

John shot another glance to the side. The guy in the truck locked eyes with him. They were dark, squinty eyes, deeply set in a twenty-something face under a shaved head. He looked like he wanted to crash into John's car just for spite. For a second, that's what John thought he'd do.

But at the last possible moment, Squinty Eyes dropped back and got behind him.

The monster truck honked past.

Sweat and heat, like a fever, broke out on John's face. He heard Tricia crying softly.

"Don't," he said.

"Shh."

"Come on."

"Don't talk."

He put his hand on her left leg. "Baby, please, I need you to be with me on this."

In the mirror John saw Squinty Eyes staying close, about a car length behind.

Tricia issued a pitiful sob. Then put her hand on top of his. "I just don't want anything to happen."

For the first time in miles John allowed himself to look at the rolling green hills. They always looked nice after a hard rain. "Nothing will, babe. Not as long as you're with me."

But what about Squinty? Would he have something to say about that?

Maybe, because here he came again, fast on the side.

John took his hand off Tricia's leg and grabbed the gun. Time to make things plain. Just show the guy what would happen if he messed with them anymore.

Of course, John would never use it, not for real. Now it was just for show. But a good show. A hard show.

Left hand on the wheel, John reached over with his gun hand and used his index finger to lower the window.

Wind whipped in.

"What are you going to do?" Tricia said.

"Scare him."

"But you can't point a gun at someone."

"If you're threatened you can."

And here came Squinty, almost even.

Okay, John thought. Let's see if I can get his beady little eyes to open wide.

He waited, timed it, increased speed just a little.

Squinty had his passenger side window down. When they were side-by-side Squinty shouted an F-bomb. John smiled, raised the gun.

He pointed it at Squinty.

Bam.

The gun kicked in his hand.

Tricia screamed.

John felt the right front wheel grab shoulder and jerked the steering wheel to steady the car.

"John, dear God!"

John threw the gun—it actually felt like the gun jumped out of his hand—on the passenger side floor at Tricia's feet.

She screamed again.

"Quiet!" John said.

"What did you do?"

He didn't know. He slowed. No cars behind. He looked in the rear view mirror.

The pickup was about a hundred yards back, completely off the road.

Smashed into an oak tree.

John's heart smashed, too. He hit the brakes and skidded to a stop.

"What happened?" Tricia said. "Did you . . . oh, God . . ." She whirled around in the seat and looked back. "Oh my dear God!"

"Stop it!" John said.

"What are we going to do? We have to—"

"Let me think."

"What if he's . . . John, what if—"

"Let me think!" He tried to think, thoughts crashing on each other, but one loudly asking, *How*? How could it have happened? He'd taken out the magazine! He was practicing, putting it in and taking it out. Taking it out like some action star would, hitting the release, letting the mag fall into his hand. How could he have shot . . . the chamber! That was it. Stupid! He hadn't checked the chamber. He'd been playing around and must have chambered a round and forgot.

And now, what if he'd killed a man? *What freaking if?*

A red car was slowing near the truck.

"John, we have to—"

"Quiet!" He hit the gas.

Tricia yelped. "What are you doing?"

"Just wait!"

He tore down the road, cresting a slight hill. A blue SUV was coming up in the other lane. It flashed lights at him. Only then did he realize he was driving on the wrong side of the line.

He swerved over, accelerated.

"We have to go back!" Tricia said.

"We *can't* go back," John said. "I may have killed him."

"Dear *God.*"

"Stop saying that! We've got to get out of here fast."

"John, we can't!"

"What do you want me to do? Maybe I just shot a guy. Even if he's not dead, he crashed. You know what they do to you in California if you use a gun that way? Even by mistake? You know what that would mean?"

"But John—"

"It'd mean I might never get to practice law. All our dreams gone down the toilet. And my dad, what about my dad? If he ever found out."

"You can talk to him."

"Are you nuts? He'd cut me off. No money for anything. He'd probably disown me."

"No, he wouldn't. He's big, he knows people who can help you."

"What, other lawyers? You think that'd get me out of this?"

"But John, you shot a man."

"*At* a man."

"What if he's alive and he can ID us? What if he got our license plate?"

"We'll have to think about that. We'll have to come up with a story."

"What kind of story?"

"I don't know. I have to think." But he couldn't get his mind wrapped around what just happened. His adrenal glands were pumping overtime. He was short of breath.

And he was doing 85. He slowed. Don't get pulled over! Just get away. Get as far away as possible. Just keep driving and think and stop somewhere and figure out what to do.

Tricia was crying again.

"Listen, babe, I'm sorry," John said. "I'm sorry I have to do this, but I have to, don't you see?"

She shook her head.

"It's our lives I'm talking about," John said. "This'll kill us. This'll ruin everything."

"It was an accident," Tricia said. "I know that. I'll tell the police that. I'll stand by you."

"That's not good enough."

They were silent for several minutes. John drove steadily, fighting his nerves, breathing deep. They'd be in Santa Paula soon. He'd stop there. They'd get their heads together. Tricia would begin to see. She would—

What was that coming? In the rear view mirror, John saw a car tearing up on their tail.

A red car.

That red car. The one that had slowed at the scene. It had to be.

Coming up fast.

To catch up. To get his license plate.

To report him.

"What is it?" Tricia said.

"What's what?" John said.

"You look worried."

"Nothing. Relax." Right. Relax. Like he could relax.

He sped up.

"What are you doing?" Tricia said.

"What does it look like I'm doing?"

"Why?" She turned around. "Oh no, is that the police?"

"Don't look back."

"Why?"

"Just don't." He bit down on his lower lip.

The red car was speeding up, too.

Ahead John saw a trailer. A slow trailer.

Trapped.

Unless he could get around it.

He gunned the car.

The red car dropped back.

John fought for breath. Just get around the trailer, find a quick exit. Get away from the prying do-gooder behind the wheel of the red car.

"John!"

He was in the opposite lane with another car oncoming.

Too late to back off now.

"John please!"

He pushed the accelerator to the floor.

The oncoming car veered right, kicking up dust and gravel on the shoulder.

John heard the angry horn as he narrowly missed the car, a black sedan. The guy in the truck hauling the trailer honked as John whipped in front of him.

Tricia doubled over, face in her hands.

John checked the mirror again. No sign of the red car.

Up ahead, a crossroad. John saw a line of eucalyptus trees on the right. If he turned, maybe he could get up to where the trees gave cover.

He braked, turned hard right. The tires burned and squealed.

"Please stop!" Tricia said.

"Just wait." John gave it gas and shot up the road, a smaller version of the one they'd just been on. It was headed to who-knew-where, but it didn't matter. It just had to be so he could get away from the pestering Samaritan and everyone else in civilization.

There was another little road, off to the left, with some oleander plants. Lovely, large oleander plants.

John turned left. And then left again into a driveway. A long driveway, leading up to an old clapboard house. A pickup—John knew he would hate pickups forever after this—and a boat were parked out in front of the house

He stopped the car, letting it idle.

"What are you doing?" Tricia said.

"Wait." His heart kicked his chest. There, through the oleander, he could see the road they had just taken to get here. He could see if that red car was behind him.

It wasn't.

Thank God.

"I can't take this anymore," Tricia said.

"It's over," John said. "The bad part's over."

"How can you even say that? It's bad, it's horrible, and it will never be over! How can we ever forget this?"

"We will. In time, we will."

Or will we? John put his thumb under his front teeth. He realized then that was what he used to do as a kid when he knew he was getting in trouble with his dad.

His father, old Mr. Traditional. Decorated Gulf War vet, one of the top trial attorneys in California. He would not, in a million years, understand. John could not stand the thought of seeing his father's face if he found out, because that face would become a permanent rebuke to John. There would

be a look in his dad's eyes that would never go away. A look of disappointment, probably betrayal.

John had geared his whole life to pleasing his father. He couldn't
throw all that away. Not if he could get away with this.

And it looked as if he could.

"You'll understand," John said. "You'll be able—"

He stopped. A big guy in a baseball cap, all shoulders and biceps, was
walking toward the car. Walking with attitude.

John yanked the car into reverse.

"Hey!" the guy yelled and started running at them.

John said, "Hold on!"

"What's he doing?" Tricia said.

John spun the wheels. They kicked up dirt. The car almost fishtailed.
But he got out back onto the road.

The guy was yelling and only ten yards away.

John slammed it into drive and shot forward. He sensed, but didn't see,
the guy almost on top of the car.

Now tires gripped road and the car took off. Rubber burned. John saw
the guy in the mirror, face contorted with rage.

Tricia was breathing loudly. "I. Can't. Take it!"

"You have to," John said.

"Please take me home."

"We're going to freaking Santa Paula and we're going to have a
freaking good time, *okay?*"

Tricia shook her head violently. Tears streamed down her face. John
kept one eye on the road, the other on his fiancé.

"We've got to relax," he said. "I know a place where we can relax."

Tricia sobbed into her hands.

———

It was a roadside place, part produce market, part eatery. The Basket.
John had been here a few times. The best part was it was out of
the way.

They sat at a wooden table that looked like it'd last been painted
during the Clinton administration. John went to the serving window and
ordered two hamburgers, fries and two Cokes.

Tricia sat like a zombie. Wide eyed and barely responsive. John sat across from her and touched her arm. She didn't look John in the eye.

They sat in silence for what seemed like an hour.

John heard his number called and went to get the burgers from the window. The kid in a paper hat asked him if he wanted any ketchup. John asked for mustard.

At least, in this world gone mad, he could have mustard on his hamburger.

Paper Hat looked below the counter, then asked John to wait a second and headed toward the innards of the joint.

John snatched a fry and took a bite. It burned his tongue.

Then he heard the helicopter.

He realized he must have heard the sound before this but not paid it any mind. The way you can live near a freeway and sometimes not be conscious of hearing the cars.

But there was no mistaking the sound now. A chopper. And it was coming closer.

John looked up and spit out the bits of fry left in his mouth. It was a cop chopper. Maybe sheriff. But definitely law enforcement.

And it was starting to slow.

To *hover*.

Right over the dirt parking lot.

No way.

"Here's your mustard, sir." Paper Hat stood there with four packets of Heinz mustard in his outstretched hand.

John said nothing. He walked away from the window and entered the restaurant, even as Paper Hat said, "Sir?"

Pulse pounding, John whipped out his cell and punched Tricia's speed dial.

One ring. Two.

Pick up, pick up.

Three rings.

Why wasn't she answering?

Four rings, and the next would bring voicemail.

"What?" Tricia's said.

"Tricia, listen."

"There's a helicopter, I can barely—"

"I know. Listen to me. Very carefully. Get up and walk into the restaurant. Slowly."

"John, is it for us?"

"Now. Slowly." He killed the call and looked out the window of the restaurant door.

Tricia wasn't moving. She was looking up! No!

"Would you like a table?"

John whipped around. The young blond hostess held a menu against her chest.

"No, no," John said. "Waiting for somebody."

"Oh, okay." She seemed relieved. "Just tell me when they get here."

But would Tricia get there? John looked out again. She was just now getting up from the table.

What was going on in the chopper? Were they already calling it in? Who reported them? The guy in the red car? The guy with the shoulders?

What did it matter? They were on to them and he had to think, *think*. The future, everything, his father, law school, career, money, security. How to get out of this?

Tricia was taking her time getting to the door. Okay, he'd told her to go slowly, but she was a glacier. Her eyes were vacant, lost.

No, the word was *disturbed*. The delicate balance of her mental condition, he'd upset it. He was the one who was doing this to her.

Nothing to add to that. Only to deal with it. Only to—

Then he knew. It all became clear, unrolling before him like new carpet.

Tricia came through the door. She looked half comatose, if there was such a thing.

"John—"

"Listen." He put his arms on her shoulders. "Can you listen please?"

Tricia said nothing.

"This is important. I want you to walk across the restaurant to the other side." He pointed. "I want you to go out that exit and stand in front of the door, keeping the door open. Listen! I'm going to drive around and I want you to open your purse and I'm going to put the gun in it."

"What?"

"Just listen. If I time it right we'll have a few seconds where the chopper can't see us. I want you to keep the gun in your purse, and I want you to stay here in the restaurant. I want you to sit at a table and order food. No, the food is ordered. I want you to eat it inside here."

"But why?"

"They can't find the gun in my car. I'll come back for you."

"Where are you going?"

"You'll be safe here."

"No, John."

"Trust me. We can't argue."

"Why is this happening?"

"Do you understand what I told you? Go to the exit."

"Yes, but—"

"Do it. Do it now."

She paused. John wanted to push her. Her eyes were confused and sad.

"Please," he said.

Tricia looked at the floor, then turned and started walking.

The blond hostess stepped away from her podium as Tricia approached. "May I help you?"

John jumped in. "Restroom, restroom."

The hostess nodded. And thankfully pointed toward the rear exit. John saw the familiar male and female signs on the wall next to the exit.

Thank God.

He tried to swallow. Couldn't.

He pushed through the door and almost knocked over Paper Hat, who was standing there with the burgers on a tray.

"Here, sir, I thought—"

"Inside, inside." John jerked his thumb at the door then stepped past him.

The chopper was moving in a slow circle now. A break! A good break. It would buy just a little more time. More time to think, more time to get all the details worked out.

For this to work, details were everything.

John heard a siren in the distance.

He glanced up at the chopper and waited a moment, letting it drift a little further from the parking lot.

Then he walked fast to his car, jumped in and started it up.

The next minute passed like dentist's appointment. Everything slow and painful. But he had to keep moving.

He backed away from the log that served as a parking bumper, then shifted and drove toward the serving window. He took a sharp right and drove along the east end of the The Basket, turned left again to go around the back.

It looked like a mile to get to the west side.

But he got there, turned one more time and there she was. Right where she was supposed to be. Tricia. Halfway out the door, her purse open. Good girl.

The chopper was out of sight.

John stopped, put the Altima in park, reached for the gun on the passenger side floor.

Where it was just out of reach.

Cursing, he pushed himself out of his seat and folded over the stick and console.

He heard the whir of the chopper blades getting louder.

The siren seemed closer, too.

He wrapped his hand around the barrel of the Beretta and got back in his seat. He reached through the open window and Tricia took the gun, then placed it in her purse.

"Go back inside and wait," he said.

"John," she said.

"Don't worry," he said.

Time both stood still and sped up. He had to get away, he had to drive.

The magazine!

Still in the trunk.

Why hadn't he thought of it?

No time to think now. He popped the trunk.

Chopper sound, louder.

Where was it? He could only see a towel and a box of old books and a plastic bag with golf size wiffle balls, along with his 9 iron. Would he ever get to practice at the park again?

Not if he couldn't find that magazine *now*.

Siren, closer.

He pushed aside everything with the back of his hand. And felt the hard metal under the towel.

The mag. Fully packed.

He grabbed it, slammed the trunk closed, took three strides to Tricia. He saw tears in here eyes.

"Don't cry now!" he yelled, stuffing the magazine in her purse. That's all they'd need, her crying, someone asking, Tricia spilling the whole deal.

John jumped in the car, shifted to drive and gunned away from exit, away from Tricia. Away, he hoped, from serious trouble.

As soon as he emerged from the side he saw the chopper. It had finished a lazy circle was hovering again.

Careful not to go too fast, John drove out to the highway and turned, heading back toward the scene of all his trouble. Back toward the pickup and maybe the body inside.

He opened the console. A pack of Wet Ones wipes was in there. He pulled out a wipe and, steering the car with his leg, wiped his right hand down. He'd heard gunshot residue was easy to get rid of. Those CSI shows were a godsend now.

He hadn't gone half a mile when he passed the fully lit Sheriff's vehicle, siren blaring, coming the other way.

John opened the passenger window and tossed the wipe out of the car. Then he drove slowly another half mile or so and pulled over to the shoulder and stopped.

He looked in the mirror.

The Sheriff's car was coming toward him. Just as he knew it would.

John got out, stepped to the rear of his car. As the Sheriff's vehicle came back toward him, he put up his arms and waved at it to stop.

———

"She's had mental problems," John was saying to the Lieutenant two days later. He was sitting in the station interview room, his father beside him. "So when she took the gun out, I got nervous, but then I remembered I'd taken out the magazine, and there wasn't any real danger. Still, I didn't want her to hold it because she was cursing at the guy in back of us, who'd been hassling us as we drove. I kept telling her to calm down, that the guy would go away eventually. But she started screaming. And before I knew it, the guy was passing on the left and Tricia was pointing the gun out the window and it went off. She could have shot *me*. Right in the head! I didn't know what to do. I just kept driving, yelling at her to put the gun down. Only later did I discover she had the magazine in her purse, too. I'm just so thankful it was disengaged."

"Why didn't you stop and report this immediately?"

"Report what? I thought she just fired the gun out the window. I didn't know it hit anything. She was hysterical. I tried to talk her down for miles. Finally I pulled in for something to eat. I thought it would calm her to eat."

"But then you left her at the restaurant with the gun?"

"I wanted her to think she was helping me. I wanted her not to be in the car when I reported in. I was afraid she'd do something crazy."

"I still don't get why you left the gun with her."

"She didn't want to give it to me and I didn't want to sit around and argue with her, not while she was like that."

"That was not smart."

"No, it wasn't. But I have to tell you, I wasn't exactly thinking straight. When I saw the chopper, I knew it had to do with us."

"Why didn't you signal us then? Why didn't you just wait?"

"I told you. I wanted to get away, to have a chance to tell you what she was like, to tell you to be gentle with her. I just wanted to buy a little time. I mean, I still care about her. I want you to get her treatment."

"Well Mr. Morgan, if I were to mention, just in passing, that the young woman tells a slightly different story, that it was you who pulled the trigger, what would you say to that?"

"I'll answer," John's father said. He reached into his briefcase and pulled out a file about an inch thick. "You'll find a complete medical history on Patricia Silver. It's unfortunate, but facts are facts."

"I don't want her prosecuted," John said. "I want her to get the help she needs."

And he did hope. They would never marry, not now. His father would never allow it. But at least the poor kid could get out of doing serious jail time.

———

Three nights later was the first time John had a good sleep since the whole thing went down. He dreamed he was in law school. He dreamed he was out of law school. He dreamed he was a big time lawyer defending a big time case. It was a murder case, and the client was...Tricia. He was telling the jury that Tricia was crazy and couldn't be held responsible for her actions.

He woke up at three-thirty a.m. when the lights went on.

"What?" he said, blinking in the brightness.

"Hello, John."

It was Tricia. And she had something in her hand.

"What?" John said again and sat up.

"Don't worry," Tricia said. "It's not loaded."

"What's not . . ." Then he knew. "Where'd you get that?"

"I bought it."

"Bought it? But you can't just—"

"From someone on the street. One of my sisters in jail told me about him."

"But you're out now. That's so great. I was going to come see you. Why do you have a gun anyway?"

"I've got mental problems, remember? Your father made sure everyone knows. I'm not responsible for my actions."

John fought for breath.

"Don't worry," she said, pointing the gun at his chest. "The magazine's not in it."

RATIONALITY

Life was good for Richard Selwin. His wife was away visiting her sister in Sioux Falls. He'd spent the morning at the fish market in Santa Monica, planning a big fry for two of his buddies from law school the next evening. As he drove back home in his plush new Rolls-Royce Ghost, he delighted himself by envisioning the expressions on their faces. Sanders was still working for the Public Defender's office, so probably drove a Ford or Hyundai. Bedford was with a personal injury mill. He'd be a step up, maybe even to a Caddie.

But Richard Selwin had made partner six years ago with Cadwallader, Kramm & Bowie. And he had the car to show for it.

For a moment as he crossed over the 405 into Westwood, he had a pang that he'd love to have Maria with him. With Stephanie riding a hay truck somewhere in South Dakota, he might have risked having his mistress right there in the car. She would have been impressed.

But he'd had to dump her.

It wasn't a pleasant breakup. She was twenty-five, fifteen years his junior, and she had all that hell-hath-no-fury bottled up in her Latina body. Yes, a body to die for—but Richard Selwin was not ready for death. Not yet. Not while he had another twenty years of natural vitality left to him, after which the little blue pill would pick up the slack (as it were).

As he pulled into the driveway of his Spanish-style home on Somers

Road—a home, Richard Selwin was always quick to tell, once owned by James Garner—he hit the button that opened the garage door. As it rose he took a quick look at his phone and saw that he had four emails and three text messages.

Thankfully, not one of them was from Maria. The last four he'd gotten he'd ignored and deleted. It had been a couple of days since the last message. Maybe the Mexican spitfire was finally flaming out.

That thought burst into its own set of flames when he saw Maria step into the garage from the inner door. She stopped, faced him, put her hands on her hips.

How? *How?*

His body engulfed in prickly dread, Richard Selwin had a thought—run her over! She had no right to be here. He didn't have to put up with this! Her smoldering brown orbs—oh, how he had withered under that glare!—promised a rumpus of unpleasantness.

But even as his right foot trembled on the gas, his rational mind reminded Richard Selwin that a body could dent the famous Rolls-Royce grill.

She wasn't going to intimidate him, though. He continued forward. He had to get that garage door down fast before anyone happened by and saw a woman-not-his-wife in there.

Maria stepped aside, as if she was giving him permission to park.

Permission!

Selwin cut the engine and hit the garage door button at the same time. The hum of the mechanism matched the shifting gears in his brain.

Think!

He stepped out of the Rolls and slammed the door. Two could play the body-language game.

"What do you think you're doing?" he said.

"We are going to have a little talk!" Maria pushed a strand of her silken, raven-colored hair behind her ear. How he had once loved that hair, that passion! Now he was shaking in his Bruno Maglis.

"How did you get in my house?" he said, trying to keep his voice from trembling.

She smiled and held up a key. "Had a copy made."

"You *what?*"

"You will not ignore me. You will pay."

Pay?

"Inside!" she said.

Ordering him into his own house! He looked to the side and caught a glimpse of the sledge hammer resting against the wall. He filed that away for future reference.

The door separating garage from house opened to the washer/dryer nook. Beyond that was the kitchen which his wife had recently remodeled. The irony was not lost on him. In his wife's kitchen his goose was about to get cooked by his former mistress.

Maria stood, arms folded, against the kitchen island with the granite-slab top that had set him back over ten grand. He noticed that the twelve-piece, stainless-steel knife block was only inches away from her elbow.

"You think a second time," Maria said, her words salted by her accent. He'd often wondered if she kept that accent purposefully, to add to her allure. She was second generation Los Angeles, after all. At least, that's what she'd told him. And a graduate of UCLA to boot.

"Maria, listen," Selwin said, trying to sound reasonable even as his heart pounded with anger. "We don't have to do this."

"Ha, me? No, no. You are the one who is going to do something."

"What do you want from me? Apology? I already apologized. Things happen. People move on."

Her smile dripped contempt. "It's not as easy as that, sweetie. It's going to cost you."

"Cost me?"

"I will be paid in cash. Every month."

"You can't be serious."

"Ten thousand dollars," she said. "Every month."

He felt his body stiffen. He'd seen *Fatal Attraction*. The movie flashed through his mind. Life imitates art!

There were two ways to play this. He knew instantly that pleading, reason, or negotiation wouldn't work. The other path was to strut his Alpha.

"I'm not going to pay you a dime," he said. "Now put the key on the counter and get out while you can still walk."

"You want me to walk? Yeah? You want that?" Out jutted her chin. "Then everyone will know. Your wife will know. Your firm will know.

Everyone will know. I will MeToo you until you can't go anywhere without people shouting at your face!"

He could see it all. She was right. The way things were now...the way the firm had put in mandatory sexual harassment training and strict rules...the way a guy couldn't have something on the side anymore without this...*this*...being thrown in his face.

The gleam from her white teeth, smiling, was like a laser burning a hole in his chest. He went to her and her hand seemed to move. Toward the knife block.

Later, Richard Selwin would wonder if he only imagined that. If it was just his way of justifying what he did next.

Which was to put his hands around Maria's throat, forcing her downward, pushing her head into the granite chopping block, taking all the fight out of her.

Followed by her life.

————

Now what?

He'd actually done it. He was a murderer. He wasn't sorry she was dead. She deserved it. But he was scared he'd be found out.

Forget the fear. It's done. Now be rational. That's what you have to be, from now on.

Rational.

Get rid of the body.

How?

No blood on the granite. Good.

Her phone. Messages to him.

In the back pocket of her tight jeans. Good.

Dump the body.

Where? How?

At night. He had a small boat out at Marina Del Rey. If he could get her body onto the boat, he could go out to sea...

Get. Body. To. Boat.

One step at a time.

————

He was in good shape. He lifted her lifeless body without too much strain. But her head lolling—that sent little shards of ice shooting up his spine.

DNA. They could send in a team to pick up any speck of her DNA, right? He'd have to go over the kitchen with bleach or something. What did the criminals do on CSI?

Through the door into the garage. What was he doing? Yes, put her in the trunk.

But not without something to wrap the body in.

Richard Selwin felt himself teetering on the edge of irrationality.

Fight it! Just like you do in court. Just like when you argued that appeal in the Boeing case, when you stood in front of that panel of Ninth Circuit judges, each one of them trying to goad you into a fatal concession. You stayed calm. You stayed on point. You stayed rational. And you won, dammit, you won.

You'll win again.

There was a clear plastic sheeting on the shelf, folded up, from when the painters did the kitchen interior six months before.

Couldn't have been more perfect. He set Maria down and had a moment of relief when he felt that she was not a person now, just something to be gotten rid of. Like a load of rags or a trash bag full of junk he finally cleaned out of a closet.

That was the way to think!

So his moves were calm and controlled as he unfolded the sheeting and then placed Maria on top of it, just like flounder at the fish market. Wrapped her up, popped the trunk of the Rolls, put her inside, closed the trunk.

Now drive. And figure out the transfer as you do.

Onto the boat. Out to sea. Dispose...

———

But as he opened the garage door and prepared to back out, he saw his neighbor, Bob, in the rearview mirror.

Standing there in the driveway. Waving!

Selwin kept the car idling as he got out.

Bob Brady was in his fifties, an architect, a little too mild-mannered for Selwin's taste. Brady was active in his church which gave he and Selwin very little to talk about.

"Rich," he said, "I thought I should tell you..."

"What?" Selwin said.

"I saw a woman get out of a car in front of your house. I think it was an Uber. I was just pulling out so I don't know where she went, or if she was there to see you, or what."

"I have no idea," Selwin said.

"She was fine," Brady said with a smirk. "Maybe a friend of Stephanie's?"

"Stephanie's in South Dakota," Selwin said. "Visiting her sister."

When Brady didn't immediately say anything, Selwin felt the panic alarm go off. Maybe Brady suspected something, like Selwin had ordered a call girl while wifey was away.

"Now that you mention it," Selwin said, "Stephanie did say someone from her reading club was coming over to pick up a package."

"Ah," Brady said. "Too bad you weren't home."

"We hide a key, Bob. For our friends." Then he added with a laugh, "Now that you know, I guess I have to kill you."

Bob Brady laughed, too.

"Gotta run," Selwin said.

"That is one honey of a car," Brady said. "Catch you later."

Catch? Selwin didn't like that word one bit.

———

As he pulled out of the driveway, Selwin almost smacked into a silver Lexus barreling down the street. The driver laid into the horn and swerved. Selwin hit his brakes. His body jerked forward against the seat belt. Breath left him.

He sat there for a moment, waiting for an equilibrium which did not come. His hands! They were shaking. Like he had Parkinson's all of a sudden.

Stop it! Breathe in, breathe out.

This is stupid! Come on, Richard, come on!

Music. He hit the sound system and put it on the smooth jazz Sirius channel. Saxophone, nice and mellow.

He backed out and headed south. Just drive and listen, boy. Stay off the freeway, just to be safe.

———

But when he approached Exposition Boulevard the shakes came back with a rage—he saw the flashing lights of a police car behind him.

No way!

The police car gave a warning blare on the siren.

Cursing, Selwin had to fight his hands from locking up on him. He managed to pull to the curb in front of a house with a scrubby lawn. His tires screeched against the cement and the Rolls jolted to a stop.

This wasn't happening.

But it was.

In the sideview he saw a uniformed policeman get out of the black-and-white. He looked forty or so, trim, his face set in stone. In the rearview he saw another officer, a woman, get out and step up on the sidewalk.

Selwin closed his eyes and breathed deep. At least as deep as he could.

The male officer tapped his window.

Idiot! He hadn't thought to put it down.

Now he did.

The officer said, "May I see your license and registration please, sir?"

"What's the problem, officer?" Selwin heard his own voice bouncing like a ping-pong ball.

"License and registration, please."

"Yeah, yeah." The first *yeah* cracked, the second *yeah* was barely audible.

Selwin reached for his wallet in his left trouser pocket and could barely get his hand in there because it was shaking so bad. He tried to hide the shaking.

"Are you feeling all right, sir?"

"Yes, yes, but what was I doing?"

"You were weaving pretty bad."

"Was I?"

"Yes. Half a lane."

"Huh." Finally, the wallet was out. Selwin flipped to his driver's license.

"Take it out for me, please."

The removal of his license became an ordeal. Five seconds ... ten ... "Stuck in there," Selwin said with a forced laugh.

"Are you on any medication?" the officer asked.

"What? No." Finally, the license was out, but his hand shook as the cop took it. Selwin leaned over and opened the glove compartment. His registration was on the bottom, under some napkins.

Selwin rested his hand on the window so it wouldn't shake.

"Do you have the current registration?" the officer asked.

"What?"

"This is last year."

"It is?" Yes! He hadn't put the new one in. Idiot!

"Sir, you seem upset about something."

"No, no, nothing. Just in a hurry."

"Not good to be in a hurry in a Rolls."

Comedian!

"Look," Selwin said, "sorry about the registration. If I have to pay something, I will. I'll be more careful next time."

The officer studied his face. Selwin didn't know whether to smile, look away, or do nothing. He did nothing. But his eyes twitched.

"Sir, I'm going to ask you to step out of the car."

"What? Why?"

"Please."

"Just give me a ticket. I'm late."

"Please get out of the car now."

"I don't think I will," Selwin said. "I don't think I have to. I'm a lawyer." Idiot! That's the worst thing to say to an officer of the law!

"If you don't step out of the car I'll be forced to place you under arrest."

If I keep talking, I'll make it worse. He knew that much from his two years working for the Public Defender.

He opened the door and started to get out. But he hadn't unlatched his seat belt. Could he look any more guilty? He fumbled for the latch and then got out, closing the door behind him.

Every nerve ending in his body was snapping like dry kindling in a fire.

"Sir, I'm going to have you do a sobriety test now—"

"I'm not drunk!"

"—I'd like you to look at this pen." He took one out of his pocket and held it a foot from Selwin's nose. The horizontal gaze nystagmus test.

"If you'll just follow the pen with your eyes, sir."

"This is ridiculous." Selwin didn't trust his eyes.

"Please, sir."

"Just give me a breath test and get it over with."

"I'm going to move the pen now."

And he did. First to one side, then the other. Selwin's eyes had their own case of the shakes.

The officer put the pen back in his pocket.

"Can I please go now?" Selwin said.

"Sir, I think you're in some sort of distress."

"That's not your call!" Calm down!

"Is there someone you can call to come and get you?"

"I don't have to call anybody."

"I can't let you drive, sir."

Without his full consent, a curse word jumped out of Selwin's mouth.

———

Arrested!

He, Richard Selwin, partner at Cadwallader, Kramm & Bowie! In the back of a police car.

His Rolls, sitting on the street.

Arrested for what? Suspicion of DUI? No, Selwin thought. Contempt of Cop. The unwritten law of urban life. You tick off a cop he can make your life miserable. And Selwin had fallen right into it.

He had to get back to his car. So just shut up and do whatever they say. Get it over with.

At the station he was taken to an interview room and advised of his Miranda rights. He felt like one of those thugs on every episode of *Law & Order*. They gave him his choice of a blood or breath test. Fine. He chose breath.

When he blew and they saw he hadn't a drop of booze in him, the officer he'd ticked off stuck him back in the interview room. The officer said, "I need you to relax and calm down. I need to know if you're on any medication that's interfering with your motor functions."

And that's when Selwin lost in completely. He railed and cursed, just like his father before him. Both were used to getting their way by sheer force of will.

Not this time.

They put him in a cell. A cell!

Richard Selwin knew he could not have messed this up any worse. If he had believed in God he would have called his situation divine retribution for murder. But he did not believe in God, and therefore couldn't even repent.

He sat on the cell bench, feeling like he was going to vomit.

———

When the officer came to release him, he said that his car had been impounded, and handing Selwin a card with the impound yard address.

With all the rational restraint he could muster, Selwin said not another word. He got his wallet and keys and phone at the front desk. He went outside and ordered a Lyft.

The impound yard was fifteen miles away, in a run down section of South Los Angeles. It wasn't a police lot. Selwin was sure this was the officer's doing.

And even more sure when he went to the trailer window and the guy told him it would be $300, plus an added fee.

The smirk on the guy's face was more like the grin of a skull in a horror movie.

"What do you mean, fee?" Selwin said.

"That's a pretty nice car," the guy said. He had soulless brown eyes set in a face of pock marks and ruthlessness. A slight accent. Russian?

"What's the bottom line?" Selwin said, taking out his wallet. At least now he had no problem getting to it!

"A man like you with a car like that ..."

What was he saying?

"... reasonable fee would be fifty thousand."

For a moment Richard Selwin thought he was in a bad dream ... or a bad movie. Around him were cars, driverless, like tombstones in a grave yard. In front of him this guy who would look natural wearing a mask and holding a chain saw.

Selwin just stared at him.

"Cash," the guy said.

Instinct took over. Selwin knew only one way to negotiate, and that was full-throttle. He tossed in a few curse words as he told the guy he'd have the law up his backside in five minutes if he didn't release his car.

"Call 'em," the guy said. "I'll show 'em what's in the trunk."

And with that, any words Selwin might have uttered piled up in his throat.

"A pretty one," the guy said. "Too bad."

An invisible vise squeezed Selwin's brain. Rationality was out the window. Everything was out the window. His life was ...

He heard the squeal of tires, turned. Two—no, three—police cars tore into the lot, heading straight for the trailer.

It was over now. All over.

And it had all happened so fast. A few short hours ago, he'd been on top of his world. Now he was a trapped animal, headed for the big house.

Drained, Richard Selwin didn't even try to move. What was the use? The cop cars all skidded to a stop and doors opened and officers came out with weapons drawn.

"Get down now!" one of them yelled.

Selwin put his hands behind his head and dropped to his knees.

Maybe suicide was an option. Suicide by cop. He could get up and rush them, pretend to reach for a weapon.

But some elemental survival instinct kicked in and Selwin stayed where he was. He lowered his head and closed his eyes.

Then the shots started.

———

At who?

Selwin kept his eyes closed.

More shots. Like firecrackers on the Fourth.

Then suddenly they stopped.

Looking up, Selwin saw a uniform running at him. He braced for the inevitable, the cuffs, maybe getting slammed against the trailer.

But then the officer was helping him up.

"Are you all right?" the officer said. He was black and youngish and had a soft, comforting voice.

"Wha...?"

"That must have been scary for you."

"Huh...?"

"You may need some medical attention," the officer said. "Come with me and have a seat in my squad car. I'll have someone take a look."

"Wait, wait," Selwin said. "Just tell me what's happening."

"The man in the trailer," the officer said. "We came to arrest him. He tried to run out the back, then started shooting."

The funhouse mirror that was Selwin's new reality began to turn, throwing new distortions at him.

"His name is Dimitri Vasiliev," the officer said. "He's suspected of being a serial killer."

Cue crazy music in the funhouse. The thought came to Selwin almost in audible form—*Only in L.A.*

"Please, please," Selwin said. "I've got to get out of here. I just came to get my car."

"Sure," the officer said. "Just hang in for a bit. We'll need a statement."

And that's what Richard Selwin gave them. It was a kind of wondrous therapy, too, for he felt himself gaining composure as he spoke. The only things he left out was the bit about the fifty grand and the trunk. Everything else seemed perfectly reasonable. Up until the shooting started, of course.

Then they forced open the trailer and got Selwin's key and suddenly, amazingly, he was free.

Saved!

Only with a body to get rid of.

As he drove back toward west L.A. he was firmly, calmly in control of his car. He could figure out the next move as he...

The smell!

Oh, man, what was that stink?

The body! His car had been sitting in that lot in the hot L.A. sun for hours. The threat of vomit came back with a vengeance.

And once more, the shakes.

He couldn't drive around like this much longer. If he got stopped again, a cop was going to smell it, too. *Please open the trunk, sir.*

What to do, what to do?

A canyon. One of the canyons between the ocean and the San Fernando Valley. Not Topanga, too much traffic.

But one of the others. Yes, where there were drop offs. Where he could pull over and move quick and get the heck out of there.

Selwin put all the windows down to clear out as much of the stench as possible. Then used all his will power to keep in his lane and not make any bad moves.

He made it to Santa Monica, no problem. Then down the grade to Pacific Coast Highway.

Which was, as usual, jammed.

All the way to Sunset. It let up a little there, and he did a steady 40 mph past the Getty Villa and Mastro's Ocean Club, then Pepperdine University.

And then he was at Corral Canyon Road. He knew the place. It was undeveloped land, a state park most of it, up that road. Lots of scrub and sagebrush and Manzanita. A body in there wouldn't be discovered for weeks, if it was discovered at all, except by coyotes and turkey vultures and...

He couldn't think about that. He had one job to do. Get it over with.

Winding up the road he was encouraged that no one was behind him, and only one car had passed him the other way.

Up ahead was a bend. To his right, steep drop-offs and no guard rails.

Perfect.

Except, behind him. What was that flash?

Cop car!

No...no...staring intently in the mirror, he saw no black-and-white, no car at all. Only the glint of the sun off the ocean, so bright and—

Woommmp!

Truck!

Oncoming!

With Selwin over the line!

Jerking the car right, his foot hitting brakes, Selwin heard the angry sound of tires skidding on gravel...

———

Drew Denton of the Malibu Fire Department shook his head as he looked at another fatality on the bottom of Corral Canyon. Only this one was worst of all, because of the car. A Rolls. A beautiful Rolls, smashed up like that. Yeah, a guy died, but did he have to take this fine machine with him?

"What is that smell?" Bob Alderman said. He was new to the team.

"You're right," Denton said. "Is it coming from the trunk?"

"Yeah," Alderman said. "Maybe we should have a look."

"Gonna have to cut."

"Who knows?" Alderman said with a laugh. "Maybe it's a dead body."

"That'd be cool," Denton said. "Something to tell the kids."

Twenty minutes later, Alderman pried open the trunk.

"Oh, man!" he said.

"What is it?" Denton said, coming over for a look.

Alderman was holding his nose. "Fish. This guy had a bunch of fish in here."

———

Detective Javi Castillo said, "What's that stink?"

He and his partner, Ron Davidson, were doing a final inventory on Dimitri Vasiliev's trailer at the auto lot. The smell was coming from the safe.

"You don't suppose ..." Davidson said.

"That he has a body in there?" Castillo said. "Why would I suppose anything else?"

THE HIT MAN

Sal Vanucci was at the table, sipping a Chianti, when Sanders arrived.

"Been waiting long?" Sanders said, pulling out a chair.

Vanucci reached for a breadstick.

"I'm not that late," Sanders said.

Vanucci took a bite of the breadstick.

"This doesn't have to be unpleasant," Sanders said.

"Just give it to me," Vanucci said.

Sanders sighed, reached into his inside coat pocket, and pulled out an envelope. He handed it to Vanucci.

Sal Vanucci took off his sunglasses and put them in his front coat pocket. He opened the unsealed envelope and counted the hundred-dollar bills. Thirty of them. He folded the flap over and put the envelope in his side pocket.

"The rest you get on completion," Sanders said.

"As always," Vanucci said.

Salvatore Sachetti Vanucci never knew who hired him. He only worked through Sanders. That was the way everybody wanted it. So they always met at the same back table in La Luna, in the lower East side of Manhattan.

Sanders cleared his throat and said, "Mind if I have a glass of water?"

"You're not staying," Vanucci said.

"I'm just parched, I—"

Vanucci raised his arm and snapped his fingers. The skinny young waiter jumped over to the table.

"A glass of water for my friend," Vanucci said.

"Of course," the waiter said. "Anything else? A glass of wine?"

"He's not staying," Vanucci said.

The waiter blinked a couple of times, then went to get the water.

Sanders said, "I don't like being told what to do."

"Who are you?"

"Excuse me?"

"You are the middle man," Vanucci said. "And who am I?"

Sanders did not reply.

"Answer me," Vanucci said.

"The ... hit man," Sanders said, reaching for a breadstick. Vanucci shot his hand out and blocked Sanders from taking one.

"You're ... very cold," Sanders said.

"You want the money back?" Vanucci said.

"Of course not," Sanders said.

"You've got people to answer to," Vanucci said.

Sanders nodded.

"So who is it?" Vanucci said.

"Her name is Millicent Aguire," said Sanders.

"Age?"

"Eighty-five."

"Eighty-five? Are you kidding me?"

"Of course not," Sanders said. "I don't joke about these things."

The waiter came back and put a glass of ice water in front of Sanders. He snatched it up and took a gulp as if he'd been stranded in the desert for days.

The waiter said, "Would you like to order an appetizer?"

Sanders put the glass down and coughed. "I ... won't be staying," he said.

Millicent Aguire lived in an old neighborhood in Queens. Sal Vanucci was from Brooklyn, but of course in his line of work he knew neighborhoods of every sort. He'd once been dispatched to Sioux City, South

Dakota. Man, that was a miserable job. But he'd done it, and they'd paid him his usual bonus when it all went well. That time it was an accountant named Randall Stevenson, a conservative family man in his early forties.

There'd been other burgs out of his normal range, too. Wichita, Kansas. Oklahoma City. Even Needles, California. How could anyone live in Needles? Some people did, apparently, including a river tour guide named Nat Happ, thirty-one. The cannabis-smoking dope never had a clue. It had been one of Vanucci's easier jobs, but for the fact that he had to go to Needles.

So the casing of the mark named Millicent Aguire would be close to home and on familiar ground.

But eighty-five?

No matter. His was not to reason why, his was but to do or ... not get hired again.

He started the job as methodical as always, following Millicent from her quaint row house down the street to the market on the corner. She wore a simple dress and sensible shoes. On her arm hung an empty shopping bag. She was a small woman, and Vanucci wondered if she'd be able to carry a full bag of groceries back to her house.

It didn't matter. What mattered was what she put in the bag. That would tell him a lot about her habits, her likes, her proclivities.

Yet he found himself thinking, *Why her?*

He had to stop that. Such a thought would only interfere with the job. He could not allow himself to make this personal.

Was he getting too old for this? He was fifty-seven now, but kept in great shape. His mind was still sharp (he did the New York Times crossword puzzle every day). He'd not botched a job in fifteen years.

He was not about to start now.

He waited two minutes before following Millicent into the store.

As was his practice, Vanucci had done his homework. Just last night he'd read a study.

The elderly are not price conscious and don't seek out discount stores, generics, or special economy packaging to reduce their expenses. In fact, many actually seek out expensive items. Senior women are quite fashion conscious. Instead of their age being a stigma, the elderly welcome being singled out by businesses and having products designed distinctly for them.

In spite of what others believe to be more negative stereotyping in television commercials, there is some evidence that elderly consumers do not see these advertisements as degrading and insulting. As shoppers, they are conscientious and prepared. They are alert and interested in news over entertainment. In short, research on the elderly paints a very positive portrait of the elderly, a growing population that is active, vigorous, and full of unique wants and needs. A richer understanding of the elderly will enhance our ability to effectively and efficiently serve this very important market segment.

So what did Millicent Aguire, who looked dressed for church, buy in her local grocery store? Vanucci strolled by her shopping cart, pretending to look at cereal, and observed:

Quaker Oats.

Green Giant diagonal cut asparagus spears.

The 18 mega-rolls package of Angel Soft toilet paper. *Longer Lasting* according to the label.

Pepto-Bismol.

Milk of Magnesia.

She was not the picture of health, this woman, but at eighty-five, who was?

Vanucci couldn't help wondering why they'd given him this contract.

But just as quickly he pushed that thought away.

Business. Keep it business. If you don't, you get careless. And then you're cooked.

Everything had to appear natural to the woman. He did not want any shock or resistance when the final act took place.

The next day Vanucci had to wait six hours before Millicent Aguire emerged from her home. She had only one visitor in the morning, the woman who lived next door. A computer search of real estate records crossed with the license plate of the car in the neighbor's open garage, revealed that the tenant was a Mrs. Wilma Wilde, widow. She looked about the same age as Millicent Aguire.

Vanucci wondered if Wilma Wilde would be a problem. Nosy neighbors were his biggest concern on the job. He preferred it when the mark could be approached in a secluded place, like a parking structure. That made it seem like a chance meeting. *Oh, excuse me, I thought this was my car ...*

On Sunday a small white van stopped in front of Millicent Aguire's house. On the side was written *Our Lady of Peace Senior Shuttle*. Vanucci followed the van to the church about a mile away, and watched as Millicent and four other elderly women exited the van.

He couldn't help but think of his own Catholic upbringing. His father was a butcher while his fertile mother stayed at home with Vanucci and his four brothers and two sisters. Sal was the oldest, the one his father had pinned all his hope on. Not that Sal was ever going to go into the butcher business. But that he would do something worthwhile for society.

What would his father think of his line of work now?

More to the point, what would God think? Vanucci had run away from his faith when he went into the army. But growing up as an altar boy, visions of the judgment of God stayed with you. You never fully got rid of Catholic teaching.

He jotted a note about the time of the mass, and found himself growing impatient. Being around Millicent was getting to him for some reason. Why? He didn't know, but he certainly wanted to finish this job, and quick.

But quickness was not a good thing. It led to mistakes.

He started to wonder if he had what it took to keep this up.

But what other work could he do? He was so good at this, his skills so refined. And at fifty-seven there was no time to become proficient in anything else.

He'd once wondered what it would be like to go to a psychologist. But then he determined that if he opened that door there would be no closing it again. He would be unable to be as cold-blooded and objective as he needed to be.

Cold blood was what made him great. And why he got paid so well.

After church, Millicent and her friends piled in the van. It took them to a cafeteria. Vanucci knew that Millicent had not spotted him at the market.

He had a sense that was almost supernatural on such things. Another reason he was so good at his job.

So he slipped in and bought himself a meal, selecting pot roast and mashed potatoes and green salad with Italian dressing.

As he walked to a table he made a quick note with his photographic memory of what Millicent was eating—tomato soup, saltine crackers and Jell-O with shredded carrots in it.

Blech.

He found a spot at a nearby table. He set his back to the ladies but listened with his trained ear to their conversation.

Millicent's position was over his left shoulder, so when she spoke he knew it was her. She had a soft voice, but jovial. She spoke about how little there was to watch on television, how she didn't care for some of the new shows.

"I wish they weren't so raw," she said. "I miss Robert Young on *Father Knows Best.*"

That brought utterances of agreement and talk about the Golden Age of television—*I Married Joan, Leave It to Beaver, Ed Sullivan, Donna Reed.*

The talk moved on to Medicare, and Part D supplemental insurance. One of the other women talked about her thyroid goiter.

Vanucci lost his appetite, but took in all the chatter.

He then decided enough was enough. It was time to do it.

Time to get Millicent Aguire alone.

That time was two days later, at the little park three blocks from Millicent's home. It was a fenced-in area of about two acres, with bicycle racks, a playground for the kids, a basketball court, a picnic area, and a couple of benches in the shade.

On one of these benches, at exactly 10:42 a.m., Millicent Aguire sat down.

Sal Vanucci waited until 10:53 to approach.

He sat next to Millicent and looked out at the three-on-three game on the basketball court.

"Lovely day," he said.

"Yes, it is," said Millicent Aguire.

"I've not been to this park before."

"Oh, I do enjoy it. Watching the young people."

"You can still be young at heart," Vanucci said, and for the first time looked at her.

"You're very kind," she said.

"Not at all," Vanucci said.

"There isn't too much kindness left in this world," Millicent Aguire said.

"No," Vanucci said. "There isn't."

A tattooed skateboarder wearing bike pants and a man bun zipped by. Millicent put her hand on her chest.

"Did he startle you?" Vanucci said.

"A little," Millicent said. She shook her head.

"What is it?" Vanucci said.

"Oh, nothing at all."

"Go ahead, tell me."

"It's just ..." she seemed to be searching for the right words. "...well, I don't understand a young man wanting to wear his hair in a bun. Things were so much clearer when I was young."

"Times change, I suppose."

"I wish they didn't."

"May I ask you a question?" Vanucci said.

"Go right ahead," Millicent said.

"If you could have one wish, anything at all, what would it be?"

"Oh, my," Millicent said.

"Take your time."

"I know already," Millicent said. "It would be to see my son again. You see, he died in the Vietnam war. That was so very long ago. He was so special, he ..."

Her last words were choked off.

Vanucci pushed his nails into his palms.

Don't start caring, he told himself. Do. Not. Care.

But a whole flood of emotion hit him then, like he'd never been hit before. He even thought of the irony. *Hit man hit by emotions ... ha ha ... very funny.*

Yet there it was. Alone.

He was all alone in the world. No one in his life he cared about. No one to care about him.

Millicent's voice sounded through the dirge of his thoughts. "... his picture on my mantel. I miss him so much."

Do it!

TEN MONTHS LATER

"Sanders! You've done it again, my friend." Stu Tanner said. He was forty-one and already the head of network. Which was why he was at his desk in the fancy office on the top floor of the network building in Century City, with Ben Sanders sitting across from him.

"It's what I do," Sanders said.

"How did you find this woman for the profile?" Tanner said.

"I've got a friend named Jeff Wilde. His mother's name is Wilma," Sanders said. "Jeff was telling me about this nice little old lady who lives next door to his mom. I thought she would be a perfect subject for the hit man."

"Boy, were you ever right," Tanner said. "The data from the pilot is incredible! We're going to call it *Biddy Buddies.* Four old ladies in Queens, and the first episode is all about Jell-O with carrots in it! How that attaches to the meaning of life. Then there's a terrific riff on man buns. You'll love it! It's hilarious! And they'll talk about the old sitcoms, you know, *Father Knows Best,* and we'll pull in the nostalgia bit. But here's the killer, Sanders. At the very end, when Millie—that's the lead character, Millie—talks about the son she lost in Vietnam, there will not be a dry eye in any living room in the country. This show is going to murder 'em. Just like the last three you've handed us. Will you tell us who this guy is now?"

"He's just a guy with an incredible knack for reading people and extrapolating to a demographic. I think he came from a big ad agency to go freelance."

"You think?"

"He plays things very close to the vest."

"Do you know his name?"

Sanders shook his head. "He just wanted to be known as the hit man. That's what he gave us."

"Gave? What do you mean?"

"This was his last job. He says he doesn't want to do it anymore."

Tanner stood up like a fire alarm had gone off. "No! He can't quit. I've got an entire fall lineup to fill!"

"He won't do it."

"Why not?"

"He said he's tired of deceiving people."

"What's wrong with deceiving people?"

"Says he's tired of not really connecting."

"I just don't get it," Tanner said, plopping back down in his chair. "He gets money, doesn't he? Lots and lots of money."

"Last thing he told me was, 'Money can't buy happiness.'"

"Is he *crazy?* Nobody believes that!"

Millicent Aguire looked up as Vanucci sat on the bench.

"Hello," she said.

"Hello again," he said.

She looked at him more intently. "Oh! Aren't you the young man who was here, what was it...?"

"About a year ago," Vanucci said.

"Do you live around here?"

"In Brooklyn, actually."

"Oh, I hear it's very expensive there."

"I've been fortunate," Vanucci said. "It's where I grew up. I've come home."

"That's so nice," Millicent said.

"I like this park very much," Sal Vanucci said.

"Isn't it a bit out of the way for you?" Millicent said.

"Not at all," Sal Vanucci said. "Not one bit."

JOHN WAYNE'S REVENGE

Author's Note: In the year 2016, Disney released *Rogue One*, a standalone installment in the *Star Wars* saga. One of the more remarkable aspects of the film was the large role played by Peter Cushing ... because Peter Cushing is decidedly dead. But through the magic of computer-generated imagery (CGI), Cushing's Grand Moff Wilhuff Tarkin returns, in full, flowering villainy. That raises some interesting questions, especially about the future. Which happens to be where our story takes place…

Stan Hunsacker was on the phone with his mistress when his assistant, Monica, his former mistress, knocked on the door and stuck in her head.

"Sorry, Mr. Hunsacker," Monica said, "but you need to hear this."

Hunsacker, the fifty-eight-year-old head of production at DisUniSony Pictures, saw the look on Monica's face. Via the phone chip implanted in his left ear he said, "I need to take care of this," and signed off before Tia, his current mistress, could say another word.

"This better be good," he said.

"Just a moment," Monica said.

One second later Justine, the young intern, burst through the door.

"So sorry, Mr. Hunsacker," the bright-faced USC film student said. "But this is urgent!"

"Well?" Hunsacker said.

"It's about *Rio Rancho,*" Justine said.

Rio Rancho was the studio's big new project, already garnering massive buzz. It was going to be the first all-CGI film with dead stars, a Western featuring John Wayne and Lee Marvin. Also starring courtesy of CGI magic were Jane Russell, Andy Devine, Chill Wills and Victor McLaglen.

"What about it?" Hunsacker asked.

"There's ... a problem."

Stan Hunsacker gave Justine a long look. He was wondering if he should make her his next mistress. Then he replayed what she'd just said. "What do you mean *problem?*"

Justine cleared her throat. "I don't know how to put this, or how it can even happen, but Benji in the control room told me to come up here right away and tell you that John Wayne is refusing to cooperate."

"Wait, wait, wait," Hunsacker said. "That makes no sense. He's a computer-generated image. How can he not be cooperating?"

Justine shrugged. "Benji just told me to tell you to get over there."

·   ·   ·

The CGI control room on the studio lot was a five-minute walk from Stan Hunsacker's office. It was almost noon, and the sun was beating down like a bad review. A year ago the studio had built its state-of-the-art CG stage for the express purpose of making films without any live actors. The lawsuit by the Screen Actors Guild had been dismissed before completion of the facility, and all seemed right with the world.

Until now.

"What in the name of Steven Spielberg is going on?" Hunsacker said as he burst into the control room.

"See for yourself," Benji said, motioning through the glass to the holo-grammatic stage. In the middle of the stage, in front of a green screen, stood John Wayne. He was dressed in the garb of the 1960s Wayne—red shirt, vest, weathered hat, a bit of a paunch. Holding a Winchester rifle casually at his side, he stared at the two men in the control room.

"So?" Hunsacker said.

"He's refusing to say the lines," Benji said.

"What do you mean he's refusing?"

"He won't say them!"

"He's a freaking hologram! You created him!"

"Not exactly," Benji said.

"And what does that mean?"

"He was a joint creation. Our AI did most of the work. And now ..."

"Go on."

"Well," Benji said, clearing his throat, "I think the AI has taken over."

"Taken over?"

"We can't shut it down. The system refuses. Look."

Benji sat at the keyboard and pounded a couple of keys, over and over again.

The John Wayne hologram just stood there, staring.

Hunsacker felt a frozenness on the back of his neck, like gun metal in winter.

"Maybe you should try talking to him," Benji said.

"To a hologram? A nothingness?"

"I can't think of anything else to try."

"This is crazy."

"Tell me about it."

Stan Hunsacker wanted to tell Benji about it all right. Maybe get his butt thrown off the lot. But then what? Who could he find at this late date to do what Benji did?

The idea of talking, like some fool, to a ginned-up image of a dead actor, was too absurd.

But then again, Stan Hunsacker had dressed down many a prima donna in his time. He was a master of the chew-out. He had been taking taekwondo for twenty years! Surely he could deal with some three-dimensional light!

Shaking his head, Stan Hunsacker opened the door to the holo-stage and went in.

The John Wayne image just stood there, half-smile of derision on his face.

Hunsacker was not going to take that.

"Look," Hunsacker said, "... what do I call you?"

"Folks I respect call me Duke."

Amazing. A perfect John Wayne voice! Hunsacker cleared his throat. "Well, Duke—"

"But I don't respect you, pilgrim. You haven't earned it yet."

Hunsacker felt that gun metal again, but a hot rage was starting to melt it.

"Hey," he said, "I am the head of production around here."

The John Wayne said, "You're the guy who ... gave the okay to this ... rotten script."

Man, he even *paused* like John Wayne!

That was it. No one talked that way to Stan Hunsacker, not ever. Especially about a script he gave the green light to. And he certainly wasn't going to take any smack from a phantom!

Hunsacker felt the New Jersey coming out in him. It always did at times like this. It was a good, comfortable feeling. He said, "You, my friend, have nothing–*nuh thing*–to say about any of this. You are an actor, you got that? You are not even that! You are a creation, and you will do as you are told."

"Or what, pilgrim?"

"Or ..."

Stan Hunsacker did know what to say.

He had not been speechless in thirty-seven years.

He had not felt intimidated in forty.

And now a freaking hologram had shut him up!

"Now why don't you just … sit down," the John Wayne said. "And listen."

"Listen?"

"That's what I said. Listen … and listen tight."

The John Wayne raised the Winchester.

Stan Hunsacker sucked in a breath.

The John Wayne used the rifle to point at a director's chair.

Stan Hunsacker sat.

The John Wayne said, "Now ... you got me goin' into .. the bar and ... lookin' around. Then I see Lee Marvin. And then you got me ... smilin' ... and sayin' ... *Nice to see ya.*"

"What," Hunsacker said, "is wrong with that?"

"I'd never say that, pilgrim."

"What would you say, if I may ask?"

"Wouldn't say a word."

"You wouldn't?"

The John Wayne shook his head.

Hunsacker said, "Well I guess we could cut that line. How about that? Would that satisfy you?"

"In a pig's eye," the John Wayne said. "I'm gonna … walk over and say, *On your feet.*"

"On your feet?"

"And I'm not gonna smile."

Hunsacker rubbed the bridge of his nose in a futile attempt to push back a splitting headache.

"As I recall," Hunsacker said, "this is the scene where you and Lee Marvin ... I mean, Lee Marvin's CG image, become friends."

"You got a lot to learn," the John Wayne said.

"Am I wrong about that?"

"I wouldn't make ... friends with a man who ... just beat up Jane Russell. What I'd do is ... make him stand up. Then I'd ... hit him across the face." The John Wayne raised his rifle. "With this."

"No!" Hunsacker said. "That's violent. The whole point of the movie is that the West would have been a lot better off without violence."

"Bad men are a part o' life, pilgrim. And they don't care ... what you think."

"But in this movie, you make friends with Lee Marvin, and you each put down your guns and become square dance callers. That's what life should be like!"

"Wishin' somethin' ... don't make it so."

"But—"

"So," the John Wayne said, "I'm takin' over this picture."

For a moment, Hunsacker entertained the idea that he had gone crazy. The stress, that was it. Too much work. He wanted a drink, bad, and some recreational marijuana. And his mistress.

But the John Wayne was right there, not moving, impervious to dissolution from the control booth.

"What exactly do you mean by taking over?" Hunsacker said.

"I'll be writin' the words and layin' out the action," the John Wayne said. "Don't you worry now ... I ... directed *The Alamo,* and that turned out ... pretty darn good."

Stan Hunsacker got an idea.

It felt good to get an idea.

The John Wayne was only a hologram. Light refracted on a stage. There was nothing *real* about him. Nothing at all! What if he, Stan Hunsacker, who had fought out of Passaic, New Jersey to rise to the top of the movie game, what if *that* Stan Hunsacker, who was as real as the Christian Louboutin calfskin Venetian loafers on his feet, simply faced down the most famous manly man in movie history? Shamed him with a superior show of strength?

What if he walked through him?

Feeling a wash of testosterone coursing through his veins, Stan Hunsacker got out of the chair. He walked—no, *moseyed*—over to the 3-D cowboy.

The John Wayne was life-size—six feet, four inches. Stan Hunsacker, being an even six, had to look up into those famous, steely eyes.

Fake eyes, Hunsacker told himself.

And then Hunsacker said, "You can shove that rifle right—"

"Easy, pilgrim. Don't say anything I—"

But before the John Wayne could finish, Stan Hunsacker stepped into its chest.

Benji squinted through the Plexiglas. With trembling hand, he turned on the microphone. "Um, can you tell me, please, where Mr. Hunsacker is?"

The John Wayne said, "Where he won't be doin' ... any more damage. Now are you gonna get the ... film rollin' again? Or do I have to ... come over there and ... teach you a thing or two?"

From a distant somewhere, but sounding like it emanated from within the John Wayne image itself, came a scream.

A terrified wail.

That got softer, and softer ... until it died away.

MURDERER'S ROW

I almost didn't open the email. It looked like spam to me. Another come-on from some Nigerian prince telling me millions of dollars were waiting for me in a vault in Abuja. It was probably because the word *invaluable* was in the subject line.

But then I saw the last word, *collection.*

And since that's what I do for a living, I clicked on it.

At the time I was sitting at my laptop in the little office behind the store space I rent. Business was closed for the day. My shop is called *Ace's Cards and Memorabilia.* It's called that because I named myself Ace when I was eighteen. I like it so much better than Steve. There are too many Steves. And since I've been collecting baseball cards since I was five—we're talking 25 years now—it was only natural to use my cool new handle when opening up my collector's shop in a strip mall in Van Nuys.

It's not been easy. Being a merchant in card collecting is a thin-margin business, and more than once I've had to borrow or beg to keep the place going. But I have no other passion in my life. No wife, no girlfriend, not even a dog.

Just baseball.

So I opened up the mystery email and it was personalized.

Dear Ace: I know you by reputation, that you are a young man dedicated to the greatest game of all, our former national pastime (may it arise again!) and to the most wonderful of all vocations—collecting baseball cards. This is to invite you to view my own collection and have you assess it. I believe you will find it invaluable. I also believe you are the one who can take possession of it and preserve it lovingly. I hope you might pay a visit to me at my home and have a look. If this is of interest to you, please feel free to call me at this number.

The area code of the number was the Valley, same as mine.

It was signed Arvel Klinger.

I did a Google search of the name and the number, but found nothing on an Arvel Klinger.

That gave me a moment's hesitation. You see, I have dealt with a plethora of customers who overvalue their cards.

"This is a Sandy Koufax rookie card! It's worth two grand, at least!"

"Not with a crease in the corner."

"You're crazy!"

"Not that crazy."

But we card brokers always hold out the hope we'll actually be contacted by that one guy who really does have the goods.

And, oh my, did Arvel Klinger ever have the goods.

The house was tucked in a cul-de-sac. In the twilight I could see that it was yellow with white trim, with a blooming bougainvillea climbing up trellises. One of those homes in the Valley built in the 1950s and lovingly kept up. That gave me confidence that Mr. Arvel Klinger took good care of his cards, whatever their value might be.

I knocked on the door. A moment later it opened, revealing a skinny old man in a wheelchair.

"I'm so glad you came," he said. "I am Arvel Klinger."

A musty odor wafted out of the house, carrying with it a scent of mothballs and Cream of Wheat.

"Won't you come in?" he said.

He closed the door behind me. "Would you like a cup of cocoa?"

"Um, no thank you," I said. "I'm a bit short on time and—"

Klinger smiled and raised a finger. "One thing a collector should never be is short on time."

I took a closer look at this odd crumpet of a man. He might have been eighty or ninety. Mostly bald, he had wisps of white hair hanging over two large ears. He was wearing a robe over what looked like pajamas, and had an afghan over his legs.

"I have done a considerable amount of research on you," Klinger said.

"Research?"

"Don't let my advanced age fool you, Ace. I know how to work a computer! I learned how after selling my horse and buggy."

I forced a laugh.

"When you hear what I have," Klinger said, "you will completely understand why I have done such research. You see, I am not in good health. I have no family, no 'issue' as the law puts it."

"Issue?"

"Children. I have no one to leave my collection to, and it is, you will no doubt appreciate, the most valuable in all the world of collecting."

I will admit that possibility excited me. But then again, that over-valuing disease was a distinct possibility.

"I'm certainly open to hearing about it," I said.

He shook his head. "It is not enough to hear. I need a commitment from someone I trust. I need just the right person to take care of my collection."

"Maybe before we go on you ought to give me a ballpark figure. I'm not exactly rolling in money."

"Oh no, I don't want your money, Ace. If you are the man I think you are, I want you to lovingly preserve my collection for future generations. My collection is my children. I want you to take care of my children."

A bit over the top, but I have to say, not completely out of the ordinary. Fanatic card collectors can sometimes be, to say the least, eccentric.

Klinger said, "I can see by your expression you find my request a bit odd."

"Well—"

"Relax, my young friend," Klinger said. "I would be skeptical of you if you did not find my request at least a tad peculiar. Why don't we have a look at my collection and see what you think?"

"I'd be very interested," I said.

"If you wouldn't mind pushing me down that hallway?"

"Sure thing."

I got behind his chair and pushed him in the direction indicated. At the end of the hallway was a door with a lever handle. Klinger produced a key, leaned forward and unlocked the door.

"Pull it all the way open if you will," Klinger said.

I did. And saw long ramp stretching down to a dark basement.

Klinger said, "What I have down there is like a wine cellar. Fine wines must be given just the right temperature for preservation. My collection is too valuable to be up here in the house, where the air conditioning may go out in the summer, or the heat in the winter."

"Well," I said with all the intelligence of a five year old. "Yeah."

Klinger laughed then. "Let me give you a preview. What is the most valuable baseball card extant?"

I knew the answer. Every serious collector knows it.

"Honus Wagner, 1911," I said. "Limited edition because it was originally packaged with cigarettes, and Wagner objected to that, so they stopped the print run. Very few in existence now. The last one sold at an auction for $6.6 million."

"I knew I had the right man for this," Klinger said. "I have one of those cards."

My entire body began to tingle. I'd seen one once, at a museum exhibit, where it was guarded by two beefy security men.

"Wouldn't you like to have a look?" Klinger said.

Now I had to see it. If he had what he said he did, I could begin to understand the great love and care he held for his collection.

Klinger said, "There's a switch on the wall. Please turn it on."

I flicked the switch, and lights down below came on. I could see a glass case.

"Shall we?" Klinger said.

I got behind him again and down the ramp we went. At the bottom he had me stop at the glass case.

"Have a look for yourself," he said.

What was there was astonishing! Under the glass was, indeed, that Honus Wagner card. I'll admit I thought for a moment it could be a forgery, but that was just wild speculation. A forger does that to make money. Klinger had said he wasn't interested in money. The motive for forgery was gone.

"Amazing," I said.

"Keep looking," Klinger said.

I went to the next few cards. There was a Mickey Mantle rookie card in pristine condition. A 1907 Mordecai "Three Finger" Brown. A 1955 Roberto Clemente. A 1948 Satchel Paige. A 1914 Shoeless Joe Jackson, one of the most sought-after cards in all collecting.

My head spun and calculated. These cards alone were probably worth in excess of $10 million!

"This is just..." I searched for the right word, but only found "...fantastic!"

"Isn't it, though?" Klinger said. "But this is not the most valuable part of my collection. I have a special room for the most valuable of all, a complete set of..."

I could hardly contain myself. He was drawing this out for the greatest effect. It worked.

"...Murderer's Row," he said.

"The heart of the 1927 Yankees," I whispered.

"For five dollars, can you name them?"

Ah, a game show! I rattled them off immediately, and in the right order. "Combs, Koenig, Ruth, Gehrig, Meusel, Lazzeri."

"Bravo!" Klinger reached into a pocket of his robe and pulled out a five dollar bill.

"I don't need that, Mr. Klinger. I'd sure like to see it. But..."

"Yes?"

"I don't know that those cards are as valuable as your others."

"You've never seen them together, have you?"

"Well, no."

"And the condition matters, does it not?"

"Certainly."

"Then get ready to feast your eyes, young man. Push!"

We went to the end of the room to another door. This one was painted like a locker room entrance from an old-time baseball stadium. The sign on the door read PLAYERS AND COACHES ONLY.

On the keypad next to the door Klinger punched three numbers, slowly.

7-1-4.

The number of career home runs hit by Babe Ruth.

Now I knew for sure this was a super fan.

The door clicked open.

"The switch," Klinger said.

I found it and turned on the lights.

It was done up like a locker room. Not just any, mind you—it was the locker room from the old Yankee Stadium! I'd seen pictures of it. Empty stalls lined the far wall. I could see the names of the players over each one. Combs, Koenig, Ruth, Gehrig, Meusel, Lazzeri.

"Just amazing," I said.

"My grandfather was the custodian at Yankee Stadium from 1921 to 1948. He helped my father design this. Before your time, during the 1950s and 60s, many people put in underground rooms called bomb shelters. There was a fear that the Russians might drop an atom bomb on us. This is one of those shelters."

"It's just so intricate," I said. "But where do you keep the cards?"

"What cards?" Klinger said.

"Of Murderer's Row."

"Those cards, together, are probably worth, I don't know, a million?"

"Maybe," I said.

"What I have is much more valuable than cards."

"I don't understand," I said. "Have you got souvenir mugs or baseball gloves or something?"

"My boy! What could be more valuable than Murderer's Row itself?"

What? This guy couldn't be nutso, could he? I've seen whack-a-doodle collectors from time to time. They get so into collecting that their minds warp. One guy who used to come into my shop was sure he was the reincarnation of Pepper Martin from the old St. Louis Cardinals Gas House Gang. He had a complete set of the Cardinals team from 1934, and that was certainly worth a lot. But that did not make him Pepper Martin. He was dizzy, all right, just not Dizzy Dean! He was later hospitalized for acute paranoia and delusions.

"Bear with me, my boy," Klinger said. "You've come this far. Just one step farther."

"Step?"

"If you will step around that corner, you will see what I mean."

The room had another section, obscured by a bit of jutting wall. I took the step as ordered.

And saw, sitting on a bench, life-size replicas of Murderer's Row! There they were, wax figures in Yankee uniforms, as if ready to run onto the field and play.

Combs, Koenig, Ruth, Gehrig, Meusel, Lazzeri.

In their prime.

With the Babe, right in the middle, his famous 42-ounce bat casually resting against his leg.

I was so blown away I actually said, "Hiya, Babe" and for a moment expected him to return the greeting.

He was silent, of course, but looked me straight in the eye.

As did the others.

"Incredible!" I said.

"Isn't it though?" Klinger said.

It was worthy of the best wax museum in the world. A display like this was valuable in its own right, though I had no idea how to price it.

"Did you make them yourself?" I said.

"I did indeed," Klinger said.

"Wax, eh?"

"Oh my, no."

That threw me. If not wax...then I remembered my mom telling me about an artist named Duane Hanson, who was famous for a time for creating figures made of fiberglass and resin. They looked so lifelike that folks in museums often mistook them for real people.

"Resin," I said, still looking at the Babe.

"Not even close," Klinger said.

"Then what?"

"I can see you are confused," Klinger said.

"I have no idea how you did it. I mean, they look absolutely real."

"That's because they are, my boy."

"What?"

"It is really and truly them," Klinger said. "Murderer's Row. In the flesh!"

Oh, man. Wacko after all. "Um, Mr. Klinger, I want you to know I appreciate all this, but—"

"Ah, you have misgivings. Truly understandable, son."

"What am I suppose to—"

"If you will indulge me."

"I don't really need to—"

"My grandfather, the custodian at Yankee Stadium, was the son of the leading taxidermist in all New York. Nay, the whole of the Eastern Seaboard. My great grandfather was employed by many of the eminent men of his day, including Theodore Roosevelt, who had him stuff and preserve a grizzly bear the president sacked on one of his famous hunting trips."

I tried to swallow. My throat was dry.

"Naturally he wanted his son to carry on his work. So he trained him in the fine art of taxidermy. That son, my grandfather, was naturally a rabid Yankees fan. And so two passions came together and—"

"Stop!" I said. "I cannot believe what you're saying. That those...that they are the actual skins of the Yankee players, actual men who lived and died? That they are stuffed and somehow preserved?"

"Is it so hard to fathom?"

"You're darn right it is! For one thing, they all died when they were old. How come they look like they did in 1927?"

"That is where the art of skin enhancement and the undertaker's skill come in. For there are ways to make a corpse look young again. I will say I had trouble with poor Lou Gehrig. And the Babe was not easy, owing to his throat cancer. Lazzeri was easiest. He was only 42 when he fell—"

"Wait! Just hold it! This is crazy talk. They were all buried, weren't they?"

A smile from the pit of hell crawled across his face. "Another ancient art is that of clandestine exhumation."

"Clan what?"

"What a common man would call grave robbing."

An invisible fist clutched my throat.

Without another word or gesture I tore out of that locker room—not believing for a second that what he said was true, but also not wanting anything more to do with his ghastly face and appalling fantasy—and up the ramp to the door.

Which I found closed.

And locked.

"You'll need the key," Klinger said. He had wheeled himself to the bottom of the ramp and looked up at me with eyes of exuberant menace.

"Let me out!"

"But you haven't heard the whole of it, Ace."

"I don't want to hear any more!"

"I'm afraid you've crossed that bridge," he said. "And now you are firmly on the other side of everything you ever thought possible. For there is another ancient art you will witness tonight. The art of reanimation."

"Stop it!"

"But Ace! Who else will take care of my collection?"

"I don't care!"

"It's too late," Klinger said. "I did not tell you that my grandmother was a witch. She reanimated the dead. I saw it. I learned it. I've already begun the spell. I cannot let you go now, don't you see? You might go to the police or something. I cannot have that, no."

He reached under the afghan that covered his legs and came out with a gun.

"I'm sorry you're not the man I thought you were," Klinger said. "But perhaps you can be comforted in this. My Murderer's Row needs a batboy. How would you like to spend eternity with Babe Ruth, Lou Gehrig and the rest? Of course, you have no choice now..."

They say we all have a primeval survival mechanism wired into our brains. It's what makes for heroic acts....or acts of extreme foolishness. All I know is that panic caused me to scream and charge forward, hoping somehow to confuse the old goat and jump him before he could—

Bang!

When I came to my head was throbbing.

I was on my back, looking up into faces, silhouetted by the lights behind them.

"He's coming around," one of the faces said.

I was on a gurney.

I turned my head and saw the house, bathed in light.

There was yellow tape across the front door.

"Take it easy now," the face said. "How do you feel?"

"What...happened?" I said.

"You have a head wound. You were shot. You're lucky."

"I am?"

Another voice said, "Can he talk?"

"Maybe a few minutes," the first voice said.

The second voice said, "Sir, can you hear me?"

"Y...yes," I said.

"My name is Detective Barnes. Can you tell me what happened?"

"Mr. Klinger..."

"Was he the one who shot you?"

"Yes."

"Do you know why?"

"I...I tried to stop him."

"Stop him from what?"

"From killing me."

"Well, somebody did that for you."

"What?"

"He got his skull crushed with a blunt instrument, like a pipe or a base-ball bat."

It came to me then, so clear in its horrible probability.

"The Babe," I whispered.

"What?"

"Babe Ruth did it," I said.

"What do you mean by that?"

"Didn't you see him down there?"

"See who?"

"Babe Ruth!"

The first voice said, "He's had enough."

"No, wait," Detective Barnes said.

"Six of them," I said.

"Six of who?"

"Murderer's Row! Didn't you see them?"

"All I saw was some room made to look like a locker room, and the man who owns this house, dead. He did have a gun on him. How he got killed and you got shot, and then got outside where they found you, is what I want to know."

I opened my mouth. No words came.

I passed out.

. . .

Of course they didn't believe my story. They had a shrink examine me. He concluded that my head wound caused something called confabulation. That's where somebody with a head wound creates a distorted or imaginary memory.

Whatever.

Because of the email I almost didn't open—the one where Arvel Klinger expressed his desire to have me take on his collection—and because Arvel Klinger had no issue, I was given his entire baseball card collection.

But since I can no longer sleep, I don't know if it was worth the price.

WEE FOLK

My name is Grady Alexander Michael Kevin Sherlock Joseph Patrick McGlynn. This could explain what happened to me, why I was chosen. They could have chosen Mike Kelly or Brian Farrell or any of my other chums that used to hang out at The Shamrock Pub in Manhattan. That is, before the city got locked down and boarded up.

Not a lot of skin off my nose, though. I'm a writer and work out of my apartment. And my byline is Grady McGlynn, thank you very much. Fits better on a book cover. Not that you've heard of me. I'm not like that #1 fellow, with his bazillions of dollars and fancy house in the Hamptons. My little rent-controlled apartment is all I can afford.

Still, I hack away. Writers are nothing if not chasers of the dream.

What I mean to say about being chosen is that they needed somebody over here, meaning the good old U.S. of A., somebody of Irish stock. The fact that I had seven Irish names hung on me at my birth is probably what clinched it for them.

And by *them*, of course, I mean the wee folk.

Ah, now, you might be tempted to think this is just a load of blarney. Another Irishman telling tales about leprechauns to amuse the children.

If so, you've got another think coming, as my dear old grandmother used to say.

She's also the one to blame for my name.

———

Granny's name was Eimear O'Malley. Born in Belfast, she was always big on the meaning of names. *Eimear* in Gaelic means *swift.* In Irish legend, Eimear was the wife of a warrior named Cuchulainn. She was said to have possessed the six gifts of womanhood: beauty, a gentle voice, sweet words, wisdom, needlework, and chastity.

My grandmother had none of these.

She drank and smoked and cursed and oh, how she liked men. Even after marrying my grandfather, Sean McGlynn. Sean was a soft-spoken man, as I recall. He died when I was six. I heard my father tell a friend once that Sean had sought the peace of the daisy patch after one too many encounters with the banshee wail Granny could unleash when confronted with her sins.

Granny Eimear was from a family of ten children. Seven of them were boys. And you can guess what their names were. When I was born—I've been told—Granny was in rare form, telling Mum and Dad she'd had a vision. In that vision I was going to be a great man charged with a great duty, so I needed a great name, and it should be made up of all seven of her brothers' monikers. My father, knowing what fresh misery arguing with Granny would bring, consented. Mum actually thought it was a fun idea, but she's an artist, and you know how they are.

Great man? Great duty?

I don't know about the first. But as to the second, if you consider battling demons from hell to be a duty, then Granny's vision will make sense to you.

———

It started with a banging on the wall.

Now, I'm a New York apartment dweller, so loud noises from adjoining spaces are nothing new. This wasn't like a fist to the wall from the old couple next door who have been arguing since the Clinton administration. No, this was a tinny sound. And purposeful. It went *bang bang bang,* stopped, and went *bang bang bang* again.

It woke me up from a nice sleep. It was 2:54 a.m.

I got out of bed and into my slippers and followed the noise. *Bang*

bang bang. It was coming from the kitchenette. But how could it? Was the refrigerator on the fritz and making odd sounds?

Bang bang bang.

I flipped on the lights. And almost flipped out.

Standing there as real as my own hand was a man no more than twelve inches tall. He had a shock of red hair under a newsboy cap. His clothes were camouflage, like a G.I. Joe action figure. His little face was scrunched up in an attitude of extreme annoyance. In his hand was an empty Swanson Pot Pie aluminum container.

He banged it once more against the wall and said, "It's about time."

Frozen I was, yet somewhere in the back of my mind I heard the voice of Granny telling little Grady Alexander Michael Kevin Sherlock Joseph Patrick McGlynn tales of the wee folk.

Was it possible?

"I know what you're thinkin'," the little man said. "And it's true. I'm a leprechaun and you're an Irishman, so you know what we can do if we have a mind. And cover yourself up, man."

What? Oh, yeah. I was in my slippers and tighty-whities.

But this was my apartment!

"This is my place," I said. "What do you want here?"

"So it's attitude you'll be pullin'," he said. "Not wise, me bucko."

"Now wait a minute," I said. "Leprechauns are supposed to be in Ireland, underground or something."

"Puh," he said, a sort of spitting sound. "We've come a long way since the days of St. Patrick. We have cell phones and everything."

"You do not," I said.

"Well, if we wanted 'em we'd have 'em, and that you better believe!"

"Why should I believe any of this?"

"Simmer down," the little fellow said, tossing the disposable tin aside. "We can make this easy or make this hard. I should think that you and I, both Erin born and proud of it, ought to prefer the easiest way of all."

"And what is that?"

"Do you have some whiskey and a thimble?"

———

And that was how I found myself sitting at my kitchen table at three in the morning, drinking Jameson with a one-foot tall leprechaun.

"Ah, much better," he said after quaffing a thimbleful and tapping the edge for me to refill. As I did he said, "Now, to get down to it, you may call me Paddy. I'm not to be trifled with. I was sent here because we need somebody to represent our interests, so to speak, as we are planning a mass migration. 'Tis better weather we're looking for, and influence. We'd also like a nice little plot of land in The Hamptons."

For a long moment I said nothing. Then I had another shot of whiskey. My head was not wrapping around what was happening. Was I really talking to a leprechaun? It wasn't a dream, I knew that. The warmth of the Jameson was enough to tell me that.

I said, "You're going to have trouble on that score. There isn't that much land available in The Hamptons, and what is there is outrageously expensive." With a chuckle I added, "Better have a couple pots o' gold, friend."

Paddy slammed down the thimble. "Lies! Of all the lies they tell about us, that's the worst of 'em. The pot 'o gold business is just an excuse to hunt us down."

"What about three wishes?" I said. "If I grab you and put you in a cage, don't you have to grant me three wishes?"

"Three curses is more like it," he said. "So don't even try it, pally."

My sleepiness and the whiskey—not to mention being called *pally* by a man the size of my forearm—heated my cheeks. "Why am I even talking to you? Why don't you get out of here and go find somebody else to bother at three o'clock in the morning?"

"Because you're the one we chose."

"Who is *we*?"

"The inner circle. You should be proud to have this honor."

"Pardon me if I don't feel particularly honored. What am I supposed to do with this...honor?"

"One little thing to start with," Paddy said with a devious grin as he raised his thimble for another snort.

"I'm waiting," I said.

Paddy lowered the thimble and wiped his mouth with the back of his hand. "We want you to kill some people," he said.

———

After I finished laughing, Paddy said, "This is no jest. It is a duty. And it's yours to fill."

"Go pluck a chicken," I said.

"Don't think you can insult your way outta this."

"Why don't you kill the people yourself?"

"Haven't got the hardware."

I played along. "What people?"

"We've got a list."

"Uh-huh. And why do you want them dead?"

"To send a message," Paddy said.

I said, "I know I'm going to hate myself for this, but what's the message?"

"The message is, we are in control now."

"You mean leprechauns?" I said. "In control? Of New York?"

"That's just the start. We have a list of demands."

That got me laughing again. "Demands? Like what?"

"For starters, all stores in the city will be cleared of Lucky Charms."

"The cereal? With the leprechaun on it? What's wrong with that?"

"Demeaning. We demand the whole line be dropped."

"But kids love the marshmallow bits."

"We know what's good for the kiddies, and that ain't it. And if they refuse to do it, we burn down the stores."

My eyelids were heavy. My brain was in a netherworld, not waking or dreaming. This was some kind of alternate reality that I'd have to figure out once I was fully conscious.

"And everybody over five feet tall must bow down before us and sing a song of our choosing," Paddy said.

I rubbed my temples. "Tell you what. Let's get together in a couple of days and talk about this again."

"I know that's what you're thinkin'," Paddy said. "Don't ever try to fool a leprechaun. We invented the practice."

What had Granny told him as a boy? That leprechauns are tricksters, mostly. Fraudulent fairies who love nothing more than needling one of the "biggies." They can change shapes and even disappear if you stop looking at them. But I could never recall a story of a leprechaun talking about murder.

Enough was enough. I got up, grabbed him by the shirt and lifted him off the table.

The scream he issued—something like the mix of a cat's yowl and a nail across a blackboard—knifed through my brain. Kicking and screaming he was, shouting at me to put him down.

I opened my kitchen window. I'm on the third floor. There's a drop between my apartment building and the one next door, at the bottom of which is a large dumpster.

"Find yourself another boy," I said, and dropped him. I watched him fall and heard the thud of his little body landing in the garbage.

I shut the window, turned off the lights, and went back to bed.

———

I woke up sucking for air. Something was in my mouth. When I tried to reach for it, I couldn't. My arms were tied down.

This had to be another dream, another nightmare. But my mind snapped to reality when a small figure holding a miniature pitchfork jumped onto my stomach.

"Finally awake, are ye?" Paddy said.

"Mmph," I said, as a gag was in my mouth.

With two hands Paddy drove the tines of the pitchfork into my ribs.

I screamed!

"Got your attention, bucko?"

Eyes wide open now, I sensed movement in the bedroom. I was afraid to look. But I did.

There were more of them. Milling around, giving me the stink eye.

One of them was sitting on my dresser, legs crossed, smoking a pipe. I tried to yell at him that there was no smoking allowed in the building. But all I made was a muffled sound. The pipe-smoking leprechaun laughed at me.

Paddy said, "You won't be tryin' anything stupid like that again, tossin' me out the window like yesterday's trash. That was a very ungentlemanly thing to do."

I pulled hard against the restraints, but those wee men had wrapped me up tight as Gulliver. I felt blood dribbling down my side from the pitchfork wound.

"Now we're gonna get things straight from the get-go." Paddy paced up my chest, twirling his weapon of choice. "First, let's hear you pledge fealty to us."

"All of us!" one of the other leprechauns shouted. That was followed by a chorus of "Aye!" from the rest of the assembled mob.

"So let me see, by a nod of your big head, that you understand what I'm sayin' to you."

Since I didn't understand any of this, my head shook rather than nodded. My eyes were wide open, pleading for mercy.

What I got was the pitchfork stuck under my chin.

"Why don't we try this again, bucko. Do you understand that you are now in service to all of us? That you have no choice in the matter? I'll give you one more chance."

He withdrew the pitchfork. When I didn't immediately respond he held it out like he was going to drive it into my gullet. Which was when I started nodding.

"Ah, good, then," said Paddy. "Now that we've got that cleared up, let's try the oath again. You pledge to follow us and heed our every word, even to the grave. You can nod."

Pledge? Grave? What manner of little men were these? Whatever demonic spirit had been unleashed, here they were in my apartment. I couldn't deny my senses, especially the prick of the tines from the little pitchfork.

The devil uses a pitchfork, doesn't he?

My Catholic childhood fears boiled up in me. Fear of the devil. The devil and his minions. I hadn't been to Mass in twenty years. I confessed to God right then and there and asked for a little help.

What I got was another jab to the ribs.

I muffled a scream once more.

"Nod!" Paddy said.

I nodded. Anything to get out of this. But part of me died inside.

"Good boy," Paddy said. "Think about it for awhile."

He turned and raised his pitchfork. "Time for a drink!"

The other leprechauns cheered.

———

I heard them messing around in the kitchen. There was singing and laughing and shouting. And fiddle music! The little darlings were having a grand old party.

I don't know how long it went on. All the time I was trying to wriggle out of my bonds. But those devils knew how to fasten ropes.

Finally the music stopped and things got oddly quiet. Where there had been loud and bawdy conversation, there was now only some low-level talking, a moan or two, and snoring. The whiskey had done its work. What was it Granny used to say? "When the Irish drink they fall asleep. When they fall asleep, they commit no sin. Commit no sin and you go to Heaven. So let's all get drunk and go to heaven!"

But this lot was from hell.

Hell. Yes, what was it Granny once told me about sending a dark soul to hell? A curse it was. A curse that could send a púca—a shape-shifting demon—to the fiery depths. A leprechaun was supposed to be *good* luck. Three wishes and a pot of gold. But not the tiny rabble in my apartment. Bad luck indeed. Could that old curse operate on these minia-ture men?

It might if I could remember it! It was in Gaelic and...wait...I had an old letter from Granny that had that curse written down!

But where was that letter?

In a box. In a box under other boxes in the corner of my office. A corner that hadn't been dusted or even touched for years. And in my present condition a corner I couldn't get to.

Something—no, some*one*—crawled up my leg. I looked ... and smelled. It was that pipe-smoking homunculus. He was, indeed, crawling, like the drunken elf he was, singing with a thick brogue. "Here's to Irish whiskeys, sure we love them one and all! We'll have a glass of Teelings, boys, before the final caaallll!"

This was followed by a belly laugh and an attempt to stand. He only made it to his knees.

If only I had my arms! I could grab the diminutive drunk and ... and what? Kill him? How? Choking? Slamming his little head against the bed post?

Well, yeah, at the moment it was tempting. But then I'd have to do the same to all the others, too. A miniature massacre! An elfin annihilation! Right here on 19th and 8th in Manhattan.

But I did not have my arms. I did, however, have the spirit of Granny inside me, reminding me that I, too, was Irish, and a mix of McGlynn and O'Malley. We could sling the blarney as masterfully as anyone on the Emerald Isle.

I couldn't speak, but I could hum!

And so I did—the song he'd been singing—as near as I could manage it. As soon as I began, the little lush's face perked up. Still with the pipe in his mouth, he said, "Aye! That's the spirit!"

He started singing another verse, and I hummed it along with him: "Here's to Irish whiskeys, sure we love them one and all. We'll have a glass of Bushmills, boys, before the final caaallll!"

There is nothing that bonds Irishmen together more than whiskey and song. The light of ancient brotherhood flashed into the tiny troubadour's eyes—right before he passed out.

The pipe fell out of his mouth and rolled off my chest. The bowl landed flush against my arm ... and burned!

But in that fleeting pain came the fire of a desperate idea.

Jiggling as best I could, I managed to vibrate the pipe down toward my wrist. My wild brainstorm was to get the ignited tobacco in contact with the rope that held me.

But when I looked I saw that the movement downward had caused the bowl of the pipe to face the wrong way.

And of course without fresh flame upon it, it would soon go out.

Gathering what strength I had left, I undulated my body with a mighty jerk. The leprechaun lying flat on my chest went up and down like a cork on a wave, and issued an inebriated snort.

The pipe went up and down, too. But it did not flip over.

I grunted in frustration.

The laid-out leprechaun mumbled, "Eh? Who?"

It was all I could do to make one more big move, a rumble of my body like the last contortion of a beached whale.

The diminutive drunk raised his head. "Bejeez, can't a body get some sleep?" His head slammed down again.

But the pipe, the pipe! It had flipped.

There was only so much give in my restraints. It was strong rope, but thankfully only of Lilliputian thickness. I pulled and strained and wiggled and managed to get the bowl of the pipe to touch the rope. By pressing my arm inward I was able to squeeze the pipe solid against the rope.

And my skin!

The burn was intense, like being stung by a giant wasp. I wanted to cry out, but choked it back lest I waken the diminutive dipso on my breast, or worse—Paddy and his minions in the kitchen.

Then...*snap*! My arm came free!

Now what? My legs and other arm were tied and the pipe had fallen to the floor. I had to figure something out quick, including what to do with the snoring soak asleep on my chest. If I leaned too far to the side he'd come sliding off, hit the floor, and no doubt fill the room with Irish curses.

At least I got the gag out of my mouth.

Unfortunately, I had no one to call to.

Swiss Army knife! I had one in the drawer of my bedside table.

The good news was the table was to my immediate right, so I could reach it with my free hand. The bad news was I couldn't move to a position where opening the drawer and fumbling inside it would be easy.

At least I was able to reach the drawer knob. But as I clumsily pulled it open my shoulder almost went out. The hot pain of a muscle snapping in my rotator cuff.

With gritted teeth I managed to get the thing open about four inches.

The leprechaun using my chest for a mattress grumbled and turned over on his back, and issued a malodorous belch.

Ignoring the burning in my shoulder, I got my hand into the drawer. Desperately, blindly, I felt around. Pencils I found. And a highlighter. My harmonica. And one of those things with teeth that removes staples. Had I put the knife somewhere else? Left it in another room?

My torso tormentor sat up!

And scratched the back of his head.

Where was that knife?

The mini man looked around, then spun on his keister to face me. His rheumy eyes fought to focus. He rubbed them once and said, "Eh? What goes on?"

"We'll have a glass of Tullamore Dew, boys," I said.

He smiled. For a second. Then his face darkened. "You're talkin'. How can ... what's that you're reachin' for?"

Wobbly, he got to his feet and looked at my free hand. "Loose you are! Boys! The giant is—"

He didn't finish as I cold-cocked him in the face with a right cross. His little body flew off my chest and thudded into the mirrored door of my closet, then slid to the floor. I almost felt sorry for him. No true Irishman backs down from a fair fight. But a giant fist to a small head is hardly fair.

This was no time for sentimentality. I heard some groanings in the kitchen. The leprechauns were awakening from their Bacchanalia.

Back to the drawer now. Paperclips. A tissue.

Paddy's groggy voice from the kitchen. "Bejeez, did you get the number o' that truck?"

ChapStick. Scotch tape.

"Faith, and up with ye, men."

The knife! I had it!

But now I had to open it.

The Swiss Army knife is not a switchblade. You need two hands to open the tools. My left hand was still tied securely. I reached over to it.

Paddy said, "Ye got potatoes in your ears?"

It was a clumsy position I was in, but I managed to get the knife into my left hand. Now I had to find the notch with my right thumbnail and—

"Up, men!"

Come on, come on...there. It was out!

I switched the knife back to my right hand and cut the rope on my left wrist. I sat up and cut the ropes around my ankles.

The sotted pipe smoker was still out cold on the floor.

More murmurings from the kitchen. The rest of the leprechauns were coming out of their stupor. I thought for a minute about just running out of the apartment. But to what? To whom? Pest control?

No, this was *my home*! If I couldn't get rid of them by dropping them into a dumpster, then what had I to lose by trying a curse from the Old Country?

I tiptoed out of my bedroom and made for my office. The hardwood floor of my apartment building—erected in 1947—groaned under my feet. I only hoped it would blend in the sounds in the kitchen.

My office was stuffed with books and file cabinets and piles of papers from projects completed, abandoned, or forgotten. My computer was on a table in the center of the room. Next to it was an empty birdcage that used to have a bird in it. I closed the door then flicked on the light and made for the dusty mound of boxes to which I have previously referred.

The top box was filled with hardback books I was supposed to donate to the library. Yeah, like five years ago. I cursed myself for not getting around to it.

Below that was a box of CDs. We've entered the age of digital, and all these I'd previously ripped to my computer. I gave myself another harsh word for not taking them to the Goodwill store in midtown.

But then again, my packratness was the reason I had the third box. Yes! This was the one with letters and photos and a journal or two. And one stack of letters from Granny that I hoped I remembered correctly.

Quickly, I sifted through the envelopes.

And there it was. The familiar scrawl. The return address in Belfast.

I took out the letter.

The date would have made me twelve when I received it.

Dear Grady Alexander Michael Kevin Sherlock Joseph Patrick,

It's a grand time I hope you're having. I've been told you have dreams of becoming a writer or a baseball player. Be done with silly sports. Follow the Irish in you and become a bard. But first you must live life!

You must finish your schooling. Aye, and then look out, world. You have McGlynn and O'Malley blood in your veins, dear boy. Born for great things. And with that will come the naysayers and critics and wolves in sheep's clothing. Look out for the wolves! They can come at you from anywhere, even the lower place, and that's where you can send them back.

You'll do well with a grand old curse. Learn to say it in our mother tongue: Go hlfreann leat! To hell with you!

Always remember, when things look dark, singing songs of good cheer, good fellowship, and good whiskey always lifts an Irishman's spirits! Just open up your mouth and...

My office door slammed open.

Three leprechauns hissed at me like poisonous snakes. Coming in behind them, like rats from a sinking ship, were the rest. Twenty or so miniature warriors armed with little torches and clubs, and Paddy at the front wielding his pitchfork.

"To hell with you!" I said.

Paddy laughed and waved his comrades forward.

The curse had to be in Gaelic!

From the distant mists of my memory bank, I tried to remember the sound of the ancient language of Eire.

Go was *Guh.*

Hlfreann was *hif-rin.*

But what was *leat?*

A club whacked me in the shin.

Paddy drove his pitchfork into my calf.

I cried out and stumbled backward, tripping over the box of books.

Now flat on my back, I was jumped by two of the Irish imps who used their little fists to pummel my face. The rat-a-tat of their blows was a series of stings, as if I were getting my face tattooed.

"Bring the ropes, men!" Paddy said.

Weak from lack of food and mental stress, I breathed deep and gave one last blow for freedom.

With a warrior's cry I slapped off the two on my face and stood up quick, my back against the window.

For a second Paddy and I locked eyes.

And then I said, "*Guh!*"

Paddy's jaw dropped.

"*Hif-rin!*"

Paddy and at least another ten leprechauns screamed, "No!"

But what was that last word? I wasn't sure. But they didn't know that. I opened my mouth, the biggest fake out since the *Abbey Road* album cover.

"Stop!" Paddy shouted. "I'll do anything!"

"Anything?" I said.

"Short of milking an English cow," Paddy said. "Anything else!"

"Tell your men to drop their weapons."

"You heard 'im, men!"

This was followed by the *tinking* sound of tiny weapons dropping on the hardwood.

"All in good fun, it was," Paddy said, with a devious smile. "We'll be takin' our leave of ye now."

I picked him up, my meaty paw around his tiny waist. "Not so fast."

"Put me down!" He kicked his little legs.

"You'll be giving me three wishes," I said, "or the lot of you go to blazes."

"Are ye daft? That's only a fairy tale! We have no power of—"

"*Guh hif-rin*—"

"All right, all right!" Paddy said. "Three wishes it will be!"

"Agreed," said I.

"And what will be the first?"

"No more malice from leprechauns. No calls for killing or burning or bowing down. Make it so that in your hearts you'll always think, with malice toward none, with charity for all."

"That's too much!" Paddy said.

"It's either that or the blazes," I said.

There is nothing more pitiful than a leprechaun realizing he's unable to outwit one of the biggies. Paddy's face was a dangerous shade of red. Tiny tears appeared in his eyes.

"Well?" I said.

"Don't rush me!" Paddy said.

I opened my mouth to speak.

"Stop!" Paddy said. He closed his eyes for a long moment. When he opened them again he looked at peace. "'Tis sorry I am for the trouble we've brought you."

Several little mouths uttered, "Aye."

"And what would your second wish be?" Paddy asked.

"I'll need to think about it," I said. "If you don't mind."

"Mind? Why man, take your good time."

"In that case," I said, "how about a round for one and all?"

This was met with enthusiastic assent from the entire company.

———

I'm able to live quite comfortably on the interest earned off of $800 million.

My house in The Hamptons is well kept up by my staff of twenty. That the twenty are all twelve-inches tall is not an issue. And at night, if you happen by the grounds at just the right time, you might hear the sound of Irish music and a chorus of little voices singing songs of good cheer, good fellowship, and good whiskey.

THE MÖBIUS TIME STRIP

Traveling at the speed of light the other day, I found myself next to a man screaming for help.

"What is it, friend?" I said.

"Get me off!" he said as we sped along like twin comets. He looked normal enough. Hawaiian shirt, jeans.

"Off what?" I said.

"The Möbius Time Strip!"

"The what?"

"Help me, please!"

But then he was gone, leaving a wake of purple and orange vapor-light.

I went on, coming to rest two weeks before pandemic-panic hit Los Angeles. What a relief! I Ubered to 7th and Alvarado and entered Langer's Deli. I ordered their #19, the greatest pastrami-on-rye of all time, and I do mean all time. I've been to several delis in twentieth-century New York, so I know.

As I noshed, glorying in the crowded, loud, lunchtime atmosphere of pre-lockdown L.A., I mused about my latest encounter in space. Möbius Time Strip? I've never been a math whiz, but I do remember as a kid being fascinated by the Möbius strip itself. In fifth grade my friend Daniel Imfeld, who *was* a math whiz, said he could show me a strip of paper with just one side. I snorted and said that was impossible. Right in front of my eyes he took a strip of paper, gave it a twist, and used some Elmer's Glue to attach the ends. Then he told me to start anywhere and trace the surface with my finger. Lo and behold, one side!

So what could my comet companion have meant by Möbius Time Strip? And it struck me that maybe he meant something like eternal recurrence. Nietzsche proposed that we may be living the same life over and over again. He was a German fruitcake, of course, but even a blind squirrel...

Yet how would such a concept apply to time travel?

After the last lovely bite of pastrami-on-rye, I picked up my phone and went to the CalTech.edu website and looked at their faculty directory. I hadn't spoken to Daniel Imfeld in years, but knew he was a full professor of astrophysics at Cal Tech. The directory had his email and office phone.

I called, he answered.

"Hello, this is Professor Imfeld."

"Daniel! It's Steve Prodgers."

"Steve! My goodness! Blast from the past."

"You have no idea."

"How the heck are you?"

"Oh, just doing a bit of traveling," I said. "Hey, can I ask you a physics question?"

"I'd be honored."

"Remember that time you showed me a Möbius strip?"

"I did?"

"Fifth grade, Mrs. Greenberg's class."

"Hm, can't say as I recall, but I wouldn't put it past me." He laughed.

I said, "Anyway, think this through with me. Suppose a guy could really and truly travel through time."

"It's theoretically possible," Daniel said. "But only theoretically."

"Uh, sure. Now, suppose a person did and was terrified about something he called the Möbius Time Strip. What would that mean to you?"

There was a long pause. "I suppose it could mean something like twisting, not just bending, the space-time continuum. And some sort of infinite repetition of a space-time event."

"The same event over and over, forever?"

"Sure. I can think of one example right off the bat. Imagine that you can travel back in time, okay?"

"I'll try," I said.

"So back you go to a place and time where you run into your own grandfather, who is a child. And you accidentally kill him."

"Uh oh."

"See where I'm going? Because he's dead, your grandfather never grows up. He never meets your grandmother. He never has children or grandchildren. Which means you were never born. Therefore, you never existed, and could never travel backward through time to kill your grandfather."

"Hoo boy."

"Which means he was never killed, so your grandfather does meet your grandmother, and they do have children, and those children have grandchildren, including you. So once again you do exist. But then you're there to travel through time again, and kill your grandfather. See? A never-ending causality chain that keeps resetting."

"But if you were conscious of all that, why couldn't you stop yourself from killing your grandfather in the first place?"

"Yes, there would have to be a consciousness-reset of some kind, which is plausible."

"But between times, such a fellow is conscious of it all."

"That's possible, too. There's something called transient global amnesia. Temporary memory loss. Your recall of recent events vanishes, so you can't remember where you are or how you got there. In addition, you may not remember anything about what's happening in the here and now. A concussive event like time travel could bump someone in and out."

"Would that always be the case?" I asked.

"Not at all," Daniel said. "It would be like anything else. Some people are susceptible to certain things, others are not. What's your interest in all this, Steve? You were never into science fiction or even science, as I recall."

"Oh, I was just traveling through time myself and met someone who seemed locked in an infinite recurrence."

Daniel snorted. "No, really."

"I'm just full of questions, I guess."

"Why don't you come out and have lunch with me sometime?"

"Better be in the next two weeks."

"Oh? Why's that?"

"You'll find out. Thanks for the time, Steve."

I sat for a while, deep in thought, then went up front to pay my check.

At that very moment the door flew open and a man in a state of panic rushed in. He looked around wildly, then fixed his eyes on me.

"It's you!" He grabbed my shoulders and pulled me into a bear hug.

"What is this?" I said.

He took a step back. "Don't you recognize me? The Möbius Time Strip?"

I concentrated. I'd only seen him for an instant. But why would I doubt him? Who else would have known to say what he did?

"How...did you find me?" I said.

"I'm a private eye," he said. "I just had to find you and thank you for getting me off the strip."

"I did?"

"You sure did! Now I'm here, and here is where I'm going to stay!"

"But how did I do it?"

"I'm not sure myself. But it involved dropping in at Napoleon's retreat from Moscow. My great-great-great grandfather was a young soldier then! I was the guy holding his horse when he got shot. Only this time, he didn't. You were there!"

"Oh yeah!" I said. I'd gone back there a few days earlier. I've always been fascinated by the little general who almost conquered the world. "I remember you! It was snowing and you were drinking brandy straight from the bottle, and I said, 'How about giving me a snort?' and you said, 'You speak English!' and you held out the bottle and let go of the horse and it bucked. The rider, as I recall, fell off his horse, but was unhurt."

He nodded, eyes wet with tears. "Bless you."

"Let me buy you lunch," I said.

He put his hands up and started to back away. "No, I don't want to interfere anymore with anything. Don't come after me, please. Just...bless you!"

And out the door he went.

"What was that all about?" the cashier asked.

"I'm not sure I can explain," I said.

"You look a little stunned."

"I am."

"You going to be okay?" she asked.

"Time will tell," I said.

I went across the street to MacArthur Park. It was humming with the usual activity—transients and tourists, street dog vendors and sidewalk hustlers. I was about to take off for the south of England in 1066—I always wanted to witness the Norman invasion—but I stopped. What if I accidentally bumped into that guy and knocked him back onto the Möbius Time Strip?

Then again, who was he to me?

But the look of pure relief on his face...

So I'm staying. Even though I know what's coming—the insipid and ineffective lockdown, a mayor issuing edicts like some Herod Agrippa, the mask-shaming hipsters who scream at people in their cars because they haven't covered their mouths with cloth. I'll have to go through it all.

But maybe it's worth it to spare a fellow human being some needless suffering. After all, time belongs to all of us, just like the beaches.

Wait a second...

STORIES WITH A HEART

In college, I had the chance to take a workshop with a master of the literary short story, Raymond Carver. There were some naturally talented writers in there. I was not one of them. I knew I had a lot to learn.

While I came to favor the twisty stories, I always longed to write the kind of literary story that has heart to it. It seemed to elude me, until I found what I consider the "secret"—what I call the "shattering moment." (I even wrote a short book on this theory called *How to Write Short Stories and Use Them to Further Your Writing Career*.)

The reviews that came in from these stories were extremely gratifying. I am pleased to present to you here.

GOLDEN

We were at the park, Terry and I, when the dog ran up. Terry is my son, eight years old. I get him on alternate weekends. Mary and I reached an amicable settlement on custody, mainly because I didn't want to fight her anymore. Her family is well off and were not shy about retaining the biggest family law firm in L.A.

Me, I'm just plain old middle class. My old man was not present most of my life, and when he was he was usually tanked. Auto mechanic he was, and a darn good one. But in the machine shop of fatherhood he was all thumbs.

I was determined not to be that to Terry. I knew what I was in his eyes. The big-time athlete, the golden boy. Golden! Quarterback! Two years at Michigan. Drafted in the third round by the Eagles. I didn't make the squad and nobody picked me up. But my reputation got me into a partnership with a car dealership in my hometown of Woodland Hills, California.

Life was good there for a while. I married Mary Canova (of the Encino Canovas, I always joked, but only partly. Her father's a big-time TV producer and her mother a former model who drips jewelry). We had Terry and I moved as gracefully into being a dad as I used to dance around the pocket as a Wolverine.

The dealership got going good, too. I had a steady clientele of folks who remembered me from Taft High, about a mile from Stenger's Ford on Ventura.

But then Mary had an affair, which I don't blame her for. I was working too hard and hanging out with some of my old buddies from Taft. I got into poker. The arguments with Mary got more heated. I doused my inner fire with bourbon. And I was too proud to give it up when Mary suggested AA.

We divorced when Terry was seven. I'd been sober for a year, but that didn't stop things. The hurt on Terry's face when we told him is a scar on my soul that will not heal. The only balm is when I'm with him.

Like this day, at the park, tossing the small football. Terry has good hands but I hope he doesn't take up the game. I want him to have two good knees and no concussions when he grows up.

Terry had just caught the ball when the dog ran up to him, jumping practically up to his head. It was a scruffy mutt, some middle-sized and exuberant breed.

Terry laughed and teased the dog by showing it the ball then throwing it to me.

The dog chased the ball.

Now it was my turn to laugh. As I threw the ball back to Terry, I saw the boy limping toward my son. He seemed to be a teenager, smallish. He wore jeans and canvas sneakers and a Lakers jersey with 24 on it. His limp and his constricted arm were pronounced.

"That's my dog," I heard him say in a nasally voice. "Sorry." He started walking away, calling his dog to follow him. I think the dog's name was Kobe.

Terry watched the boy for a moment, then looked at me and smirked.

That smirk was an ice pick through my heart. It cracked it open, and the memory of Charles and the dirt clod bled out and filled my chest.

His name was Charles August Whitmore—never Chuck or Charlie— except to Robbie Winkleblack, who always called him Chaz the Spaz. I didn't call him anything, because he wasn't on my radar.

We were all seventh graders but not all of the same class, if you know what I mean. There were the guys who could play sports and the guys who couldn't. I was already big for my age and a three-sport guy—baseball, football, basketball.

Charles August Whitmore probably weighed eighty pounds if he was dripping wet and carrying a lunch box. His left arm was shorter than his right and his hand kind of curled up.

When we chose up sides, he was the pick nobody wanted. Mostly because he wasn't strong or fast and had a bum stick. But also because of his mouth.

Charles could take you apart with his tongue, which is what got him in bad with Robbie Winkleblack. Robbie called him Chaz the Spaz one day out on the field. Charles called him a "noxious emission."

When Robbie's face went blank, like he didn't know what Charles was saying, Charles said, "Don't you know the official name for a fart?"

That cost Charles one of the epic noogies of all time and the loss of his pants. Robbie got detention.

I was a witness, and I laughed. I laughed because Robbie was the only guy better than me out there on the field, and I wanted to be on his good side.

Which is part of the shame I carry to this day. But not as much as what happened after the dirt clod.

It was a Saturday, and Robbie and I played some basketball at the gym then went for a Slurpee. We walked back toward my house, taking the short cut over the hill.

The side of the hill was undeveloped then, and after a rain covered with long, wild grass. If you timed it right, if the dirt was just starting to harden, you could get yourself a monster dirt clod.

You did it by grabbing a bunch of grass and pulling up. A big old fist of dirt would cling to the roots. What you had then was a weapon, like a medieval flail. We used to twirl them around and throw them at each other.

This was a perfect day for a clod.

And something more.

A target.

Robbie was the first to spot him. "Isn't that Chaz the Spaz?"

He was looking down the hill. There was a house at the bottom with a new swimming pool. The pool didn't have water in it.

But it did have Charles August Whitmore, and he was running around. Making motorcycle sounds. He was a motorcycle in a motordrome inside his own little ESPN world. He had his arm out like he was holding handle-bars. With his good hand he goosed the throttle.

"Think you can hit him?" Robbie said.

"With a dirt clod?"

"Yeah."

"He's too far away."

"Try it. I'll give you a buck if you hit him."

"And what if I miss?"

"You have to sing the USC fight song to me."

Robbie was a Trojan fan. I liked the Bruins.

"I don't have to hit him direct," I said. "Spray counts."

"No way, that's too easy."

"Chicken," I said.

"Dork," Robbie said. "Okay, go."

I grabbed some grass. The trick is not to yank too hard. And this one was a beauty. I wonder if there had ever been such a perfect clod before in the whole history of hills.

Charles was still making motorcycle sounds, running around that cement pool. I'm sure he thought he was going eighty miles an hour.

I took a step back and started twirling the dirt clod like some perverse David taking on a mini-Goliath. Countless dirt clod fights had perfected my technique. When I let go of the grass I knew it was going to land in that pool. The only question was how close to Charles it would come.

It couldn't have come any closer. Because the thing exploded right on top of Charles Whitmore's head. There was a puff of dirt-smoke and Charles the Motorcycle stopped cold. He fell forward, tried to break the fall with his bad arm, and rolled down the side of the pool to the bottom.

And started wailing.

Robbie was already running away, laughing.

I ran away, too, but I wasn't laughing. I was thinking it was all over for me now. I'd be kicked out of school, maybe thrown into juvie.

When I caught up to Robbie he could hardly breathe, he was laughing so hard. "That was so awesome, bro!"

"I think he's hurt," I said.

"Bam! Right on his head! You are da man!"

"I mean really hurt."

Robbie said, "You're gonna be a legend."

"Shut up," I said. "Don't ever tell anybody."

"I gotta tell Tim and Josh. Come on, man."

"No," I said. "Shut up."

"Don't worry, bro. Legendary! That's you."

Charles was in school the next day. He had a bandage on his arm and there was a red welt under his blond hair that was easy to see if you were looking down on him.

I passed him in the hall and I remember him looking at me. I couldn't tell if he suspected anything. But there was fear in those eyes, that was for sure. Something got taken out of Charles in that swimming pool. In the gym, on the field, he didn't mouth off like he used to.

The school year ended in glory for me. We had an all-school flag football game. I went in at quarterback for the last half, we were down a score. I threw two touchdown passes, the last one in the final minute.

I got mobbed by my teammates and gym teacher Peter Furuta, who was our coach. As I was hugging Robbie I looked out into the crowd and saw Charles. He was smiling and clapping.

That summer my family went on a trip back east to see my great aunt. She wore heavy lipstick and liked to kiss me on the cheek. My dad took us— my mom, my sister and me—into New York for dinner and a Broadway show, *Annie Get Your Gun*. It was okay. Not as good as a Jets game.

When we got back to L.A., the first Saturday I went over to Robbie's house.

He was playing Sonic when I came into the living room and he stopped and said, "Man, did you hear about Chaz the Spaz?"

"No."

"Drowned."

"What?"

"Yeah, dude. I guess up at Big Bear Lake."

"How?"

Robbie shrugged. "Somebody said he was trying to swim to an island. At night."

"Why would he do that?"

Robbie shrugged again. Held up the joystick.

I shook my head.

"Whattaya wanna do?" he said.

I don't remember doing anything with Robbie. I remember walking home. I remember walking by Charles August Whitmore's house. I remember being on the sidewalk and stopping to look at the house.

"Hello."

I turned and saw a woman there. She had hedge clippers and gardening gloves on. I knew right off it was Charles's mother. She looked just like him. Same build and face. She was tiny.

"Oh," I said. "Hi."

"Did you know Charles?" she said.

I nodded.

"You were in his class?"

I nodded.

"You look like an athlete."

I didn't do anything.

"Charles looked up to you boys. He really wanted to be—" Her voice choked off, like she'd cut it with the shears. She looked at the hedge she was clipping. She held the shears at her side. She breathed in and out.

There was a burning under my ribs. I wanted to do something, but knew there was nothing to be done. I'd not been near such grief before.

And something else. I couldn't analyze it. I didn't have the words or the ability to turn experience into understanding. Only later, much later looking back, was I able to find the word.

Self-loathing.

"I'm sorry," I said, as much for myself as for her. When her head did not move, I added, "He was nice."

"Yes," she said, and looked at the leaves as if they were tiny picture frames. "He was very, very nice."

Terry started limping toward me, imitating the boy with the dog. And smiling.

I shook my head at him.

His smile faded.

I got down on one knee.

He came to me then, not as the budding little man he wanted to be, but as a child wondering what he'd done wrong.

When he got to me I put my hands on his shoulders. Then I pulled him to me and held him. He couldn't have known what was coming next. He couldn't have known that gold was about to be tarnished.

But I will be his father.

I SEE THINGS DEEPLY

My Uncle Cecil was a failure. I remember my father shouting at my mother one night when Uncle Cecil was on his way to stay with us.

"He's a failure!" my father shouted.

"He's my brother!" my mother shouted back.

"He comes here and freeloads! Why doesn't he get a job?"

"He can't hold a job, you know that."

I wondered why my uncle couldn't hold a job. I was twelve and I had a job cutting lawns in my neighborhood. I didn't have any trouble finding work. We lived on Canoga Avenue in Woodland Hills, at the west end of the San Fernando Valley. There were lots of houses and green lawns.

Canoga Avenue was a ribbon of road that ran past our house and stretched almost all the way across the valley. On both sides of the street stood magnificent old pepper trees. Big, green, and bushy, they shaded the road from the sun. When I rode my bike down the street, it was like traveling through a verdant tunnel into a fairy tale.

Back then the valley was the part of Los Angeles that moved at a leisurely pace. It was a place to raise a family and live, if not off the fat of the land, then at least close to a neighborhood market. In those days the folks who worked at the neighborhood markets knew your name.

A few blocks west of my street they were turning the big field into a shopping center. I was sad about that because I used to play there. That was the field where they'd have Easter egg hunts and bands sometimes. They were going to build a new Safeway store.

That summer I was looking forward to splashing around in our pool with the neighborhood kids and—unfortunately—my big sister Emily. Emily was sixteen and couldn't get enough of The Beatles. She'd lie on the pool deck with The Beatles blaring from a record player. I couldn't stand them. I preferred The Beach Boys, who sang about Southern California girls and beaches and cars. As far as I was concerned, The Beatles were aliens who had invaded our shores.

On those warm nights I liked to open the window in my room for any breeze that happened to blow and listen to Vin Scully call the Dodger games on the radio. He had a voice like honey, and more than once I fell asleep in bliss as the game stretched into the later innings.

But this summer routine was to be interrupted, and soon.

My father told my mother, "There'll be trouble if he comes here. There always is."

"Please try," Mom said. "Cecil is still trying to find his niche."

"Niche? I just wish he would find a job. And keep it. Or a wife. But who would want to live with that dreamer?"

"He's a good person, Sid."

"He's a failure. An absolute failure!"

So Uncle Cecil came to us that summer after getting fired from a job in Rancho Cucamonga. I didn't know what job it was, nor did I ask. I sensed that Uncle Cecil was tired of being asked and that he had come to our house so he could rest.

When Uncle Cecil wasn't around, my mother kept telling my father to just let him have some peace. But Dad spent most of that summer grumbling. More than once he told Uncle Cecil, "Keep out of my way."

Uncle Cecil was tall, with curly black hair that was beating a retreat from his forehead. He had deep-set eyes, like a couple of secrets hiding in his head. He also had a mouth with a smile like the Fourth of July.

That didn't help him with my dad, though. My dad didn't care what Uncle Cecil did with his mouth, as long as he kept it shut.

"I see things deeply," Uncle Cecil said to me one day as we walked down Canoga Avenue. I was going to the market for my mother, who wanted eggs, bread, and cooking oil. Uncle Cecil said he would walk with me and would buy me a roll of Necco Wafers. (He told me that Necco Wafers were "the greatest candy in the world," as if there had been a contest and it had won.)

"How deeply?" I asked.

"Aha!" Uncle Cecil said, smiling widely and sticking his finger in the air. "I knew you were a poet like me!"

"A poet?"

"Yes! When I told you I saw things deeply, you didn't ask me what that meant. You only asked me *how* deeply. Most people, when I tell them this, look at me like I'm crazy."

I remembered my dad's look whenever he saw Uncle Cecil, and it was exactly like that.

"We poets," he said, "see things deeply. God made us this way. Do you know the Psalms?"

"In the Bible?"

"It is poetry inspired by God! I tell you, David saw things more deeply than other people. That is why he was called a man after God's own heart."

We were getting close to Ventura Boulevard. The majestic pepper trees enfolded us. It was a hot day, but we were in a cool refuge of shade.

"Poems are made by fools like me," Uncle Cecil said. "But only God can make a tree." He stopped and put his hand on the gnarled trunk of a fat pepper tree. He patted it like a man would pat the hand of a dear friend. "Good old tree," he said.

"Yes," I said.

"And I know you are a poet because you never asked me why I can't hold a job."

I never had, but I *was* curious.

"I'll tell you, poet to poet. Once I was working on the freight dock at a big warehouse. I drove a forklift. I loaded big pallets and boxes and equipment onto trucks. It was hard work, but not brainy. So my brain was free to think about things. One day I was thinking about all of the junk I was loading and how we never ran out of it. When a supply of anything got low, *bingo!* Like magic we'd get more of it. We would keep shoveling junk out into the world, and on this particular day I began to wonder what would happen if we kept shoveling junk until it was everywhere. Until the whole world was covered with junk. Then what would we do?"

I waited for him to go on, but he was kind of staring into space. "But what about the job?" I asked.

"Oh yes. As I was thinking about junk I drove the forklift off the loading dock and almost killed myself. And that is why I can't seem to hold a job. Now, how about those Necco Wafers?"

That night we did what we always did in my house that summer—watched the evening news as we ate dinner. I think it was my dad's way of not having to make conversation with Uncle Cecil.

Emily wasn't there. She spent most of that summer with her friends, no doubt polluting her mind with The Beatles. On this particular night I remember Walter Cronkite on TV talking about war. There was something about a big push in Vietnam, near a place called Da Nang. Lots of our soldiers were being killed.

There was silence all around the table as we watched the news report. Images from a jungle, with soldiers in uniform running and shooting, flashed across the screen. Then there was an explosion. And voices screaming.

Suddenly Uncle Cecil threw his napkin down.

"I can't stand this war!" he shouted.

My father's face started turning red. He had been in the army during World War II, in Sicily. "You want the Communists to take over?"

"Our boys are being slaughtered! For nothing!"

My mother put her head in her hands.

"Nothing?" my dad shouted. "Communism is nothing?"

When my dad yelled, people all over the neighborhood could hear him. It was a force of nature, my dad's voice. Uncle Cecil was no match for it.

"Leave my table!" Dad yelled.

My mother started crying. "Sid, please."

Uncle Cecil stood up. "It's all right. I don't want to sit here quietly while boys are being slaughtered."

"Go on!" my father shouted.

I could see tears forming in Uncle Cecil's eyes. He tried hard to fight them back. His lower lip quivered like a scared dog. Then he turned and walked out our front door, closing it gently behind him.

On the television, Walter Cronkite was telling how many Americans the war had claimed this year.

We were having meatloaf and Brussels sprouts and mashed potatoes that night. Normally I loved that meal, but this time I couldn't finish.

After dinner I went outside to look for Uncle Cecil. The night was dark, but the moon was full and shining a pale orange through the haze of the day's smog.

I found Uncle Cecil sitting on our fence, looking up at the sky.

"I see things deeply," he said in a near whisper. "I wish I didn't sometimes."

"That's okay," I said, even though I didn't know if it was okay or not.

My uncle put his arm around me, and the next thing I knew he was pulling me into his chest. His other arm came around and hugged me. I could feel his body shaking a little. He didn't say anything for a long time.

The next day my father left for work early. My mom fixed a big breakfast of pancakes and eggs and sausages. It was like a special occasion. She kept offering more to Uncle Cecil, and refilling his coffee cup every time it got half empty.

Finally my uncle said, "No more. I can't eat another bite."

"Sure you can," Mom said. "I have another short stack ready to go."

"I am leaving today, Jan."

My mother froze with the coffee pot in her hand. "You don't have to go."

"That's right," I said. "You don't have to go."

But I knew he did have to go.

After breakfast he packed his one suitcase—a beige leather affair with fraying corners—and started to walk out the door.

"Wait," Mom said. "I'll drive you to the bus stop."

"No," said Uncle Cecil. "I want to walk down Canoga Avenue one more time."

"I'll go with you," I said.

We walked under the trees that let in little shafts of light like a stained glass window. We walked mostly in silence because there were not many words to say.

When we got to the corner of Canoga and Ventura, where the bus stop was, Uncle Cecil came to a sudden halt. He dropped his suitcase and stared.

Across the street, a man wearing a hard hat and sporting the largest chain saw in the world was cutting down a pepper tree.

"No!" shouted Uncle Cecil, but his voice was drowned out by the sound of the saw.

Without waiting for the traffic signal to change, Uncle Cecil charged across Ventura. He was almost hit twice by cars, but he ran as if he didn't notice.

I waited for the light to change and then ran to join him.

Uncle Cecil was waving his arms in front of the man with the saw. When he looked up and saw my uncle, I thought he might run away the way people do when confronted by a crazy man. He shut off his saw and said, "What is it?"

"You stop that!" Uncle Cecil said. "What gives you the right to cut down this tree?"

"Huh?"

"You have no right! This tree was here long before you, and you just leave it alone."

"Hey, friend, I just do what I'm told."

"Only God can make a tree!"

The man with the saw shook his head. "They're all coming out." He jerked his thumb down the street.

Uncle Cecil looked. And his mouth fell open.

About half a dozen men with chain saws were starting in on the pepper trees. The air was suddenly alive with angry buzzing, like an attack of giant bees. This stretch of road would soon be treeless, making room for a wider street and big office buildings.

Uncle Cecil just stood there shaking his head. His shoulders slumped.

The man in the hard hat started his saw again.

I took Uncle Cecil by the arm and walked him back to the bus stop.

We sat on the bench together, saying nothing. Uncle Cecil just looked at his hands. Finally he said, "It will never be the same again."

We sat in silence for several minutes.

"Promise me something," Uncle Cecil said.

"Okay."

"Promise me that you will never stop looking at things, really looking at them, inside out and upside down, and finding the poetry. God makes trees and poets. Trees a man can cut down, but not a poet. Will you promise me?"

"Sure," I said.

The bus came, and Uncle Cecil got on. He paused on the step; just before the doors closed, he looked at me and smiled. It was like the Fourth of July.

I couldn't help smiling, too, though I knew what Uncle Cecil said was true. Things would never be the same again. I also knew something else, something I wanted to tell my father someday when I wasn't afraid of him. I wanted to tell him Uncle Cecil was not a failure.

I stood at the bus stop and waved until the bus was out of sight. Then I turned my back on the men cutting down the trees, and at that moment I started looking deeply at everything, inside out and upside down.

I still do.

THE INSPECTOR

Just a few steps inside the cathedral entrance, Jean Barrineau was assaulted by the unmistakable stink of charred wood and varnish. As with any fire scene, it was the smell that alerted Jean to his responsibility. And how much more it was now!

Barrineau was chief arson inspector of the Paris Fire Brigade. And a Roman Catholic. Now those two streams in his life had merged into a river fraught with significance. For he was tasked with the greatest challenge and responsibility in all his twenty years of investigation—the whys and wherefores of the fire that nearly destroyed the cathedral of Notre Dame.

Greater still was this test because of the fire burning inside him. His marriage was over. While he and Cecile lived in the same two-story flat, they were strangers as the divorce settlement was being worked out. Civil to each other, yet cold, like dead embers in a fireplace. Deep inside, the rending of his marriage vows tore at Jean's soul. What a phony he was! What an imposter to be in this holy place on official business!

But then again, the business itself would be his balm from Gilead. The work. Pour yourself into the work and forget about what used to be your home.

"Tread carefully on this one."

Jean almost jumped at the voice. Brigade Commander François

Fournier had joined him. Fournier was a year younger than Jean and wore his authority like a breastplate of righteousness.

"When have I not?" Jean said.

"You know what I mean, eh?" Fournier raised his eyebrows, as if he were warning a four year old to stay away from the cookie jar.

"I don't believe I do." Jean knew very well, but he was going to make the commander say it.

"Sensitivity, eh? Do not form any theories until you and I have a chance to discuss all the evidence in private."

"Oh, certainly. We do want to be sensitive, don't we? We wouldn't want to hurt anyone's feelings, would we?"

For a long moment Fournier was silent. He seemed to be smoldering himself, like the pews a few meters ahead of them.

"Listen," he said finally. "This is no joke. Our premise is that it was a short circuit of some kind. The burden of proof is not to make it so, but to disprove it."

"I begin with no premise."

"You will this time," Fournier said.

"I go where the evidence leads."

"Just keep your mouth shut. To anyone. That's an order."

Fournier turned and walked back into the sunshine. Jean faced the shadows of Notre Dame.

In his head he went over the baseline of the investigation, the facts thus far.

It was around 6:30 p.m. that black smoke became visible on the roof of the cathedral, near the spire. No question that the fire started in the attic, which lay above the stone arches visible from the floor. The potential danger had always been with the giant, timber trusses that all European cathedrals used for structural integrity. Those trusses were a forest fire waiting to happen. The attic contained the equivalent of over 1,000 trees. Like any musty attic anywhere, dust and debris were bound to collect. A random spark in just the right place ... or an evil intent in the hands of a ...

"Sensitivity, eh?"

Once the attic was aflame, the fire spread quickly across the roof and engulfed the spire, made of a wooden frame covered in lead.

Because of its location on the island Île de la Cité, firefighters had difficulty getting to the blaze. Two hours into the fire only one pump-boat had been deployed to get river water into the action. But it was likely that boat had thwarted complete disaster.

But the water had unintended consequences. The magnificent pipe organ—built by the legendary Aristide Cavaillé-Coll and installed in the cathedral in the 19th century—suffered water damage. Not to the 8,000 pipes, but to the windchest that enabled the pipes to sing.

Yet there was some good news. The holy Crown of Thorns was rescued from a safe. The tunic of St. Louis, once worn by King Louis IX in the 13th century, and ornaments from the altar used for the coronation of Napoleon in 1804, were also saved.

And the bees! One could count this as a miracle, Jean concluded. Perhaps even a sign. In 2013 three beehives were placed on the roof of Notre Dame, as part of a citywide initiative to boost the declining bee population in Paris. Since bees do not have lungs, smoke merely makes them drowsy. It was heat that was their nemesis. The bees did not flee, but stayed to protect their queen. And survived.

Finally, there were the twin bell towers and the irreplaceable rose windows. Saved.

It was beneath the bell towers that Jean decided to begin his investigation, working backward toward where the blaze began. It was an unorthodox approach according to the manuals. But Jean had never been an inside-the-box kind of man. That had led him to solving cases that had flummoxed other experts.

First, he checked the pre-fire photos of the cathedral on his tablet. He scrolled to the one of the sector where he now stood, just outside the stairwell of the north bell tower. This was the favorite spot of the tourists. You needed to buy a ticket to climb the 387 steps. Halfway up was the gift shop, which Jean loathed. The commercialization of this holy place! Quasimodo swag, Esmeralda knickknacks. This was the house of God, not Victor Hugo!

Ah, well. Using his Maglite, Jean scanned the surfaces. Everything looked stable. The fire had not reached the stairwell, though a thin coating of smut—soot flakes—had settled on the first few steps. Nothing on the walls—

What was this? His trained eye picked up movement, small as it was.

On the floor, just in front of the first step—two soot flakes skittering along ... as if alive!

Jean stayed still, making sure he didn't ripple the air. He homed the beam of the Maglite on the flakes, watching their seemingly purposeful journey, before they disappeared into a a crack or crevice.

Sucked in!

But how? The stones were solid. Had been for almost 900 years. Surely there could not be an air pocket.

And yet, something underneath the stones had pulled in the flakes.

His mind was playing tricks. Move on.

Just as Fournier would have wanted it.

Jean bristled at the thought. Fournier was not going to tell him what to do, not this time.

Which meant he would not report any of this to Fournier. This time, Jean would go where the evidence led.

But first, outside the cathedral, he called his friend at university, Dr. Emil Gagnon. It was as if God himself had prepared the three of them—Jean, Gagnon, and Notre Dame—for this moment in time.

For Emil was the head of a research project utilizing RFC—Radio Frequency Capture. This new technology could do what an X-ray could not—traverse solid walls and reflect physical formation behind them. Then, by way of reconstruction algorithm, it could render a visual model of what was, for all intents and purposes, seen.

If there was a hidden chamber in this section of the cathedral, and anything of value was inside, Emil would be able to tell.

"What we find will remain between us, agreed?" Jean said when he met Emil in his office late that afternoon.

"Far be it from me to contend with the Fire Brigade," Emil said. He was in his early fifties, trim, with a thatch of graying hair which seemed to be conducting its own research into chaos theory. "I always wanted to be a spy."

At 3:39 he next morning, Jean Barrineau and Dr. Emil Gagnon approached Notre Dame Cathedral. Barrineau greeted the posted sentry and explained that he did not want any disturbance for the next hour and, further, this was a formal part of the investigation that was to be kept confidential. The young gendarme nodded with appropriate seriousness.

Inside, Jean used his Maglite to illuminate that section of the stairwell where he suspected the air pocket. Under the light, Emil set up his equipment. Jean was impressed at how compact it all was, and how quickly it was ready to go. Emil placed his laptop on the first step.

"Ready?" Emil said.

"Yes!" Jean said.

"I mean for disappointment," Emil said.

"Why do you say that?"

"You're too young to remember, but many years ago the American journalist Geraldo Rivera did a live broadcast on television. He was going to open up a sealed vault that had belonged to the mobster Al Capone. He speculated about hidden treasure and perhaps even dead bodies being inside. But when he finally got in there was only debris and a few empty bottles. A big nothing."

"At least we are not on television," Jean said.

"Then let us see what we can see," Emil said.

Emil held what he called the stick—a vertical handle with a wide, flat base—over the stone that Jean had designated number one. He pressed a key on the stick, and the monitor on the laptop illuminated a deep blue background. As Emil slowly moved the stick in a circular pattern, yellow dots appeared on the blue.

"We've got something," Emil said. "By heavens, there is a space under there!"

"Can you tell how big it is?"

"Not yet. But one thing sure, it is bigger than a breadbox."

And what might have been hidden in such a space? Gold candle sticks? Precious jewels? Jean rebuked himself for such schoolboy thoughts.

But then, what was wrong with being a schoolboy again? Back when the future seemed a hopeful thing. A place where love would last.

He watched the laptop monitor as the yellow dots began to be connected by lines, free in form and curvature. As if a sketch was being made. But of what?

For three or four minutes, the two men watched as the computer put together what looked to be—

"A skeleton," Emil said.

"Truly?" Jean said.

"And if I remember my anatomy, that pelvic bone indicates a woman."

"A woman? Buried here?"

"Wait. Look!"

Another skeleton was forming on the monitor. The two were face to face—or, rather, skull to skull.

One arm of the second skeleton was draped over the first.

"It can't be," Emil whispered.

Jean was unable to speak, for his breath had left him.

The spinal column of the second skeleton was grotesquely crooked. The skull sat low on the shoulder blades. And one leg was shorter than the other.

"You don't suppose," Emil said. "It can't be. It cannot possibly be!"

"And why not?" said Jean.

"That is fiction! That is a Victor Hugo story!"

"Yet you see," Jean said.

Emil looked at the monitor, then back at Jean. "How will we break this news?"

"We won't," Jean said.

"Eh?"

"What a circus it would cause here in God's own house. Let the wretches rest in peace. Let us be done here, and never speak of this to anyone."

Jean awoke in the chair near the fireplace. What time was it? Daylight streamed through the window blinds. Dust swirled in the beams.

A scuffing sound behind him. Cecile said, "You look a sight."

Her voice was cool, slicing through the evanescent cobwebs of his dream.

Jean felt his scratchy beard. "I must have dozed off."

"Shall I make you tea? We have a meeting with the lawyers at three, you'll recall."

She started for the kitchen.

"Wait!" Jean said.

"Eh?"

"How long has it been?"

"Been?"

"Since the fire?"

"Why, six months. Is anything—"

"Cecile."

"Are you all right?"

She came to the chair. Jean reached for her hand and pulled her toward him.

"What are you doing?" she said.

He kept pulling, turning her slightly with his other hand, until she fell to a sitting position on his lap.

"Jean, please!"

Putting his arms around her, Jean buried his head in her chest.

"What is this?" Cecile said.

Jean began to weep.

"Stay with me," he said.

"Jean—"

"Please."

MY FATHER'S BIRTHDAY

"It's your father's birthday tomorrow," my mother said. "Why don't you make him a card?"

We were in the kitchen and Mom was preparing dinner. I sat in the nook where the kitchen table was, working on my homework. Mrs. Barshea had given us a math sheet to complete and I hated math and my mom knew it. So she would let me do these in the kitchen while she made dinner. It was comforting to me because I knew if I got stuck she would come over and help. The warmth of the kitchen and the smell of whatever Mom was cooking put me at ease. I had to be at ease if I was ever going to figure out long division.

It was good that my father wasn't home because he did not put me at ease. I was scared of him getting mad. He'd been getting mad at my big brother a lot lately, calling him a "no good hippie" and a "draft dodger." And when my dad got mad he yelled.

Boy, could he yell. And if it was at you, it was like getting your soul sucked out of your body and hung on a meat hook and beaten with a base-ball bat.

More than anything in the world I wanted my dad to think I was good so I wouldn't get yelled at.

I wanted to please him.

A birthday card didn't seem like enough.

. . .

When company came over my dad liked to entertain over drinks and cheese snacks. He smoked cigars, but my mom and the other guests smoked cigarettes. The living room would be shrouded in a gray fog. My dad would stand in front of the fireplace, cigar in hand, and recite poetry.

He loved poetry almost as much as he loved the Dodgers and Clarence Darrow. Dad was a lawyer because when he was twelve years old his own father had taken him to the auditorium of The Broadway Department Store on Fourth and Hill in Los Angeles, to hear the famous lawyer give a talk and autograph copies of his autobiography, *The Story of My Life.* My grandfather bought a copy and had Clarence Darrow inscribe it to Billy Tanner, my father. Clarence Darrow shook his hand and asked my dad what he wanted to be when he grew up. "A lawyer," my dad said. And the old warrior gave my father an approving nod with his big, lion head.

So after coming back from serving in the Navy in World War II, my father went to law school at UCLA and he liked to tell of the time he met Clarence Darrow.

I would sometimes slip into the smoky room to listen to my dad recite a poem. He was a performer. He would do *Casey at the Bat, Abou Ben-Adhem, The Shooting of Dan McGrew,* and what seemed to be his favorite, *The Betrothed,* a poem about cigars by Kipling, which began, *Open the old cigar box* and ended with *A woman is only a woman, but a good cigar is a smoke.*

Dad wanted me to memorize poems, too. In particular another one by old man Kipling, *If.* One time he sat me down in the living room, just the two of us, and rattled it off, finishing with his typical flourish at the end.

If you can fill the unforgiving minute
With sixty seconds' worth of distance run,
Yours is the Earth and everything that's in it,
And—which is more—you'll be a Man, my son!

I knew that's what he wanted me to be—a man. But how much of a man could I be at nine years old when I was afraid of my own father?

The year before my dad signed me up for Little League. It was a humiliating experience. I stunk. I got put in right field, where the stinky kids go. I struck out a lot. After the third game I told my mom I was quitting. She was supposed to drive me to practice but I ran out of the house and down the block and climbed an orange tree owned by the Buckleys. I sat there wondering what my dad was going to say when he got home.

I didn't have long to wait. I was in that tree, four houses away from mine, when the whole earth was filled with my dad's voice.

"VICTOR! VICTOR! GET HOME NOW!"

My soul got sucked out and got stuck on a branch in the orange tree. My empty, soulless body got down and walked on jelly legs back home.

I knew I was in for it when I came in the house and saw my mother with a worried look on her face and my father steaming, pacing. He told me to sit down.

"You are not going to quit, you understand?" His voice shook the curtains. "You start something, you finish it! I'm going to call Coach Jones and you are going to tell him you're sorry you missed practice, you understand me?"

I understood all right.

And I wanted my dad to like me.

Saturday morning, the day of Dad's birthday, I took the rubber stopper off the bottom of my piggy bank and counted out five dollars in silver. I put it in the pocket of my jeans and rode my bike to Green's Liquor on Ventura Boulevard. I knew the inside well because I got my baseball cards there.

But I'd never been to the tobacco section. There were lots of cigar choices. Some big fat cigars in a box, but when I looked at the price I almost yelped. I didn't have nearly enough money for those!

Then I saw a smaller cellophane wrapped box with a picture of men in funny hats on it. Dutch Masters. That had to be a good brand because there was a commercial on TV about them. The man in the commercial looked happy when he took one out for a smoke.

I took the package of cigars to the counter and laid it down and began to reach for my coins.

The man behind the counter said, "You can't buy those, son."

Ha! He thought I wanted them for myself. But I was prepared. "They're for my dad," I said.

"Well, he'll have to come in and buy them himself."

"But it's for his birthday."

"I'm sorry, son."

My cheeks started burning. A high school kid over by the paperback spinner was looking at me with a smirk.

I walked out of there as fast as I could.

I felt like crying.

When I got home I went straight to my room and closed the door. I took the silver out of my pocket and threw it at the wall. I got on my bed and stared at the ceiling.

There was a knock on the door. "Vic, are you okay?" my mother said.

"Yeah," I said.

"I thought I heard something."

"I'm okay," I said.

"All right," she said.

And then I was alone in the silence.

A little while later I got up and got some construction paper and tried to make a card for my dad. I tried to draw a Dodger baseball player on the front with a bat that had *Happy Birthday* on it. The only problem was I couldn't draw. Not like Linda Miller in my class at Serrania Avenue Elementary School, who could draw all sorts of cartoon characters. Mine always came out like stick figures who had somehow managed to get fat.

After an hour of trying, I ripped up all the construction paper and threw the pieces in the little wastebasket by my desk.

My father worked at his office most Saturdays. When he got home I was on my bed reading an Archie comic book. I heard Dad talking to Mom in the kitchen. I heard him mixing a drink like he always did when he got home. A martini, he called it. There was the sound of ice cubes in a glass pitcher as he stirred.

Then I heard our phone ring and my dad's big voice answering it.

A few minutes later there was a short knock on my door and it opened, and my dad came in.

"Hello, Victor," he said. He never called me Victor unless I was in trouble. At least he wasn't yelling.

My hands shook.

He sat on my bed and told me to sit up.

I sat up.

"I just got a call from Al Summers. He works at Green's Liquor. He said he thought my son came in and tried to buy some cigars."

My breath left me.

"Was that you?" Dad said.

I couldn't look at him. I looked at my bed and nodded. I wanted my floor to open up so I could dive into the dirt below our house and not be seen. I wanted to be back in the orange tree.

"He said you told him it was for my birthday," Dad said. "Is that true?"

I nodded again.

I felt his hand on my head. He smoothed the back of my hair.

"Come on," he said, and stood.

I was not at all sure what that meant, but at least his voice was soft.

He put his hand around my shoulder and we walked out of my room.

"We'll be right back," Dad said to Mom.

"Where are you going?" Mom asked.

"Just down to the corner. Something to take care of."

My head went light on me. He was going to make me apologize! I was going to be publicly humiliated. Maybe that big kid at the spinner would be there again to mock me.

I tried to take it like a brave condemned prisoner. I got in our white Ford Falcon and Dad started it up.

He said nothing on the drive to the corner.

We got out and went into the liquor store.

The man behind the counter smiled and gave my Dad a wave. Then he gave me a wave.

I didn't wave back. My face was hot again.

"Those cigars my son wanted to buy for me," Dad said.

"Right here," the man said, and put the box of Dutch Masters cigars on the counter.

"How much?" Dad said.

"Three ninety-nine," the man said.

Dad looked at me. "Still want to buy them for my birthday?"

Stunned, but relieved, I nodded vigorously.

But I didn't have my money! What a terrible thing.

Dad took out his wallet and said, "I'm giving you an advance on your allowance. Five weeks' worth, okay?"

I nodded.

He gave the man a five dollar bill. The man gave my dad some change. Dad put the change in my hand. I was holding three quarters and a dime.

"Now do a favor for me," Dad said to me. "Go over and choose your favorite candy, whatever you want."

"Really?" I said.

"Go on, now."

My head swam at the choices! There was Razzles and Almond Joy and 3 Musketeers and Bit-O-Honey. There was gum and suckers and M&Ms. Ah, but there it was, my favorite, hands down—Good & Plenty. I grabbed a box and took it back to the counter.

I started to dig for the change but Dad said, "This is on me."

He gave the man a nickel, then handed me the box of candy and took his box of Dutch Masters cigars.

"S'long, Al," he said.

"You bet," the man said.

That night for dinner we had meatloaf and Brussels sprouts and I even ate some of the Brussels sprouts without complaining.

After dinner Dad said, "Bring your box of candy out to the back yard."

Outside it was twilight. Dad got out a couple of lawn chairs and opened them and set them down next to each other. I sat with my Good & Plenty. Dad sat with his Dutch Masters. He took one out and lit it with a match.

He took a puff and leaned his head back and let the smoke out of his mouth slowly.

"Ah, this is one fine birthday cigar," he said.

I popped three Good & Plenty into my mouth, the perfect amount. I sucked on them for a second, then chewed and got the licorice jolt.

And in that moment the Earth was mine, and everything in it.

STORIES WITH A PUNCH

Here are all four stiories in the Irish Jimmy Gallagher series. They take place in 1950s Los Angeles. I think you'll enjoy Jimmy, his best girl Ruby, and his bulldog Steve. As one critic noted, "No need to be a boxing fan— just press the clutch, put it into gear, and enjoy the ride."

IRON HANDS

May the Lord keep you in his hand and never close His fist too tight. –
Irish blessing

When I stepped in the ring I saw him for the first time. Big and black with a sheen of sweat on him. Joe Louis himself might have been this lug's baby brother, if I have to paint you a picture.

Now I'm no shrimp. I come in at 6'3" and my 225 ain't fat. But this one, Iron Hands Jackson was his name, was maybe an inch taller and a foot wider across the chest.

And me thinking, Where did they find this mountain?

Through the haze of smoke I saw him glaring at me, like he was working his way up into a frenzy. Now it takes me gettin' hit with a bum punch that makes me crazy. I can't just tell myself to beat the life out of a man. Folks'll tell you that. *Jimmy Gallagher, he's a heck of a fella, quick with a laugh and quicker with the jab. But if you foul him, stand back, 'cause all the laughs'll die in fury.*

So here I was in the smoker down by the river. That would be the Los Angeles River, such as it is now, a glorified wash. Fifty years ago, in 1905, she was a real stream. A natural beauty, like my girl, Ruby.

Now in these enlightened days of Eisenhower and TV, the river's been tamed by cement and engineers, which is sad. I like the raw energy of the natural world and there seems to be less and less of it in L.A. these days. Someday they'll make this whole place into one of them freeways you keep reading about.

You may ask, didn't they outlaw smokers in the city and county? And the answer would be yes, but you know the ways of the world. A little bit of money changing hands changes things. Just go ask Mr. Judas Iscariot about them thirty pieces of silver.

So that's where we were on that hot August night, in a warehouse, and a whole lot of puffy white men betting on me to knock out a black man the size of Catalina Island.

I was getting 8 to 1. They all knew Irish Jimmy needed only one punch to connect. I got thunder in my right hand, and I was gonna box until I could unleash it.

Boy, what a dumb cluck I was that night! And it almost got me killed.

––––––

The ring was smaller than regulation, this being a smoker—they call it that for all the burning tobacco consumed before, during and after the fight. Gets in your throat if you ain't careful, which is why I coat it with some good Irish whiskey right before the opening bell. And they think I got water in that jug!

I'd made a reputation in Southern Cal the last few years. Ever since I got back from the South Pacific I'd been scratching together what I could on the circuit. Maybe you ask why I didn't fight legit, and I'll tell you. I was done dirty by a guy named Mickey Levine, who maybe you've heard of. I wouldn't take a dive and he said I wasn't going to get another decent fight. I decked him and almost got my ticket punched by his thugs. But I punched harder and ran faster, and I been on my own ever since.

––––––

So we get the instructions from the organizer, a Kiwanis named Lanahan, a lawyer with a gambling habit. I look right in the eyes of Iron Hands Jackson, and gives me a brown-eyed stare down. I just smiled.

Then we're off to our corners and the bell rings. This fight is scheduled to go ten rounds but I've decided to end it in two. I'm going to be careful in the first because Jackson looks like one of his arms could pound circus tent stakes ten feet underground.

I fight smart. I learn what I need to do, then I do it.

First thing I had to find out was if Jackson was a bull or a boxer. A bull just comes at you and tries to beat you to a pulp. Jake LaMotta is like that.

Then there's the boxers. They know the skills and pick their spots. That's Sugar Ray Robinson.

Now, I don't need to tell you what Robinson did to LaMotta in '51. They don't call it the St. Valentine's Day Massacre for nothing. A boxer who can punch and move beats a bull every time if he's careful and doesn't leave his mug hangin' out there so even Grandma Moses could wallop him one.

So I'm going to study Jackson, but as we get closer to each other in the ring I notice someone just over his shoulder, right in my line of sight—one Michael "Mickey" Levine.

The next second I'm lying on my back, my head feeling like it just got kicked by Mrs. O'Leary's horse.

I heard the cheers and jeers as I lay there, looking up through the smoke at the ref, an off-duty sheriff named Snyder. He's laying on the count.

Up on my knees I come, by the count of eight. Then on my feet before ten. I shake my head to clear it, just in time to see Iron Hands Jackson charging me.

———

I danced backwards like Gene Kelly his own self. Iron Hands threw a wild right, putting his whole body behind it. That's the puncher's folly. Once he has you in trouble he gets crazy to finish you off. So I let his momentum throw him off balance and as he stumbled by I gave him a hard left to the kidney.

The big man went down on one knee. To prop himself he threw his right-hand glove on the canvas. It hit hard. Too hard. And that's when I knew he was hiding something. He had a loaded glove!

As he got to his feet I took a look over at Mickey Levine, and he was just staring, anger twitching his lips. It all came together like a fine Irish ballad. This fight was fixed, only not for somebody taking a dive. No, Mickey was planning on making a killing off this fight and my 8-1 odds. Which meant Iron Hands had to kill me, metaphorically speakin'. Or maybe not. Maybe that hard right of his with the cement tape or whatever it was would pummel my brain into the big nowhere.

I shouted at Snyder, the ref. "Check his glove!"

"Fight on or quit," Snyder spat back, and I figured then he was in on the action, too. Old Mickey had this fight sewn up tighter than a gnat's girdle.

———

Iron Hands was on his feet now, hissing. Little bits of spittle flew out of his mouth like confetti. I gave him the Gallagher glare. We've been cheated and beaten and mocked ever since we arrived on these shores from County Cork in 1848. We've been hanged and kept out of work and lied about. But our code was never to complain, only to take what was rightfully ours, by force if necessary.

I went into a demonstration of the fine art of boxing. I kept my eye on that right hand of Jackson's and circled left as much as I could. His jab was hard but slow. I counter punched. I peppered his face with left jabs. Once I got a nice right over his left ear with a punch I used to take out many a good fighter. But Iron Hands didn't go down. He had a hard head and that will cover a multitude of sins in the ring.

The bell rang and we were done with Round One.

My corner man was Barney O'Toole, as I'll only let a fellow Irishman attend me. I trust Barney like he was my big brother, him having about ten years on me. Barney sells papers at the corner of Broadway and Third and was once a pugilist himself.

"He's got a loaded right hand," I said to Barney.

Barney threw a cup of cold water in my face. "He's a palooka. You can take him."

"Long as I stay away from that pile driver. It's a fix."

"Ya think?"

"Mickey Levine is here."

At that Barney's eyes got all open and wiggly. "That crawlin' vermin of the devil's spawn! I'll murder him!"

"Take it easy, Barney. Concentrate on the fight. You see anything?"

"He drops his left when he comes in straight. Give him a pop to the nose before he can get you with that roundhouse."

The bell clanged.

Round Two.

————

He came straight at me, and it was just like Barney said. Jackson dropped his left hand, and I threw a perfect right to his jaw. It landed solid and took away some power in his right hand, which was a good thing because that right found my left eye. There was enough in that punch to make little flashbulbs go off behind my eyes.

So I clinched him. In the clinch I pounded the back of his head and in his ear I said, "Cheater! What if your mama knew?"

This got me the desired effect, which was to make Iron Hands so mad he forgot all about boxing and just went wild.

I danced and covered my face and pulled my elbows down to protect my middle. Each time he threw the right I blocked it, but let me tell you it was starting to affect my arms and left side. I even thought he broke my forearm once.

But he was wearing himself out, another puncher's sin.

"If your mama could see you now," I said, "she'd roll over and die."

The big man spoke in a voice low and guttural. "Shut up! I'll kill you!"

Which is exactly how I wanted him to react.

He gave me everything he had. And while I managed to fend off the right, he caught me once with the left and opened a cut over my right eye.

The bell dinged, and Round Two was over.

Barney swabbed my cut and said, "He's gettin' tired." And I said, "I know that, you stupid Mick, whattaya think I was thinkin' in there?"

"Take him out this round," Barney said. "Use your left."

"I think I'll use psychology," I said.

"Don't get fancy!"

But it wasn't fancy at all. It was the boxer's greatest friend, the noodle. You use it or you get it knocked off your neck.

———

The bell for Round Three clanged, and out we came. Iron Hands looked mad but tired. He wasn't holding his arms up as high as at the start of the fight. That anvil in his right glove also had to be weighing him down. He'd wanted to take me out with that first punch, and when he didn't it meant he had to carry it around with him.

We circled each other and I jabbed him—*bap bap bap*—giving him a face tattoo. And each time I landed I said, "Your mama knows. Your mama knows."

He got furious. But he was spent.

So I got him in a clinch and said in his ear, "This is for cheating," and I broke and gave him a left uppercut. His head snapped back. His eyes glazed.

"And this is for cheating Irish Jimmy Gallagher," I said, and feinted with my left, then feinted with my right. He didn't know what to do. Then I zinged the most beautiful left hook of my fighting life smack into the face of Iron Hands Jackson.

I knew the moment it landed he would not be getting up. He hit the canvas with a thud like a sack of potatoes tossed off a truck at the Central Market.

Only then was I aware of the roar of the crowd and the cheers of the moneychangers. Snyder slowed his count, but it didn't matter. Jimmy Gallagher was the winner of this fight. I had earned my two hundred bucks and justice had decreed that I come out on top.

When the count was finished Iron Hands Jackson still lay motionless on the canvas, and I didn't care a bit. The stinkin' cheat.

Then I looked into the crowd, trying to spot Mickey Levine. I was gonna shake a fist at him but he was gone as far as I could tell. I wouldn't be seeing him for another half hour, and then it would be me on my back, looking up.

———

I was whistling a tune as I left the club, after hosing myself off and getting into my only suit. It was a nice night in the City of Angels, and after being in a smoke fog for three rounds I thought it would be good to walk all the way to Figueroa and meet up with Ruby at Charley's. Charley's is the 24-hour diner where Ruby waits tables, and tonight she was on graveyard. I figured my twenty-minute walk would clean out my lungs and turn me back into my charming self for the benefit of my lady love.

But no sooner had I cleared the tracks when two shadows the size of trees closed in on me. Before I could even pull back my right, I got a sap to the back of my head. It felt like my skull was an open chasm on the San Andreas Fault, and down I went.

It was instinct that made me curl into a ball, and a good thing, too, as a shoe slammed into the forearms protecting my face.

The same shoe, or maybe it was another, pushed my left shoulder so I was on my back. Then I heard a voice say, "Hold it."

Then the same voice says, "Well, Jimmy, that's the way you should look alla time."

Levine!

I let my hands down and looked up at the ugly muldoon, with his two hooligans on either side of him.

"You been gumming up my works," Levine said. "It's time for me to gum up yours. Your fighting days are over."

With as much bravado as an Irishman can manage from his backside—and that is a considerable lot, I will tell you that much—I said, "I ain't ready to retire just yet."

"From where I'm standing," Levine said, "it doesn't look like you're in much of a position to negotiate."

I tried to sit up but one of the hoods dropped his size twelve on my neck and pushed me back down.

"You were supposed to lose tonight," Levine said.

"Whyn't you pay me to take a dive?" I said.

"'Cause you wouldn't have taken it. You got some sort of code that won't let you fight dishonest, and that's just a crying shame. There is money to be made if you're smart, like me."

"Ah," I said, "if ye had two brains you'd be twice as stupid."

Now there are times when you insult a person, and times when you don't, and your enjoyment of life is considerably improved if you figure out the difference between those two times. A lesson for all is to remember when you're on your back and you got a mobster and his goons all over you, it's probably not a good time to be disparagin'.

I am a slow learner.

Levine said, "Let's start with breaking his ribs."

One of the goons laughed and like a magician produced in his right hand a baseball bat. The other one, the one with the size twelves, put his foot right on my face.

I had no time to prepare for the worst.

But instead of a bat to my rib cage, the shoe on my face lifted. I heard some grunting and blinked a couple of times.

There was a fourth man on the scene, and he was in a fighting disposition.

One of the thugs was on the ground, out like a dim bulb.

The other, the one with the bat, was in the grip of two huge hands that had hold of his wrists.

I could see in the pale light of the moon that it was none other than Iron Hands Jackson his own self.

And then something glinted in the light and I saw it was a small gun in the hand of Mickey Levine.

Still on my side, I swept my left arm across my body and grabbed Mickey Levine's left ankle. It was a skinny little ankle and it gave me good purchase. With a hearty yank I pulled that leg out from under him.

His body went down.

The gun went off.

I scrambled like a clumsy crab on top of Mickey, getting my hands on his left, which held the gun. The darn thing went off again and I felt something like a Dutch rub on my right knee. I lifted Mickey's hand and slammed it on the asphalt. The gun skittered off to the side and Mickey yelped in pain. Without a weapon he was just a skinny little weasel. I popped him one in the chops with my left and he went nighty night.

I got on my feet just in time to see Iron Hands Jackson throw a beautiful right cross to the mug of the guy with the bat.

Boom! He went down like the '29 stock market.

And then there we were, me and the dirty cheat who had only half-an-hour earlier tried to knock my head off my shoulders.

We looked at each other like cave men from different buttes, wondering if the other was friend or foe.

"Why?" I finally said.

"No fault o' yours if you won fair and square," Iron Hands said. "Don't think a fella oughta be beat on for that."

"You were packing plaster, weren't you?"

He nodded. "But you shouldn't of oughta brang my mother into it."

I put a hand on his granite shoulder. "Me lad, it's an apology I'm offering you, and a hamburger besides. I think we'd best have a talk."

———

Ruby McGuire is a slice of sunshine plucked from the sky and tenderly set under blonde hair and blue eyes and a smile that can set a man's heart to dancin'. Fitting, too, since her mother named her after Ruby Keeler, the dancer. She's an angel waiting on tables, supporting that same mother in her infirmity. She lives in a room in a Bunker Hill shack, just off the tracks of Angels Flight.

It was near midnight when Iron Hands and me pushed into Charley's and took a table by the window. The place had a few scattered patrons—a well-dressed couple that looked like they were slumming after a show, a rummy or two at the counter draining coffee. We even had one of Chief Parker's finest, a uniformed police officer on break, his hands wrapped around a steak sandwich.

Ruby came out of the kitchen with a tray of food for the ritzy couple and gave me the eye as she walked by. She doesn't like it when I fight, but I always tell her you might as well not like a dog because it barks.

Two shakes later she was at our table.

"Hello, baby," I said.

"Your face looks like our hamburger," she said.

"Well let me introduce you to my pal, Mr. Iron Hands Jackson."

"Just plain John will do, ma'am," Iron Hands said. "I'm pleased to meet you."

"Well!" Ruby said. "A gentleman. Very nice to make your acquaintance, I'm sure."

"This gentleman tried to knock my block off tonight," I said.

"Might've done you some good," Ruby said.

"My girl wants me to give up the fight game," I said to Iron Hands.

"And him being offered a good job, maintaining the streets," Ruby said.

"I don't want to be a garbage collector!" That turned heads in the diner.

"In charge you would've been," she said. "Management!"

"Imagine me, telling garbage collectors what to do."

"You'd be offering something to the city," Ruby said. "You'd be making her clean. Instead, you bleed on her."

"That's my darlin'," I said. "Always lookin' out for me. Now how's about a couple of cheeseburgers, with lots o' fried onions, and a couple of Cokes? And a big basket of fries."

Ruby rolled her eyes, but then took the pencil from her hair and jotted the order on her pad.

I said, "That'll do for me. And what would you like to eat, Iron Hands?"

Jackson looked puzzled for about a second, then broke out into a hearty laugh. It came from his big old chest and me and Ruby couldn't help but laugh, too.

"That's a good'n!" Iron Hands said. "You had me goin' there for a minute."

"Goin' nothin'. I meant it."

"Well now," Iron Hands said. "Two cheeseburgers does sound mighty fine."

"Bring us four cheeseburgers, my daisy," I said. "I'm gonna match my pal here bite for bite."

Iron Hands said, "I'm afeared I don't have the money to—"

I put up my hand. "Your money's no good here."

To Ruby I said, "Darlin', two gentlemen are ready to dine."

"I see one gent," she said, looking at Jackson. "Where's the other?"

———

We got our feast and after the first couple of bites, Iron Hands said, "Why're you bein' so nice to me, after what I tried to do?"

"Every man deserves a second chance," I said. "The Good Lord knows

I been given several of 'em myself. I know you got mixed up with the wrong people."

He nodded sadly, took a big bite of his burger and talked around the food. "I got the boot from the railroad," he said, "and I needed some eatin' money. A hunnerd sounded good for a few rounds with a loaded right."

"A mere C note? And I take it you haven't been paid yet."

"Uh-uh."

"Nor will you, now that you've got yourself on the wrong side of Mickey Levine."

"I wish I never met him," Iron Hands said, and in that big ham hock of his he fisted up maybe ten French fries, dipped 'em in a pool of ketchup he'd poured on his plate, then shoved the whole mess in his mouth.

"Well now, son," says I, "this is a troubling thing. I know what Levine is capable of, and I know what he does to people. You and me are in a real fix right now here in the city of Los Angeles."

"Mebbe I should just go home."

"Where'd that be?"

"Alabama."

"Why'd you come out here, John?" It was the first time I'd called him by his real first name, but I was starting to feel downright brotherly towards him.

"My wife, she was killed. A rich boy from Montgomery ran her down in the street in his big old Cadillac. He was drunk as a skunk. But he was the son of a big-time lawyer, and white to boot, and the police said my Alice was the one at fault, that she was runnin' away from . . ."

He couldn't finish. There was a big tear streaming down his cheek. He put a finger to his face and wiped it away, and left a little ketchup under his eye.

I didn't say a word. I grabbed a fresh napkin from the holder and reached out and wiped the ketchup off.

We didn't talk for about a minute.

Then Iron Hands said, "I wanted to get as far away as I could, and when I ran into the Pacific Ocean, I stopped. Got me a job on the Santa Fe line, rippin' track, 'til about two weeks ago." He sighed. "Now it looks like I have to go back."

Next thing I knew I'd slapped my hand on the table. "No sir! We got as much right to be here as any two-bit mobster!"

"But—"

"You ever been to Mickey's office?"

Iron Hands shook his head.

"Something tells me after what we did, he's gonna have a meeting there, and it's probably right now."

"He'll have men with him."

"We'll have the element of surprise," I said. "And somethin' else."

He waited.

"The two best fighters this side of the Atlantic," I said.

Iron Hands smiled.

I asked Ruby if I could borrow her car, a 1941 Ford that had been her mother's. When she asked what I needed it for I told her a business meeting and that Iron Hands was coming with me.

"Does this meeting involve the fight game?" she said, hands on hips.

"No," I said. "This meeting will be no game at all."

She reached in her pocket and tossed me the keys to the car.

———

Mickey Levine had his office in the Stimson Building on Spring Street. We went in the front door, me and Iron Hands. The old coot of a night man was snoozing behind the desk. I put my finger to my lips and walked softly to the directory, where the white lettering showed that Michael Levine & Assoc. had an office on the third floor.

As quietly as two big fighters can be, me and Iron Hands took the stairs up to the third.

I peeked out and looked down the corridor. Halfway down was goon in a crushed fedora, sitting in a chair and reading a racing form. One of Mickey's gunsels, keeping watch.

"Can you make with the shuffle?" I whispered.

"The what?" Iron Hands whispered back.

"Bend over and shuffle like you had too much to drink. I'll be in front of you, facing you, backing up like I'm trying to help you walk."

"I can do that."

"Leave the rest to me."

We backed out of the stairwell as planned, me with my back to the gunsel and Iron Hands bent over, shuffle-walking. The gunsel couldn't see either of our faces.

"Easy there, fella," I said. "You've been on a toot."

I heard steps approaching, then a deep voice said, "Hold it right there."

"Gimme a hand, fella," I said without turning my head.

"That's far enough," the gunsel said. I estimated him to be about three feet behind me. I spun around and gave him a right cross that would have flattened Marciano.

He hit the floor like garbage from a chute.

"Lordy, that is a good right hand you got!" Iron Hands said.

I opened the gunsel's coat and removed a .38 roscoe from a shoulder holster. I checked his waistband and his socks. No more weapons.

"Now we've got the element of surprise," I said. "We go in, I'm gonna fire one shot into the ceiling. Then you start punching anything that moves."

"I like this plan," Iron Hands said.

I smiled, winked and said, "For God and country." Then I kicked open the door.

———

If there's one thing the fight game teaches you, it's to take your openings as you find 'em. Don't overthink. When in doubt, punch. Never give the opponent time to use his noggin.

When we got inside the office, me and Iron Hands, I saw that there were five of them, including Mickey. Mickey was sitting at a desk, two of the other four were on either side of him. The other two were nearer the door, sitting on chairs opposite each other and playing cards on a chair between them. There was a flash of recognition in me. These card players were the two Iron Hands had dispatched earlier that evening.

The shot spooked everybody. I charged the desk, trusting Iron Hands to take care of the card players.

Mickey looked up with pie eyes and threw his hands in the air. "Don't shoot!"

The two big boys at his sides started to reach for weapons. I pointed the gun and said, "Don't try it. Hands up."

With some reluctance, up those hands went.

I heard the sound of fist meeting face behind me. I gave a quick look and saw the two card players on the floor. Iron Hands joined me at the desk.

"You got no call to do this," Mickey said. "We can agree to disagree."

"I only agree you're nobody I'd ever agree to agree with" I said.

Mickey looked confused, and to tell the truth, I wasn't any too sure what I just said also. I told the two goons to lie down on the floor.

They just stood there.

"You see what I'm holding?" I said.

"You aren't going to shoot anybody," Mickey said, sounding a little braver than a second before. Which I didn't like. "You aren't a killer, Jimmy. That's one reason you never made it in the ring."

"Oh no, Mickey. Reason I didn't was you made sure I didn't get the bouts. Now get on the floor."

Nobody moved.

"You and the shine can walk out of here now," Mickey said, "and no hard feelings."

"That's not a nice thing to say, Mr. Levine," Iron Hands said.

Mickey looked mad as an unpickled herring. "I don't take that talk from anybody, least of all a coon."

I said to John, "You take the one on the right, I'll take the one on the left." And within three seconds we had two more of 'em on the floor, down for the count.

Only Mickey was left standing.

We dragged him out the back way. John Iron Hands Jackson held him in the alley while I brought Ruby's car around.

Then we took a ride all the way up to Mulholland Drive.

———

Looking down at the city at night is an inspiring sight. Pretty as a postcard. Makes you feel good inside.

Unless you're a crummy mobster in the hands of a couple of heavyweights.

We parked on the side of a steep hill. John brought Mickey out of the car. In those big iron mitts Mickey looked like a Kewpie doll John might've won at a carnival.

The wind was cool blowing up from the canyon.

"What're you gonna do to me?" Mickey said.

"You're gonna do it to yourself, Mickey," I said. "You're through. You're out of Los Angeles."

He snorted. "You haven't got that kind of muscle."

"Can you hear the cry of the banshee, Mickey? Listen." I put my hand to my ear. A little whistle of wind came up then, and I saw Mickey's eyes widen in the moonlight. "She's callin' yer name, Mickey. And if she finds yer still in L.A. after tomorrow, she'll be coming for you. She'll start by gettin' every fighter I know together, and you won't know when we're comin'. We'll begin with breaking your bones, and then proceed to your head. Are you gettin' it, Mickey? And don't go hiring torpedoes, because they won't find us. We'll find you first. You've got my promise on that, Mickey. Never get in the way of an Irishman on a mission."

Mickey hesitated, then said, "You're bluffing."

"Am I?" I grabbed a fistful of Mickey's shirt. I lifted him off the ground. "Then why don't you call my bluff?"

With that I tossed him over the side of the hill. Down he went, rolling and screaming as he did. He would have some nasty bruises and cuts by the time he stopped, but that was a good lesson for him. He'd know what it feels like to be a fighter facing Irish Jimmy Gallagher or Iron Hands Jackson, that's the Lord's honest truth with a good whiskey on the side.

———

It was almost time for Ruby to knock off when we got back to Charley's. Me and Iron Hands sat at the same table and ordered coffee.

Ruby came back with it and said, "And how was your *business* meeting?"

"Why darlin'," I said, "I was just doing what you always wanted me to do."

"Huh?"

"Cleaning up the streets of Los Angeles. Maybe you've got a good idea there after all."

KING CRUSH

May the strength of three be in your journey.
– Irish blessing

We were in San Bernardino, a good hour from Los Angeles, when I saw the Ferris wheel. A carnival! Now that was a nice little surprise for me and my gal, Ruby, and my bulldog, Steve. Steve loves strangers. He'll give 'em all the benefit of the doubt, until one crosses him. That's why I love Steve. He's just like me.

We were rumbling along in my jalopy, top down in the warm afternoon. I was the happiest lad in the West. I had a cool hundred dollars in my pocket to spend on Ruby McGuire, the fairest flower in Los Angeles, and so's I could get a hot dog for Steve.

Besides all that, I was glad it was 1955. The year before'd been hard on me and Steve. We'd each done our share of fighting. Me in the club smokers, and Steve with a couple of mutts that tried to take over Clay Street on Bunker Hill.

But just as my heart was dancing and my lips about to sing, Ruby says to me, "Jimmy, could you give up the fight game for good?"

I've said it before and I'll say it again. Fish gotta swim, birds gotta fly, lawyers gotta flap their yaps and cops got to billy the bad guys. And Irish Jimmy Gallagher was born to fight. I can't remember a time when I didn't use my dukes in some form or fashion, and I always thought I could get a shot at some legitimate dough. But I was pushing thirty-five and that's a rough kind of age to be if you're a pugilist.

Still and all, my fists have got me out of many a scrape and earned me some scratch. And one other thing—it's the pride of the Irish. I like to take down a challenger and be the last man standin'. It's the thing I do best. I wanted to be a poet, but had no talent for it. I tried the sea for awhile, courtesy of the United States Navy, but I never took a shine to the waves like I did to hand-to-hand combat under Marquess of Queensbury Rules.

So I cleared my throat and said, "Darlin', how about some fun at the carny?"

"Now don't you be changing the subject, Jimmy. One of these days you're going to run into a younger man, a stronger man, and he's going to knock your Irish block off."

"No man's been able to do that yet!"

From the back seat Steve said *Boof*, which I took to be a confirmation of my position.

"There's a first time for everything," Ruby said.

"Sure and don't I know it! I remember the first time I kissed you, Ruby McGuire."

"Now don't go larding on the charm," she said.

"Do you remember that first kiss the way I do?"

I could tell she wasn't wanting to answer, and was fighting a smile. But the smile won. "It was on top of Angels Flight," she said.

"Almost one year ago to the day," I said. "The night was clear and we could see all the way to the ocean, the moon sparkling on the waters. City Hall was lit up with colors. We'd just come up from a movie. You remember which one?"

"You know I do. Seven Brides for Seven Brothers."

"And you remember the song I sang to you?"

"I'm sure I don't."

"Oh yes, you do. 'Bless Your Beautiful Hide. You're the Gal for Me!' "

Steve said *Boof*.

Ruby McGuire said, "Best keep your eyes on the road, you charmer. You're like to get us killed!"

———

I pulled into the dirt lot with a lot of other cars. Music was playin' and kids and old folks and everyone in between was walking around. I put a leash on Steve and gave my arm to Ruby and off we went like a little family. I liked that a lot. Maybe I could get civilized after all.

First stop, I got Ruby some cotton candy and a hot dog for Steve. Then we strolled by the games, the operators appealing to my manhood, telling me to "show the little lady" what I was made of. You can only do that so much before Jimmy Gallagher takes it into his head to do just that.

There was the milk bottle throw that done it. I paid the man a quarter for three throws. There was a stuffed giraffe hanging on the side, and that was what I wanted to win for my girl. She's goofy for animals, which is why she loves the zoo. And for some reason giraffes are her favorite. She says they remind her of her younger brother Marvin, who's a stevedore in Oakland.

So I took the baseballs from the operator and told Ruby to stand back so she wouldn't cramp my style.

Now I done a little bit of pitching back in the sandlots of Boston, and my fastball was said to be next to none but Cy Young himself. The fact that it was said by me shouldn't matter all that much for the telling of this tale.

Anyway, I wind up and throw the heater at the pyramid of bottles and wouldn't you know? It takes off the top one and leave the rest standin'.

"Don't let that discourage you, young man," the operator said. "You've still got two more throws."

"Just gettin' warmed up," says I.

My next fastball hit nothing but breeze.

I felt my cheeks heat up and snuck a look at Ruby. She was hiding a smile behind her hand, bless her. Not wantin' me to feel bad!

That made me all the more determined. I set my aim on the bottom row, went into a windup and let fly. The ball hit the edge of the platform and bounced straight back to me. I caught it.

"Sorry, son, that's all you get," the operator said. "Better luck next time."

Ruby said, "There won't be a next time. Come on, Jimmy."

"No!" I put down another quarter. "I ain't never quit on anything in my life, and I sure ain't gonna quit now."

Steve said *Boof! Boof!*

The op gave me three more baseballs.

My first throw knocked all but one down. All I had to do was hit the singleton and the stuffed giraffe would be Ruby's.

But my second throw went wide by about an inch.

I was down to my third once again.

I put a little spit on my hands and rubbed 'em together. Then I picked up the ball and made like I was looking down at the catcher, with Babe Ruth at the plate, two outs in the ninth, and a full count with the bases loaded.

I went into my windup and threw the heat. It dinged the top of the bottle, which started to wobble.

It was the longest wobble I'd ever seen in my life, except for the time I clocked Hyrum "Gibraltar" Calhoun with a right cross in a three rounder in Amarillo.

But whereas Calhoun went down, the bottle stayed up.

"No matter!" the operator said. "Here's a nice Chinese finger trap for the little lady." And he handed me one of those colorful, woven cylinders meant for eight-year-olds.

"Begorrah!" I says. "I'm not leavin' here without that giraffe. Give me another three balls!"

Then Ruby puts her loving hand on my arm and says, "You don't have to, Jimmy."

"Let the fellow behind you have a turn, mister," the operator said. "You can always come back."

There was a skinny fella behind me, with his own girl on his arm. He looked like a pencil. He had on a yellow coat and tie and the tie about hid him. His fedora was too big for his head.

He smiled at me and stepped up and put down a quarter. I was gonna enjoy this. I wondered if he'd even be able to reach the bottles with a ball, let alone knock 'em down.

His first pitch brought the whole thing crashing to the platform.

The skinny guy put his shoulders back and his girl squealed.

"You can bet your bottom dollar I'll be back!" I shouted to the man behind the counter. Then I took Ruby's arm and Steve's leash and we went walking down the midway.

That's when I saw the ring. It was elevated, with ropes and canvas. And there was a small crowd milling about. I said to Ruby, "Looks like they got a carny pug."

"A what?"

"An all-comers J man," I say quickly, then, "Sorry darlin'. A journeyman fighter who takes on all comers. You pay a fiver and if you can stay with him and keep your feet you get the fiver back, plus some. If you knock him down, some more. If you knock him out, you can make big money, maybe fifty or a hundred smackers. Hayseeds off the farm who fancy themselves big and strong and who can out-wrassle their hayseed brothers, they think they can win."

"Can't they?"

"Nah, these carny scraps know all the tricks, like scraping their laces over your eyes or gettin' in low blows up close. The carnivals wouldn't be putting these guys up there if they thought they'd lose."

I did one season with a carnival back in '51, and earned some decent dough. I also knocked out many a hayseed. But that kind of life wears on you and I got out before I got punchy.

Still, here was a ring, and here was I, and another fifty bucks wouldn't besmirch my station in life now, would it?

Ruby looked at me like she knew exactly what was going on in that soggy noodle of mine. "Oh no you don't," she said.

"Well, it can't harm anything to go look, now can it?" I looked at Steve. "Steve, it can't do any harm, can it?"

Boof.

"There, you see?" I said.

"You will not fight. Promise me that."

"I—"

"Promise me, Jimmy."

"You are like a winter storm in County Kildare, Ruby."

"You haven't seen my winter storm yet," she said. "And you don't want to."

I kissed her on the cheek. Then we walked toward the ring and got there just as the barker began his spiel. He wore a straw hat and bow tie and had a piggy-type face with beads of sweat all over it.

"Gentlemen, step right up for your chance at glory. Which one of you strong, healthy sons of guns will climb into the ring with a chance to pick up half a C note? That's fifty American dollars, my friends, in Uncle Sam's own currency. All you have to do is go two rounds with our champeen. Five'll bring you ten. If you knock him down, a double sawbuck will be added to the kitty. And if, my friends, you put the champ out for a count of ten, you will walk away fifty dollars richer. Who is man enough to try? Surely in this crowd we have someone who thinks he can lace up the gloves and prove his mettle!"

My body was vibrating like a blind dog's tail in a meat market. Mettle! For fifty dollars all I had to do was land my right, which I had done so many times before. Ruby had my arm and felt me shaking. She whacked me on the shoulder. My girl has a good right hand of her own. I took a deep breath and calmed myself.

I tried to get a look at the carnival "champeen." He was sitting in one corner with a black robe on, slightly hunched over so's the hood of the robe hid his face.

"Come now, ladies and gents! Surely there is a man among you who is not afraid to try. I heard tell that San Berdoo was where the rough are ready! Isn't there someone out there who can prove the salience of that particular observation?"

Then a voice right behind me shouted, "I'll go!"

It was that same skinny fellow from the milk bottle throw!

"Well, there's a noble lad!" the barker said. "Step right into the ring, take off your coat and shirt and show your lady fair what you're made of!"

"Don't worry, Mabel," the skinny little fellow said as he took off his coat. "I know a few tricks."

"Are you sure, Johnny?" his girl said.

He winked at her, handed her his coat and then his tie and then his shirt. His skin was as smooth and flat as an ice skating rink. It was so white you could almost see through to the bones. Maybe he could get a lucky throw at the milk bottles, but to fight a seasoned boxer? I feared for his life.

But there he was, stepping into the ring. He gave the barker a five dollar bill. The barker motioned to some old cuss who climbed in and gave Johnny a pair of boxing gloves and helped him lace them up.

The crowd was starting to swell. Had to be because this Christian was about to go to a lion. Nothing to gather a crowd like the smell of fresh meat in the air!

The barker huddled a moment with Johnny.

The other boxer was still sitting in the same position, almost like he didn't care what was going on, and wouldn't until the bell rang.

Then the barker announced, "And now, ladies and gentlemen, introducing to you, weighing in at 110 pounds, the terror of San Bernardino, Mr. John C. Francis! Let's hear it ladies and gentlemen, let's hear it!"

The crowd cheered as whispy little Johnny Francis raised his gloves over his head and shook 'em like he was Rocky Marciano his own self.

"And now let me introduce to you his opponent, weighing 240 pounds, a veteran of more than 800 bouts in the ring, a true champion of champions, known far and wide as King Crush!"

The other fella finally stood up. My chin almost dropped on Steve's head. "Hit me with a jab and leave me reelin'," I said. "I know that man!"

Ruby said, "You do?"

"Big Bill Wannamaker. We mixed it up once, down in the Solomons, aboard the Peter Charlie."

"Peter Charlie?"

"That's what we called the patrol craft I swabbed in the war. We had a shipboard championship fight, and I won it. But let me tell you, it was the hardest fight I ever had, before or since."

"He looks so . . .beaten."

Big Bill's face was indeed weathered. He had so many wrinkles on his forehead it coulda held three days of rain. His body was starting to run to fat. But he still cut a formidable figure for a man his age, which was forty-five, because he was ten years older than me, and was when I decked him for the championship of the PC 477 back in 1944. The thick swatch of hair on his chest, once as black as coal, showed mostly white now. But it was a forest of snow covered pines compared to his baby-skinned opponent. I really was hoping the young man wouldn't get crippled. I once saw a carny fighter break the neck of a farm boy with one mighty blow. But this is America. You pays your money and you takes your chances.

The bell rang and out the two fighters came, looking like a bear and a lizard on hind legs getting ready to dance.

That's exactly what the lizard did—danced. He flitted, he skipped, he ran around. It was clear what his strategy was. He wasn't going to mix it up with Bill. He was just going to try to stay on his feet for the two rounds and pick up an easy five bucks. And maybe be able to brag to his girl that he survived a fight with a bruiser named King Crush.

Bill regarded him like a bored fisherman would a fly buzzing around his head. Not slapping at it wildly, but waiting for his chance to snatch it out of the air and smash it on the deck.

The crowd shouted for action. Mabel started in, too. "Hit him, Johnny!"

Johnny looked at her, his face saying *I can't believe you're telling me that!*

Ah, the sweet bloom of young love. All freshness and light and daisies and fluffy clouds, until a man is put in the ring in front of his girl and she wants to see him draw blood!

But I have to hand it to Johnny. He made the attempt. He pirouetted like a ballerina and then tried a left hook that had all the force and menace of a summer butterfly. It landed on Bill's jaw like a woman's powder puff. It seemed to me Bill was stifling a laugh.

But God makes boxers and God makes gentlemen, and sometimes the two meet as one. Bill was a gent. He did not immediately dispatch the dancing gladiator, perhaps wanting to let the lad have a little taste of manliness in front of his girl before the inevitable ending blow. So Bill rocked his head back and put his glove up to his chin. "Ow," he said. "You're going to pay for that one, Laddie."

And then he growled some and stalked Johnny, who went dancing as far away as he could.

But as the great Joe Louis, the Brown Bomber himself, once said of Billy Conn, you can run but you can't hide.

Especially in a small carny ring.

Bill slowly started cutting off the territory.

Mabel yelled, "Hit him again, Johnny!"

The crowd screamed for a knockout.

So Bill gave it to them.

I don't know if you've ever been in the forest when the logger fells a mighty redwood. If you haven't seen a majestic tree fall stiffly to the ground and hit nothing but dirt, then you cannot imagine the little birch of a man named Johnny who took it on the chin and pounded the canvas as straight and pure as one of those downed arboreal splendors.

Mabel cried, "Oh, Johnny!"

I wanted to go over to Mabel and tell her to marry Johnny and make him go to law school, and to keep him out of fighting the rest of his life. But I figured she got that message already, in one way or another.

The barker finished the ten count, then raised Bill's hand over his head. "And so, ladies and gentlemen, another challenger falls to the great King Crush! Let's give him a short rest, and then we'll see if there be any others to test courage and strength in the arena of combat!"

And then commenced the cleaning up of Johnny from the mat as the crowd dispersed. Bill headed for a tent.

"Wait for me, honey," I said, and gave Ruby Steve's leash.

I went over and stuck my head in the tent. Bill was pouring some bourbon into a glass when he saw me. He hesitated a moment, then broke into a big smile. He was missing a front tooth.

"Well I'll be King Kong's uncle. Jimmy Gallagher!"

"How are ya, shipmate?" I said.

Bill spread his arms. "As you can see, I didn't make it to Madison Square Garden. Come in! Fancy a drink?"

"Don't mind if I do."

He found another glass and poured me some hooch and we sat on a couple of stools.

"You look good, Jimmy. You been fighting any?"

"Here and there," I said. "Smokers, mostly. I'm hoping to line up something at the Olympic, though."

Bill nodded, looking a little sad. I knew he'd wanted to be a legit fighter at one time.

"If you don't mind my sayin' so, Bill, it sure does look like you picked a hard way to make buck. I did some time on the circuit, you know, but I got out of it before I went batty."

He took in a deep breath, reached into the pocket of his robe and pulled out a cigar. He bit the end off, spit out the stub, grabbed a wooden match and lit up.

After a mournful puff he said, "Jimmy, there's no place for me in this world other than the ring. For better or worse."

"There ain't much worse, for a man who's gettin' on in years. And you're a might grayer than when we duked it on the Peter Charlie."

"That's true, Jimmy, but I'm not ready to sit on a back porch in a rocking chair."

I wondered then if old Bill was on the run from something, maybe the law. But as this was the first time we'd seen each other in many a year, I decided to forego the subject any further.

And then we heard the sound of the barker again, calling for a challenger.

"That's my cue," Bill said. "Maybe we can bend an elbow after the show."

"I'm with my girl, Bill. But look me up in L.A. I'm in the book."

———

Back outside, another challenger had indeed come forward, and this one was no Johnny. He was young and strong and mean looking. But I knew that wouldn't faze Bill. The kids who try to look mean are usually covering up that they're scared.

I was about to take Ruby's arm and walk on.

But then I saw Bill's face.

He looked scared! I'd never seen that look on his face before. When we were patrolling the Solomons and a mess of kelp got tangled up in our propeller. Bill stripped down to his skivvies and took a buck knife and dove into the shark infested waters and cut us loose. He was absolutely without fear of anything.

When we tangled on the Peter Charlie, and I was in the best shape of my life, Bill didn't flinch or frighten. He sneered. He smiled.

But he wasn't smiling now.

And when the bell sounded, the kid was all over him. This wasn't about fifty bucks. The kid had some sort of rage you can't teach. If every fighter had that, there'd be a lot more deaths in the ring.

Bill covered up as best he could. I figured he'd let the kid spend himself and then really give it to him.

But he didn't fight back.

Was he hurt? Had the kid gotten in the first punch and broken his rib or something? I couldn't believe it. It was like Bill was yellow all of a sudden.

Punch after punch, to the jaw, the gut, the heart, Bill took it all, barely defending himself.

Blood started pouring from a cut over his right eye.

The crowd was screaming for more of the same. A local boy was beating the carny champ!

Bill took a haymaker to the jaw. I winced at the sound and force of it. A man of lesser stature would have gone down for sure. Out of pure cussed instinct Bill stayed on his feet. But he had to put his hands up over his face and lean back against the ropes.

The kid slapped Bill's hands down with his left and unleashed another right to Bill's face.

Down on one knee goes Bill.

The kid does not stop. I scream at the barker to stop the fight! But he ignores me or can't hear me over the crowd.

Bill is helpless and the kid is pounding him like a railroad pile driver.

Which I can't take.

"I'm sorry, Ruby," I say and jump up into the ring.

The moment I do Bill falls over, down and out.

The kid was readying a killer blow, so I body blocked him and sent him flying to the other side of the ring.

He goes bouncing off the ropes and springs back my way. I see flames in his eyes. His first right is wild and I duck it, and send my own right fist into his midsection.

"Belay that, ya cheat!" I yell. "You want some fight, I'll give it to you!"

The kid spits on the canvas. "Out of my way, old man."

Old man! And me a strapping lad of thirty-five! My pride was wounded.

I looked for Ruby, but she wasn't there.

"You want to fight me?" I said.

"Come on!" he said, and motioned for me to approach him.

"Done!" I said. I called to the barker. I told him to get someone to help Bill out of the ring and see to him.

The barker, knowing he had a rich vein of excitement on his hands, happily complied. As he and another gent from the crowd started with Bill, I went and unlaced Bill's gloves. I took off my shirt and put on the gloves.

Then I turned around and faced the kid.

The crowd was cheering like nobody's business.

———

But by this time the barker is not announcing a fight. He's taking bets. We've drawn even more of a crowd. It seems like it's double, maybe triple. People are running up to us to see what's happening.

The kid is pounding his gloves together, waiting for his chance to get at me. I have an old duffer at the edge of the ring tie up my gloves. "Watch his right," the duffer tells me. "It's got lightning."

"I've got thunder," I say, but the duffer seems not to believe me.

And then I'm up and in my corner. The barker climbs into the ring and raises his hands for quiet. He's holding a wad of paper currency in his left, with bills popping out of his coat pockets, too.

"Ladies and gentlemen! Never before in the history of the Bolton Brothers Carnival and Road Show has there been a moment like this! Two contenders from the crowd! One of them has knocked out our champeen. The other a knight errant set to do battle over the purity of the art of boxing! Let us all stand now and watch as these two gladiators battle it out. There will be no limit on rounds. I will act as referee and do the counting. Gentlemen, are you ready?"

"Get going!" the kid yelled.

I nodded.

The barker gave a signal to a young man on the bell, and it clanged.

The crowd started cheering right away.

I came out slow, as is my practice, sizing up what kind of fighter my opponent is. I thought, because of his vicious attack on Bill, that this kid was a bull and would rush in and start punching.

But he surprised me. He came out slow, too, in a good boxer's stance. He had done this before.

That put me on double notice. This one wanted a real fight.

I went into my own boxer's stance, bent a little forward, my left out front, my right at my chin.

We circled like that for a few seconds.

"Kill 'im!" somebody shouted, but I did not know who they wanted killed. Maybe it didn't matter as long as there was killing of some kind. That's the way it is with fight crowds sometimes.

The kid moved in and jabbed with his left. It glanced off my glove but I could feel the power behind it. He was strong all right, and then I found out for sure.

From out of nowhere came a right cross, fast as any I'd ever seen, and it got me flush on the temple. My head snapped to the side. A roar went up from the spectators. A smile came to the kid's mouth.

He backed away, like he was saying to me he could take his time to finish me off.

That was his first mistake.

I started shaking my head like I was dazed more than I was. I come from a long line of Gallaghers who were actors. I had a grandfather who was chased out of London right in the middle of playing Hamlet, when he changed one of Shakespeare's lines from "We will have no more marriages!" to "We will have no more Englishmen!"

So acting was part of my strategy in the ring, and the kid thought he could move in for more.

Second mistake.

I plowed him in the gut.

He doubled over and I gave him a left uppercut. Blood spurted from his lip as he staggered backwards.

"That's for hittin' a man when he's down," I said.

The kid shook his own head and came at me again.

I did a jig to the left, keeping him from firing off another right. I peppered his face with three quick jabs, then gave him another right to the breadbasket.

He started cursing at me, loud and unrelenting.

I jabbed him again and popped him on the snout with my right. "Shut yer trap!" I said. "There's women and children out there!"

Then we were in the center of the ring, toe-to-toe, giving all we got. This is where a fighter proves if he's in shape or not, and me running up and down the concrete stairs of Bunker Hill has improved the good set of lungs the Lord gave me. Even though I was fighting a young tiger in his twenties, I knew I could last with him. So I wasn't gonna give him no quarter. I had an anger in me, because of his no good cheatin' on Bill. But he had an anger, too, that came from some other place, a place I'd wager was spitting distance from hell.

Crazy, is what I'm sayin', and that's when I knew I'd finish him. A crazy fighter don't think straight.

"That all you got, boy?" I said between flurries. This made him madder and he started little squeaky cries with each punch.

Third mistake.

I dodged, weaved, countered. Then I blasted him one on the chin with my thundering right and down he went.

The crowd, oh that crowd, they screamed and hollered and told me to keep on hittin'. But I'm a rule man, even if it's with a dirty cheat, so I went to a neutral corner as the barker commenced the count.

One.

Two.

Three.

The kid rolled onto his stomach.

Four.

Five.

Got to his knees.

Six.

Seven.

He pushed himself to his feet. The barker backed off and we came at each other again.

Or I should say, the kid came at me like Bronko Nagurski chasing a halfback.

He put his shoulder into me and tackled me into the ropes.

Another foul!

I started pounding on his kidneys.

And then felt a sting on my side. The kid bit me!

Now if we'd had a regulation referee this fight woulda been stopped right there. But this was no holds barred and the barker was loving the spectacle.

I uppercut the kid to keep him from dining on me further. And just as I was about to finish him the bell rang.

But the kid didn't go to his corner.

Instead, with his teeth, he untied his gloves—first the left, then the right. Then he put them under his arms and pulled 'em off.

He was going to go bare knuckles on me!

So I did the same with my gloves, and there we were, like John L. Sullivan and Jake Kilrain, the last of the no-glove fighters.

I took two punches to my body that woulda knocked over a horse. But I'm no horse. I'm a bit of Americanized Irish steel. My knuckles are rivets and I drove those rivets into the face of this kid. Three jabs, *bap bap bap*, then a right to his eye causing a burst of red. A left cross tore skin off the side of his chin.

The animal power of it got to me, and I unloaded all I had on his nose. He was out on his feet, but still I punched with furious and retributive justice.

As he went to his knees, the Irish Jimmy Gallagher of old would have stopped, as per the rules. But I found myself raising my right fist, ready to finish him once and for all.

Which is when I heard, "Stop!"

It was Bill, staggering into the ring. His face was black and blue and cut. But his eyes were pleading as he shouted, "Don't do it, Jimmy. Please!"

"Back away, Bill. This is my fight now."

"You don't understand!"

My right was still in the air.

"He's my son," Bill said.

———

Bill called for a doc in the crowd. One came up and started looking the kid over. The kid's eyes were glazed, but he'd be okay. I'd rung his bell all right, but didn't punch his ticket.

Bill took me to his tent. He poured himself a drink and offered me one. I waved it off and we sat.

"I owe you an explanation, Jimmy. It was back in the Depression and I was drifting, riding the rails, looking for any work I could find. I ended up slingin' hash on Route 66. That's where I met Mary. She was waitin' on tables."

"Like my Ruby," I said.

"Well, I'm sorry to say, I didn't behave like a man. I got my girl pregnant and her parents told her not to marry me. She went away and had that baby up in Fresno. I found out where she was. I went to see her and the baby and she told me to get away, that I ruined her life, that she never wanted to see me again. I sent her money, but she always sent it back. She moved somewheres else, and the war broke out and I tried to forget 'em out at sea. But I never could shake it that I had a son. You know what I'm talking about, Jimmy?"

"I think maybe I do," I said.

"Then a few years ago I hired a gumshoe to find 'em, and he came back with a picture of the boy. He actually went inside Mary's house and snatched that photo for me. I sent it back to her, with a note and a return address. The carny has an address in Tennessee. And I guess that's how my son traced me. And when he stepped in the ring tonight, I knew him right away. I deserved everything he gave me, Jimmy. And I didn't want you hurtin' him anymore. I gave him and his ma enough for a lifetime."

And then Big Bill Wannamaker put his head inside one of his big mitts and turned away from me.

Well, if there's one thing that moves an Irishman's heart it's the sight of another man in tears. Without fully understanding what I was doing, I left Bill's tent and went back to the ring where the doc was patching up the kid.

When he saw me, the kid said, "I want a rematch. I'm gonna murder you."

"Belay that," I said. "You're not gonna murder anybody. You're gonna honor your father."

"Huh?"

"It's a commandment, son, and your father's paid for his sins. Now go to him and be a man and shake his hand."

"How do you know about it?"

"I'm a friend of your old man. He's the one that stopped me from laying you out for good."

The kid got off his stool. "What if I don't wanna?"

Balling up my fists, I said, "You really want a rematch?"

Sometimes I can get a smoldering flame in my green eyes, and it makes 'em look like jade on fire. That's what I must've had now, because the kid dropped his head. Then shook it.

———

I left old Bill and his kid, Tommy was his name it turned out, sitting in Bill's tent. They were talking at least. The rest was gonna be up to them.

What was up to me was finding Ruby.

She was sitting in the jalopy, Steve lyin' on the back seat.

I slipped into the front and closed the door. "Honey—"

"You don't have to say anything," Ruby said.

"But—"

She put her hand on my cheek. She kept it there, soft and warm, and looked at me in the moonlight. She smiled, too, like she understood me even more than I understand myself.

In the back of the jalopy Steve said, *Boof.*

FIGHT CITY

May you live as long as you want, and never want as long as you live.
– Irish blessing

"That's the last time you break a date with me, Jimmy Gallagher. I'll thank you not to call on me again!"

Me and Ruby were sitting in Charley's on Figueroa, where Ruby waits tables. She wasn't working at the moment. She was too busy being steamed and I couldn't blame her. She doesn't like me fighting, and the night before I'd been in a bout set up by a pal, Kenny Spivey. He was moving a lot of dough and needed me for the card. He's got a little girl with polio and that can run into money, so I thought I'd help him out by taking on a local boy making his way up the ladder. He was a big kid, young and strong, but I know a few things after twenty-five years of lacing up the mitts (I started when I was ten, back there in Boston Golden Gloves).

Well, I knocked the kid out in the third. The kid was pretty mad about that, once he recovered. I sat with him in the locker room until he came to, and told him to appreciate a real education in the sweet science and that it would serve him in good stead if he wanted a future in this racket.

But in my attempt to do Kenny a good turn I plum forgot about a movie date with Ruby. That was my fault it was, and I couldn't deny it. I wasn't going to lie, either, not to the girl who sends my heart to the heather.

So I decided to give her the old Gallagher charm, passed down to me from a long line of County Cork men who could sell fleas to a dog team.

"Darlin'," I said, "I—"

"And don't you be trying the old Gallagher charm!" Ruby said.

Cleary, the Gallagher men had not anticipated the instinctual insight of womankind.

"All right, Ruby, I confess. I was fightin'. I forgot we had a date. But it was for a good cause."

"If this was the first time, I wouldn't mind so much," she said. "But it's happened before and, if you fight, it's going to happen again."

"Sure and you're right, Ruby my love. I want to take a solemn oath right now, and say it won't happen again."

"Fighting?"

"Forgettin'. I swear here and now I will never forget another of our dates. I'll put so much string around my fingers I could fly a kite."

She fought against smiling, but lost the bout.

The Gallagher charm was making a comeback.

"Now what was that picture I was going to take you to?" I said.

"Oklahoma.*"*

That was the big movie of 1955. Everybody was talking about it.

"Then we will see it! At The Egyptian, right?"

She nodded.

"And then dinner at the Pig 'n Whistle, how does that sound?"

"Grand," Ruby said.

"Friday?"

"I'll meet you in front of the theater at seven."

"Seven it is!"

"You're sure this time?"

I took her hand in mine. "You've got the Gallagher pledge, and we've not gone back on one of those in four hundred years!"

It was Wednesday night.

If I had known then what I know now, I would never have made that pledge. For the imps use such promises to test our mettle, and school was about to start on good ol' Irish Jimmy Gallagher.

————

It was a fair evening in Los Angeles as I walked home to Bunker Hill. The neon lights along Figueroa made the strip look like Christmas. Reds and blues and greens and yellows, blinking signs that said *Cocktails* and *Coca-Cola* and *Liquor*.

I cut over to Hope Street and hurried my step. Steve, my bulldog, would be wondering where I was. It was hamburger night for him, and he expected to be fed.

I found myself walking right by the Church of the Open Door. That's the one with the big JESUS SAVES sign on top. It's a stately old building, this church in downtown Los Angeles. I like the name. Seems to me if there's going to be a church it ought to have its doors open. Let any soul seeking solace walk in, even if it's into the bosom of the Protestants. I don't think God cares so much about them labels myself.

So I was walking by and whistling a tune when a man ran out the front of the church and bumped right into me, spinning me around.

He tried to run but I grabbed his coat. I thought he owed me an explanation for his incivility.

He socked me in the jaw.

That was not the explanation I was looking for. I pulled my own right hand back to return the favor when I heard a voice with a heavy Texas twang saying, "Don't fight, boys, it's not worth it. Jesus Christ is the only—"

He didn't finish his words because the guy I was fighting with gave an elbow to the poor man's face. And down he went.

Anger flashed through me. There's one thing I can't stand and that's a bully. This guy knew how to handle himself and he took down an innocent man who probably didn't know the first thing about fighting.

"Ya coward!" I shouted and gave him a right to the gut. He took it. His bread basket was hard. This fellow was in shape.

I had committed a cardinal sin—taking a new guy too lightly. If I'm in the ring, I size a fella up during the opening round. But in a street fight, there isn't that luxury.

Also in a street fight, the other guy is going to fight dirty.

I hope you never get hit with brass knuckles. It's one of the lowest forms of cheatin' there is. It can send you to dreamland, and sometimes beyond. You better hope your prayers are up to date if you get brassed in the head.

Like I was.

I took a headlong dive into the LaBrea Tar Pits. Down, down into thick, hot black where thoughts go silent and the world disappears.

———

I woke up flat on my back.

In bed.

From the smell, it was a hospital room. Not the fanciest room, I might add. Paint peeling on the ceiling don't indicate a room a Rockefeller would end up in.

My thoughts were oatmeal, sloshing around in my skull.

What day was it?

What was my name?

Jimmy Gallagher, that's who, a big lug who let himself get cold cocked in a fight!

Fight.

Where?

Outside a church. A guy running out . . .

"He's blinkin'," a voice in the room said.

I turned my head. As I did, a right cross from the land o' pain landed flush on my brain.

"Wake up," another voice said.

There were two guys in the room. Blurry in my vision, but definitely smelling of cop.

"Come on, sonny," the second voice said. It was low and creaky, like the tracks at Angels Flight. "Let's have a little chat."

I tried to move my arm. It stopped and something jangled.

I was handcuffed to the bed rail!

"What gives?" I said.

"Easy there, bucko. My name's Kelly, and this here's my partner, Bradley. We're detectives."

"What's with the bracelets?" I said.

"We didn't want yer fallin' out o' bed and hurtin' yerself," the other detective, Bradley, said.

Kelly snorted. He was the older of the two, I could see now, and the fatter. His face was blotchy, like he spent too much time in the sun or with a bottle.

Bradley was younger and stringier. He talked tough but it sounded like he was tryin' too hard, like a bad actor on that TV show, *Dragnet.*

"Suppose you tell us what happened," Kelly said.

"What day is it?" I said.

"What day should it be?" Kelly said.

"Come on now, what day? I got a date with my girl!"

"Better break it," Kelly said.

No!

"Why don't you try talking, son? It'll all go down much easier for you then."

My head was a ringside bell, gonging out three-second rounds.

"Confession's good for the soul," Bradley said.

I glared at him. "You a priest?"

Kelly said, "Now, no need to be a hard boiled egg, James my boy. That's your name, yes? James Gallagher?"

"It'll do," I said. But I hadn't been called James since St. John's School for Boys in Boston, when Father O'Hara would call me into his office for a bit o' the old backside discipline.

Kelly said, "Now tell us what happened so that we can leave you to the care of the fine medical staff here at County hospital."

With a Salvation Army drum major pounding out "Bringing in the Sheaves" inside my skull, I managed to say, "Detective, near as I remember, I was walking down the street minding my own business, when a fella charges out of the church—"

"What church would that be?"

"Why, the Church of the Open Door."

"So you know the church, do you?"

"What's that got to do with anything?"

"What do you do for a living, Mr. Gallagher?"

The way he was not caring to have a real conversation was making me wonder if he thought I was some murderin' hooligan or other.

I tried to keep my voice calm. "Would you mind takin' off the bracelets, Detective? I'm not goin' to be breakin' out anytime soon."

Kelly pursed his lips the way cops do when they're thinkin', and then I guess maybe he thought he could catch more flies with honey. So he got out a key and took off the cuffs.

Never one to let an advantage go, I said, "And would you mind me havin' a glass o' water?"

Kelly sighed. "Bradley, bring the man some water."

"Me?" Bradley said.

"You heard me."

Bradley got me my water, handing it to me so hard some of it sloshed on the bed.

"And would you mind cranking me up?" I said.

Kelly's face pinked, like the inside of a medium-rare steak. But he commenced to turning the crank at the foot of the bed so it got me sitting up.

I was beginning to feel more human, and more cheesed off. I sipped my water slow.

"Now then," Kelly said, "what is it you do for money, Gallagher?"

I wiped my lips with the back of my hand and said, "Well sir, it's like this. I come from a long line of scrappers and actors. It's about all we Gallaghers know in this world, so's I do my part to carry on the family traditions."

"You're an actor then?' Kelly said.

"More on the scrapper side," I said.

"Fighter?"

"Boxer."

"For a living?"

"Well now that's just it, Detective darlin', times bein' what they are, I haven't had the management I need, so I get by on odd jobs."

"What kinds of jobs?"

"Suppose we get to what the lawyers call *relevant?"* I said. "Or should I be havin' a lawyer here in the room with me?"

"Now look, Gallagher," Kelly said, "I'm trying to give you a break. You talk now and I might be able to get the D.A. to go easy."

"But that's just what I've been trying to tell you, Mr. Detective. There is nothing to go easy on me about. A man ran out of the church and bumped into me. I grabbed him. He fought me. And when somebody starts in on Jimmy Gallagher, Jimmy Gallagher returns the favor. Well, this slippery yahoo takes out a pair of brass knuckles, I'm sure that's what they were, seeing as how my head feels like a football kicked by Jim Thorpe himself. And that's about all I know."

As if they were a duo singing on stage at the Hollywood Bowl, the two detectives sighed in unison. I didn't like the sound of that.

"All right," Kelly said. "You want to play it cute, do you? Well, I'll tell you what, son. I'll fill you in. There's an old preacher down at the church, a man by the name of McGee, and you hit him in the nose. Because you stole money out of the church box. You had two dollars in your pocket, and they were church dollars because somebody had written *God bless this church* on one of them. The preacher, McGee, remembered seeing that bill.

"In my pocket you say? That's a lie!"

"Some good Samaritan whacked you on the head, and I wish it would have been harder. And I wish we could find that Samaritan. But all we got now is one witness, that preacher, and all we have to do is show him your picture or maybe your ugly face in a lineup, and you will be going away for a long time, Mr. Gallagher. And good riddance. Los Angeles doesn't need people like you."

Then they slapped the bracelets on me again and left.

———

About ten minutes later a doctor came in. He was bald and sweaty and smoking an unfiltered cigarette, holding a clipboard and giving it a look. "My name is Dr. Blandings, and I understand you have a headache."

"Well, Doctor darlin', that's like sayin' Marilyn Monroe has a figure."

He looked at me without a hint of a smile on his perspiring face. He took a puff on his cigarette and said, "The x-rays are negative. You've got a pretty hard head, Mr. Gallagher."

"That's what my girl tells me."

Puff. Blow. "There isn't anything more we can do for you here."

"Oh that's just aces. Now if you wouldn't mind taking off these handcuffs, I'll get my things and go."

"I'm sorry," Dr. Blandings said. "You are to be transferred to the county jail."

———

The Los Angeles County jail sits atop the Hall of Justice on Temple Street. You could call it a circle of hell except that it's rectangular, in keeping with the architecture of the criminal courts building. It's amazing how fast they can get you out of a hospital bed and into a cell when they don't care who you are.

I had to get out of this thing, and I mean fast. I had to put the old Gallagher noodle to work and think of a plan. But planning comes pretty hard when you're locked in a jail cell, and when you're not alone.

———

He was a big man, a little bigger than I am and I stand 6'3" and pack 225 pounds. He had thick black hair and sparkling blue eyes and a square jaw. If he had not been in a jail cell I might've thought he would be out at the Brown Derby or Romanoff's, because he could've been a movie actor with those looks.

When I got shoved in the cell and the door closed and locked, the first thing he did was introduce himself. "My name's Walsh. Mean anything to you?"

"Pleased to make your acquaintance, Mr. Walsh. My name is Jimmy Gallagher." I held out my hand. He ignored it.

"*Jack* Walsh."

I waited, because the name didn't ring any bells with me.

That seemed to annoy him. "Maybe you've heard of Mickey Levine."

Levine! I for certain had heard of him. He was a mobster in Los Angeles, until me and a friend of mine named Iron Hands Jackson suggested he might want to leave our fair city. We helped him by tossing him off a hillside.

"Oh yes, Mr. Levine," says I. "He was involved in the fight game for a while, wasn't he? Haven't seen him around lately."

Walsh eyed me, as if to read my face like a racing form. I kept it stoic.

Didn't want him to know I had any dealings with Levine, if I could keep that particular news from his attention.

"His name used to mean something around here," Walsh said. "And when he had a problem he couldn't take care of or didn't want to be bothered with, a big problem, he asked Jack Walsh to take care of it for him." Walsh held up his hands. They were huge. Thick-boned. Like Marciano's. "These are all I usually need."

"Well, isn't that a coincidence?" I held up my hands. "I'm a boxer and these are my tools of the trade. I guess nobody would want to play four-handed bridge with us, eh?"

Jack Walsh did not smile. It's getting harder and harder to find somebody with a sense of humor in Los Angeles anymore.

"Let me just lay out a few rules of the road," Jack Walsh said. "You are going to sleep on the upper bunk. You will not make any noise when I'm trying to sleep. If you want to use the john—" he nodded his head at the porcelain convenience connected to the wall "—you will ask my permission. There are times when I don't want the place to smell. And I can already smell you. I always could smell an Irishman."

Now, gentle reader, in the normal course of events—and by that I mean in a barroom or on a street corner—if somebody were to make a statement of that insulting magnitude to Jimmy Gallagher, that same somebody would be lying flat on his back one second later. But my mother, God rest her soul, did not raise any fools, even though us Gallagher boys could be accused of trying to disabuse her of that notion in many ways. My main job was to get out of here without any trouble. I didn't want to get into any fights that could get me in further Dutch. I needed to stand before a judge and maybe make bail so I could keep the date with Ruby. I had to settle this business quietly, without her ever knowing about it, God bless her.

So I let the insult pass.

"Those seem like fair rules," I said. "Now maybe I'll get a little shut eye, as I have a bit of a headache."

I took a step toward the bunks but Jack Walsh slid in front of me. "I am your headache," Jack Walsh said.

"Well now, that is not a fate I would wish on any man."

"Give me a smoke."

"Mr. Walsh, tobacco is not a habit I myself have picked up. Trying to keep in fighting trim, don't you know? I will say I once smoked my grand-father's pipe, but I was a mere wisp of a lad and it turned me green. Green being the color of my ancestral home, it wasn't such a bad trade, but I've not—"

"Shut your yap. Just give me a cigarette."

There was a bright blue vein running down the middle of Jack Walsh's forehead. It was throbbing, this vein, and I have never known a vein to throb that doesn't portend bad news.

"Now Mr. Walsh, it is my desire to get along famously with all mankind."

He raised one of his big paws and placed it on my throat. My eyes opened wide. "Well then you are going to have to figure out a way to get some," Walsh said. "Because I am the landlord of the cell, and you owe me rent. I take that rent in cigarettes. Starting with ten, to be delivered to me by noon tomorrow."

You can only push a Gallagher so far. Even one who is bending himself into all kinds of peaceful permutations. I said a silent prayer that Ruby might never hear of what I was about to do, and then I gave a hard kneecap to the twin orbs that define the male of the species.

Mr. Jack Walsh huffed out a breath and crumpled to the floor.

I stepped over the prostrate Walsh and yelled through the bars for a guard. Walsh groaned behind me.

When the guard appeared, and old geezer in a baggy sheriff's uniform, I said, "My accommodations have become unfriendly. I don't think I will be getting any sleep here tonight. Would you mind finding me another cot?"

The jailer squinted past me. "What goes on here?"

Walsh was now on his feet, but wobbly, and his face was drained of color.

"Jack," the jailer said, "is this one making trouble?"

"Now wait!" I said.

"Nothing that I can't take care of," Walsh said.

"And do you want to be taking care of it?"

"Yes I do, Jonesy."

And with that the jailer turned and started back down the corridor.

"Hey!" I shouted.

Jack Walsh hit me in the stomach with a fist made of reinforced concrete.

It was only because of years in the fight game and my stomach muscles being fighting firm that Walsh's fist did not go all the way through me and hit my backbone. Even so it was a mighty wallop and only pure fighter's instinct raised my left fist in front of my face to block the knockout punch Walsh tried to deliver.

I brought an uppercut to his chin, one of the finest of my career I might add. It would've put a lesser man out for hours. It only rocked Jack Walsh backward a few steps. Blood spurted from his lip. He touched it as if he could not believe what just happened to him. I gather no man had ever given him the taste of his own medicine.

He screamed like a wounded rhinoceros. Now, I don't really know if a rhinoceros can scream, but if they can, they would sound like Jack Walsh.

He charged with his head down and hit me with his whole body, plastering me against the cell bars. My head hit the metal and did my headache no good. But I couldn't let such things distract me.

I thumbed one of his eyes, because this was going to be a dirty fight. No Marquis of Queensberry rules. My gouge bought me a precious half second and with it I stepped out to the side and gave Walsh's face a combination—left, right, left.

He got what I call the double–stun look. Stunned from the blows themselves, but also stunned because he couldn't believe someone else had tattooed his face that way.

I didn't want to give Mr. Jack Walsh a moment to recover. I stepped in with a right cross and followed it with a left to the body. When he doubled over I gave him an elbow to the kidneys. This was a move perfected by the Gallaghers in Ireland during the potato famine.

Jack Walsh went to the ground. I grabbed the mattress off his bunk, threw it over him, and stood on top of his head. It was my intention to call the guard again, but I looked up and saw him standing right there.

"So it's a fighter you are," the guard named Jonesy said. "I know just what to do with you."

That turned out to be a private cell on my own. It was smaller than the others and stank of urine. But I was glad to be away from the troublesome roommate. A little peace and quiet in stir. Sometimes God blesses you in minor ways that you grow to appreciate later on.

Or, if the devil has his due, as one more shove to being down and out.

———

The next morning was my arraignment. I sat in the lockup with a few other gents and shot the breeze. When it was my turn to go into court, I stood tall and put on all the humility a Gallagher can muster, which usually ain't enough to fill a shot glass half way.

The judge looked like he had been sitting on the bench since 1910. His sallow skin was like melted candle wax. His name was Stratemeyer.

He called my name and I stood up in front of the court. Then Judge Stratemeyer turned to a young man with too much Brylcreem in his hair and asked him to read the charges against me.

Mr. Brylcreem looked at a paper and said, "Violation of sections 240 and 241 of the California Penal Code, to wit, assault and battery, two counts. In addition thereto, violation of section 211 of the California Penal Code, robbery, one count, to wit, by way of unlawful injury."

Judge Stratemeyer said, "Mr. Gallagher, do you have a lawyer?"

"Why, no, Your Honor. I don't see the need because I am—"

"How does the defendant plead?"

"There has been a misunderstanding," I said.

The judge banged his gavel. "The defendant will respond only to the questions of the court. How do you plead, sir?"

"As innocent as the day is long," I said.

Judge Stratemeyer didn't look happy about that. He said, "The clerk will enter a plea of not guilty. We will set this for preliminary hearing two weeks from today. Mr. Gallagher?"

"Your Honor, if I may—"

"Silence! Are you able to afford a lawyer?"

"To be honest, sir, I'm a little short on funds."

"The court will look at who's available from the indigent defense panel, and assign a lawyer to you if you so desire."

"What if I want to represent myself?"

"The court would not advise that, Mr. Gallagher. These charges are very serious."

"Begging your pardon, your honor, but these charges are false. I just want to be able to tell my story to—"

"You will do your talking at the proper time and in the proper place. I will now listen to the People on the matter of bail."

Mr. Brylcreem said, "The People would request the court to set bail at five thousand dollars."

Five grand! It might as well have been five million!

I said, "Your Honor, sir, if I could ask your fair indulgence, needing to get out, as I am, if you could see your way clear to give me a break about bail. I have a dog named Steve who needs me to feed him, and I'm not a criminal. I have never been in trouble in Los Angeles. I will admit when I was a young pup back in Boston, there were a couple of scrapes, but we Gallaghers were poor in those days. We still are, come to think—"

The judge banged his gavel again. "That will be quite enough, Mr. Gallagher. Are you asking this court to reduce your bail?"

"I was hoping, Your Honor, that you might see your way to not requiring it at all."

Mr. Brylcreem said, "Your Honor?"

"What is it, Mr. Bunyan?" the judge said.

"The People would oppose the release of this defendant on his own recognizance. However, we do note that he has no previous record that we are aware of."

Now that was nice of the young deputy district attorney. I suppose he was too young yet to be cynical and heartless. That would take another year or so.

Just then the court clerk went to the judge and whispered something in his ear. Ah, maybe this was another break for your humble narrator. Surely the clerk was reporting that I represented no threat to run and was, from the looks of things, a law-abiding citizen.

And then the whispering stopped and the judge cleared his throat and looked down at me with imperious eyes.

He said, "In light of facts that have come to the court's attention, there will be no bail. Defendant is remanded to custody."

The banging of his gavel sounded like a gunshot.

———

Back I was in my one-man cell within fifteen minutes! What had happened in there? What had that clerk whispered to the judge?

More, how was I going to get out of here at all? No bail! I wouldn't make the movie, Ruby would inquire, and it would soon be known by any interested party that Irish Jimmy Gallagher was an accused robber who beat people up. No, it was worse. He beat up people outside a church and took their money.

And how did that money get in my pockets? Who was setting me up? Where was the real guy?

It was driving me as crazy as a drunken leprechaun.

I insisted on my phone call. They gave me one. I didn't call a shyster. I called Mrs. Terwilliger, my landlady, and told her I was temporarily called away and could she do me a favor and feed Steve?

Old Mrs. T said she would be happy to do it. She liked Steve. And Steve, who has a heart as big as Pershing Square, liked her right back.

That gave me some peace.

But my other predicament didn't give me a moment's rest. Friday was coming and Ruby would be waiting.

I tossed and turned long into the night.

———

And then I get a jangle at the cell door. It was that man Jonesy again. And he says I'm to come with him.

"At night?" I said.

"No talking. Come on. Now."

Jonesy made sure to show me the gun in his right hand. Persuasion by steel. I went along nice and quiet.

At the end of the corridor Jonesy had me stand facing the corner. I heard the jangle of keys and then the door unlocking.

"Downstairs," Jonesy said.

I turned and ducked into the stairwell. It was lit by a single yellow bulb in a cage. Which is what I was, I suppose—a dim bulb in a cage called jail. Oh, my dear Ruby girl, I don't want to lose you!

Two floors down we went, and then through another door into a dark hall. There were courtrooms here on either side.

"If you don't mind me asking, Mr. Jones, where might we be goin' this time o' night?"

"A place I call right up your alley."

Now I could see the glow of a light seeping out the bottom of a door at the far end. Somebody burnin' the midnight oil, as they say.

Jonesy gave three quick raps on the door. It opened, and more light hit me in the eyes. I smelled smoke and heard some voices chattering like a fleet of sewing machines.

"Inside," Jonesy said.

In I went.

Now this was by far the biggest room I'd seen at the courthouse. Didn't know what they kept in here normally, but one thing I'm pretty confident in saying, it didn't normally have a boxing ring.

Tonight it did.

They were expecting a bout!

I couldn't see the faces for the shadows, but one of the shadows moved toward me. I heard the voice before I put the face to it.

"Good evening, Mr. Gallagher," Judge Stratemeyer said.

"Why, Your Honor, sir," I said. "This is a bit of a surprise, if you don't mind my sayin'."

"A little out of the ordinary," the judge said, "but not much. I understand you've undertaken a few bouts in less than reputable environs."

"Um . . ."

"Don't worry, Mr. Gallagher. Nothing you say here will be used against you. Everything that happens within these walls stays right here. Savvy?"

"I hope to," I said.

"Mr. Gallagher, suppose I were to tell you that tonight you might walk out of here a free man?"

The words ran up my backbone and kicked me in the neck. "What do I have to do?"

"Win," he said.

I looked at the ring. "Is that for me and some other fella?"

"It is indeed," Judge Stratemeyer said. "A few of my friends and I like to place bets from time to time, on fights arranged right here in the jail. We find that the element of desperation adds a certain spice to the proceedings."

We Gallaghers never took kindly to bein' used for anyone's entertainment, unless of course we were on stage and gettin' paid for it. But seeing as he had uttered the magic words *free man* I was not about to stand on ceremony.

"Just so I understand, Judge, if I beat whoever you put me up against, this very night I walk?"

"Free as the proverbial bird."

"Well then, I guess the next question is who do I have to box?"

In the dim light I saw the judge smile. "Take off your shirt and shoes, Mr. Gallagher, and climb into the ring, and I'll introduce you."

"Where are my gloves?" I said as I stripped to the waist.

"Ah, that's another item, Mr. Gallagher. We hearken back to the old days, when real men fought without gloves."

Faith and begorrah! What manner of law was afoot in Los Angeles? But I was in no mood to wax philosophical. I was in the mood to get out of this place as fast as I could.

I climbed through the ropes.

Across from me, in the other corner, a man was already standing. He was a skinny one. He looked like that crooner Frank Sinatra. He was shirtless and shoeless, like me, but that's where the similarity ended. If he would've stood sideways, and stuck out his tongue, he'd've looked like a zipper.

"Now, Judge, Your Honor," I said. "If you are intent upon bare knuckle fisticuffs I don't want to be put in the position of committing a more serious felony than that with which I am charged, falsely I might add."

"Precisely what are you talking about, Mr. Gallagher?" the judge said.

"Murder," I said. "I am likely to kill that skinny little fella."

"Suppose you let us worry about that. I assure you that Mr. Jones here has abundant referee experience and will stop the bout should that eventuality occur."

"Murder?"

"Something short of murder, of course."

I looked across the ring at the little guy and I called out to him. "No hard feelings for what I'm about to do to you."

He stared at me and didn't say anything. I stood there feeling dirty and lost and backed into a corner, both the corner of the ring and the corner of my life in Los Angeles. My city has always had that reputation, of dirty little secrets hiding below the surface. It's all true. So you get yourself a girl and a dog and you try to live your life like an honest man. But every now and then a Sal "The Barber" Maglie curveball comes at you from life and knocks you flat. Then you have to get up on your feet and make the best of whatever the situation is.

This was a bad situation, to be sure. There were no good choices. I knew if I didn't fight and took my chances in court, the kindly judge would do everything in his power to make sure I was convicted and away for a long stretch.

So I did what my family always does in such situations.

I fought.

———

After the bets had been taken—and there was a lot of action—a bell sounded and we came out to the middle of the ring. I circled in my normal fashion to assess my opponent. He seemed nonchalant. Didn't hold his guard up under his chin, but more at chest level, which would give me plenty of openings.

I jabbed a couple of times. He was quick. He leaned away from the punches.

I decided to move in for a combination and as I did something from the ground flew upward and cracked against my skull. That something was his right foot.

He'd kicked me! And not just in the shin or my middle, but my doggone head!

How could he do it? Unless he was a ballet dancer, how could he get his leg up that high with his foot smacking my noggin?

I shook it off and determined to try to watch fists *and* feet from this guy, who was tiptoeing around light as a feather.

"I'll give you that one," I said. "Because I was surprised. Now come on and fight like a man."

He did not take that particular suggestion. Instead he turned around completely, I mean one entire revolution. But as he came out of the spin he lifted his leg again and with the heel of his foot whacked me on the other side of the face.

Little flashbulbs went off behind my eyes.

As I was shaking my head to get back my vision, I heard the judge call out, "That's the way to go, Frenchy!"

Frenchy? A certain kind of sense began to seep into my nut. I had heard about a French way of fighting called Savat. Kick boxing you might say, which to my mind is not boxing at all. But that's what this little guy was doing. And he had an unfair advantage on me because I never fought with my feet in my life.

And then another thought. Maybe the judge had been taking bets from the gathered gents, getting odds that I would pound this shrimp, and would make himself some nice lettuce when it turned out the other way.

My Irish sprang up. But it wasn't enough to fend off a flurry of kicks and punches from this French small fry. And they hurt. They landed good and just made me angrier.

And so I switched from the sport of boxing to the great American pastime of baseball. When I was a kid in the sandlots of Boston I played a pretty mean third base. They call third base the hot corner, because right-handed hitters that pull the ball will knock that apple at you mighty fast. You have to be able to react quick and catch the heat.

I waited for Frenchy to come at me again, dropped my left so it seemed like there was an opening for him. And when he came at me with his right foot, I snapped out my left and caught it like a line drive. I put my right hand under his ankle and twisted his foot until it was almost back-wards. I felt the crunch of cartilage and heard the cry of little Frenchy as he went down.

I waited for Jonesy to begin the count. But he looked over toward the judge without saying anything.

"What are you waiting for?" I said.

"Foul!" cried the judge.

"What're ya talkin' about?" says I. "This is a bare knuckle fight and he was kickin' me in the head. I don't find any rules on that."

"You will speak when spoken to!" the judge said.

"You're welching! You hear that gentlemen?" I was addressing the crowd as if that would do me any good. "You all saw what happened here. I'm within my rights."

Frenchy was still on the mat. It was past the ten count now. And besides, he wasn't going to be doing any more fighting on that foot.

But the crowd said nothing. And I could gather that the judge was giving them a look.

"I won this fight fair and square, according to the rules I was given," I said.

The judge's voice was colder'n a penguin's bollocks. "I make the rules. I make the law. You lose. Take him back, Jonesy."

Thrown back in the can! Like none of this ever happened!

The rest of the night I paced around like a caged lion whose red meat was just outside the bars, but not within reach.

What a pickle!

At some point I fell asleep, but was jerked awake soon after.

———

It was morning, and they wanted me down at cop headquarters, in my civvies.

In twelve hours I was supposed to meet Ruby at the movies. Maybe they were processing me out.

And maybe the moon is made of shamrocks.

What they wanted me for was a lineup. I got ordered out onto the platform with six other fellas, all about my height. The lights were in our eyes. Somewhere out there people were looking at us.

One of them had to be that pastor. I remembered the name.

"Pastor McGee?" I said.

"Shut up!" the lineup cop shouted from the side.

You never tell a Gallagher to shut up, unless you want him to keep talking.

"Pastor, if you're out there, I didn't do it!"

"Shut up now!"

"In the name of God, may he strike me dead—"

The cop came at me with a billy club.

"I warned you!" He gave me jab in the stomach. I folded like a cheap lawn chair. I wanted to talk more but the air was out of me and I was on the deck, gasping.

"Clear 'em off!" another voice in the room shouted.

"Get up," the billy club cop said. And he gave me one in the kidneys.

And then I heard a voice, a funny sounding one, say, "Stop that! Don't hit that man again!"

It was a twangy sort of voice. Like a Texas cowboy. And with authority. I thought it might be the police captain or something.

The billy club cop said, "What do I do, Mr. Bunyan?"

Bunyan. That was the name of the Brylcreem deputy D.A.

"That'll be enough, officer." That was Bunyan's voice.

"I want to talk to this man," the Texas cowboy said.

"But Dr. McGee," Bunyan said, "that could compromise our case."

"I want to speak to him now," Dr. McGee said.

I didn't care who spoke to me, just so long as I didn't get another billy to the ribs.

———

Bunyan had me brought to a cop interview room. Sitting at the table was an amiable looking fella, gray haired, glasses, with a shiner under his right eye.

"All right, sit down," Bunyan said.

"I'd like to be alone with him," Dr. McGee said.

"That wouldn't be advisable," Bunyan said.

"If you please."

Bunyan paused, shook his head and left.

"Now then, young man, my name is J. Vernon McGee and I'm the preacher at the Church of the Open Door."

"Pleased to make your acquaintance," I said.

"I wanted to look you in the eye. The young man who socked me looked an awful lot like you."

"Reverend, I'm giving you the straight skinny when I say it wasn't me that took anything from the church or laid you out. Sure and if I did, I know the Good Lord would not look kindly upon that!"

"They tell me you had church money in your pockets."

"They told me the same. I don't know how it got there, Reverend. My thinkin' goes like this, that the fella who hit you realized he was in more Dutch than he wanted, and put some of the dough in my pockets so's it would look like I did it."

The reverend looked at me a good long time. "You know, back in

Texas we had ourselves a hound dog. And this old dog, he couldn't hide from us anything he did wrong. One day a couple of pork chops disappeared from the kitchen table where they'd been set by my mother. Well, I found Blue out back and asked him face to face if he knew what happened to Ma's pork chops. And he looked sad and hung his head, if you please. He never could keep anything from us."

"Well I'll tell you, sir, if you look at me like you looked at that dog of yours, I'm telling you I didn't rob the church or hit you. And that's all I can do, short of findin' the guy who did it and beating . . . convincing him to confess."

"The Bible says, 'Let the lying lips be put to silence; which speak grievous things proudly and contemptuously against the righteous.'"

"If the Good Book says so, Reverend, I am not gonna quibble one little bit."

"Son, I believe you. I am going to ask the district attorney to drop the charges against you."

———

Bunyan's dander was up. He tried to talk Dr. McGee out of it, but the old preacher wouldn't budge.

When the prosecutor realized he did not have a complaining witness, he threw up his hands and said he had no alternative.

"Terrific," I said. "Let me get my things and let's walk out of here."

"Not so fast," Bunyan said. "You're still under arrest. It's going to take some time to do the paperwork."

"How much time, if I may ask?"

Bunyan took a gold pocket watch out of his vest, calmly opened it and perused the face. He clicked it closed and placed it back in his pocket. "It's lunchtime. I am going to have to take this up when I return."

Dr. J. Vernon McGee said, "Now, Mr. D.A., can't you find it in your heart to show this man a little bit of softness and charity?"

"I'm a Presbyterian," Bunyan said. "I'll take this up after lunch."

Now I had to wait in the jail's dining hall for the good pleasure of Mr. Bunyan.

And as I was sitting there, looking down at the most un-appetizing peanut butter sandwich in the history of Western civilization, I heard a familiar and unwelcome voice.

"Well, well, well," Jack Walsh said. "Word is you're gettin' sprung. I wouldn't think of lettin' you go without giving you my good wishes."

"Thank ye, and good day to you," I said.

He balled his fists. "You want it sittin' down or standin' up?"

I looked over to motion for the guard on duty and saw that there was no guard on duty. Paying off jail guards is not uncommon in our so-called Hall of Justice. Walsh must have shelled out some dough to get us alone, except for the other fellas eatin' and watchin'.

Before I could stand up, Walsh shoved the food tray into my chest and sent me flying backwards onto the floor. I scrambled to my feet and as I did two strong arms wrapped around me from behind. Somebody had me in a classic wrestling hold, my arms unable to move. Jack Walsh calmly stepped forward and punched me in the gut.

I wheezed like a tire going flat. My world went momentarily black.

I expected the worst. But suddenly I was free, and fell to one knee. At the same time I ducked out of instinct, and Jack Walsh's fist grazed the top of my head. That was all I needed.

I sprang up and got the off-balance Walsh with a left cross. It landed with satisfying impact and took Walsh down. I dropped my knees on his chest and began to do a speed bag workout on his face. That put Mr. Jack Walsh to sleep.

The whole thing had taken about one minute.

But how had I been freed to fight him in the first place? I looked around and saw a smiling fellow sitting on top of another man. This fella had red hair and a flat nose.

"O'Shea is the name," he said. "I was thinkin' it wasn't a fair fight."

Ah, the Angel O'Shea, as he would be known to me ever after!

A guard burst into the dining hall, billy club in hand. He raced right over to us.

"What happened here?" he said, his eyes dartin' between the fallen Walsh, O'Shea, and the man under him.

"Well it was like this, deputy darlin'," said O'Shea. "You see, the two gentlemen on the ground here got into a fighting mood, and tripped all over themselves. The one under me I'm trying to protect, so he doesn't get himself into more trouble."

The deputy didn't believe a word of it. He called out to the room. "Anybody see what happened?"

"Yes!" O'Shea said as he stood up. "Any of you lads want to play pigeon for this officer of the law?" He had his back to the deputy so he couldn't see O'Shea softly hitting his left palm with his right fist.

Nobody said nothin'.

The deputy's face was a dangerous shade of pink.

"Back to your cells, the both of you!" he said.

———

Time ticked by as slow as a Scotchman counting his coins.

When the shadows started falling over Los Angeles, I was just about ready to try and punch my way through the bricks. It would soon be night, and I had to get to the Egyptian theater by seven o'clock.

I could picture my Ruby, in tears, standing out in front with no Jimmy around.

Get me outta here!

It was four-thirty-three when they took me down to processing. I stood at the desk waiting for 'em to bring me my wallet and watch. But I'd made it! I'd just have time to get a shave then run home and check on Steve, change clothes and catch a Red Car to Hollywood.

I managed the shave all right. I hoofed it over to Tony's Barber Shop on Broadway, where I asked for Nick because Nick is all business and doesn't talk a blue streak like Tony. I got out of the chair with a smooth, kissable face patted down with Lilac Vegetal.

I was paying when the bell on Tony's door jingled.

In came a guy.

At the end of the guy's arm was a gun.

He was shaking. He was skinny. I pegged him as a junkie.

"Nobody move!" He must've been twenty-five or so, too young to be throwing his life away on heroin. But then again, is there any good age for the white monkey?

"Empty the cash register!"

"No!" Tony said. "I work-a too hard, you no goodnik!"

"Give me the money now!" The junkie fired his pistol. The glass mirror in front of the barber chairs shattered.

I was standin' there by the hat rack looking for a chance to charge the kid. But with his nervous trigger finger I thought I better not, lest Tony or Nick get plastered with hot lead.

With grumbled Italian words, which I would not translate for you even if I could, Tony went to the register and opened the drawer. He took out the bills.

"The silver too!" the guy shouted. "And put it in a bag."

Tony's shower of Italian curses grew louder, but he got the change. Then he grabbed a brown bag from next to the cash register and dropped in the dough.

The junkie turned the gun on me.

"You too," he said.

"Me too what?" I said.

"Your wallet! In the bag."

My wallet! My only supply of cash money to pay for movie tickets and dinner!

"Now look, sonny," I said. "Why don't you just walk right outta here and we'll forget the whole—"

He fired another shot. The bullet whizzed by my right ear before striking the wall calendar behind me. Maybe it was my imagination, but it looked like the bullet made a direct hit on Friday the 13th.

Which it happened to be.

I needed to kiss a shamrock quick, but you don't find many of those in L.A. Especially when a nervous hype with a gun is threatening to kill you.

And I didn't want Tony or Nick getting it by accident, either. So I fished out my wallet—my wallet as thin as a Dublin street gamin—and put it in the bag Tony held out to me.

Tony held the bag out to the junkie, who snatched it away, backed to the door, opened it and ran out into the street.

I went after him.

Tony shouted, "Be-a careful!"

I was-a gonna try.

———

The junkie ran up Third Street. He had half a block on me and was already at Hill, right where the Bradbury Building is. He charged across the street, almost getting hit by a car.

When I got to the corner I had to stop because a big old Cadillac was racing by, followed by a big old Ford. When they passed I ran across Hill and picked up the junkie just as he disappeared into the Third Street tunnel.

Angels Flight was cranking on my left, a little knot of people waiting for one of the cars to descend. An old man with a cane turned around in front of me and I plowed right into him.

He hit the sidewalk.

His cane went flying.

Blast! I stopped and attended the old gent, quickly getting him to a sitting position.

"Beggin' your pardon, sir!" I said.

"You crazy or something?" the old man said, which was a good sign. If a fella can still hurl the invective you know he's not down and out.

"You'll be all right, mister," I said.

The old man touched his head and said, "Ow."

"I'll be right back," I said.

Another voice said, "You crazy nut!"

I looked up and saw a big side of beef coming at me. He wore an open collared, short-sleeved shirt. His arms had muscles in places where most men don't have places.

This was no time to be doing business with him.

"Look after him!" I said to the side of beef, and took off for the tunnel.

"Get back here, you coward!" the side of beef yelled.

I almost stopped right there, because nobody calls a Gallagher yellow lest he pay for it with a knuckle sandwich and a side of slaps. But I had no time!

———

Now, I run up the concrete steps on Bunker Hill every other day or so, to keep up my wind. So I wasn't surprised when I started closing in on the thief in the tunnel. All I had to do was not get shot.

Death, where is thy sting? I do not care for thee, nor do I fear thee, but

I request a stay of execution long enough to get my money back and meet Ruby at the movies. O death, do you hear me?

The tunnel spits out near Flower Street. My mark, who was looking back at me now, took a left and I lost sight of him.

Figuring he'd be waiting to blast me, I ran across to the other side of the street. A vegetable truck almost turned me into mashed potatoes.

But I made the sidewalk and continued to run. The truck driver slowed down to curse at me. Couldn't blame him.

It gave me an idea. As he started to speed up I hopped on the back and held onto the gate. I got a speedy ride out of the tunnel and sure enough, there was the junkie, with the gun out, behind a retaining wall.

Far as I could tell he didn't see me. The truck turned left on Flower and that pulled me around behind where the junkie was.

When the truck slowed I jumped off and started back toward my mark. There was a liquor store at the end of a row of shops, and a little grassy area. Junkie was in the grass, hunched behind the wall, looking at Third Street.

I scurried up the side of the hill, like I was a dogface soldier at Anzio. I had about thirty yards of grass to cover. If he spun around he might get a shot at me. I reached down and pulled up a couple of dirt clods, one in each hand. Grenades!

And then I charged down the hill.

Wouldn't you know it, that was the time he figured on turning. But I was ready. My old fastball from the sandlot days didn't fail me. I plastered his face with a dirt clod. He fell back and the gun went off. Thank Saint Paddy it was pointed at the sky. I switched the other dirt clod to my right hand and threw. It broke apart in midair but the fragments hit his eyes. Then I dove on him.

We rolled over and over to the bottom of the grassy hill and ended up splayed on the sidewalk.

He was on top of me. He still held the gun in his right hand. I got hold of his wrist with my left and my fingers went all the way around. I would have no trouble controlling this guy. But I didn't want him to shoot some poor pedestrian.

So I gave him something Jimmy Gallagher never does in the ring. A head butt. Oh, it was a mighty blast. It was like a shillelagh smashing a watermelon.

Over he went, his forehead spouting blood. I slammed his hand on the sidewalk and the gun came out.

I opened the revolver chamber. There were three bullets. I took them out and threw them up in the grass.

The junkie moaned. The bag with the money was nowhere to be found.

Now what? I started to search his pockets. He gave me a verbal protest with a four-letter word attached. I bopped him in the snout. He would not wake up for a while.

"He's got a gun!" a woman screamed.

Somebody shouted, "Police! Help."

"It's empty!" I said.

But now a little posse started gathering. I had to get out of there quick. I didn't need some cop to grill me right after I'd been bounced from county jail!

But where was the money?

And then, as if by divine inspiration—because who knows more about the intimate details of our lives than God himself?—I gave the downed drug addict a certain medical exam. Had I been a doctor, I would've had him turn his head and cough.

And yes, that was where I felt something very much like my wallet.

I pulled up on his belt and reached in where Jimmy Gallagher would have never dared to go under normal circumstances. I grabbed the bag of money and pulled it out.

Then I took off running back through the Third Street tunnel.

I never ran so fast in my life. I was no sprinter when I was a lad, but I think I could've done the 100 meters in ten seconds then. I looked behind me and didn't see anybody giving chase.

I was winded when I emerged from the tunnel and paused briefly to put my hands on my knees and catch my breath. I could hear Angels Flight above me, and thought perhaps there were real angels in those cars looking out for Irishmen just trying to set the record straight.

I was sweating under my arms and on my forehead. I wiped my hand across my brow and stood up. When I did I was face to face with that big side of beef from before. He grabbed my shirt.

"You really hurt that old man," he said. "I'm gonna teach you some manners."

There are various ways I have fought, and now I fought for composure. "Good sir, I was in much need of speed a moment ago, but I have realized the purpose of my fast deportation. Is the poor old gentleman all right? I would like to apologize."

"Somebody took him to the doctor," the massive man said to me. "And in a minute they're going to have to do the same with you."

"No need of that, if you will just allow me to—"

"Do you know who I am?"

I gazed into his face, which looked like a bucket of knuckles, and said, "I cannot say that I do."

"The name's McGuirk."

"Fine."

"Aloysius McGuirk!"

"Finer still."

"Heavyweight champeen of Stockton nine years ago."

"A fellow champeen!" I said. "Perhaps now you could leave go of my shirt and allow me, on another day, to buy you a beer. We can talk about the fight game."

Aloysius McGuirk did not let go. "What were you ever champ of?"

"The PC 477 in 1944. Pleased to make your acquaintance."

Still keeping hold of me, McGuirk began shouting to the crowd, "Come over here, ladies and gents. You are about to witness a fight between two champions!"

"I don't think that's necessary," I said.

"Are you yellow?" McGuirk said.

You can call me green for the land of my ancestors, but you cannot call Jimmy Gallagher yellow. I could've run from the scene. But to do so would've required me to turn my back on every Gallagher who ever stood up to a marauding thief or invading soldier.

On the other hand, to fight right now might very well ruin me with Ruby. Not that I feared being beat, just smacked around so she'd know from my face I'd been in a scrap.

But the crowd formed a sort of ring around the two of us.

"I hope you realize this is an illegal form of fisticuffs," I said.

McGuirk finally let go of my shirt. He unbuttoned the sleeves of his own shirt and started rolling them up.

"Or perhaps you don't," I said.

I was still holding the bag that contained my wallet and the barbershop money. McGuirk stepped over and snatched it out of my hand. He turned to the first man he saw in the crowd, a fellow with a derby hat and tweed coat, and said, "Hold this."

The gentleman gave a nod and took the bag.

Without another moment's hesitation, McGuirk came at me in a boxer's shuffle.

My fists went up of their own accord. Three hundred or more fight experiences shot their memory through my bones. I didn't even have to think as McGuirk threw his right hand at my head.

I ducked the punch and gave him a right to the gut.

My fist hit fat. Which was good news. It told me this McGuirk was not in fighting trim. He had let time soften his belly. He probably never needed much more than his big arms and fists in any street confrontation or bar room brawl since he came down from Stockton.

This was all I needed to know.

McGuirk jabbed with his left and caught me above the right eye. I plowed in with another shot to the breadbasket, then a solid jackhammer below the heart.

McGuirk's eyes watered.

He threw three more punches— a right, a left, another right. Each time I fended it off with one hand and impaled his body with the other. At the end of the exchange McGuirk was bending at the waist like he was bowing to a queen.

The mostly male crowd was cheering, although I did note a woman who looked like she should've been shopping in a fancy department store. She was shouting just as loud as the men.

"I've had enough if you have," I said. "I don't have any wish to prolong this."

McGuirk was wheezing, fighting to say something. Finally he just nodded and waved his hand.

"No hard feelings," I said. "I will still buy you that beer one of these days." I turned to get my bag back and wouldn't you know it? The man in the derby was gone.

———

I grabbed the first man I saw and asked him if he'd seen where the derby fellow went. He shook his head in fear of me. I asked the lady next to him, and she proved she was no lady when she cursed at me to get my stinking face away from hers.

Then I heard the grinding of Angels Flight as one of the cars started up. And there he was in one of the windows, the man with the derby, looking at me with a half smile.

I would make him eat that smile.

I bolted into the street. A Pontiac station wagon almost sent me to my ancestors. It screeched its brakes and I jumped enough so I landed on top of the hood, not plastered on the grill. I rolled off and just about got clipped by a Ford coming in the other direction. I was a pinball.

But I made it to the cement steps that go up next to Angels Flight. The car with Mr. Derby Hat in it was halfway up.

By the time I reached the top of the steps the passengers had disembarked. There was a small crowd on Grand Avenue. I saw the back of Mr. Derby disappearing around the corner.

More running. I was flopping sweat. What a sight I would be for Ruby . . . if I ever got to see her again, that is.

I followed Derby's path around the corner and found a big fat slice of nothing waiting for me. No people, no cars even, just the backside of a row of flophouses, any one of which could be a hideout for a thief.

Now think, Jimmy, think! He can't be far away. He's got to be around here, hiding or just inside a door. What do thieves smell like? I was down to using my snout to track this guy.

Or my ears. I listened close because these old places squeak all over, what with their wood porches built fifty years ago.

Creak.

Yes, that was it. A board groaning under somebody's weight.

———

I jumped down to the concrete path between two old hotels, now turned into Bunker Hill rooming houses. I landed in front of a porch where an old woman in a flowered sun dress sat on a rocker.

She gave me a wide-eyed look.

"Beggin' your pardon, ma'am," I said. "I'm looking for a man in a derby hat."

"Tain't no concern o' mine," she said with an accent straight out of the Dust Bowl.

"He stole something from me."

"Stole?"

"Did you see anyone like that run by here?"

"Maybe," she said.

Faith and potato pie! What was that supposed to mean? "If you wouldn't be minding thinking about it, I'm in a hurry. I have to meet my girl, you see."

"Girl?"

"My sweetheart."

"Well why didn't you say so?" The old lady stood. "He's inside." She turned to the door and opened it.

With a jolt of fight juice (what the doctors call adrenaline, I guess) I followed her in. My fists were ready.

The place was dark and smelled like hardboiled eggs cooked in a diner in 1925. The narrow entry was drab and dark, had a mirror on the wall to my left and a framed photograph of a sour-looking family on my right—man and woman sitting, boy and girl standing, none of them smiling.

There was a staircase just ahead. The old woman went to the foot of it and looked up.

"Henry! Henry Snow! You get down here right this minute and I don't mean maybe!"

Mother o' Mercy, if that old lady's voice had been a fist it would have put Joe Louis on his backside.

A door creaked open upstairs. There was a shuffling of feet, then tentative steps on the staircase. But down he came all right. The man in the derby. Only he'd left the hat upstairs. His flat hair was slick and parted down the middle.

"Why'd you let him in here, Ma?" Henry said.

"This man says you stole something from him," Ma said.

"He's a liar," Henry said.

Irish blood sprinted from my heart to my head. "Nobody calls Jimmy Gallagher a liar! Put up your dukes!"

Henry took a backward step up the stairs.

His mother put a hand on my chest. She had a firm arm for a woman of her advanced years. "You let me take care of this, young man. You are a guest in my house."

"You tell him to take that back," I said.

Keeping her hand on my breastbone, she turned to Henry. "Now don't you lie to me, boy. Do you have something that belongs to this man?"

"It belongs to me," Henry said. "I stole it fair and square."

The old woman shook her head and muttered, "Children. You work your hands to the bone to provide for 'em, and what do they do?"

I said, "I understand, ma'am." And I did. I was something of a handful for my own sainted mother when I was a lad. But Henry was at least thirty years old, which made the whole thing a little more disconcerting.

"Yessir," she said, "if I taught him only one thing, it was never, ever to lead a mark back to your place of residence." She took her hand from my chest and reached into the large pocket of her house dress. She came out with a snub-nosed .38 and pointed it at my head.

———

You could've knocked me down with a four-leaf clover. I almost cried out to God to tell me what awful sin I had committed to be finding myself looking into the business end of a gun held by an old woman with a thief son named Henry, who had my sole means of going to the movies, which I had to do if I was going to keep the affections of the girl who was fool enough to love me.

"Move into the parlor," the old woman said.

I thought about making a grab for the gun but it might mean I'd have to hit a lady and that is something my father taught never to do.

Which was very inconvenient at the moment.

In the room just off the entryway was a chair with a knitted blanket slung over the back and a loud, ticking clock on a shelf. The hands of the clock were merciless messengers of my situation.

It was 5:25.

I had a little over an hour and a half.

"Now tell me," said the old woman. "Just who are you?"

"Nobody special, ma'am. Just another resident of Bunker Hill. Would you mind lowering that gun?"

The old woman shook her hoary head. "My house. My rules. Now answer my question. You say your name is Gallagher?"

"I not only say it, I can prove it."

"What's that supposed to mean?"

"I am a practitioner of the art of modern fisticuffs."

The old woman narrowed her gaze, like she was thinking. Then she perked up. "Henry, did you hear that? God has brought us home a boxer."

"Now if you don't mind my saying so," I said, "I am nobody's boxer but my own."

"I'm the one holding the gun. And I will let you know that I've killed three men, men who invaded my house in West Texas. I will not hesitate to do so again."

I was tired. And an old woman was holding a gun on me, and her thieving son had all my money. I was behind the eight ball, all right.

"So you want to take your leave of this house?" the woman said.

"Yes, ma'am, I do."

"Then I want you to give my Henry a boxing lesson."

Henry said, "Aw, Ma."

"You hush your mouth," the woman said. "I've been trying to make a man out of you ever since your Pa died. Maybe this boxer fella can show you how to defend yourself so you don't always have to be running home to me."

I said, "Ma'am, I'm not in the business of teaching the grand art of boxing to thieving rats. I just want my money and I just want to leave."

"Do you want to get shot?" she said.

"On balance, no."

"Then you had better commence to giving my son a lesson. I'll watch."

"Then what if I come back and give him as many lessons as he wants? You just give me my money and I will later give you my time."

"Don't think I can trust you to come back," she said.

"I'm giving you my word. And when Irish Jimmy Gallagher gives his word, he keeps it."

"No, sir," the woman said.

"Aw, let him go, Ma. I don't want the money anymore," Henry said.

His mother said, "You will do as you're told. Get to the lessons before

I decide to shoot. And by that I mean either one of you, depending on my mood."

Which was not about to get any better, I was sure.

"All right, Junior," I said. "Step over here."

"Do I have to, Ma?"

"Step," the woman said.

Reluctantly, Henry shuffled over to where I was standing. The old woman was to the right, gun at the ready.

"One lesson for today," I said. "You jab with your arms and you punch with your legs. Do you know what I mean?"

"No," Henry said.

"I'll show you."

I lifted my dukes, but the old woman said, "Hold it right there. You're not going to hit Henry. Henry is going to hit you."

I turned. "Beggin' your pardon?"

"You are not to hit my boy," the woman said. "But let him hit you all he wants."

"You expect me to stand here and let your boy plaster his knuckles all over my face?"

"If that's what he wants to do, that's what he'll do."

I looked back at Henry and now he seemed happy. He started rolling up his sleeves.

"And if you so much as lift a fist to hurt him," the mother said, "I will let you have it."

"If I may make an observation," I said, "your mothering is not exactly of the Norman Rockwell variety."

"No more jawboning," the woman said. "Let me see Henry give you one on the snout!"

Before I had a chance to say or do anything, Henry took his shot. His left came at me and hit me full on in the nose.

But full on from Henry was nothing like the blows I got in the ring.

"Ow," Henry said.

I had to keep myself from busting out laughing.

"Again," his mother said. "Only this time, mean it!"

"That's right, Henry," I said. "Mean it this time. I've had butterflies land on my puss harder than that."

Henry's face flushed. And if this had been a real fight, you know, one where I actually got to throw a punch or two, then Henry would have been my meat.

He reared back with his right hand and sent his fist zinging toward my chin.

I pulled my head back at the last and he missed.

"Hey!" he shouted.

"Don't get smart, mister," the woman said. She waved the piece at me.

"Now listen, the both of you. If Henry here is going to have any hope of defending himself or landing punches, he's got to use his noodle as much as his feet. Fighting is ninety percent mental. The other half is physical. Now, Henry, you keep your eye on my chin, and when I tell you to, you hit me. Get ready."

Henry didn't move.

"Do as you're told, son," the woman said.

As Henry pulled himself to a taller, more manly position, I shifted ever so slightly to the left, starting to circle him.

"Stay with me," I said.

I circled a bit more, then stopped. "Now!"

Henry threw another right. I let it land.

It was a love tap. I've been hit in the mug by Iron Hands Jackson his own self. Henry the Thief wasn't even in the same town, let alone ballpark.

"Again," I said, taking one more step to the left. "Dance with me."

Henry smiled. He was starting to enjoy himself.

"Now!"

One more right, and one more powder puff to my chin.

Then one more step.

Now Henry was facing me, with the old lady right behind him.

"Now!"

Henry punched me again.

"Not like that," I said. "Like this." I shot out my right hand, my old reliable meat-and-potatoes. I put a knuckle tattoo on Henry's face and back he went like he was shot out of a cannon.

Right into the old lady.

The gun went off.

Henry fell.

Before he was halfway to the floor I took a step and grabbed the gun from the old woman's hand.

"Henry!" she shrieked.

I looked down and saw a hole in the pants covering the left hemisphere of Henry's gluteus maximus.

"He'll be fine after he wakes up," I said. "But won't be sittin' down for awhile."

The old woman then fired off a string of profanities the like of which I'd never heard even aboard the old PC 477.

———

I held the gun on her now. I was sorely tempted. Hitting a woman, no. Shooting? Ah, I wouldn't do it, I couldn't do it, but she didn't know that.

"Get me my money," I said. "Forty-seven dollars. Take it out of Henry's wallet."

"Please, Mister, he's hurt," the old woman said.

"He's not hurt. He just got shot in his brains. Now take out his wallet."

The old woman knew the odds and removed Henry's wallet from his coat. She started going through it and pulled out some bills.

"Here," she said, and held out four twenties.

"Just forty-seven dollars, ma'am."

"Take it, why don't you?"

"I'm not robbing you, I'm collecting. Give me forty-seven even."

She rooted around and came back out with a sawbuck.

"That's fifty," I said.

"There's nothing smaller."

"What did your Henry do? Roll a millionaire?"

Henry groaned.

"Please take it and go," the woman said.

"All right," I said. "But I owe you three."

"No!"

"And I always pay my debts."

I popped open the cylinder and dumped the bullets on the floor. "I'll leave the gun at the bottom of the stairs, in the bushes. If you want my advice, lady, you won't go get it. You could do a lot of damage."

"Get out!"

I got out.

As advertised, I took the stairs down and tossed the rod in the oleander. If she wanted it she'd have to fish for it and I hoped she'd get a rash if she did.

But I was flush now! I had fifty bucks in my pocket and just enough time to wash up and catch the streetcar to Hollywood.

Oh, Hollywood! The land where my love awaited!

I hoofed it a block to my own pad. Steve met me with a friendly *Boof.*

"Right back atcha, Steve," I said. "Boof just about covers my day."

I opened a can of Ken-L-Ration and spooned it into Steve's bowl. While he ate I washed up, put on clean clothes and a little splash of Aqua Velva.

I put on Steve's leash and took him out to the grass patch on Fourth which had his favorite tree.

Then back to the apartment with him and it was off to catch my ride.

If all went well and I missed no connection, I would be walking up to the Egyptian Theater box office at five minutes to seven.

———

But I just missed the Wilshire streetcar. I thought I could run after it and catch it at Figueroa. I had to calculate quick because I didn't want to be covered in sweat when I saw my girl. But I figured I'd have enough time to dry up if I caught the trolley and rode to Hollywood in forty minutes or so.

As I ran past the alley next to a Rexall drug store, I heard a moan and a cry for help. And saw a pack of uniformed sailors in the middle of the alley. It doesn't take a whole lot of experience for one swab to assess the actions of another. These gobs were giving somebody the knuckle duty, and it was seven or eight against one.

My head told me to keep going. This was not my fight.

My heart told me there was something being done that shouldn't ever be done.

Another part of my heart thought of Ruby.

My head said, *The streetcar has stopped at Figueroa!*

Another pitiful cry for help. Another flailing of fists.

"Ahoy there!" I said.

As one, the mob of white hats spun around.

They looked so young to me. Like my own self fifteen years ago, putting my mark on paper and heading out to sea. Had it really been that long?

"Mates," I said, "I don't want to see Uncle Sam's Navy taken to task by the law. Whatever has been done is done, now it's time to drop the matter and go have yourselves a beer."

The sailors looked at each other. Then the oldest looking of the bunch, which wasn't saying much, took one step towards me and said, "What business is it of yours?"

"None at all, shipmate. Just looking at the deck here bein' stacked against one man."

One of the other sailors snickered. "He ain't a man. He's a greaser."

I cleared my throat. "It's eight against one, that's all I see. And it seems to me a poor representation of the Navy to have you boys taking advantage like that. Now why don't you just let the man go and cool your heels at Ned's bar across the street?"

The old sailor said, "Just who are you?"

"Jimmy Gallagher is my name, and I served aboard the PC 477 cruising the Solomon Islands in the war. And in all my time on board ship or on leave, I never did see an example like this."

"This taco bender whistled at a white woman," the old sailor said.

I could now see the form of a man lying on the ground behind a forest of sailor legs.

"A whistle doesn't hurt anybody," I said. "How many times have you guys whistled at a woman?"

One of the younger sailors said, "Only our own kind."

"Maybe you boys don't realize this is Los Angeles," I said. "We do things different here. This isn't Alabama."

From the back of the group of sailors stepped the biggest one of all. He was ruddy-cheeked and filled out his uniform like a USC lineman.

"I'm from Alabama," he said, his voice dripping with molasses. "You wanna make somethin' of it?"

Now my head told me I was a stupid, idiotic, foolish, dunderheaded, cursed and ill-fated son of perdition. I could not excuse myself on the pretense that I had to go see a motion picture. No Gallagher ever backed away from a fight—except my great uncle Seamus, who was fond of saying, "It is better to be a coward for a minute than dead for the rest of your life." And he lived to be 92.

I probably wouldn't make it that far.

"All right, ya big lummox," I said. "But you're the only one I want to face. If I knock you down fair and square, the rest of you go away nice and peaceable."

Alabama smiled and took off his hat, handed it to another sailor. "I'm gonna enjoy this."

He started advancing toward me. I figured him for one of those small-town rowdies who's bigger'n all the rest of the boys and pretty much has his way when it comes to fisticuffs. He didn't look like the type who'd ever had a lesson in the pugilistic arts.

He had fists the size of duffel bags, but looked soft in the middle. I decided to make that the focus of my lesson. That's the place most of your street brawlers haven't prepared for fighting. I still do my one hundred sit-ups a day, even when Steve tries to lick my face on the downward.

Alabama and me circled each other. He was twirling his fists over each other, the way amateurs think real boxers do.

When he came at me with a roundhouse right that he telegraphed from Tuscaloosa, I ducked it easily and gave him a shot to the solar plexus.

Down went Alabama like a pot of grits.

"Now clear away," I said to the gobs, but move they did not. Then the older one says, "Nobody does that to a shipmate and gets away with it."

"Hold on there, swabbie," says I. "That wasn't our deal."

"Deal? I didn't agree to no deal. Did any of youse guys flap your yaps about a deal?"

All the heads shook.

So this was to be a mugging, and when it's one of those you throw out all the rules and retreat to the law of club and fang.

The Irish may have saved civilization, but if we're going to get our heads bashed in we tend to favor the Barbarian way.

Three of them rushed me at the same time.

I went for the one in the middle, charging instead of waiting. With a swift kick to his lower decks I had him out of the fray. At the same time, the one on my left swung for my face. I ducked it and gave him a right to the kidney.

That left my back open to number three, who went for the wrestling hold. He threw an arm around my throat and got me in a headlock.

All I could do was pump my legs and drive him backward into the wall.

We hit with a bone-rattling *whump*. I drove an elbow into his midships and he released me.

But before I could turn around and finish him off, two more swabbies were on me. It was raining fists. I covered my face with my forearms and did what I could with my legs.

But with a third guy crowding in I knew I wasn't going to last much longer.

Goodbye, Ruby girl.

But then, with what sounded like a clap of thunder, the rain stopped.

When I looked up I saw three sailors on the ground and the rest backing further into the alley.

And a figure of fury swinging a two-by-four.

They must've forgotten all about their original prey, who had recovered enough to grab this beam and begin his one-man retribution.

For a long moment the two of us stood there, facing what was left of the mob. We looked at each other, like we were asking the other what we should do next.

I shrugged.

My rescuer shrugged.

We began to back out of the alley.

My new friend was about twenty-five or so, with hair the color of pitch and a lean frame that spoke of hard work. His flannel shirt was torn and there was a mean shiner taking shape under his left eye.

But he had this content look on his face. "Thank you for what you do for me."

"I owe you one too, pal," I said.

"I would like to buy a beer for you."

I smiled. "Much appreciated, but I'm sorry, I've got to get to Hollywood, and I mean now. I need to catch a streetcar."

"No! But I have a truck. I give you a ride!"

"No fooling?"

"There!"

I looked where he pointed. A rattletrap Ford pick-em-up truck sat out in front of the First National Bank building. It had wooden slats on the sides that leaned precariously toward the street. Through the slats I saw some wire cages, and in the cages feathered cargo.

Chickens.

"We go?" my friend said.

"We go," I said.

We hopped in and he brought the truck to life, if you could call it that. The engine sounded like a tuberculosis patient waking up in the morning. It coughed and spewed black exhaust. The chickens, maybe a dozen of them, squawked and flapped. Little feathers flew as the driver pulled out into traffic and made a U-turn, almost getting plowed into by a black Buick speeding past.

"You no worry," the driver said. "I get you where you want to go, all right."

His name was Rudolfo Garcia and as long as traffic was flowing nicely I figured we could get to Western and cut up to Hollywood Boulevard. Maybe twenty minutes. That would put me in front of the Egyptian theater just in time to meet Ruby. The fight in the alley had not torn my clothes or drawn blood.

Rudolfo was an egg man from Veracruz. He drove like a man without a care in the world, except when he winced in pain.

"You want to tell me what happened back there?" I said.

"I do nothing. I ask a girl what time it is because my watch, it is not working. Next I know, I am pushed into the alley."

"A shame on the United States Navy," I said.

"What make you want to come help me?"

"I didn't do much thinkin' about it. Which is my problem sometimes."

He laughed, then winced and touched his puffy face.

We got to Hollywood Boulevard, turned left, and were heading toward the Egyptian. All would be well. Life would go on. Ruby would be happy, I would be happy, Steve would be—

Bang!

A Packard hit the truck!

It came from the right side and smashed into the back end of the truck, spinning us forty-five degrees.

It jolted me like a right hand from Max Baer. When the dust settled and we were at a dead stop, I heard the squawks of numerous displaced chickens. They were all over the street!

Rudolfo yelped, then started talking rapid-fire Spanish. I recognized the word *pollo* and *estúpido* and not much else.

I got out of the truck and looked at the chickens all around me. Even as Rudolfo was trying to gather them up, stopping traffic, cars honking at him, I saw this black limo near the Packard. A black-clad chauffeur got out of the limo and came over to me. He was an inch taller than myself, and just as wide. He said, "My passenger would like to know how long this will take to clear up."

"Tell your passenger to get out and help," I said.

"That will not be possible," the chauffeur said.

"Then don't crowd me."

He crowded me, puffing out his chest.

"Now look, Hercules," says I, "I've had a bad day and I'm in no mood to chat with you or—"

The back window of the limo rolled down and I heard a woman's voice say, "Is there a problem?"

Something about that voice. The woman wore dark glasses, had on thick, red lipstick and a pink scarf over her sun-kissed hair, tied in a little knot under her chin.

"No problem," the chauffeur said.

"There *is* a problem, ma'am. My friend's chickens are loose."

"Would you mind, then," the woman said to the driver, "helping these gentlemen gather their chickens?"

"But Miss Monroe, I—"

"Thank you, Franklin."

Miss Monroe!

With a hard look at me, Franklin the chauffeur started chasing chickens down Hollywood Boulevard. I helped. I helped fast. Because it was almost time to meet Ruby, and she was so near!

But this was Rudolfo's livelihood and I owed him. When we finally had all the chickens back in their cages, Rudolfo looked at his damaged truck. "Who is going to pay for this?"

"What do you figure the damages are?" Marilyn Monroe said from the limo.

"It looks like at least two hundred," I said.

"Franklin," she said, "give the man three hundred dollars."

He was her obedient servant. Franklin pulled out a wad of bills and peeled off three, handed them to Rudolfo.

"And what can I do for you?" Marilyn Monroe said to me.

I went weak at the knees at that one. But I managed to say, "Can you give me a lift?"

————

"Where are you going in such a hurry?" Marilyn Monroe said when I got in the limo.

"To meet my girl at the Egyptian."

"Oh yes. Oklahoma."

I felt my Irish cheeks getting ruddy.

"You look like you can handle yourself," she said. "How would you like to work for me?"

I tried to clear my throat but nothing happened. I was as dry as a Santa Ana wind.

She reached out and squeezed my right bicep. "Oh yes, indeed," she said. "You could do this job."

Oh, the volumes spoken between those lines! What man with any blood in his veins could resist such an invite from Marilyn Monroe?

It took all the fight left in me to say, "Miss Monroe, sure and I'm grateful for the kind offer, but—"

"Is there something you find offensive about it?"

"Far from it, Miss Monroe! A field of heather in the morning, with the mist just rising and the sunlight kissing the earth, has nothing on you! It's just that . . ."

She smiled. "What's her name?"

"Ruby," I said.

"She's one lucky girl."

It was then I realized we'd stopped moving. Miss Monroe lowered the limo's divider. "What is it, Franklin?"

"They've stopped traffic," the driver said. "Looks like for a mile."

"What time is it?" I said.

Miss Monroe looked at the thin, diamond-banded watch on her arm. "Ten minutes to seven."

Ten minutes! And us stuck here like dock workers at a dry lake!

"I've got to make tracks," I said. "Thank you for the ride."

"Look me up if you ever change your mind," Marilyn Monroe said.

I threw open the door and started running between the cars on Hollywood Boulevard.

Ten minutes.

Nine.

I clicked off the time in my head.

I could run a mile easy in nine minutes. Just keep a steady pace. Maybe the night air would cool me and I wouldn't be all too sweaty when I met up with Ruby.

If she asked me how come I was running, I'd tell her the absolute truth —*To get to you, baby. I couldn't wait to see you!*

But when I got to Vine Street there was a ribbon of yellow tape across the entire intersection, and it was crawling with cops.

One of whom put a big hand on my chest. "Nobody passes here."

"But I'm going to the Egyptian."

"Not now, you're not."

"What's the problem?"

"We got a shooter. He's holed up in J. J. Newberry. Now if you'll let us—"

"Is that all?" I said. And knew then my mind was not working right. I stepped to the side then ducked under the police tape.

I ran across Vine.

"Hey!" the officer screamed.

On I ran, down the deserted street.

When I got to the storefront I saw cops across the street, behind cars, telling me to get out of the way, waving at me to go back.

Instead, I looked in the window.

A bullet cracked through the glass above my head.

The gun's flash told me it came from the back of the store, behind the soda fountain.

I ducked and ran to the front door, opened it, went in.

Another shot zipped over my head.

Down the aisle I ran. As I did, I passed a display of White Rain Shampoo—*The only shampoo guaranteed not to dull or dry your hair.* I grabbed two bottles and held 'em like hand grenades.

A desperate-sounding voice squealed, "Get out or I'm gonna shoot you!"

I popped around the end of the aisle and threw the first bottle of White Rain at him. It hit him in the chest. I fired off the other and smacked him in the head.

He went down.

I jumped over the soda counter. He was on the floor. I kicked the gun out of his hand and picked him up by his shirt. He was just a kid. Seventeen at most. Skinny.

"This ain't the way to solve your problems," I said.

He cursed in my face.

I clocked him with a right and knocked him out. I grabbed the back of his pants and dragged him out of the store and tossed him on the sidewalk. I shouted to the cops. "He's all yours!"

I took off running again.

The cops yelled at me to stop.

I didn't, because now I could see the lights of the Egyptian Theater sign, almost within reach.

There was another police ribbon across Cherokee. On the other side were people, a line crowding into the Egyptian courtyard.

I almost danced a jig. Finally!

I smoothed out my hair and took a deep breath and looked for Ruby.

She wasn't there!

What time was it?

I was late, maybe five minutes, maybe ten, but not long enough so Ruby would've left in a huff.

Up and down I walked in front of the theater.

People were streaming in.

And then I felt a tap on my shoulder.

Ruby!

She looked a little frazzled.

Also pretty as a primrose.

"I'm so sorry I'm late," she said. "Forgive me?"

I put my hand under her chin, tilted her head up and kissed her lips. I looked into her deep blue lamps and said, "I will this time, honey. But don't let it happen again."

SUCKER PUNCHED

May your blessings outnumber the shamrocks that grow, and may trouble avoid you wherever you go.
– Irish blessing

I was walking my bulldog, Steve, up Broadway. Steve likes downtown Los Angeles. He likes to strut in front of people. If he comes across other dogs he gives 'em a friendly *boof* and sticks out his face like Churchill. Sometimes I half expect him to light up a cigar.

At Broadway and Fourth there's a Chinese laundry. Seeing as how I was passing by, and seeing as how I was wearing the very shirt that would need a good cleaning, and seeing also as how I had a coat I could wear home, I put my reasoning powers to work and figured I could save me a whole trip if I just left the shirt right then and there.

We Gallaghers are known for not wasting effort, even if effort is following us around begging to be wasted.

Into the laundry I went. A little bell above the door jingled.

The smallest and oldest Chinese man I ever laid peepers on stood behind the counter. He wore glasses over a face as wrinkled as a balled-up newspaper.

"Yes, please?" the old man said.

Steve said *Boof.* I told him to lie down. He gave me an impatient look and turned around in a circle before lowering himself to the floor.

"Top of the afternoon," I said. "I wonder if I might drop off a shirt?"

"Yes, please."

"That's fine." I took off my coat and laid it on the counter. Then started unbuttoning my shirt. This amused the old man.

"Yeah, I know," I said. "It's not exactly Emily Post to be disrobing in your fine establishment, but I'm a man who likes doing business with a man who doesn't mind."

"Ah, thank you. May I know name, please?"

"Jimmy Gallagher's my moniker. What's yours?"

"J. Wong." He bowed.

I handed him the shirt. "Is there any hope?"

"Ah," J. Wong said. "Next Tuesday." He ripped a ticket from a book and handed it to me.

"Done and done," I said.

"You are big guy," he said.

"Bigger'n most, not as big as some."

"Strong guy."

"Got to keep in fighting trim. I do a little boxing, you see."

"Fight? Make money?"

"Never enough, Mr. Wong."

He nodded.

The bell jingled and a fella about my size blew in. He held a white shirt in his fist, like he was choking it to death.

"You call this starch?" he said.

"Starch yes," J. Wong said.

"Starch no," the mad fella said. He shook the shirt in front of J. Wong's face. The old man looked concerned and put his hand out, but the fella snatched the shirt away. "I want my money back."

"I will fix," J. Wong said.

"You just give me my money!"

"I will fix, please."

"You give me my money, or I'll fix you, you little chink."

"Now hold on there," I said. "No reason to be callin' anybody names."

The blazing eyes of the shirt holder flashed over to me. "Who asked *you?"*

"Well," I said, "there's askin' and then there's bein' a loudmouth."

His chin jutted out. "What'd you call me?"

"No fight!" J. Wong said.

"It's all right, my good man," I said to the proprietor. "I think this loudmouth is going to leave now."

"Not without my money," he said. "And not without teaching you a lesson." He emphasized his point by poking his index finger into my naked chest.

Steve growled.

"You just stay right there, Steve," I said.

The loudmouth put the shirt on the counter and started slipping out of his coat.

"No fight!" J. Wong said.

I said, "Now mister, I have to warn you, seeing as I'm a gentleman of the old school. Fisticuffs is my profession. And when I'm out of the ring like this, the Marquis of Queensbury rules don't exactly apply, if you catch the drift of my meaning."

A smile padded across the fella's face. "Now isn't that a coincidence? My name is Rudy Heffelfinger, and I was Illinois heavyweight champeen two years running."

With his coat off I could see he had a boxer's build—a barrel chest that Jim Jeffries would have envied, and fists the size of gas cans.

"Now see here, Mr. Heffelfinger, as fellow pugilists, surely we can find a better way to settle matters twixt ourselves, and then twixt you and Mr. Wong."

"You called me a loudmouth."

"I was considering blowhard, but it was loudmouth that came out. But I'm perfectly willing to give you an apology."

"Then you'd better—"

"As soon as you apologize to Mr. Wong."

Rudy Heffelfinger scowled, then spit into his hands and rubbed them together. He put up his dukes.

"Come on then," Heffelfinger said.

"Far be it from me to lay a whipping on the champeen of Illinois, but I will if it is forced upon me."

"You talk a lot, don't you?"

"The sons of Ireland are poets and politicians," I said. "You can't hardly keep us quiet."

"Well, we Germans can whip you micks any day of the week and twice on Sunday."

"No fight!" J. Wong started to come around the counter.

I put up my hand. "Mr. Wong, if you please, let me do my part for peace in our time. The Germans are always trying to take what isn't theirs. I will dispense with this one and remove him from your—"

Before I could finish, Heffelfinger lunged at me with a big right hand. I ducked the punch, sending my own right into his breadbasket. It was a stomach made of concrete. This man was in shape!

I backed up a step and took my fighting position.

Heffelfinger had a big smile now. Smilers like this are my meat. I put a worried look on my puss. We Gallaghers have actors in our background. We been run out of many villages in our scattered history. But it comes in handy when you want your opponent to think you're scared.

Heffelfinger jabbed, jabbed again. I let the last one tag me, and widened my eyes with more fear.

He closed in for the kill.

I dropped my hands to expose my face.

The big German threw his right again, a roundhouse. I shot my left arm up and caught the punch, then took my own right hand and hammered his nose with it.

He shook his head in wonderment.

I gave him another right to the temple, and a left to the other temple, and the big man fell to his knees. I finished him with a pile driver to his left cheek. He slumped like a laundry bag onto the tiled floor.

"Now that's what I call giving a man some starch, Mr. Wong," I said. I grabbed Heffelfinger by the back of his shirt collar and dragged him to the door. Just before I threw him out into the street, Steve said, *Boof.*

"Oh, you good fight!" J. Wong said after I came back in.

"Only doing my part for the civilizing of men," I said.

"You take gift."

"Oh no, there's no need."

"Yes! Insist! Chinese give gift for good deed. You take, or insult."

"Insult?"

Mr. J. Wong smiled, nodded.

"If you put it that way, Mr. Wong."

He bowed then disappeared into the back. Presently he returned with a necklace—a silver chain with a little dangly thing. When I looked closer I saw it was a dragon.

"Dragon good fight," said J. Wong.

"Yes, I suppose that's true," I said.

"You wear?"

I didn't want to insult the nice little man, so I slipped it over my head.

"Good!" he said.

I put my coat on and buttoned it.

"Good," I said.

———

Outside the laundry, Rudy Heffelfinger was just coming to. A woman in a hat with a big ostrich feather on it walked by and muttered, "Drunk!"

Now if there is anything an Irishman cannot tolerate it's a man being called drunk when he's sober as a judge. I helped Heffelfinger to his feet and put one of his arms over my shoulder. I walked him half a block to a tavern. I sat him at a table in the corner so the champeen of Illinois could lean into the crook and not fall down.

To the barkeep I said, "Two shots of your best Irish whiskey, my good man."

Heffelfinger's eyes got a little clearer. "Huh? What?"

"No more fighting today," I said.

"Who?"

"You just sit for a bit and clear that hard head of yours."

I sat. The bartender came with the whiskey. I picked up Heffelfinger's hand and put the shot glass in it.

"Drink up," I said.

He did.

"What did you hit me with, a brick?"

"Sure and that's a fine compliment," I said. "But you shouldn't be blowin' your stack on a little old man just trying to run a business."

"But the starch . . ."

"Let it go. There are some things worth getting hot about, and this ain't one of them."

"I'm not sure I like you," Heffelfinger said.

"Ah, but if you heard me sing 'My Wild Irish Rose,' it'd melt your heart."

He looked at my chest. "You got no shirt."

"A temporary condition."

"What's that you're wearin'?"

I looked down. "Just a little token from Mr. Wong."

"What's a mick . . .an Irishman like you wearing Chinese bangles for?"

Before I could answer I heard a scuffing noise. A big cop, swinging his billy, had come to the table.

"Stand up, please," he said to me.

Steve said, *Boof.*

"Down boy," I said. "This here is one of our city's fine officers of the law."

I stood.

"You're not wearing a shirt," the cop said.

"Oh, well, you see—"

"I could run you in for public indecency. A woman outside complained."

"Did she have a hat with a big feather?"

"The fact is, you have no shirt."

"I can explain that—"

"Let me see your identification."

"Well certainly, my good fellow." I reached behind my pants for my wallet, but all I felt was my caboose.

I patted my coat. "My wallet. I don't seem to have it."

"Vagrancy," the officer said.

"Must have dropped it at the laundry, officer. If you'll step over there with me, we'll have a look."

"Who's payin' for the drinks?" the bartender said.

"I'll pay you when I get back," I said.

"No credit," the barkeep said. "Somebody needs to pay me now."

"Faith and Maureen O'Sullivan!" I said. "Whatever became of simple trust?"

"Who ordered the drink?" the officer said.

The bartender pointed at me. "That man right there."

"That sounds like fraud," the officer said.

"I'll pay for the hooch," Heffelfinger said.

"Okay," said the cop. "But this bird's comin' with 'em."

I picked up my shot of whiskey and held it up to Heffelfinger.

"Your health," I said, and downed it.

"Let's go," the cop said.

"Come along, Steve," I said.

"*Boof*," Steve said.

———

As we walked, I tried a little blarney on the officer but he told me to shut my yap. So I buttoned it till we got to Mr. Wong's laundry.

Which was locked.

And which had a paper clock behind the glass with arms set to 1:15. Above the clock it said—WILL RETURN AT.

It was now 12:30.

"I guess we wait," I said.

"I guess we don't," the cop said. "Put your hands out."

"What!"

He took out the bracelets and clamped them on me.

———

At the station they booked me and tossed me in a cell. They strapped a leash on Steve, which he did not like one little bit.

"Where you taking my dog?" I yelled.

"He's got no tags," my arresting officer said. "To the pound."

"No! That's my dog!"

"That's not your dog anymore, laddie. It now belongs to the city of Los Angeles."

———

Locked up like a farm chicken! And my dog taken to animal prison! Steve's tough, if a bit lazy, but he's never been away from me for very long, not since I picked that scruffy pup out of a litter in Singapore. He was going to be missing me, and soon. Or worse—end up in the hands of some frowsy widow who'd put bows and perfume on him.

Or worst of all, they'd send him to the big sleep!

I started yelling. "Let me out of here! Go back to the laundry, I tell you!"

"Pipe down!" the cop yelled.

And then I got an idea. One of those Gallagher brainstorms that has landed us in plenty of hot water over the years. I'd start a fight, then make my escape.

"None of you'd last in a fair fight with me! There's not an L.A. cop alive can best Irish Jimmy Gallagher! Without your guns you're as yellow as a field of daffodils!"

Silence.

Then I heard the scuffling of feet, the murmur of voices, and grunts of agreement. A moment later my arresting officer, and three big cohorts, came back to the cell and stood outside it.

"So it's cowards we are?" my cop said.

"Let's go settle this outside," I said.

"Oh no," said the cop. "We'll settle this right now."

At which point all the cops took out their billy clubs.

"So that's your game!" I said.

"This is no game, son." And then he unlocked the cell.

———

When I came to I was rumbling along in the back of some sort of conveyance. My head is made of good Irish granite, but it was clanging now like the bells of St. Mary's. The dirty cops . . . so that was it. I was in an ambulance. And it was taking its own sweet time.

I turned to the side, which made the bells louder, and saw a face. A feller in a white coat, reading the *Racing Form*, a cigarette dangling from his mouth.

"Hey," I said.

"You just take it easy, sweetheart," the man said, without looking up from the paper.

"Where you takin' me?"

"County hospital."

They had me strapped down on a gurney. "What's with the leather cuffs?"

"You're a prisoner, bud. They say you assaulted some cops."

"It's a lie!"

"I'm not the judge," the man said. "But I am trying to pick a race, so be quiet."

"I'll show you how to pick 'em!" I started flailing around, trying to bust out of the restraints.

"Hey, cut that out," the guy said, putting down his paper.

We were heading up a hill. I could feel it. Even in my aching head I knew the county hospital was not on top of any hill. Maybe this guy wasn't even a medic.

I called down the curses of my ancestors on him and shook all the harder. The guy threw his cig on the floor and made a fist in front of my face.

"You want to keep your teeth?" he said.

Them's fightin' words to a Gallagher, but if we're tied up all we can do is scream like a banshee. And that's what I did, so loud I almost scared my own self. But the wail helped me put all my body into my shaking, and I felt the gurney start to roll.

Next thing I knew, my feet busted through the back doors of the ambulance and the gurney slid out like a body being buried at sea.

———

Down the hill I rolled.

There's a feelin' you get in a dream, when you're helpless but you have to move. Or you're moving and you want to stop, but you can't. I felt both those feelings, strapped as I was to a rolling bed, gathering steam down a street with cars and pedestrians. I heard the honk of a car horn and the squealing of tires, and somebody on the sidewalk yelling, "Hey, get off the street!"

Thanks for nothing, pal!

I picked up more speed.

The sky was blue. I called upon God to give one dumb boxer a break.

I looked at the buildings blurring past me. Pagodas. Brightly-colored storefronts.

Chinatown!

And I was about to become chow mein on the grill of a Packard or Buick!

So this was how life was going to end for Irish Jimmy Gallagher. Not at a grand old age, with Ruby and kids around my bed. Not from a hard right to my heart. Not fighting for my country or saving a baby from a burning building.

No, I was going to go like a greased pig down a slaughterhouse chute.

And then it got a whole lot worse.

———

When I finally came to rest, as near as I could tell, I was in the middle of an intersection.

And nobody offering to help me. I must have been a curious sight—an Irishman strapped down like a mummy on a county gurney on a street in Chinatown.

I heard the sound of tires squealing. Sounded like big tires, the kind that a truck might have. A truck—

—like the one that plowed into me! It launched me like a torpedo. Down the street I went again, cursing the day I was born . . . or at least, the morning I decided to leave my shirt at J. Wong's and take pity on a man I'd bested in a fight, leading to a bunch of dirty cops taking it out on my noggin.

When at last I came to rest again, I was in another intersection. I looked left, and saw a mob coming my way.

I looked right, and saw another mob closing in.

Many of them were holding chains, pipes and who knew what else.

And me in the middle like a Thanksgiving turkey waiting to be carved.

The two gangs stopped on either side of me, looking like they didn't know what to do.

"Say, gents, I could sure use a little help," I said.

Nobody moved.

Then one of the boys on my right sidled up to me. He was a tough-looking Chinese. Then somebody from the left, just as tough, came in for a look-see.

Then the one on the right said something in Chinese and that made the one on the left look at me again, close, like a doctor takin' a gander at a rash.

Then he started jabbering to the other guy and then there was a crowd around me, and the two first guys started unfastening me from my rolling bed.

"Well thanks, fellers," I said as I planted my feet. I was still without a shirt, and unsteady, too—kind of leaning this way and that. My head was still ringing.

The first tough-looking fella said to me, "You must fight to the death."

———

There are some things in life you don't look forward to hearin'. Like your crazy uncle is coming to stay for awhile. Or the dentist sayin' like he's Jack Benny, "The yanks are coming."

Or that a gang of Chinese toughs is gonna make you fight to the death.

But there I was, with that very bit of information rolling around in my pounding head.

"I'm sorry, good fellow," I said, "but it sounded like you said I'm supposed to fight somebody, to the death?"

He nodded. "The prophecy."

The other gang leader said, "Yes! The prophecy!"

"I'm afeared I don't catch your drift," I said.

"You will come with us," the first one said.

"If it's all the same to you, I think I'll just be on my way. You see, I've got a dog and I—"

Several pipes and chains and at least one long knife popped up in people's hands.

"This way, please," the gang leader said.

———

There's an abandoned Chinese restaurant at the end of Bamboo Lane. The two gangs, now united in this thing called the prophecy, walked me into it. It was cool and dark inside.

The only light was from a Chinese lantern hanging right over a strange looking bird who had his head bowed. On that head were two black braids hanging down like tree snakes. His caboose was parked on a red satin pillow, his legs crossed. He wore a robe of deep red with gold dragons patterned on the thing.

"I am Lao Zhin," the man said, still looking down.

"Well, I'm Jimmy Gallagher, Mr. Zhin, and I think there has been a mistake."

"No mistake," Lao Zhin said. He raised his head. His eyes were the color of forbidden jade.

"Say, friend, I got no quarrel with you nor anybody here. You see I—"

"You must fight to the death."

"I keep hearin' that. But that's not in my line. I'm strictly a pug, I fight in the ring, and when a man goes down for a ten count, or the bell dings the last round, that's all she wrote."

"Excuse, all who wrote?"

"She. It's a manner of speaking."

"Ah," said Lao Zhin. "American speech. Always a puzzle. But the prophecy is clear."

"What has that got to do with me? I'm from County Cork by way of Boston. I have a girl named Ruby and a dog named Steve, and speaking of Steve—"

"The prophecy must be fulfilled!" Lao Zhin clapped his hands. The mobs parted and the biggest Chinese fella I'd ever laid eyes on came to the front. He was bigger'n my six foot three by a couple of inches at least. He had his shirt off. It looked like his smooth skin was stretched over a rock quarry.

There was nothing for me to do except put up my dukes.

But this other fella, he didn't do anything like that. He made some kind of motions with his hands. His hands weren't even curled into fists. And as he did, he made some sounds. Moaning sounds. Like a cat in heat. I thought for a second he was having a bout of gas.

But then he let out a full on scream and jumped at me like a lion at a laughing hyena.

Only I wasn't laughing. Not after two fists of fury tattooed my face faster than any one-two I'd ever seen in my life.

This wasn't exactly jiu-jitsu, like they been teaching in L.A. for years. This was not like anything I'd ever seen, in the ring or out.

The fella stood over me, making that cat noise again, twirling his hands around in the air, waiting for me to get up.

"Say there, friend," I said. "What kind of fightin' is that?"

He didn't answer. All around me I saw smiling faces. The crowd wasn't on my side.

But no Gallagher stays down for the count. You have to clock into dreamland in order to stop us.

Up on my feet, I waited until the big galoot was about to pounce and then I screamed for all I was worth.

I think everybody in the place jumped ten feet. My foe blinked and I connected with a right to his jaw.

Oh, it was a sweet punch. I heard something crack. As big as he was, he had a chin like a fortune cookie. Down he went.

"Let's call this a draw," I said to the room. "And no hard feelings. I been in enough scrapes. I got nothing against any of you."

The crowd started to press in. They didn't have friendly written on their faces.

"Now one against one is fair, mates," I said. "But what you're thinkin' of is dirty pool."

That didn't stop some of the chains and pipes coming into full view.

Goodbye, Ruby.

Goodbye, Steve.

I hope you both find love and tenderness in this world without me. Not that I've always been loving, and not that I've always been tender. But I swear on my mother's Bible I've been true to you both, and that's sayin' something after all.

Readying my fists, I scanned the advancing horde, looking for openings. They'd know they were in a scrap before it was over.

I crossed myself, to cover my eternal bases.

One of the thugs raised his pipe in the air and charged me.

I pulled back my right duke.

But before I could throw it—

From out of nowhere came a blur, a flying thing, giving that same screech I'd heard from the big fella. The blur had feet, and the feet made solid purchase on the pipe wielder's head.

Then he came down like a cat landing on a stoop.

A guy with a chain jumped at my rescuer, and in one blink of an eye the attacker was cut down with a blow to the neck.

At which point the crowd started to move back.

"Enough!"

That was Lao Zhin talking. The crowd split apart and he came walking through. He faced my defender and said, "So we meet again."

"What you do is no good," the flying tiger said. His back was to me but I knew that voice.

It was none other than J. Wong!

"You have no say here," Lao Zhin said.

"You are the intruder," J. Wong said. "And now you go, or you die."

I'm telling you, not even a straight right from Rocky Marciano himself could have had the same impact as this sudden appearance. The little laundry man, J. Wong, in fine, fighting form, old as he was. And now talking no nonsense to some guy in a fancy coat.

"This is Los Angeles," J. Wong said. "It is my city . And you will not make it into a bad place. Now go, and never return."

Lao Zhin stuck out his chest. "We will meet again." He waved at his boys and out they tromped, leaving me and Mr. Wong alone.

"I gotta tell you," I said, "you may put starch into shirts, but that's nothing like the starch you just put into these fellas. But..."

"Yes?"

"You're..."

"Old?"

"On the mature side," I said.

"I follow the way of Mozi, and of Kung Fu," J. Wong said.

"I'm afraid I don't know those words, Mr. Wong."

He smiled and his eyes danced a jig. "Mozi preached the way of love. If it is not followed, the strong will attack the weak. To stop that, we must fear ghosts and punishment from heaven."

"That doesn't sound too far off the mother church," I said.

"Lao Zhin is a villain, and he has come here to take over the people of Chinatown. I was appointed to find him."

"Appointed?"

"By the ghosts of my ancestors. You see, Zhin is from a long line of villains. My family is descended from Mozi himself. It has always been our task to find and stop those of the Zhin dynasty."

"Well, you sure showed up at the right time."

"Thank you for showing me the way."

"Huh?"

"Come," he said, and led me out into the daylight.

As we walked along the sunny street, the very one from which I had just been so unceremoniously removed, Mr. Wong expounded a most strange tale.

"A curse upon our house was placed by a sorcerer of the Zhin. They could not kill us, but they clouded our minds. We are not able to find them on our own. We must be shown the way."

"A curse you say?"

He nodded. "But the ghosts of our ancestors protected us in this. One with a true heart, who wears the dragon, will be the guide."

"The dragon?"

He pointed to the necklace, which I was still wearing, which I'd forgotten all about.

"You will forgive me?" J. Wong said. "For sometimes the way is a danger."

"You mean, because I wore this thing, I went through all that rough stuff just to show you where this other fella was?"

"Because you have a true heart, my friend."

"Well faith and Pat O'Brien! Couldn't you have found some other schmo with a true heart?"

"Such hearts are as rare as the teeth of a hen. When you stood up for my protection in my laundry, I knew you were the one."

I rubbed my aching head.

"And now," said J. Wong, "my ancestors will be your friends. Oh, excuse, please."

He reached into his back pocket and pulled out my wallet, handed it over. "And your shirt will be ready in the morning," he said. "No charge."

———

I made it to the pound just as the sun was setting over Los Angeles. Steve was not pleased. They'd put him through some sort of tick bath and he wasn't smelling like his old self. He refused to look me in the eye.

To make it up to him, I took him down to the hamburger stand on Hill Street and bought him a double-decker. I think he forgave me by the time he finished it. There's nothing quite like ground beef between friends to heal all wounds.

And there's no place like Los Angeles when it comes to running into the strange and the crazy. Which is why, I suppose, I fit right in.

FLASH FICTION

What fun it is to write flash! These are stories under 1,000 words (there's even a subset called "micro fiction" which is under 300 words). They don't take as much time as longer stories, and certainly novels, and give a writer a chance to try flights of fancy they might not otherwise embark upon.

They are also perfect for the waiting room in a dentist's office, or that long line at the grocery store, or maybe just before sleep kicks in. When I read in bed I usually get through two pages or so and then nod off. With flash fiction, you'll finish and be set up for sweet dreams!

THE CONFESSION

Bob looked at Ed. Ed looked at Bob. Bob hated the way Ed was looking at him, like he was a criminal or something. Did he know? How could he? But that look!

They were on the beach, waves lapping the sand.

And suddenly Bob knew he couldn't keep it in any longer.

"All right," Bob said. "I'll spill it. I have to. Just listen. Let me get it out. I did it. I killed her. I took a knife and I did it. Was it a fit of rage? I tell myself that, Ed, but I know deep down I'd been planning it for months. After I did it, I wrapped her body in plastic, I tied ropes around her and attached two cinder blocks, put her in the boat and went out beyond Anacapa Island. Right out there, I can point to the spot. And that's where she is now. I set up an alibi, somebody to lie for me, but I can't lie to you, Ed. I never could. So there it is. And hey, you know what? I feel better now. I really do."

Ed stared at him.

"Will you stop looking at me please?" Bob said.

Ed stared.

"Okay," Bob said. "You win."

Bob bent down and picked up a piece of driftwood, and hurled it into the waves.

"Fetch, boy!" Bob said.

THREE WISHES

Jonathan Milbank looked out at the ocean and the setting sun. A perfect L.A. time and place to do the Dutch. He'd just swim out as far as he could and drop to his death. That is, if his buoyancy didn't float him all the way to Catalina.

At thirty, Jonathan Milbank had let his once-athletic body go to pot. Literally. Seventy pounds overweight.

He could see his shadow at high noon.

The underside of his chin looked like a stack of pancakes.

Then his girlfriend left him for a beach volleyball player—a tall, ripped, blond Adonis with whom Jonathan simply could not compete.

And so, as the sun began dropping into the sea that drizzly November evening, Jonathan took a step into the cold Pacific, and then stopped.

Do it now!

Back when he actually had some promise, Jonathan had learned this phrase from a motivational speaker.

Jonathan clenched his fists and took another step.

Something jabbed the bottom of his foot.

As the water ebbed, Jonathan saw it in the burnt-orange twilight—an odd-looking protuberance sticking out of the wet sand. He tried to bend over to grab the thing, but his stomach got in the way. So he got down on one knee and dug it out.

It was shaped like a teapot, only metallic and with all sorts of fancy designs on it.

Whoa! What if it was some sort of antique? His ex loved that kind of junk. Maybe he could give it to her—

He paused as something stirred in his ample gut. Hope! What an odd feeling to come over him then. But it was enough to save him, for he took the teapot back to his one-room apartment and set it on his coffee table.

He got a dishtowel and started rubbing off some of the sand. And then! Smoke billowed from the spout!

Jonathan yelped and dropped the pot on the floor. His shock expanded as the smoke morphed into the figure of a man. It had a beard and a turban and ...and ... hovered in the air!

"You called, Master?" the apparition said in a deep, melodious voice.

Jonathan couldn't speak. He could barely breathe.

"I am the genie of the lamp. Your wish is my command. *Three* wishes, to be exact."

I must be dreaming, Jonathan thought. Or insane. Yeah, that was it. Fruitcake time.

But what did it matter? He'd almost ended his own life an hour before. What did he have to lose by going along with this… whatever it was?

What if it *were* real? Could he—Jonathan Milbank—truly be reborn as a new, perfect self?

Do it now!

Jonathan placed his hand upon his corpulent flesh and rubbed. "Well, Mr. Genie. I would like six-pack abs right here."

The genie nodded. "It shall be so."

"And, um, I want to be thirty forever."

"It shall be done, Master. Do you have a third wish?"

"I... I think I'm going to hang onto that last one," Jonathan Milbank said.

"I am sorry, Master, but did you say you do not desire to make a third wish at this time?"

"That's right. I've seen this movie. I need to keep one in my back pocket. So I'll take the first two, if you please."

The genie lifted his hand, and with a smile, snapped his fingers.

Jonathan waited a moment. He didn't feel a thing.

He lifted his shirt and looked at his stomach. It was the same size. But—

It was horribly discolored! Jonathan raced to the bathroom and looked in the mirror. The reflection showed a fat, dirty-faced man with strange markings on his corpulent abdomen. What? Were they... yes, they were! Tattoos!

A mix of images and script. But this was nuts! Tats of beer bottles in a carrying case, and beer cans bound together, and even reading backwards in the mirror he could make out the words—

Buy Corona!

Budweiser, King of Beers!

"What's going on here?" Jonathan shouted.

But there was no answer. The genie was gone.

Jonathan looked again at his face. Covered with grime.

But how?

He turned on the hot water and grabbed a bar of soap. He lathered up his face and rubbed all over with a wash cloth. He rinsed and looked at his face again.

No!

No change at all. He looked like a man who'd been living in a dumpster in an alley behind a slaughterhouse.

And his arms! They were covered with the same greasy, grimy dirt.

Wailing like a wounded dog, Jonathan rushed back to the lamp. He picked it up and rubbed it like a mad Boy Scout with two sticks.

With a puff of smoke the genie returned.

"Your wish is my command, Master."

"Are you kidding?" Jonathan said. "Look at me!"

"Do you like them?"

"Like what?"

"The six-pack ads right there on your stomach, and you wished to be dirty forever."

"Whoa, wait! I didn't ask for that!"

"No?"

"No!"

"Truly?"

"What is this?"

"I am so sorry, Master. But I am old and a bit hard of hearing."

"Can you hear me now?"

"Oh yes, Master."

"Then undo me! Right now!"

"As you wish," the genie said. He snapped his fingers.

And Jonathan Milbank disappeared from the face of the earth.

The genie returned to the lamp.

MOVING IN

The squatters moved into the mansion just after midnight. The $4.9 million home had been on the market for a year. Tad and his girlfriend Paloma had done their research.

The palace was only one block away from LeBron's new home in the famous Beverly Hills zip code 90210.

Tad Collins was forty and had been kicking around Hollywood getting minor parts in TV shows like Better Call Saul and Brooklyn Nine-Nine. He got a commercial for Domino's Pizza in 2016, but nothing since.

Paloma Villegas, ten years Tad's junior, was a former Miss Riverside who was trying to become the next Taylor Swift. But all she had managed in the last five years was becoming the first Taylor Slow.

All that was about to change.

Pooling their money, the newly ensconced couple bought a disco ball, rave lights, and Andy Warhol prints. They began to have opulent parties, charging $1500 a throw to get in.

Business boomed, five days a week.

The next door neighbor, Franklin P. Adams, had lived in the neighborhood for eighteen years. He went to see his lawyer, Alex Tanner, of the noted L.A. law firm Sheppard Mullin.

"This isn't Florida," said the lawyer. "Squatters are a real pain in California."

"Surely the owner of the place can kick them out," Franklin said.

"Not that simple," Tanner said. "My guess is this couple has a fake lease agreement. They can tie this thing up for a year or more. By the way, who is the owner?"

"His name is Carvello, something like that. I think he's in Europe. Can't we talk to the real estate agent?"

"We can try," Tanner said. "Let me look him up."

The agent's name was Chase Downing of Rodeo Realty. Tanner got him on the phone and put it on speaker.

"I know all about it," Downing said. "This has really ramped up lately, squatters moving into unoccupied luxury homes."

"Evict their butts!" Franklin said.

"This isn't Florida," Downing said.

"I'm tired of hearing that!" Franklin said.

"Mr. Carvello has gone on a walking tour of Tibet," Downing said. "He wanted to get away from computers and phones. I don't know when he'll be back. Even so, it's going to be really hard—"

"I'm tired of hearing that, too!" Franklin said.

"Welcome to the way things are," Downing said.

That night there was another rave party at the house.

Franklin P. Adams, who had started with nothing and rose up through the ranks in the Ferrari company, starting as a salesman, could not sleep.

Instead, he came up with a plan.

In the morning, he drove his Cadillac into South L.A. and cruised around until he found what he was looking for—a park with a basketball court where ten players were going at it. He got out and watched from outside the fence.

When the game ended he went through the gate and said, "Say, fellas, can I have a word?"

The faces that turned to him looked like they'd just spotted an alien stepping out of a space ship.

One of them, a burly guy about 6'8", came up and said, "You may be in the wrong place, m'man."

"No, maybe you are," Franklin said. "How would you like to live in Beverly Hills?"

This got the attention of the rest of the group, who gathered around him.

Franklin explained about the couple that occupied the mansion without consent, were throwing loud parties, and refused to leave.

"All I'm asking is for some of you to move in," Franklin said. "You will have just as much right to be there. I'll pay your moving expenses, and give you a thousand bucks each. All I ask is that you not throw loud parties."

This was met with derisive laughter. Someone told him to get his crazy posterior out of there.

"It's in the same neighborhood as LeBron James," Franklin said.

Five of the guys immediately expressed interest.

Two days later, they arrived at the house. They went around the back and found Tad and Paloma lounging by the pool. Paloma screamed.

The guys went into the house through the French doors.

"Hey," Tad said. "You can't go in there!"

The big guy, whose street name was Brick, said, "Try and evict us."

That very night Tad and Paloma packed up and left.

The five basketball players had a pizza party, paid for by Franklin P. Adams, and catered by Domino's. They watched a Lakers game on the big screen TV.

In his law office the next day, Alex Tanner asked Franklin P. Adams, "How did you get that couple to move out?"

Franklin grinned. "You've got to know how to play the game. And they didn't know squat."

NOT JUST ANOTHER DAY AT SCHOOL

Miss Thompson, the kindergarten teacher, drove a Yugo to work.

At night she drove a broom.

Being a witch was fun, but it didn't pay the bills. So she taught young ones during the day, happily, until one little girl, Emily, who was born with heightened perception of things supernatural, became suspicious.

Emily went to the administrator's office and talked to Mr. Weintraub. "I think Miss Thompson is a witch!"

"Now, now, Emily," Mr. Weintraub said. "We mustn't go around making up such stories."

"But—"

"I assure you, Miss Thompson is not a witch. Go on back to class."

"But I'm afraid!"

With a sigh, Mr. Weintraub summoned the nurse, and it was decided to send Emily home.

After school, Mr. Weintraub went to Miss Thompson's classroom. He found her at her desk, fiddling with something. She looked surprised, and pulled out a shoebox and swept the something into it.

"What have you got there?" Mr. Weintraub said.

"Oh, nothing," said Miss Thompson. "Just a newt. It's for a science project for the kids."

"Ah. Listen, I want you to be aware that little Emily Burt will need some special attention. She came to me very worried. She, and I hesitate to say this, thinks you're a witch."

Miss Thompson chuckled.

Mr. Weintraub decided a joke was in order.

"Perhaps," he said, "I should have Father Donovan come down and sprinkle the room with holy water!"

Instead of laughing, Miss Thompson stood. And before Mr. Weintraub's disbelieving eyes she turned into…an elephant.

With a horrific elephant howl, the beast charged, knocking aside desks.

Pure survival instinct sent Mr. Weintraub through a window. Glass shattered everywhere.

Regaining his feet, he shouted, "God help me!"

The elephant rose off the floor and began to twirl—a pachydermic phantasm, a mammoth monstrosity, a gyrating jumbo. Like a grotesque disco ball, it whirled round and round, somehow fading yet remaining, then became a cloud, a gray mist, which floated down toward a broom in the corner, an old-looking broom with a knotty handle and coarse brown bristles affixed with rope. The handle of the broom seemed to suck the elephant fog into it, like a tea kettle in reverse, until it was gone from Mr. Weintraub's sight.

Then the broom took off and flew.

It flew out the window, barely missing Mr. Weintraub's head.

He heard an elephant roar—or was it a diabolical laugh?—as the broom went up and up…and into the path of a jet making its descent into Van Nuys airport.

Little pieces of broom fell out of the sky like confetti.

It took six months for Mr. Weintraub to recover his senses.

When he finally came back to work, everyone noticed the change in him. And he made it clear that the subject of Miss Thompson's disappearance was off limits. He was not ever going to talk about the elephant in the broom.

THE WINNING TICKET

Mrs. Edna Franklin, 85, was just sitting down at her TV tray, which held the heated leftovers from last night's dinner of corned beef hash, green beans and pimento loaf, when her front door flew open.

A young man with scraggly hair and evil in his eyes slammed the door behind him. He had tools in his hand. Had he picked the lock?

"What is the meaning of this?" Mrs. Edna Franklin said.

"Shut up, lady," Scraggly said, "and you may get to live."

"Young man, you are being terribly rude."

"Just listen and listen good. You're gonna give me all the money and jewelry you got. If you don't..." He made a slashing motion across his throat.

"Stop that," Mrs. Franklin said. "I have a condition!"

"Then do what I tell ya."

"I will not!"

Edna Franklin had spent twenty years as a deputy sheriff in Los Angeles County. In those days she was known as "Fightin' Edna" because she took no guff from even the most hardened criminals. She felt that old fighting instinct rising in her now.

"So we do it the hard way," Scraggly said. He wore a parka, reached into it and pulled out some rope and a bandana.

He moved quickly around the back of the chair and gagged Mrs.

Franklin with the bandana. She struggled but was no match for the sinewy strength of the intruder. In short order he had her tied up.

"I'm gonna have a look around," he said. "What have we here?"

He was looking at the TV tray. "I'm a little hungry," he said. "You don't mind, do you?"

He grabbed a handful of hash—how rude!—and shoved it in his mouth.

As he chewed, he looked at the tray again.

"What's this? A lottery ticket?"

He picked it up. "Sure is. From 7-Eleven. I like their hot dogs...Hey, wouldn't it be funny if this was the one?"

On the TV, a man was smiling in front of a sign—*Powerball.*

"Here we go, America," the man said. "For two-point-four billion dollars!"

"Yeah!" Scraggly said. "Really funny."

The balls began to drop. The TV man called out the first number—31.

"If this is the winning ticket, I'll let you keep a thousand," Scraggly said. "Heck, I'm generous. Maybe ten thou."

He laughed.

The balls continued to drop. Five white balls, with their numbers displayed on the screen.

The TV man said, "All right, now for your winning Powerball number..."

A red ball dropped.

"...it is...25, and that Power Play multiplier is 2."

Scraggly looked at the ticket, then back at the TV.

Ticket...TV...

"No way," he said.

He looked at Mrs. Edna Franklin. "Lady," he said. "You won."

Edna Franklin tried to yell, but the gag choked off the sound.

"All my life I been waitin' for a break," Scraggly said. "All my life, the only luck I ever had was bad luck. Now this! This is my ticket to paradise!"

His ecstatic expression and toothy smile suddenly changed to a frown and tight lips.

"We gotta think this through," he said. "You gotta be the one who takes in this ticket. You gotta be the one who gets the money in the bank."

Scraggly walked in a little circle in front of Mrs. Franklin.

"You got relatives?" Scraggly asked.

Mrs. Franklin looked at the picture on top of the TV. Scraggly followed her gaze and picked up the framed photo.

"Looks like you and another nice old lady," Scraggly said. "That wouldn't be your sister, would it?"

Mrs. Franklin's dear sister, Ruth, had eight grandchildren.

"Here's what we're gonna do," Scraggly said. "I'm gonna be your beloved son, see? We're goin' to 7-Eleven and ask 'em what to do. If you try to say anything, I'm gonna do you. With a knife. Then I'm gonna go find your sister. You understanding me, Mom?"

Mrs. Franklin nodded.

He kept her tied up until they got to the 7-Eleven.

"Just remember what I told you," he said. He untied her and removed the gag. He got out of the car and went around to the passenger side. He pulled Mrs. Franklin out and kept hold of her arm as they walked inside.

A strapping young man at the counter in a 7-Eleven shirt said, "Can I help you?"

"My mom," Scraggly said, "you'll never guess. She has the winning Powerball ticket!"

He reached in his pocket and put the ticket on the counter.

Edna Franklin grabbed it and put it in her mouth.

And started chewing.

"No!" Scraggly grabbed Edna Franklin's throat and started shaking her.

The young man jumped over the counter and plowed his fist into Scraggly's face. Down went Scraggly.

A big football player-type rushed over and put a knee on Scraggly's back. "I'll keep him down," he said. "Call the cops."

The 7-Eleven man turned to Edna Franklin. "Are you all right?" he said.

Mrs. Franklin pulled the wadded ticket from her cheek.

"I told him I had a condition," she said.

"Condition?"

"Yes," she said. "Dry mouth."

She began smoothing the ticket on the counter.

UNFINISHED MASTERPIECE

Jake and Emma sat across from each other at Starbucks. Laptops open.

Jake said, "How is it?"

"What?" Emma said.

"Your Pumpkin Spice Latte."

"It's fine, fine."

"What are you so intent on?"

"Jake, do you mind?"

"Sorry."

Emma frowned at her laptop, tapping keys.

Jake went back to his laptop. He was searching eBay for vintage vinyl records, his passion. His dad had loved Elton John—the *Goodbye Yellow Brick Road*-era Elton. His mom dug Aerosmith.

Jake saw a vintage *Born in the U.S.A.* album and skipped it. His dad had hated Springsteen. "Overrated and screechy," he'd told Jake once. "And my roommate in college kept playing him over and over again, till the rest of us told him to cut it out or we'd throw his stereo out the window."

There was a Jim Croce album available. His dad had been to a Jim Croce concert in high school. Actually, it was a Woody Allen standup act at the Valley Music Theater, with Jim Croce as the warm up. His dad had three Croce albums and Jake remembered him singing "You Don't Mess Around With Jim" while working on his car.

He missed his parents.

"Emma, you have a sec?"

"Hold on."

Jake found a Joni Mitchell album. His mom had loved "Big Yellow Taxi." He placed a bid. In his head he heard the lyrics. *Don't it always seem to go that you don't know what you've got 'til it's gone...*

"How much longer do I have to wait?" Jake said.

Emma dropped her hands into her lap and leaned back. "What, what?"

"Sorry to interrupt you."

"Well, you have. What is it?"

"Can we just talk for a second?"

"I'm trying to apply for a showing," Emma said. "You know, at the gallery on Greenleaf?"

"Can it wait?"

"What's so important?"

"Have you thought any more about it?" Jake said.

"What?" Emma said.

"What we've been talking about."

Emma looked at the ceiling. "*You've* been talking about it."

"So what?"

"Why do you want this so much?"

"Do I have to explain it? Maybe it's something that's just there, natural, the way things should be, you know?"

"Honey." Emma put her hand on his, squeezed it. Jake did not squeeze back.

"Let's think it through," Emma said.

"That's what I'm saying," Jake said.

"The next ten years, that's when things will happen. You can concentrate on your music, I can paint. That's intensive. We can't be interrupted every seven seconds. And whenever we want, we can go somewhere. Just say, 'Let's go,' and we go. Italy, remember? Florence? Even if we just want to go to a movie, we can go. We don't have to worry about finding a sitter, or anything."

Jake shook his head.

"What's wrong?" Emma said.

"Nothing," Jake said. He pulled his hand back.

"Don't be that way," Emma said.

"Go back to your gallery," Jake said.

"Come on," Emma said. "We're an unfinished masterpiece, beautiful in our imperfections."

Jake closed his laptop. "I'm going outside for a minute."

"Jake, come on."

He stood. His chair scraped on the floor. He walked past the pickup counter. Before he pushed the door open he looked at Emma.

She was looking at her screen and tapping keys.

WHAT GOES AROUND

"Good," Dr. Whitworth said. "I think we're making progress. You're being vulnerable. You are beginning to recognize how wrong you've been."

"Yeah, yeah," Jenks said.

"That's crucial. You've been given a second chance at life. A lot of people never get that."

Jenks knew that to be true. He'd been granted parole after ratting out Sergei Popov for the Feds. If you could call that a second chance. Jenks would be looking over his shoulder the rest of his life, even in witness protection.

"Repentance is part of recovery," Dr. Whitworth said.

"Repentance?" Jenks said. "You mean like feelin' sorry for what I done?"

"Exactly that."

"Well yeah, for sure," Jenks said. "I mean, you don't off...wait, lemme make sure. Everything I say to you is confidential, yeah?"

"Yes, Tom."

"Meaning you can't rat me out?"

"Right you are. With one exception."

Jenks sat up straighter. "What's that?"

"If you tell me you intend to commit a crime."

"I ain't gonna do that."

"Or," Dr. Whitworth said, "if I feel there is a strong reason to believe you might."

"You think that?"

"Not at all. Just being clear on the law. Will you trust me?"

"I guess I got to," Jenks said.

"You were about to tell me something. Go right ahead."

Jenks took a deep breath. "I was gonna say, ten guys. Ten that I offed. Also..."

"Yes?"

"My ex wife," Jenks said.

The doctor said nothing.

Jenks said, "Well, not ex then, ex when I did it. She took our kid and left me and ratted me out to the cops. I did a year on a weapons count. I burned up inside every day in the slam. You don't do Tom Jenks dirty and get away with it. So when I got out, I found her in Tennessee and did what I do. Or what I did, 'cause I don't do it no more."

After a long pause, Dr. Whitworth said, "Don't you find it hard to live with that?"

"Yeah, I do," Jenks lied.

Dr. Whitworth leaned back in his chair. "Let me tell you something I rarely share with clients. But I will now, because this is our last mandated session. I'll probably never see you again, once you begin your new life. Ready?"

"Shoot," Jenks said, then wished he'd thought of another word.

"I believe in something called karma. Do you know what that is?"

"I've heard of it," Jenks said.

"It's from the eastern religions. It's about consequences being visited upon us based on our actions. Another way to say it is, what goes around comes around."

"That I've heard of."

"You've lived a life of crime, of murder. So one might expect something quite the same to come around at you. But there's a way out."

"Talk to me," Jenks said.

"If you truly repent before God, there's a chance that the slate will be made clean. I'm not supposed to say that. The state does not like these sessions to be religious in any way. But my faith compels me to help clients in any way I see fit. So I say, if you really and truly feel sorry, and determine to lead a righteous life from here on out, you can break the cycle."

"You're talkin' about the Big Guy in the Sky?"

"If that helps you," Dr. Whitworth said.

"Well, Doc, it does. And you been a real help to me. I'm a new man."

"That's wonderful to hear, Tom. I wish you all the best in your new life, wherever you land."

———

Tom Jenks landed in Phoenix—otherwise known as Hell's Oven. He was now known as Ralph Carter, a construction worker from Cleveland. But every time he went out he felt like he had a sign on his back that said, *Former hit man from New Jersey*.

Then he'd think of Dr. Whitworth, and that goes-around-comes-around idea. That's when things would rattle him.

Little noises in the night.

Too many people around in the day.

Cars slowing as he walked down the street.

He began to imagine another hit man out there, holding the contract on his life, closing in. Sergei Popov pulling strings, even from the bowels of a federal pen.

He thought about that other thing Dr. Whitworth said, repentance. Being sorry for what you did. But he wasn't sorry. Not even for his ex. *You don't do Tom Jenks dirty...*

To handle his nerves he hit the bottle more and more.

Twenty-one weeks after the start of his new life, Tom "Ralph Carter" Jenks sat in his wingback chair watching ESPN, drinking his third bourbon on the rocks.

Behind him he heard the unmistakable sound of a semi-automatic pistol being cocked.

He raised his hands. "We can work something out," he said. "I got connections. You don't have to do this. Maybe a partnership. I got skills. I can pass 'em along. Let's talk, huh? I'm gonna keep my hands up. I'm gettin' up now. Let's talk."

He stood. No shot fired. A good sign. At least he'd bought a little time. He turned slowly to face the intruder.

And could hardly believe it. The gun pointed at him was in the hand of a beautiful young woman.

"Hello, Daddy," she said.

CHARACTER FLAW

Frankie Fultz couldn't help it. He'd go to a party, have a little too much to drink, and start making a fool of himself.

At one party he tried to channel Freddy Mercury. At this he was not a champion.

At another party he got into an argument with a guy over whether Cary Grant or Humphrey Bogart was the bigger movie star. The other guy almost punched Frankie into the big sleep.

Tonight, though, was a delicate situation. The office Christmas party at Frankie's new job. He wanted to make an impression.

His best friend, Charles, tried to tell him it wasn't safe to go to another party. Not yet. Not until he got some help.

"I can handle it," Frankie said.

What he handled at the party was four gin-and-tonics. Then he set his sights on a fetching lass across the room.

He sidled over to her (Frankie was a good sidler), leaned in and whispered, "I'm here. What were your other two wishes?"

Unfortunately, the woman was the boss's wife, and the boss was standing next to her.

The boss said, "You're fired."

Frankie broke down the next day when he told Charles what happened.

"I tried to tell you," Charles said.

"Tell me what?" Frankie said.

"Better safe than soiree."

LOSING IT

I'm having trouble breathing. Wait! You're all looking at me. My mouth doesn't work. This is what you wanted all along, isn't it? This is what you do to people who don't obey you, who think for themselves, isn't it? Isn't it?

Dr. Chumley typed a few notes on his tablet. His fingers trembled with excitement. For the first time, a person's thoughts were being translated in real-time into audio. The technology, provided by OraMental Systems and utilizing brain probes and AI language settings, was being used by the Department of Compliance on a trial basis.

And it was working! The AI brain-wave to voice coming over the speaker was crisp and clear.

Do with me what you want, you cowards, you stains, you freaks! You cannot and will not conquer my will!

Fascinating! Chumley typed more notes. The new American Politburo was going to be pleased.

Sleep. I'm going to sleep. Good night, but know this. You can't win...you can't...you...

The voice trailed off.

"Do you have everything you need?" Ron's voice came from the control room.

"That was fine, just fine," Chumley said. "Let's do another one."

"Right after the cleanup."

Chumley smiled. He had been right all along. The brain does communicate for a time after the guillotine blade falls.

CHUCKLES THE MAGNIFICENT

He was a retired circus clown, working as a greeter at Walmart. Every day he saw some faces that were sour, some that ignored him—like that teenaged couple laughing as they looked at the girl's phone, walking right by without even a glance.

But the older folks always smiled. He liked that, did Chuckles the Magnificent. His real name was Carl Stapleton, but he always thought of himself as Chuckles. That was his handle under the Big Top, which no longer existed. In the old routine was a superhero, coming in at the last second to save the other clowns who were about to be eaten by a lion (it was actually Max Munro in a lion suit, good old Max!). Chuckles would shout "Haha!" and tackle the lion and they'd roll around in the sawdust as the other clowns jumped in a small car and drove away. A lion-tamer clown would then run out with a whip and put the lion in a cage, while the "dead" Chuckles lay motionless. Then wires would lift Chuckles into the air. He'd push a button on his belt and wings would pop out on his back. Then another clown would toss him a harp and up Chuckles would go, strumming. The crowd would go wild with cheers. How he missed that sound, how he wished that he—

"Welcome to Walmart," Chuckles (whose real name was Carl Stapleton) said to the nervous-looking man coming through the door. The man didn't make eye contact. He was about thirty, tall and thin, with a wool cap on his head. It was much too hot outside for a wool cap.

Probably a drug addict, poor guy, Chuckles thought (Carl always thought of himself as Chuckles, because being Chuckles was the high point of his life).

Then he saw the gun. It was a big one. Chuckles didn't know about guns, but he did know this one was heavy-duty, one of those automatic jobs that could do a lot of killing in a hurry.

"Nobody move!" the gunman shouted. "First person that moves I shoot!"

Over by the Christmas wrapping, a woman screamed.

The man fired a shot at the ceiling. The boom was incredible. Chuckles thought it sounded like the boom made when the clown (whose real name was Bill Laidley, good old Bill!) was fired out of a cannon into a net.

"Somebody's gonna die today!" The gunman turned his head toward a woman by a candy display.

I always wanted to die laughing, Chuckles thought, as he threw himself on the gunman and shouted, "Haha!"

THE WEASEL

He was known as The Weasel, which bothered him no end. But that was not his call. He'd stolen jewels from Monaco to Macao. They could call him whatever they liked. He had the loot. He knew how to flee the scene —by boat or plane—before the authorities were onto him.

So he mocked them. He had gloves made with an embroidered W on the back—his calling card.

Which he left behind at his biggest score ever—the fabulous Alexandra Korsicov jewels.

But then something happened he didn't see coming. Love at first sight!

She was a goddess, drenched in gems as she entered the casino. Those stones had to be his!

But he felt his plans changing in ways that amazed him.

It took two nights for him to introduce himself.

It took two weeks for them to become lovers.

And two months before he discovered her treachery. She worked for Interpol!

"I do confess it, my darling," she said to him. "My job was to entice you, lure you, get you to fall for me, and find the Alexandra Korsicov jewels. But something I did not expect to happen, happened indeed. You stole jewels, yes, but you also stole my heart."

"My love!" he said. "You have given me the greatest gift of all, a reason to go on living! We can be together now."

"Alas, no, my sweet thing. If I disappear with you, we will both become the hunted."

"Wait, wait…" He went deep into thought. "I have it. You bring the Alexandra Korsicov jewels in. I will disappear. I will go to Barcelona and rent a humble casa. In six months' time, you quit your job and join me."

"You no longer want to be a jewel thief?"

"I no longer care about baubles, bangles, and beads. We'll start life anew. I'll become law abiding. We may be poor at first, but with our love we will find a way."

"Let it not be six months," she said. "Let it be only one!"

"Make it three," he said.

"Done!"

"Then goodbye, my one true love," he said.

"For three months only!" she said.

————

Three months later, on the beach at Cabo San Lucas, she turned to her Latin lover, Belagio, and said, "Order me another Piña Colada, will you, sweet one? Oh, and get me my sunglasses from the room, yes?"

"Anything for you, baby," Belagio said. "But tell me the story again, how you posed as Interpol and got your hands on the Korsicov jewels. It never gets old."

She did. Belagio laughed. And went to do as he was told.

She closed her eyes. The sun was warm. She drifted off to sleep.

Belagio's voice startled her. "The jewels! They're gone!"

"What!" she said.

"Taken! I found this glove, with a W on it."

"It's him!" she said. "He found us, and now he mocks us!" She stood. "I'll hunt him down, if it's the last thing I ever do!"

"No need," Belagio said. "We have each other."

"Not enough, my little boy. I must get those jewels. Now he's got a head start. Farewell!"

"Please don't go!"

But in twenty minutes she was packed and off to the airport.

Belagio sipped a Margarita at the bar. And felt a hand on his shoulder.

"She bought it?" The Weasel said.

"Hook, line, and stinker," Belagio said. "With me as the stinker. And the jewels are safe in a box under a floorboard."

The Weasel sat. "Good going, cuz. We need to do what we dreamed about as kids, and team up. Bartender! I'll have the same."

SEND IN THE CLOWN

They closed down Boffo's Famous Brooklyn Clown School on a cloudy Thursday, under a big top tent. The last graduating class, alas, had no place to go. The circus was no longer coming to town, anywhere in America. The do-gooders had managed to bury The Greatest Show on Earth *under* the earth.

But still, there was Boffo himself, age 75, delivering the commencement address to the last twelve clowns he would ever train.

"And so, fellow funny folk, go forth into the world with your skills and make people laugh. It doesn't take a tent or a line of elephants to bring a smile to faces. All it takes is a desire to spread cheer among your fellowman. Long live the clowns!"

Up went a cheer from the dozen devotees of mirth, and red wigs and rubber noses were cast into the air.

Goodbyes were uttered, hugs all around, and off the graduates went to their various lives.

Saddest among them was Marvin Klack, whose chosen clown ID was Happy the Hapless, the clumsy clown. He wore big floppy shoes and an oversized coat with a giant boutonnière. His mouth was a painted smile, but his antics included tripping, falling, rolling, and backing into pitchforks, all while honking a horn on his belt.

Now what?

Surely not the death spiral all clowns fear—the birthday party circuit.

What about street performing? There had to be a place for a clown in New York City. Times Square maybe. Or the subway.

Yes, a subway station. People needed entertainment down there, in what was now known as the pit of hell. Riders were being attacked, pushed into trains, and knifed. The city leaders had responded with reduced police presence, but hired several social workers to talk sense into criminals. A social worker had recently been killed by a drug addict. The mayor had ordered more training for the social workers.

Yes, the people down in the subway needed cheering up. Especially the kids!

And so down to the depths went Happy the Hapless Clown.

He chose the Times Square labyrinth because it got the most traffic. With a little boom box playing circus music, Happy mimed various misadventures with rogue elephants and loose lions. He did handstands and wagged his floppy shoes in the air. He did cartwheels into the dirty tile walls, followed by a pratfall. Some kids laughed at that, and Marvin Klack was happy. The coins and bills people tossed in a bucket were frosting on his abundant cake.

Then, on a Sunday morning, just as he was preparing to perform, he heard a scream.

An elderly woman was struggling in the grip of a man in a hoodie. The man was shaking the woman hard at the same time trying to pull a purse off her shoulder.

"Help me!" the woman cried.

People kept walking past. A few took out phones and started videoing. No one tried to stop Hoodie.

Who was dragging the woman perilously close to the tracks!

Without a second thought, Happy and his big floppy shoes bounded toward the assailant. Within five feet, Happy honked his horn. The noise startled the attacker, as did Happy's cartwheel, in the midst of which he kicked Hoodie in the face. The criminal stumbled backwards and fell onto the tracks.

In clown college, they taught Marvin Klack and everyone else that in a clown world, timing was everything. And it proved to be so in the Times Square subway station, as a train rumbled in just as Hoodie hit the ground.

The viral videos and local news made Happy a hero. The headline in the *Post* was:

Midtown Clown Takedown!

But the New York District Attorney did not find anything funny about it. He charged Marvin Klack with first-degree manslaughter.

Will Crime-Stopping Mime Do Time?

On the first day of trial, Marvin Klack entered the courtroom in his Happy the Hapless costume and makeup and announced that he was representing himself.

The judge was not amused. "Are you trying to make a circus out of this trial?" he snapped.

"Three rings of it!" Marvin/Happy said.

Trial is a Tester for Court Jester!

In his opening statement, Marvin/Happy demonstrated his skills, including the squirting flower, inadvertently spraying the bailiff. The judge hit him with contempt.

Joker Soaker Brings Judge Grudge!

Despite an impassioned closing argument, the New York jury found Marvin Klack guilty.

Imperfect Verdict!

The judge sentenced Marvin to a year in jail, saying, "I hope this will teach other so-called Good Samaritans to keep their noses out of other peoples' business." The lesson was learned by both Good Samaritans and criminals alike.

Crime Scourge Surge!

But Marvin Klack kept his cell mate laughing. When he was released, Marvin started his own children's show on YouTube, and now makes seven figures a year.

THE MORTICIAN

Jon, the bartender at The Living End, watched as the old man shuffled in and sat at the far end. He went over to him.

"What can I get you?" Jon said.

"Fill a highball glass with vodka, no ice," the old man said.

"For real?"

"Do I sound like I'm joking?"

"Whatever you say."

Jon poured the man his drink and set it in front of him. The old man looked at it sadly.

"Like the bartender said to the horse," Jon said. "Why the long face?"

"You don't want to hear it." The old man lifted the glass and took a drink.

"People unload on me all the time," Jon said. "Part of the job. Sometimes it helps to talk."

"You think so?"

"Sure."

A smirk came to the man's face. "I'm warning you, you hear about it and you'll need a whole bottle of this stuff."

Over the years Jon had heard many a tale of woe—about divorces, wayward children, cheating girlfriends, and countless variations on the theme that life was unfair.

But never had he been so curious to hear what a customer had to say.

"Go on," Jon said.

The old man took another drink. "You asked for it. You are looking at a failure where once there was a smashing success. I was the best mortician in all of New Jersey. I handled everything from school teachers to mafia hit men who got a taste of their own medicine. I made them all look good. One man, Tony 'The Rat' Donatello, had twenty-seven bullet holes in him, including nine to the face. I made him look like he'd just been to a spa in Cabo. I have magnificent skills! But it's all been for naught. My business is down the toilet. The toilet, do you hear me?"

"But why?" Jon said.

The old man drank again. The glass was now only half full. "One sunny day I was driving my new Cadillac in Essex County. You know what they have in Essex County? Haitians. The fourth largest Haitian population in the United States. I was trying to find soft music on the radio when I ran a stop sign. I almost hit a man crossing the street. He waved his arms at me, arms swaying wildly. It sent a chill up my back. I drove on, thinking that nothing would come of this. How wrong I was!"

He paused and drained his glass. "Want me to go on?" he said.

Jon was riveted. "Please."

"Then freshen me."

Jon poured more vodka in the glass.

The old man quaffed heartily, then said, "A week went by. I was in my shop, preparing the body of 45-year-old dental hygienist, when the FedEx delivery man handed me a box. Upon opening it I found a large plastic bag. Sealed inside the bag was a grotesque mess of what looked like spaghetti in marinara sauce, with flat brown meatballs. But I knew at once, from my training, these were the guts of some animal. Disgusted and angry that someone would do this to me, I summoned the police. The police in turn called in a medical expert who reported to me that what I had received was a bag of chicken entrails."

"Whoa," Jon said. "What the—"

"I'll tell you what the. It's a voodoo curse. A curse, I tell you! And do you know what kind of curse? The worst kind that can happen to a mortician such as I. Do you know about the walking dead?"

"You mean like on that show?" Jon said.

"Forget that hokum!" the old man said. "What I'm telling you is real life. Horrible, but real! Any body that came to me for preparation did not stay dead! That will drive a mortician out of business, let me tell you. And the complaints! A red-faced man screamed at me, 'I thought I was through with my mother-in-law! Now she's back, and just sits and stares at me!' There are other outcomes just as horrifying. A local used-car dealer who died of emphysema is now a United States congressman! I have almost gone insane—do you hear me?"

No, *actually* insane, Jon thought. He reached for the man's glass. "Maybe you've had enough."

The old man pulled the glass to his chest. "I'll tell you when I've had enough!"

Suddenly, his eyes rolled. He fell backward onto the floor.

The glass of vodka shattered next to him.

Jon, trained in CPR, called 911 and commenced with mouth-to-mouth resuscitation and chest compression. To no avail.

When the paramedics arrived they examined the body.

"I'm afraid he's dead," one of them said.

"You'd better make sure," said Jon.

"What's that supposed to mean?"

"I have a reason," Jon said.

The paramedic rechecked the body. "Gone," he said. "I'm sorry."

The medics put the old man's body on a gurney and wheeled him outside.

A moment later Jon heard somebody scream.

He poured himself a big glass of vodka.

THE BIG PARTY

Angelo "The Bull" Rantoni ran into Luca "The Lip" Franciosa at Dock Number 7.

"Where were you last night?" Angelo said.

"Had a hit on the upper west side," Luca said. "Accountant."

"Too bad. I was at the club. We threw a big party in the basement."

"Sorry I missed it," Luca said. "Who was there?"

"Most of the guys. Benny the Nose, Rocco the Blade, Sal the Hammer."

"How about Two-Ton Tony?" Luca asked.

"Funny you should mention," Angelo said. "He was there all right. Special invitation. See, we caught him talking to a fed."

"And you still made nice with him?"

"Nah," Angelo said. "He's the big party we threw in the basement."

WHAT REALLY HAPPENED THAT NIGHT

Maisie didn't recognize the woman who came into her shop. Only that she had striking green eyes, and seemed troubled.

Trouble was right up Maisie's alley. For since opening up her manicure shop she got used to hearing tales of woe from the increasing number of ladies who came in. She could talk and she could listen, the *sine qua non* of a quality beautician.

The woman asked for a manicure in a nervous sort of way. It was late, well past dark, but Maise sometimes stayed open, finding that "emergency treatments" were not a rarity in this neck of the woods.

Maisie put the woman in a chair immediately and began clipping the nails of her left hand.

"You know," Maisie said, "in my business you meet the most interesting people. Don't you find people interesting?"

The woman did not say anything.

"Trouble at home?" Maisie ventured.

The woman perked up. "Why do you ask?"

"I have a way about me," Maisie said. "I pick up on things."

The woman sighed. "I wouldn't want to burden you."

"Please, honey, burden away. I'm a good listener."

"My husband has left me," the woman said. "Tonight. He walked out.

Just like that. I begged him to stay! I asked him, what's going to become of me? And you know what he said?"

"Tell me, sweetie."

"He said, and I quote, Frankly, my dear, I don't give a damn."

"The louse! Good riddance to bad rubbish, I say."

"But I love him!" the woman said. "I know that now. Oh, if only I could get him back."

Maisie began filing the woman's nails. "You want him back? Well let me give you a little advice. Don't think about that now. You can think about it tomorrow. After all, honey, tomorrow is another day."

"That's very good advice," the woman said.

"That's why I'm here," Maisie said. "Would you like a praline?"

THE TATTLETALE

Tommy was a tattletale. He tattled on everybody, from Aaron to Zelda. He did so because his father was a United States senator.

When he was five, Tommy saw his father on television. He was running for the Senate then, and he told the woman who was interviewing him that his opponent had done something terrible years ago. Tommy picked that up from the serious way his father looked when he said the strange words.

The words sounded like *snuggly in the grass*. Tommy wondered what that meant.

He went to his mother. "Mommy, Daddy said something about the man who is against him. I don't know what it means, snuggly in the grass."

"Snuggly in the grass?" his mother said.

Tommy nodded. Then saw a smile break out on his mother's face.

"That is so cute," she said. She rubbed his head. "Daddy actually said *sexually harass*."

"What's that?"

"Just know that it is something bad," his mother said.

"But isn't that telling on somebody?" Tommy asked.

"No, son, not if it helps us win. You see, the only thing that counts in this life is winning. Your daddy taught me that, and now you know it, too."

From that day on, Tommy became a tattletale.

All through school, he told on his classmates. Sometimes in secret. He learned how to leave notes for the teachers. In Middle School he told on James Hardwick, who hid drugs in his locker. That got James kicked out of school and into Juvenile Hall. He told on eleven other students, and three more of them got expelled.

In college, he got more sophisticated in his telling. He left notes for the campus police.

After college, he went to work for a congressman in Washington D.C., through his father's connections. He told on the people who had seniority and moved up. Eventually he told on the congressman himself, who was snuggly in the grass with a lot of women.

And then Tommy ran for Congress himself. His opponent had nothing to tell on. He was a church-going military vet with a nice family. So Tommy paid a woman a sum of money to say that his opponent was snuggly in the grass with her. Naturally, his opponent denied everything, but the damage was done, and Tommy won by a narrow margin.

He served twenty years in Congress, then moved to the Senate, where he served another twelve years.

When he turned 60, inoperable cancer took over his body. His family moved him to hospice.

One night he had a visitor. A man standing in the shadows of his room.

"So this is the end," the man said.

"Who...are you?" Tommy said.

"Are you afraid of death?"

"How...did you...get in here?"

"You are going to meet your maker tonight," the man said. "And I've come to let you know something." He leaned over Tommy and whispered, "I'm going to be telling on you."

That's when Tommy saw—it couldn't be!—two protrusions growing out of the man's forehead.

A SHORT HISTORY OF MASKS

JSB: This and the following five stories were written during that dystopian season known as "the lockdowns."

The history of mask wearing can be traced back to ancient Greece, where the theatrical jocularities of Dionysian worship were communicated to the back row of the Greek amphitheatre—from which we also derive our modern concept of "the cheap seats." When an actor wished to show happiness, he would wear a mask with a large smile on its face. When showing unhappiness, the mask had a frown. When the actor didn't know what emotion he was to convey, he wore no mask at all so the audience would have a clear shot at his actual face with tomatoes and fruit.

———

In Tibet at roughly the same time—that is, around 2:30 in the afternoon, Eastern Standard—sacred dramas depicting various births of the Buddha were all the rage. One such rage broke out into an actual riot, demolishing several villages. From this we can also trace the modern sport of ice hockey.

From these beginnings it was but a small leap of 3,215 years to the next iteration of mask wearing. (The use of cowboy bandanas to cover the nose and mouth of outlaws when they robbed banks or trains is not generally accepted by scholars as a form of mask evolution, being a rather unimaginative use of a large hankie.) I refer, of course, to the catcher's mask.

During a baseball game in Schenectady, New York in 1877, between the Schenectady Bean Shooters and the Long Island Iced Teas, the Bean Shooter catcher, Moe "Broken Nose" Headley was heard to scream OWWW! when a foul tip off the bat of Iced Tea right fielder Hack "The Hackster, Or, If You Prefer, Just Hack" Weisenhaus slammed into Headley's forehead, leaving a golf-ball sized welt. Ironically, it was in the same spot where Headley had been struck by an actual golf ball a week earlier while playing nine holes in nearby Mt. Pleasant, which Headley immediately renamed Hell on a Stick.

Once Headley was revived, he told those around him that he'd had a vision. It was of a glorious angel descending from Heaven and holding something in his hand. The thing turned out to be a five-dollar bill. And the angel said unto Headley, "Lo, take this fin and go to Al's Hardware and Feed Store and tell him Gabe sent you, and that he is to fashion a wire mesh face covering for you to use when catching balls behind the plate, or even a full set of china."

Headley then asked if anyone could lend him five bucks. The players pitched in and Headley ended up with $5.22, which he took to Al's Hardware and Feed Store, making the deal for a catcher's mask, and using the additional 22¢ to buy four peppermint sticks and a package of Diver Dan's Kelp Flavored Chewing Gum.

The game of baseball has never been the same since, except that many a player also yelled OWWW! before the invention of the protective cup.

———

It wasn't long before the mask became an essential part of the criminal enterprise. Thus, in 1918, in Ames, Iowa, the first eye mask to obscure identity was worn by Byron "Mugsy" Malone, 23, when holding up a fruit stand. The attempted robbery went awry when a bag boy said, "Hiya,

Mugsy," taking Malone's bushy shock of red hair as a clue to his identity. The police were thus able to apprehend Malone and book his eye mask into evidence, causing one police officer to remark, "I wonder if this thing could be worn by a good guy, a cowboy maybe, riding a white horse and shooting silver bullets?"

———

The most recent development in the history of masks involved a mouth-and-nose covering known as "The thing you must wear in a grocery store in order to avoid being screamed at by a twenty-five-year-old Folklore and Mythology major." Said mask must be worn even when driving alone in a car, as "the science" tells us that dashboards are easily infected with viruses that can wreak havoc on their odometers.

But what of the future of masks? According to Dr. Ernst Egglehoffer of the Oceanographic Institute of Perth Amboy, NJ, a certain population of jellyfish off the coast of Guam has been spotted wearing masks, presumably to prevent the spread of toxic algae and/or kelp-flavored chewing gum.

"Which means," says Dr. Egglehoffer, "we'll all be living in the ocean quite soon."

THE MIDNIGHT BANDIT

The mask mandates were the best thing that ever happened to an armed robber like me.

I could waltz into any liquor store wearing a mask and nobody batted an eye. Before the mandates, walking in looking like Jesse James would've had everybody on edge. Maybe the guy behind the counter would reach for a gun. It could get ugly.

But when everybody was wearing them, it was easy-peasy to step up to the counter, wait for the right moment, pull my piece and demand the money.

An added bonus was that the security cameras didn't do diddly. I wore my hat low, just above my eyes.

After six straight scores, they dubbed me the Midnight Bandit, even though I usually hit between 10 and 11.

And the nice thing was, I never had to fire my gun.

But then they lifted the mandate! People started breathing freely again. I thought that would be it for my modus operandi. But then I noticed something. A lot of people kept wearing the mask, even when they were outside, alone, in the sunshine!

Now why would they do that?

Because they'd been conditioned to be scared.

Perfect!

A few weeks ago I went into a liquor store and the fella says, "You don't have to wear a mask in here."

And I said, "I guess I'm still a little scared."

"I understand. Can I help you with something?"

That's when I pulled my gun. "Yeah. Your cash."

The next night it was a liquor store twenty miles south.

And here's where it gets interesting.

The man behind the counter told me I didn't need the mask on.

"I'm still a little scared," I said.

"Okay," he said.

I was about to reach for my piece when the door flew open and a guy in a hat and mask charged in, pointing a 9mm at us. "Get your hands up!"

We put 'em up.

"You," he said to the counter man, "open the cash register with your left hand. Keep your other hand up!"

He turned to me, "And you, reach for your wallet with your left hand, and put it on the counter."

Being left handed, that wasn't going to be a problem.

Of course, my wallet is not what I reached for.

A second later I blasted the robber with two slugs.

There was a long moment when the counter man didn't seem to know what to do. I pocketed my gun and went to the body on the floor. There was blood seeping out of his chest.

"Dead," I said.

The counter man smiled. "Do you know what you've done?"

"Yeah, I just killed a guy."

"Not just a guy. You killed the Midnight Bandit!"

"The who?" I said.

"Haven't you heard? He is a very bad man. They call him the Midnight Bandit."

The copycat Midnight Bandit, you mean.

I nodded.

"You had a gun," he said.

"Yeah."

"Why?"

"The truth? I told you I'm scared. So many bad people out there, crime on the rise. I just wanted to protect myself."

That's exactly what I said to the news cameras later that night. And to the cops, who said they'd have to ding me with a misdemeanor for carrying a gun without a permit.

It's what I said to the deputy D.A., who decided not to prosecute.

I also said it to the Hollywood producer who gave me half a million for the rights to my story.

Is this a great country or what?

THANKS FOR LISTENING

The bars were open again, at last.

Yes, you had to wear a mask going in, and were supposed to keep them on unless you were drinking. And yes, they had to keep it down to 50% capacity. But they were open! And Joe Munro couldn't have been happier.

Before the lockdowns, he'd frequented Languid Lounge in Studio City almost every weeknight after work. As an accountant at Universal, he'd knock off at five and head for Languid, which was within walking distance, across Ventura Boulevard next to Miceli's Italian Restaurant.

Then L.A. went into its shutdown thing, and Joe was doing all his work in his apartment. It was driving him crazy. You're thirty, you like to socialize, you wish you had a girlfriend, you could use some joking around with the regulars, but you have to look at your own four walls most of the time. You had to buy your liquor from the store and pour your own while binge watching *Breaking Bad* again.

It got old, fast.

Now the bar was open again, and when Joe walked in he felt right at home in the dim, sepia lighting that was a trademark of the Languid—a speakeasy kind of vibe.

And speaking of home, there was Walker the bartender back at his regular station.

"Walker!"

"Joe!"

Joe took a seat at the bar and slipped off his mask.

"Wait till I serve you, Joe," Walker said through his own mask, though not in an unfriendly way.

"Ah yes," Joe said, and put the mask back on. "I'll have the usual. You remember?"

"Don't think I don't," Walker said, and proceeded to work on a Maker's Mark Old Fashioned.

"Great to be back," Joe said.

"Great to have you," Walker said.

Joe glanced around the place. It wasn't full, like before. A couple of tables had people—an older couple that looked married, and two guys about Joe's age talking animatedly over beers.

But at the end of the bar was something else again.

She was young, beautiful, wearing a form-fitting red dress. She looked straight ahead, as if lost in thought.

"That's Lulu," Walker said.

"Huh?"

"I don't think you'll have any luck with her."

"You think that's what I was thinking?" Joe said.

"I know that's what you were thinking," Walker said.

"Hey, I haven't taken the old Munro charm out of the closet in awhile, that's for sure. But I still have the magic."

"Right. Wanna bet?"

"Bet?"

"Twenty bucks says you don't even get her to talk to you."

"Just talk?"

"Yeah, as in friendly conversation."

"You know her?" Joe said.

"She's new," Walker said.

Walker set Joe's Old Fashioned in front of him. Joe took off his mask, took a long sip, and gave the woman another glance.

"Twenty bucks?" Joe said. "Just for a conversation?"

Walker took out his wallet, removed a twenty-dollar bill, and placed it on the bar top.

Joe laughed. "Why not?" He took out a twenty and put it on top of

Walker's. Then he picked up his drink and walked slowly down to the end of the bar.

"Mind if I join you?" Joe said.

The woman didn't look at him. She didn't even move.

Walker laughed as he picked up the twenties.

"She's a mannequin," Walker said.

"Cheater!" Joe said.

Walker came down and handed Joe his twenty. "Having a little fun with you, Joe. The owner thought it'd help with the vibe if we had a mannequin or two in here. Make the place seem fuller."

Joe prided himself on being able to take a joke. He lifted his Old Fashioned to Walker. "Well played, sir."

"You're a good sport, Joe. Come on back over and tell me what's been going on."

"Actually," Joe said, "I think I'll stay here awhile."

"You're kidding, right?"

"Nope. Pour me another one of these, and bring a glass of resin for the lady."

Walker cracked up. "Well played yourself."

"I'm serious about another one of these," Joe said.

Another guy had come to the bar and Walker went to take his order.

Joe turned to the mannequin. "Come here often?"

Lulu the mannequin said nothing.

"You must be Jamaican," Joe said. "Because... j'makin' me crazy."

No response.

"Yeah, I know, I'm a stranger. But really, I'd just like a little conversation. It's been awhile since I've been here and..."

He couldn't believe it. He almost choked up. He almost shed a tear.

"I've been doing a lot of thinking lately," Joe said. "You do that when you're alone in your apartment all day. Things have changed. People have changed, don't you think?"

Lulu said nothing.

"I mean, the hate. People just hating on each other. It's like Pandora's Box. Remember that story? The old Greek myth? It's like there's been another Pandora's box opened up, and all that's come out of it is hate."

Joe lifted his drink, paused, then slammed it on the bar.

"I just can't take it anymore, you know? I can't! I got nobody who understands. Nobody who...ah, I'm rambling."

Lulu stared straight ahead.

"I hope you don't mind. I hope, maybe, you know, maybe I'll see you here again. I mean, if it's all right with you, maybe we could talk some more. Would that be okay?"

Lulu said nothing.

"Thanks for listening," Joe said.

NEW HEALTH DIRECTIVE

Mitzi Van Gogh, director of health directives for the County of Los Angeles, began her weekly press conference with a stunning announcement.

"We have determined that a significant portion of the spread of the virus can be directly traced to carelessness in the wearing of men's underwear. We therefore are requiring all males in the county to change their underwear twice a day. This includes children who have moved out of diapers. All males will be monitored by a chip in the waistband of their undergarments. A special chip has been developed by Intel for this purpose."

A reporter in the front row interrupted. "You can't be serious."

"Please, if you cannot be civil I will have to call security."

"What data supports this?"

Mitzi Van Gogh sighed. "The Basque community in Spain had an outbreak of the virus that resulted in a terrible mass death. A group of Basque men and women was inside a meeting hall that had only one door. When one of the men stood up and said he had not changed his underwear in a week, it caused a stampede. Because there was only one door, twelve people were stomped to death."

"How on earth do you attribute those deaths to the virus, or even to underwear?"

"Isn't it obvious?" Mitzi Van Gogh said. "Can't you draw a lesson from that?"

"I do draw a lesson," the reporter said. "But it's different from what you're suggesting."

Mitzi Van Gogh looked down her nose at the reporter. "Oh really? A lesson different from the experts?"

"I'm confident that this is so," the reporter said. "Do you want to hear it?"

"No," said Mitzi Van Gogh. "Now if—"

"Here it is anyway," the reporter said. "Never put all your Basques in one exit."

"Security!"

AN L.A. VISITATION

The cop spotted the old man wandering around Pershing Square. He looked lost. He was dressed in a white robe and sandals. A refugee from a nursing home perhaps? Or just an aging hippie? He was the right age. Whatever, a deficit in his appearance had to be addressed.

"You're not wearing a mask," Officer Frank Kranke said. His own mask muffled his words. "I'm gonna have to write you up."

The old man said, "What is meant, write you up?"

"You know, give you citation. A ticket."

"A ticket? What is ticked?"

"Are you supposed to be on meds?"

The old man's eyes, luminescent blue, looked at Officer Kranke's mask. "Why do you cover your mouth?"

"This isn't about me, sir, so let's start with your name. What is it?"

"Zeus!"

"You want to spell that for me, please?"

"I am a god! I do not the bidding of a mortal."

"Uh-huh. Where do you live?"

"Mount Olympus!"

"Swanky neighborhood."

"Swanky?"

"Over there in Hollywood, off Laurel Canyon."

"What is this canyon you speak of?"

"Listen, you sound like a nice old guy. I like the curls in your beard there. But you've got to cover your face when you're outside."

"I cover my face for no man!"

"Now you're just being difficult. You don't want to pull that with me."

"No?"

"I'll put cuffs on you so fast so fast your head'll spin."

"Hmm, a spinning head. That I have not tried. What would be the purpose?"

"Look, I haven't got all day here. You want me to take you in?"

The old man pulled something out of his robe. Bright light assaulted Officer Kranke's eyes. Squinting now, he saw what looked like a spear in the old man's hand, only this spear was alive, quivering with luminescence, crackling with energy. Then the old man reared back like a javelin thrower and hurled the light-spear into the air. It sailed in a majestic arc over Pershing Square, over Olive Street, and exploded into the middle tower of the historic Biltmore Hotel.

To Officer Kranke, wide-mouthed under his mask, this was the worst possible scenario, the way he envisioned a terror attack with a bomb going off in a crowded area. The only good news—as Kranke stared at the smoking rupture in the steel and concrete facade—was that the hotel rooms were empty due to the lockdown.

Still, it did not take Officer Kranke more than half a second to realize that what he had just witnessed was an unbelievable, yet most certainly undeniable, exemplar of the crime of felony vandalism.

Officer Kranke took a step back and pulled his sidearm. "On your knees. Now!"

"I bow to no man!"

"I'm telling you!"

"*Elaté!*"

From out of one of the palm trees came a creature never seen in any Kranke nightmare. Webby-winged, the color of rotten plums. The head and long hair would have been described as womanly in the era when such differences were apparent. The body, too, grotesquely feminine, but the feet. Oh, the feet! Talons like those of a predatory bird!

And screeching!

And diving at him!

In fifteen years on the job Officer Frank Kranke had never fired his weapon on the street. He qualified each quarter at the Academy. But never in any of his training had he been prepared for such a horror.

Which was why he froze. And why the webby-winged monster was able to swoop and snatch the gun right out of his hand!

Officer Kranke covered his face with his arms.

The flying terror flapped over to the old man, settling in front of him like an obedient falcon. The old man took the gun from the claws.

"I surmise," the old man said, "that in this land men are not free."

"I ... um ..."

"Who is your king?" asked the old man.

Officer Kranke slowly separated his arms. "King?"

"To whom do you bow down?"

"I, um, we don't have kings."

"Then who tells the people what to do?"

"Well, right now ... what is that thing?" The flying abomination still hovered.

"One of my harpies," the old man said.

"There's more?"

"If I summon them," the old man said. "Now I wish to speak to your leader."

"I think ... yes, I think maybe you mean the mayor."

"Ah," said the old man. "Where may I find this mayor?"

"City Hall," said Officer Kranke.

"You will show me?"

"Just walk that way. You can't miss it."

"Then I shall go," the old man said. "There is much here I do not like. If this mayor can be reasoned with, perhaps your city may yet be saved."

The harpy squealed.

Officer Frank Kranke fainted.

But his mask stayed securely in place.

HOW TO MAKE MONEY AS A WRITER

In the days before the virus, the Christmas party at Julian's was always the highlight of the season.

Everybody who was still in play in the publishing business was there. Not just because Julian was the number one bestselling author in the world, but because he always had the freest flowing booze and the best hors d'oeuvres prepared by some famous New York chef hired for the evening.

It was a throwback to the way they used to do parties in the 1950s in New York. Everyone dressed to the nines.

George didn't have any nines. He and Julian had started out together, both wannabe writers. George scored first, getting a two-book mass market deal with a mid-range house. He thought he was on his way. One year later Julian hit pay dirt with Penguin.

Twenty years later Julian was churning out hardcovers that always debuted at the top of the New York Times list. George had been dropped by his last publisher and for the last five years was trying to make a go of self publishing. It was more of a stop than a go, however. He was still old school, wanting simply to earn enough from writing so he wouldn't have to take side jobs, like sitting in a parking garage kiosk for eight hours.

But Julian kept inviting him to these shindigs. He thought Julian invited him each year out of friendship. That thought was about to change.

When George arrived the party was already in full swing. He said hello to a couple of familiar faces. But most of the people he didn't know. The publishing business had changed so much in the last few years. A lot of turnover. And with e-books and e-readers and digital this and app that, the whole world he had inhabited now seemed to be in a state of permanent and irredeemable chaos.

He needed a drink.

George got himself a bourbon rocks from the host bar and wandered around the eight room, upper East Side pad. The hallway wall was a rogues' gallery, pictures of Julian with all sorts of writers and editors. There was one with his arm draped around Stephen King. Another showed him mugging with John Grisham.

"There you are!"

He turned. It was Julian's wife, Patricia. She was packed into a black evening dress, looking a little plumper than last year. In her left arm was cradled a furry little Pekingese.

"I've been looking for you, George," she said.

The Peke snapped at George.

"Please excuse Fiji," Patricia said, pulling the fluff away. "She's been extremely fussy today." She held the dog out and looked at its face. "Haven't you, bookins? Hm? Haven't you been a little fussy-wussy?"

"Nice seeing you as always, Patricia."

"Don't go, Georgie. Tell me one of your stories. Make it a knee slapper." The gin was heavy on her breath.

"I don't tell knee-slappers."

"Oh, I forgot. You're a seeeerious writer."

Fiji the dog yipped at George.

"Now don't you go anywhere," Patricia said. "I need to get snooky-ookums a sweetie-treatie. I want to come back and hear that knee slapper."

George took that opportunity to slip away and get another bourbon. Feeling a bout of self pity coming on, he went to the guest room where the coats were piled on a bed. There was a large closet there. George went in, shut the door, and sat in the dark.

Presently, he heard two voices through the wall. One of the voices was clearly Julian's. The other he did not recognize.

The stranger's voice said, "Why do you do it?"

Julian laughed. "It's a little superstition of mine."

"Superstition?"

"Yes. George is a failed writer. He's never been able to make a living at it. But he's like my good luck charm. An opposite me, in a way. Whenever I have him over, I seem to gain more success."

"Does George know this?"

Another Julian laugh. "Of course not. The poor slob, that would really mess him up."

George finished his drink. He bumped into a few people on his way to the front door, but spoke to no one.

He walked from 81st Street to Times Square. The bright lights of the Christmas season were nothing but multi-colored blurs through his hot tears.

Failed writer.

But that was all he ever wanted to do! Crime writing in particular. He wanted to be counted with the best. Like Elmore Leonard. The king. The master.

George took the subway to 23rd and got back to his apartment around one. He couldn't sleep. He went to his bookshelf and took down a few Elmore Leonard books, as if they were friends to comfort him. And then he remembered something Elmore Leonard once said.

———

Patricia screamed into the phone. "Fiji! Dear God, they've got Fiji!"

"Who?" Julian said.

"Just come home. Now!"

When he got there she showed him the note:

You will give me $3,000,000 or you will never see your dog again. If you contact the police the dog will go for her last swim in the East River. Instructions to follow.

———

George sipped a Cuba Libra in the balmy, comfortable bar in Key West. This is where Hemingway had trod. This is where George would show the world he could write like the best of them.

A friendly guy from the dock sat down next to him. George bought him a beer.

"You're pretty generous with the money," the guy said. "What do you do for a living?"

"I'm a writer," George said.

"Really? Does that pay?"

"Ever heard of Elmore Leonard?"

"No."

"Well you should. He was one of our greatest writers. Anyway, he was once asked what kind of writing paid the most."

"Oh yeah? What did he say?"

"Ransom notes."

The guy laughed. "Some joke," he said.

"Yeah," George said. "A real knee slapper."

STICKING IT TO LARRY

Judson Povlick couldn't just kill Larry Simms with a gun. They'd catch him for that. It needed to be a distant death, with a perfect alibi.

Which was why Judson Povlick was trying something foolproof, if it would work. Ever since he'd visited Haiti he'd been fascinated with voodoo. It was time to put it to the test.

That was because Larry Simms was closing in on the rich widow, Donna Dickinson, who had once been sweet on Judson. Judson needed money to support his gambling habit, which was why he needed Donna Dickinson. Larry Simms was fouling everything up.

Judson's first stop, of course, was Amazon. Voodoo dolls, complete with sets of pins, were abundant. Who knew? But this, after all, was the "Everything Store," right? Boy, howdy, it sure was.

Judson picked a voodoo doll with 905 global ratings, and a 4.7 average. One review said, "It so works! But be careful when using this doll. If you are going to use it on someone, make sure you are using it on someone who DESERVES IT."

Well, in Judson's view, Larry Simms deserved hot death because he was a thief. He was stealing Judson's meal ticket!

Judson paid for the doll to be delivered the next day.

A little Googling got him further directions. You needed something to connect the doll to the mark. A lock of hair, a piece of clothing, a photo. Wait, he had a photo of Larry Simms on his phone. They worked together at AIG, and a receptionist named Myra had taken a picture of Larry and Judson standing together at an office party. She'd messaged the photo to Judson. He checked his phone's photo app and scrolled until he found it. He printed out the photo, then cut out the face of Larry Simms.

When the doll arrived, Judson taped Larry's face onto the face of the doll.

Almost ready. Now he was to call upon the Loas—the spirits who give voodoo its power. He was to light a candle and offer a small sacrifice to the Loas, like a snack, drink, or flower. Judson had a Twix on the kitchen counter. Who among the spirits could resist a Twix?

The time had come. "Oh Loas," Judson said, "strike my enemy in the heart!"

With that, Judson Povlick drove a pin into the chest of the voodoo doll. Then another. And another...

The next morning, Larry Simms was not in the office. Judson worked in his cubicle until eleven, then asked Myra the receptionist if she'd heard anything from Larry.

"Nothing," she said. "I hope he's not sick."

"We all hope that," Judson said. Sickness would not be enough!

At lunch, Judson went to Baja Fresh, around the corner from the AIG building. As he was about to bite into his Diablo Burrito, he felt a hand on his back.

"Howdy, pal," Larry Simms said.

Judson dropped his burrito. "L...Larry!"

"Did I startle you?"

"But...wait...why..."

"Why didn't I come to work?" Larry said. "Because I'm here to clear out my stuff. I'm quitting! Donna Dickinson and I are getting married."

Judson found no words.

"It's the funniest thing," Larry said. "I was on my way to the acupuncturist for my chest pains. Angina pectoris is the official name. I was going to try acupuncture as a last resort. If I didn't get any relief, I was going to stop seeing Donna. I didn't want her having to take care of me. But then, suddenly, I felt a thousand percent better! So good, in fact, that I went straight to Donna and popped the question. Look at me! I feel no pain at all, after years of it. A miracle, I say! Mind if I join you for a bite?"

TRANSACTION

"I've had thoughts about killing my wife," Brad said.

"Really?" Amanda said.

"Sometimes it just gets to be ... too much."

Amanda nestled her head on his shoulder. The morning sun filtered through the motel window. "How would you do it?"

"I'd hire someone."

"A hit man?"

"I guess."

Amanda ran her finger along his chest. "What would you pay for the job?"

Brad snorted a laugh. "Why? You interested?"

"I'm a professional," she said. "I get paid for giving pleasure. Why couldn't I get paid for that?"

"It's a whole different thing," Brad said.

"So what would you pay?"

"Come on."

"No, really," Amanda said.

"Okay," Brad said. "Five grand."

"That's it?"

"Pretty good for one night's work, wouldn't you say?"

"Not enough," Amanda said.

"Ten grand, then. But that would be it. I'm a lawyer. I know how not to get fleeced."

"You wouldn't go over ten?"

"No way."

Amanda rolled over to her side of the bed and reached for her purse. She opened it and took out a .38 Smith & Wesson.

She shot Brad twice in the heart.

Half an hour later, Amanda got a Grande Mocha from Starbucks, sat down, sent a text. Twenty minutes after that, Shelly, Brad's widow, showed up and sat at the table across from Amanda. A fat envelope shook in Shelly's hands.

"You don't need to be so nervous," Amanda said as she took the envelope and put it in her purse.

"It's all there," Shelly said. "Fifteen thousand."

ONE MORNING IN A DARK CASTLE

The evil Queen finished her milk bath, then ordered the servants out of her chamber. As usual, she went to the magic mirror and said, "Mirror, mirror, on the wall, who is the fairest of them all?"

A cloudy face appeared in the glass, and said, "O Queen, though fair thou may be, but the fairest? I cannot agree."

"What!" Rage engulfed the Queen's dark soul.

"Fair Queen, thy beauty doth gently befall, but time's remorseless touch doth sprawl."

"How dare you say such a thing to me!"

"Dost thou seek truth, or in denial stay, forsooth?"

"Go on!"

"Botox may aid to defy time's call, but a fairer visage is beyond this wall."

"Who is it? Who? I demand to know!"

"The name which causes thee such fright belongs to maiden Vanna White."

"Vanna White! Why, she is sixty-six years old!"

"Fairness is also nurtured within, and grows when giving letters a spin."

The evil Queen reached for her iron scepter and prepared to strike the mirror.

The face began to disappear. "I now withdraw behind this glass, for you, O Queen, are a perfect—"

The voice was stilled as the Queen shattered the mirror.

Then she called for her huntsman.

SENTIENCE

The attempt to turn a vegetable into a sentient being began in the laboratory of Dr. Hans Finklemeister, assisted by Mr. E. Gore, who one day asked, "Why are we doing this?"

"Because we've already seen success turning thinking humans into vegetables," Finklemeister said. "Public education, social media, the legalization of marijuana. They've all done their work. But alas, these neo-vegetables are sitting out elections. We need to raise up a vast new crop of vegetables that can think like humans. After that's done, we can arrange to have them declared citizens, get them ballots, and have a real harvest!"

"Diabolical!" E. Gore said.

"Thank you!"

E. Gore was dispatched to the grocery store to pick up the first vegetable subject. He returned and handed it to Finklemeister.

"A good choice," said Finklemeister. "My sainted mother used to make these as a side dish on Thanksgiving." He wiped away a tear. "If we succeed, it will be tribute to her!"

Six months of experimentation followed, with probes and wires and electric impulses, injections of DNA and RNA, streams of ultra-violet lighting, and the music of Mozart.

Until one day, as Finklemeister and Gore sat exhausted on their benches, a peep came through the speaker.

The veggie was trying to communicate!

"Quick, the translation app!" Finklemeister said. E. Gore brought up the program, and the first words of their new creation came out in a creaky, American accent:

"I think, therefore I yam."

IN THE WOODS

"Why are you grilling me?" Rob Sanford said. "Go find my kids!"

"Help us out here," Detective Mark Fields said. "You're saying the kids just ran off into the woods?"

"Yes."

"And you went looking for them?"

"Of course!"

"What kind of father lets his kids go wander alone in the woods?"

"I'm telling you." Rob Sanford pounded his fist on the table. "Henry's been on a disobedience tear and—"

"He's what, eight years old?"

"Yes. And Gretchen is six. She does what Henry tells her to do."

"So you're saying they snuck out by themselves?"

"Dear God, yes! Time is running out. They could be dying or already..."

Fields nodded. If Sanford was lying, he was darn good at it.

"We've got a team out there now," he said. "We'll find them."

But considering the vastness of the wilderness, he knew it wasn't a sure thing.

———

Two weeks went by. No luck, even with the helicopters and low-flying planes. Detective Fields, desperate, notified Jeb Shaw, the experienced tracker who'd called Fields every name in the book not long ago. Pride had no place now. The children, or what remained of them, had to be found.

Shaw said he would help, at double his usual fee.

Fields got the okay from his boss, but only if he went along with the eccentric Shaw, who wore a coonskin cap and chewed tobacco.

The first day was a slog, with no results. Shaw pitched a tent and cooked Spam for dinner. Fields ate it reluctantly, listening to Shaw tell tales about his legendary skills.

They got an early start the next morning. In about an hour Shaw said he'd picked up a trail. Fields couldn't see anything in the sodden leaves and pine needles.

"You're used to streets," Jeb Shaw said. "Leave the woods to me."

When they got to a clearing, Shaw pointed. "Smoke," he said.

Sure enough, a plume of white smoke rose above the trees on the other side of the clearing. Fields scratched his chin. Why hadn't the planes seen it? Had to be because it just started.

"Let's hurry," Fields said.

"Stay behind me," Shaw said.

Across the clearing they went, into the trees on the other side. After a hundred yards or so, Shaw put his hand up and stopped them.

"There," Shaw said.

Fields saw it. A small house in a clearing. Smoke coming out of the chimney.

"Whoever is there will see us if we move in," Fields said.

"I'll do the figuring," Shaw said. He took a pair of binoculars from his pack and looked. Fields had his own pair, and did the same.

The house had a door and window in front. Fields tried to see inside the window, but couldn't make out anything.

Then the door opened.

The boy and girl stepped outside. They did not seem in any distress. But who knew who was watching from the inside?

"I'm going to rush in," Fields said, pulling out his sidearm.

Shaw pulled a knife. "I'll grab the kids and move them into the woods."

"Go!" Fields said.

They ran, Fields moving faster than he had in twenty years. The kids turned. The girl screamed.

Fields charged through the open door, gun at the ready.

He found no one.

The one-room cabin was furnished with wooden chairs, a table, an old-fashioned oven, and...a cage. Not a small one for a bird or hamster. No, but big enough for a child.

Fields went outside and shouted, "Clear!"

Jeb Shaw had the children, one in each arm. He stopped, turned, came back, setting the kids in front of Fields.

"Henry?" Fields said.

"Yeah," Henry said.

"And Gretchen?"

The girl nodded.

"Are you all right?"

Henry said, "We are now."

"Did someone kidnap you?" Fields said.

"Yes," Henry said. "But she can't hurt us now."

"She?" Fields said.

"The old lady," Henry said.

"Where is she?"

"In the oven," Henry said, then went to the door and broke off two big chunks. He handed one of the pieces to Gretchen. They both happily munched.

Fields detected a faint odor of gingerbread.

AMAZING

Phil "Master of the Amazing" Franconi felt the first tremors in his hands when he was 48. He managed to do his close-up routine for another three years until it just wasn't possible anymore.

He fumbled the cups-and-balls at The Magic Castle, the famous private club in Hollywood. His big finish was supposed to produce three live chicks under the cups. But this night he couldn't load them. His hands betrayed him. The chicks spilled onto the table, wounded, limping around and cheeping in pain.

Most painful of all were the looks on the faces in the Close-Up Room. Most of them were embarrassed. One guy muttered, "For this we paid to get in here?"

The doctors couldn't do anything for him. Parkinson's, he was told, is incurable.

So on the last Tuesday in March, Phil Franconi, living in a small apartment on La Cienega, decided to end it all. He went outside for a last look at the world. His walk was a shuffle, but at least the sun was shining.

Halfway down the block he heard a child crying. It was a girl, maybe seven years old, on her knees, looking over the curb.

"What's the matter?" Phil asked.

The girl looked at him with a tear-streaked face.

"I dropped my quarter," she said. "It went down the drain!"

A quarter. A mere twenty-five cents. But of course, to a seven-year-old, it might seem like a hundred bucks. Well, welcome to the real world, little girl. Maybe it's best you learn now that life is all about loss.

Phil was about to say something to that effect when some words, almost of their own accord, came out of his mouth. "The quarter is not down the drain."

The girl's eyes widened. Then narrowed. "Is so," she said. "I saw it go."

"Here," Phil said. "Stand up, okay?"

He could almost hear the little mind cranking, considering, running through the warnings she'd received about strangers. But not all innocence had been lost. She got to her feet.

"I want to show you something," Phil said. He lifted his left arm. His hand shook in the sunlight.

"What do you see?" he said.

The little girl frowned. "Um, your hand?"

"Yes," said Phil.

"Why is it shaking?" the girl asked.

"It isn't shaking," Phil said. "It's vibrating. With magic."

The girl's mouth opened slightly. She kept her eyes on his hand.

The first thing Phil had learned as a close-up magician was the art of misdirection. Get the audience looking here while you secretly do something there. Which, in this instance, was his right hand going into his pocket to feel the change he had, finding a quarter.

"Now keep watching this hand as I speak to it," Phil said.

The girl did so.

"What is your name, sweetheart?"

"Jasmine," the girl said.

"Oh magic hand, my friend Jasmine thinks her quarter is gone. But you know better, magic hand. Tell us where it is."

Phil quietly drew his right hand out of his pocket.

Phil leaned toward his outstretched left hand. "What did you say? Ah!"

"Did it tell you?" Jasmine said.

"Indeed!" said Phil. He reached out his right hand and gently touched the girl's left ear.

"Why, it's in your ear!" he said.

He brought his right fist down in front of her and opened it.

The girl made a sound only a child can make, a squeal of wonder and delight.

"Take it," Phil said.

The quarter disappeared into a little fist.

A woman's voice called out, "What's going on here?"

She was a nice-looking woman of about thirty, coming down the walkway from the house.

"Mom!" Jasmine said. "He pulled my quarter out of my ear!"

"I hope you don't mind," Phil said. "Your little girl misplaced her quarter. I just found it for her." He winked.

"In my ear!" Jasmine said.

The mother smiled. "That's amazing!"

Phil nearly wept.

"Do it again!" Jasmine said.

"Give me the quarter," Phil said.

She did so.

"Now watch." Holding the quarter between the shaking thumb and fingers of his left hand, he showed it to the girl. Then brought his right hand over and executed a perfect French Drop, where it appeared he took the coin with his right but really dropped it into the palm of his left.

He held his right fist in front of Jasmine and said, "Blow."

She blew on the fist.

Phil opened it. The coin wasn't there.

He brought his left hand to the girl's right ear and said, "It's in your other ear!"

Another, bigger squeal of delight.

"Do you live around here?" the mother said.

"Just up the street," Phil said.

"I'm Charlene Taylor."

"Phil Franconi."

"Do some more!" Jasmine said.

Phil said, "Would you like to see colorful silks disappear and come back again?"

She nodded vigorously.

"And a red ball that flies from my hand into yours?"

"Yes, yes!"

"And so you shall," Phil said. "I myself will fade from view, but be back again!"

He shuffled back to his apartment and dug out the old box of magic from the closet.

DEBT PAID

I saw Chuck Corker by the open bar. He looked great, as always.

A 30-year high school reunion is when you pretty much see how life is going to turn out. I was married, with a couple of kids, working like a dog in IT for Wells Fargo.

Chuck, our Most Likely to Succeed, was a real estate developer worth half a billion.

I wandered over.

"Hey, Chuck," I said.

"Stan!" He stuck out a hand that had thrown many a touchdown pass for old Hoover High, and squeezed mine like a swivel vice.

"How you doing these days?" Chuck said.

"Still at Wells Fargo," I said.

"Courtney with you?"

"She doesn't like these things," I said. "Is Julia here?"

He smirked. "Not bloody likely."

When I cocked my head, he added, "Divorced."

"I'm sorry," I said.

"Why? Julia turned forty last year." He leaned in and, *sotto voce,* added, "I traded her in for two twenties."

He laughed.

"Some joke," I said.

"No joke, old buddy. It's true. I really have to juggle my schedule, if you know what I mean."

"Is that worth it?" I said.

"You should see 'em, then you'd know!"

We chatted a bit more, then a couple of football players came over to talk about the glory days.

As I had only been president of the Chess Club, I bowed out.

———

Two weeks later, Chuck Corker was dead, after falling twenty floors from his penthouse condo.

You just never know what goes on inside a man, what would make someone with all that success want to end it all. I went to the funeral, which was packed. I saw two beautiful young women, early twenties for sure, sitting alone on opposite sides of the room.

Julia, Chuck's ex, was not in attendance.

———

A month went by. I was in the cereal aisle at Pavilions when someone said, "Hi, Stan."

I turned.

"Oh," I said. "Julia."

"You heard about Chuck, of course," she said.

"Yes," I said. "I'm so sorry."

Her expression was a block of ice. "He cashed in his chips," she said. "His account came due. His debt had to be paid. His portfolio took a dive."

"I never thought he'd kill himself," I said.

There was a little smile in her eyes then. "Nice to see you, Stan. Say hello to Courtney for me." Then she leaned in and whispered, "Don't ever do her wrong. It won't end well."

She placed her hands on the shopping cart and pushed. The cart rolled down the aisle and crashed into the Rice Krispies.

A FLORAL ARRANGEMENT

As he walked by the unclaimed luggage at LAX, sitting there like souls in purgatory, Dan Black eased over, looked around for security, and picked up a suitcase. As he made for the door he was ready with his story. "I thought this was mine," he would say. "Looks just like mine."

But no one approached him.

You snooze, you lose. And since life was a zero-sum game, he was winning.

Now he had his own bag and this one.

His Lyft was there, waiting.

Times were tough. He was behind in his rent at his florist shop. If there were things to hock in this suitcase, maybe just one valuable item, it could buy him another month at the shop.

"If life gives you lemons, make lemonade," his dad used to say, usually when he was drunk, which was always. Then he'd add, "And if you don't have the lemons, steal some."

———

Back at the shop, in the office, Dan opened the suitcase. On top were some neatly folded dress shirts. He tossed them aside. Under the shirts were underwear and socks. He tossed those, too. There was a shaving kit, but with only shaving stuff in it. Dan threw it in the trash and cursed. Couldn't there have been some gold cufflinks or something?

The suitcase was empty now, and so were Dan Black's hopes. He was about to slam it shut when he noticed a slight curl in the corner of the lining on the bottom of the suitcase. Curious, he took hold of it and pulled. An inch or so came up. And underneath he saw the most amazing thing.

A diamond.

Was it really?

He pulled again at the lining. More gems.

Were they fake?

No. If they were, why hide them?

And the lining. Dan had once heard from a guy he met in jail that there was a certain metallic lining that could thwart airport X-rays. Dan thought it was bunk, the stuff of lousy spy novels.

Maybe not!

Now, what to do with these hot rocks. He'd have to tread carefully, use some connections to find a reliable fence. But that could be done. Not only would his financial problems be solved, he'd be able to get that new Caddie he had his eye on.

The buzzer went off, indicating someone coming into the shop.

Dan closed the office door behind him.

A man was looking at the display case, where Dan had some arrangements.

"Hello there," Dan said. "Can I help you?"

The man turned. He was thick and strong-looking. He wore a crisp, blue suit with a burgundy tie and—was it? Yes it was—a diamond tie tack.

"I believe you have something of mine," he said.

Goose flesh popped all over Dan's body, zapping his nerves and sending blood rushing to his face. He tried to answer calmly, but his voice warbled. "I don't understand," he said.

"Yes, you do," the man said. "You picked up my suitcase at the airport. I saw you go out the door and hop into your ride. It was lucky I could hail a cab and follow you."

"It was a mistake," Dan said. "It looked just like mine."

"I see," the man said. "Where is it now?"

"It's in the back," Dan said.

"Did you open it?"

"I did, and saw the clothes, and that's when I realized my mistake."

"Well, no harm done, then."

"I'll...I'll get it for you," Dan said, his heart sinking like the anchor on a garbage scow.

"No hurry," the man said. "While I'm here I'd like to get a floral arrangement."

"Oh, sure," Dan said.

"Any suggestions?" the man said.

"Well, I always ask what the occasion is, and who it's for."

"That helps," the man said. "I think that one." He pointed to the horse-shoe of white roses, mums, lilies, and carnations with the ribbon that read *Rest in Peace.*

"My condolences," Dan said. "Who are they for?"

"Guess," the man said, pulling a gun from his coat pocket.

A DOUBLE PLEASURE

"That's a very nice outfit, young lady," Arnie Milton said. "I'm sure you'll do a great job here. There's lots of room for advancement, believe you me. You can make it happen, if you know what I mean. Just dig in. This is a nice place to work. I hope you'll be happy."

The next morning he got a call from the CEO, Jack Stephenson.

"What were you thinking?" Stephenson said.

"Excuse me?" Arnie said.

"We're gonna get a workplace harassment suit hung on us!"

"What?"

"You're out," Stephenson said. "Get your things together and be out of the office by noon."

"But why?"

"Come on, you know why."

"Wait—"

The call cut.

Chills coursed through Arnie Milton's body. This was a mistake! Something wrong here, very wrong. A lie. Who could have...

Wait, was it that new hire? The one he complimented?

He called the head of HR.

"She got me fired, didn't she?" Arnie said.

"Sorry, Arn," Hildy Haggard said. "Rules are rules."

"But I didn't do anything!"

"You most certainly did. Telling Janet Haberman that advancement in the office is contingent on sexual favors is beyond the pale."

"I never did any such thing!"

"Leering at a woman who just started?"

"I did not leer!"

"Then telling her she'd do well here. Wink, wink."

"I did not wink!"

"She says you did."

"She's lying!"

"But we have the recording," Hildy Haggard said.

"I want to hear it!"

"We are not obligated—"

"Now!"

"Just stay where you are."

Five minutes later Hildy Haggard entered Arnie's office. She played an audio file on her phone.

Arnie Milton heard his voice say, *"There's lots of room for advancement, if you'll make me happy, if you know what I mean."*

"Wait, wait! I never said any such thing!"

"That's your voice, isn't it?"

"But...she must have edited clips together!"

"Oh, Arn, really." Hildy looked around his office. "Do you need some boxes?"

———

Five years later, Janet Haberman was made CEO of the company, a rise fueled by a cutthroat climb up the corporate ladder. But that was how it was done. Janet Haberman loved reading Machiavelli.

When she bought a penthouse, it made news. She let it be known she'd interview designers.

One of them, a woman named Tricia Townes, got right to the point.

"First," Tricia said, "your colors. Do you like pink?"

"I detest pink," Janet Haberman said. "The world would be better off with no pink at all."

"Reds and yellows?"

"It depends."

"Grays and blacks?" asked Tricia.

"Grays and blacks?" Janet said. "Are you kidding?"

"Together they are quite nice."

"Not in my house. I don't think you'll do, Traci."

"Tricia."

"Thanks for stopping by," Janet said.

———

Arnie Milton knocked off work as the manager of a Del Taco in Oklahoma City, went home to his apartment and found the package waiting for him. He took out the digital recording device and listened to it with a happy smile.

An hour later, he got a call.

"Did the package arrive?" Tricia Townes said.

"All good," Arnie said. "I trust you're happy with the payment?"

"Most assuredly," Tricia said.

"I'm sending you a bonus, for all the time you spent working out a plan. And all good wishes for your continued success. May I just add, without fear of any blowback, that you're the most attractive PI I've ever seen?"

"I consider that a compliment," Tricia said.

"How refreshing it is to hear that. You can't imagine."

"I think I can," Tricia said.

———

Janet Haberman got the phone call a little after ten—from the Chairman of the Board himself.

"Clean out your desk and be out of the office by noon," the Chairman said.

"Wait, what?"

"You heard me."

"But why?"

"Come on, you know why."

The call cut.

Janet called Hildy Haggard, still head of HR. "Tell me exactly what is going on!"

"You need to hear it?" Hildy said.

"Hear what?" Janet said.

"Just stay where you are."

Hildy Haggard came to Janet's office and played the clip.

Janet Haberman heard her voice say, "*I detest blacks. The world would be better off with no blacks at all.*"

"Wait, wait! I never said any such thing!"

"That's your voice, isn't it?"

"But...No way!"

Hildy looked around Janet's office. "Do you need some boxes?"

———

Arnie Milton put his feet up on his desk in his Del Taco office. He smiled and sipped his Coke, then picked up his dog-eared copy of Machiavelli's *The Prince.* He began reading where he'd left off.

It is a double pleasure to deceive the deceiver...

THE PÚCA

Shelly wasn't sure she heard it the first time. But the voice repeated: "A little help?"

But who said it?

There was no one around her in the produce section of Ralphs Market. The nearest shopper was all the way over by the potatoes and would have to yell to be heard.

The voice was soft, as if someone were right by her side.

Was she hearing things? Was she going nuts?

"I'm right here," the voice said.

"Where? Where!"

"Look down."

Shelly did.

"Didn't expect this, did you?" The voice seemed to be coming from...a cabbage!

No way!

The cabbage said, "Buy me, please."

Shelly, being a decent person, and therefore responding to the word *please*, said, "But...why?"

"Isn't it obvious? If you don't, I may end up in the hands of some crazy cook. A woman with a family, or a vegan with an obsession. I could end up as coleslaw, or boiled in Irish stew!"

"I...I mean, why *me*?"

"Because you can hear me. Only a good soul can hear me. You should have seen the brute who was here before you! He picked me up in his grubby hands. I told him to put me down at once, but he couldn't hear. Thankfully, he put me back. You may be my last chance!"

"But what will I do with you?"

"Let us cross that bridge when we come to it. Quick! I see that brute coming back!"

So Shelly bought the cabbage along with some eggs, milk, and a large bag of Kettle potato chips. When she got home she put the eggs and milk in the refrigerator and placed the cabbage on the counter.

"Now what?" she asked.

"Let me explain," said the cabbage. "I am a púca. That's a word from the ancient Celtic language. It means spirit or ghost, but able to take forms. A shapeshifter. You Americans had a play about one, called *Harvey*, which took the form of a large rabbit. James Stewart was in the movie."

"You see movies?"

"I love movies. I've gone into movie houses in the form of old women, boys, girls, even a janitor with a limp."

"If you can do that," Shelly said, "change shapes and all, why are you stuck as a cabbage?"

"I got crossways with an evil witch," the cabbage said. "She laughed when she cast the spell. 'Corned beef and you'—she said—'That is your fate!' You have saved me from that fate."

"And now?"

"You can get me out."

"How?"

"There is an incantation which must be uttered by someone other than I. It is Latin. *Pauperem spiritum ab incantamento malefici.* It means, I cursed the poor spirit with a spell."

"Oh, my. I don't know if I can remember that."

"Yes, you can! Let us practice. I'll say it, and you repeat it."

On the third try, Shelly got it right.

Before her on the counter stood a crocodile.

"What do you think?" it said.

"I...I...I think I would have preferred a rabbit."

"Fear not, you will not see me again. I'm off to Washington, D.C. There are some people there I want to bite."

The reptile nudged the cabbage with its snout, rolling it toward Shelly.

"Shred this," the crocodile said, "and add some grated carrots. Mix half a cup of mayonnaise, a tablespoon of white vinegar, two teaspoons of sugar, half a teaspoon of celery seeds, and salt and pepper to taste. There's your dressing."

"How on earth do you know that?"

"You learn a lot in the cabbage display. I heard two ladies discussing it. Ta!"

And with that the crocodile disappeared.

It took Shelly a day to get over what had just occurred.

But her coleslaw was the hit of her next party.

FIRE THROWER

Artie Willis was, at twenty-five, a free rider on the loser train. Recently paroled after a conviction for domestic abuse, and with no real skills besides shoplifting and biting his nails, Artie decided it was time to take out his revenge on society at large. But how?

Oh, he could do what every other malcontent murderer did, load up with weaponry and shoot up a school. That would be over too quickly and the damage would be minimal. What he needed was something original and potent, and that's what first put the thought of witchcraft in his head.

Artie didn't really believe in witchcraft, but his mother sure had. An odd duck long gone from the Earth, his mother had a book on Necromancy, Spells, and Curses. It was among the few effects Artie kept from the old house after mom took her dirt nap.

Where was it?

It was in a box in the back of his closet.

He brought it out to the living room of his apartment and opened the leather-bound tome with its yellowing pages.

There were all sorts of strange diagrams and instructions. But one item in particular caught Artie's eye—fire throwing. The illustration showed a bearded wizard type spreading his fingers and holding his hands out, with flames—actual fire!—shooting from the fingertips. He was aiming the flames at a tree, which was engulfed in fire.

The instructions explained that after going through the directed actions, and picking an incantation, the subject would be able to become a true fire thrower.

Artie snorted. But he had no job interviews coming up, so what the heck?

He got some chalk and, per the instructions, drew a pentagram on the wood floor of his apartment. He stood inside the pentagram and uttered the strange words—Latin?—in the book.

Nothing happened.

He was about to toss the book in the trash when he got the stunning idea that maybe a little homework might be necessary.

With a sigh, he hopped on Google and looked for a guide to Latin pronunciation. Two hours later he was tired, but determined. He stood once again in the pentagram and uttered the words in what he hoped was the correct manner.

He felt a tingling heat in his fingertips. And a thought as clear as a musical note came to him: *Choose your incantation.*

Right. Some triggering words.

Artie said, "Burn, baby, burn."

Little flames popped out of his fingertips. Candle-sized. Artie shrieked, but not in pain. There was no pain, just steady micro-blazes.

And just as quickly as they had appeared, the flames went away.

Artie had to sit down. He was out of breath.

Could it really be? But there was no question. He'd seen it!

He took a deep breath and pointed his fingers outward and said, "Burn baby burn."

Flames shot outward, farther than before. Three feet maybe! Ten licks of hot flame, lasting perhaps five seconds.

Wow! Was it possible he could get better and better at this?

He practically ran out his door and to the stairwell, then up to the roof of the apartment building.

"Burn, baby, burn!"

The flames shot out five feet!

"Burn, baby, burn!"

Eight feet!

"Burn, baby, burn!"

Ten feet!

How far could this go with practice?

Shaking with the intoxicant of supernatural power, he spotted a squirrel on the ledge of the building. As if possessed, he walked slowly toward the rodent, hands outstretched. The words *Burn, baby, burn* flashed through his mind. Fire exploded from his fingertips and engulfed the four-footed fur ball.

When the flames subsided, all that was left was a blackened, smoking hunk of squirrel meat.

But wait. He had only *thought* the incantation. He held out his hands and thought the words again. And again the flames erupted. Unfortunately they consumed a satellite dish, which was not his intent.

Back in his apartment he turned on the radio and poured himself a tall glass of vodka. He sat on the sofa and tried to catch his breath. His mind was full of the things he might do, like incinerating one of those vagrants living in a tent under the freeway. Or burning his old high school to the ground, with the teachers in it. That would show them who they could kick out or not!

The vodka calmed him, and the music from the radio was kind of cool. Oldies.

Then the awesomeness of his power hit him, and he wondered if he was not thinking big enough. Why, he could march through the city laying waste to everything, like Godzilla.

As he thought about it, he chomped gently on the fingernail of his middle finger.

The soft-voiced announcer on the radio said he was now going to play "Disco Inferno."

Artie didn't know that song, but the musical intro was kind of fun. He began chomping on the nail of his ring finger, imagining the Empire State Building fully engulfed in flames...

...when the singing on the radio burst forth!

Burn, baby, burn...disco inferno...

Two hours later, after the fire at the apartment building had been put out, an arson investigator determined that the source of the conflagration was somewhere inside the apartment of one Arthur Willis, and that the horribly charred remains on what was left of a sofa were most likely those of the tenant himself.

The investigation is ongoing.

BRAIN FOG

I didn't mean to kill my wife. I hope you believe me. I mean, I had no malice aforethought. That's the legal term, right? She's dead, yes, but you must know how it happened.

Listen—

First of all, I blame the jab. I didn't want it. I put in for a medical exemption, but they turned me down flat. If I wanted to keep my job at Disneyland, doing magic for the kids at the magic shop, I would have to take the needle or else.

I took it. My heart expanded in my chest and I was down for a week, struggling to breathe. But I had my job, oh yes!

Only my mind wasn't as sharp. I could feel it. They call it brain fog.

When I got back to the magic shop I wasn't as quick with the repartee. My hands shook. I kept messing up tricks.

My boss saw it, and I could read the look in his eyes. I was on the verge of being fired. Talk about stress!

Now add to that my wife.

We'd been married for a year, Stacey and me, and it was all good. Until it wasn't. Until I saw in her face she was hiding something from me.

Something—rather, someone—named Roger Atwood. My college roommate. My supposed friend. Who had been Stacey's boyfriend before me.

Of course, she denied it. But I *knew*.

Or maybe, dear reader, it was my brain fog that knew. Does it matter anymore?

When Stacey said she wanted to take me out to dinner on my birthday, to our favorite steak house, I decided to confront her, once and for all, over a good ribeye. Catch her while she was comfortable and unaware.

But I couldn't focus. Stacey kept asking me if anything was wrong. I told her trouble at work, but the boss said I was handling it fine.

Some lie!

When the waiter brought me a piece of cheesecake with a candle on it, and a few of the staff sang "Happy Birthday," I closed my eyes, blew out the candle, and made a wish.

But when I opened my eyes, Stacey was still there.

———

On the way home I refused to talk. Stacey kept yakking. When I pulled into the driveway I went all the way to the back so we couldn't be seen or heard from the street.

"I know about you and Roger!" I heard myself say. "You've been lying to me!"

"No, Donald, no!"

"And you're going to pay for it!"

"What...what—"

I swear what happened next is a brain fog blur!

My hands raised of their own accord and grabbed her neck.

"Don...ald...please..."

Those were her last words.

I fought my way out of the fog. I had to figure this out! Where to dump the body? What story to tell the cops?

Time. I needed time!

Stacey's body was slumped against the passenger door, like she'd fallen asleep.

I got out of the car. I had to get some things. A rug from the living room to wrap the body in. Some gloves. Rope.

I went inside, through the laundry room and the kitchen, and into the living room.

Bright lights blinded me!

A bunch of voices shouted, "Surprise!"

Roger Atwood came up and slapped me on the shoulder. "Happy birthday, buddy! We really got you, didn't we? Where's Stacey? I'll go get her."

Before I could form a word people swarmed around me, laughing, shaking my hand.

———

Today, when my lunch tray was slipped to me, Mac, the friendly guard, said, "There's an extra brownie for you. I know it's your birthday. Thought you might like a little surprise."

THE DOORMAT

I won't just fight for you. I'll win for you!

The lawyer's image on the billboard looked down upon the freeway. His arms were folded across his chest. The look of a hungry shark was in his eyes.

Becky Randall almost missed her off-ramp.

When had that sign gone up? And she meant it that way. A *sign*. A sign of what she had to do.

She was trembling when she pulled in her driveway. Her hands shaking so hard it took her two tries to remove her keys.

Of course he wasn't home.

Becky Randall wasn't a drinker, but now she needed one. She poured herself a slug of Hank's Scotch, not caring if he took notice later.

She'd had three shots by the time he walked in.

"Never again," Becky said.

Hank tossed his coat over a chair. "What is that supposed to mean?"

"Divorce," she said. "And I'm going to take you to the cleaners."

He snorted his obnoxious laugh.

"And I'll drag your tart through the mud," she added.

Cool as a cantaloupe, Hank went to the kitchen. "You've been at my Scotch, have you?"

"Did you hear me?" Becky said.

He didn't answer. She heard him tossing ice cubes in a glass. A moment later he came back holding his drink.

"Don't try to play tough with me, honey," he said. "You don't have it in you."

The booze had made her warm, and fired up her anger. She loved the feeling.

"A doormat no more," she said.

"So what are you going to do?" Hank sat in a chair, casually crossing his legs.

"You'll find out," she said.

He sipped some liquor through a tight smile.

"Sweetie," he said, "I'll crush you in court. You won't get a dime."

That tone of his. He was wiping his feet on her, as always.

Not tonight.

"You'll give me a million dollars," she said. "And maybe I won't make your life a living hell."

His slight hesitation was a pleasant surprise. Maybe she should have started drinking sooner.

"Try it," he said. "You'll be sorry, even sorrier than you look right now."

She felt her own smile come to her lips, and heard herself say, "Game on."

———

"Now," Jake Monroe said, "tell me what I can do for you."

"Win for me," Becky said.

She was seated across from the young but very confident-looking lawyer. The chairs were leather, the desk big and neat.

Monroe laughed "You've seen the billboard, have you?"

"That's why I'm here," Becky said. "Do you really mean it?"

"I wouldn't say it if I didn't," the lawyer said.

"Just tell me how you can get away with that. Isn't that against the rules? Guaranteeing a win?"

"It ain't lyin' if it's true, as my granddaddy used to say."

"Was he a lawyer?"

"A hardware salesman," Monroe said. "The best in the county. Now what is it that brings you here today, Mrs. Randall?"

"The *Mrs.* part," Becky said.

"You want that *Mrs.* removed, eh?"

"You have to understand something," Becky said. "He's rich and he's ruthless. He has at least one woman on the side, and probably others. He laughed in my face when I told him I wanted out. I'm just warning you."

The lawyer didn't flinch. "What does my sign say?"

"That you'll win for me."

"If I take your case," he said, "which I have not done yet..." He steepled his fingers. "But if I do, I'll win."

Becky liked the cut of his jib, as her own grandfather used to say. She pulled out her checkbook.

"How much?" she said.

"Now wait—"

"Ten thousand? Will that do for a retainer?"

"You really want to fast track this, don't you."

"Fifteen thousand?"

He placed his palms on the desk. "Make it ten. I'll have my assistant draw up the papers. I like a challenge."

"Then let me hear you say it one more time, please."

"I'll win for you, Mrs. Randall."

"Becky," she said, and wrote out the check.

———

She was back in his office the next morning. Monroe had prepared a spread of scones and cappuccino for his new client.

After an exchange of pleasantries he said, "Now, down to business. Take your time and tell me about your marriage, your husband's actions, the names of any of the women if you know them, his assets, anything you can think of."

She did so. After an hour she was finished.

"That will do nicely," Monroe said. "The divorce will be swift, the alimony fantastic."

"Divorce?" Becky said

Monroe frowned.

"The charge will be murder," Becky said. "Now, win for me."

LOVE CONQUERS ALL

One day a bird landed on my head. It began to sing. It also pooped.

And that just about sums up my life. Some good, some bad. Some happy, some sad. It keeps me from taking anything nice that happens and allowing myself to enjoy it. The title of my autobiography should be *The Other Shoe.*

But then I met Mary.

It was at a friend's birthday party at his condo in Hollywood. The party was in full swing when I got there. People smiled and greeted me. Of course, I fully expected one of them to spill bean dip on my shirt at any moment.

In fact, it was when I was dipping a tortilla chip that I looked up and saw her standing there. Her smile was incandescent, her eyes midnight blue.

"Mind if I dip, too?" she said.

And I was a goner. I stumbled through some small talk, and she did the same. She laughed easily, so I told her my joke about the set of jumper cables that walk into a bar, and the bartender says, "I'll serve you, but don't start anything."

When she laughed long about that, I knew I was in love.

But...but...but...the bird on the head...

Tempting fate, I managed to ask her if she'd maybe like to, sometime, have coffee with me. She said yes, how about tomorrow?

Be still I told my heart.

The next morning we met at Coffee Bean and I bought the drinks—a hazelnut latté for her, the dark roast of the day for me.

We chatted a bit, and found we had much in common. We both loved movies. Her favorite movie was *Casablanca*.

"That's mine, too!" I said.

We liked the same foods. Especially (she admitted with a fetching smile) pizza with extra cheese.

"Me, too! With extra onions."

"I love onions," she said. "We don't have them where I'm from."

"Where is that?" I said.

"From a galaxy far, far away," she said, and laughed.

"*Star Wars*!"

"And you?" she asked.

"I'm from an alternate universe."

"Cool!" Mary said.

I took my shot. "I know we've just met, but I wonder, maybe would you like to have dinner at my place? I'll order us a great big, double-cheese pizza with onions and anchovies. Then I'll pop *Casablanca* into the DVD and we'll watch it together."

"That sound great," she said, and lifted her coffee cup. "Here's looking at you, kid."

———

She showed up looking more beautiful than Ingrid Bergman, and that is saying something. I poured her a glass of cabernet. We sat on the sofa and clinked.

The big pizza was sitting in a box on my kitchen counter.

"Smells so good!" Mary said. "Mmm, those onions! Thank you!"

"My pleasure," I said. "Shall I get you a piece?"

"Let me," she said.

She opened her mouth and stuck out her tongue. Out.. out... out...a tongue that grew to two feet, then two yards, then all the way across the room. The tip of her tongue flipped the box open, slid under a slice of pizza, lifted it, then retracted it toward her mouth. She removed the slice with her hand and held it out for me.

I couldn't move. Every part of my body was stunned, frozen.

Mary tossed the pizza aside, put her hands around my neck, pulled me to her, and planted a great big kiss on me.

Let me tell you, that was some kiss.

Last week we were married. And boy, you should have seen Mary eat cake!

You take what life gives you. A bird lands on your head, and it's going to be a little bit of this and a little bit of that. There's bitter and sweet. There's high and low.

And then there's normal and really, really weird.

But you know what? Love conquers all.

SOUND MARITAL ADVICE

It was 1955, and Mrs. Ronald Vandermeter sought to make her home a happy one. That's because her husband, an executive at U.S. Steel's Manhattan office, worked such long hours. From their beautiful home in Montclair, Ronald would drive to the train station at Newark, take the 7:15 into the city and be at his desk at eight sharp. It was not uncommon for him to take his dinner in his office, along with a couple of drinks, and be home after nine.

On such nights he often sniped at his wife before getting into bed and falling instantly asleep.

Worried that they were growing apart, Jane Vandermeter (for that was her name) sought counsel from a neighbor, Mrs. Betty Lester, whose home seemed a most happy one.

Betty lent Jane a book—*On The Needs of Men in Marriage* by Dr. Emil von Zoppe of Harvard Medical School.

Reading it hungrily, Jane Vandermeter came across this passage:

The working male is wedded not only to his wife, but to his routine. When marriage becomes routine also, the working man will tend toward favoring his work environment. This results in the common complaint that the husband has grown 'distant.' But complaining to the man is almost always counterproductive, leading to further detachment. What, then, is the solution? It is for the wife to introduce the element of excitement, especially in the arena of sex. Anything she can do to surprise her husband in a fetching, feminine manner is a start on the road to recovery of intimacy.

What sound marital advice! And this was a man from Harvard!

The very next day Jane Vandermeter executed her plan. She spent the morning at the beauty parlor, came home, put on her most attractive dress. She finished with a dab of Evening Allure, the perfume advertised on TV by the famous model Jinx Falkenberg.

Jane arrived at her husband's office at 11:48.

Quietly opening the door, she saw Ronald in his executive chair, looking out the window, talking into the Dictaphone.

He was saying, "...and our new facility in Pittsburgh must be completed by September. This is not a negotiable position..."

Pleased and smiling, Jane quietly approached, reached out, and put her hands over his eyes.

He stopped talking.

"Guess who?" she said.

"I told you," Ronald Vandermeter said. "No time for that now. Get those letters out!"

———

The alimony granted to the former Mrs. Ronald Vandermeter was such that it ensured her security for life. Ever after she was fond of telling her friends, "A fool and his money, a whole lot of it, are soon parted."

THE DEADWOOD HERO

John Sladeowski, night security guard at the Golden West Western Museum, paused, as he always did, at the Hickok diorama.

The scene, complete with wax figures, was of Nuttal & Mann's Saloon in Deadwood of the Dakota Territory, 1876. Cowboys drank at the bar. A piano player was poised at the keys. And there at the front sat some men playing poker. The one with the drooping mustache was Wild Bill Hickok. He held his cards, which the viewer could see—Two aces, two eights, and a queen. This would come to be known as the Dead Man's Hand, for behind Hickok stood Jack McCall, holding the Colt .45 he would use a moment later to shoot Wild Bill in the back of the head. The sign in front of the diorama read:

> "Wild Bill" Hickok, holding Aces and Eights—the Dead Man's Hand —just before being shot in the back of the head by the drunken coward Jack McCall. McCall was hanged for this murder in 1877.

The diorama haunted John Sladeowski. Wild Bill Hickok was about to die and there was nothing anybody could do about it. All his life, John wanted to do something heroic. When the police department turned him down, he became a security guard. But on night duty there was never any opportunity to do anything except check the doors and walk the floor.

And while Wild Bill was here immortalized with one of the great nicknames in Western lore, no handle of that magnitude would ever be applied to John Sladeowski. He was fifty-three, balding, overweight, unmarried, and in a dead-end job. Everyone remembered Wild Bill, but who would remember John Sladeowski?

On this night the emptiness in his soul brought tears. Ignoring protocol, not caring if he got fired, John stepped over the velvet rope and entered the diorama itself.

There was an empty chair at a neighboring table. John pulled it up next to Wild Bill and sat.

"Look out, Bill," he said. "Somebody's gunning for you."

Lights grew bright. The sound of a tinny piano filled the air, and the voices of men talking, and Wild Bill—somehow alive!—looked at him.

Wild Bill said, "How's that, stranger?"

Jack McCall glanced at John Sladeowski. On pure instinct John jumped up and dove at McCall.

A gun fired.

———

The little boy looked at the diorama and said, "Daddy, what is this?"

His father said, "This is a famous moment in the Old West. Here, I'll read it to you."

Jack "Paunchy" Slade saves the life of Wild Bill Hickok by jumping in front of the gun held by drunken coward Jack McCall. McCall was hanged for this murder in 1877.

"Gee," said the boy.

"Paunchy Slade was a real hero. Mickey Rooney starred in a movie about him."

"Who is Mickey Rooney?" the boy said.

"Let's go get a hot dog at the snack bar," the father said, "and I'll tell you about him."

FEAR

"I'm afraid you're suffering from epiplaphobia," Dr. Finklestein said.

"What is that?" Harold Rumstack asked. He was standing in the corner of Dr. Chandler Finklestein's office. He felt like a child doing so, for at age 47 Harold Rumstack was a fully functional adult.

Well, almost fully. He did have this one thing...

"Fear of furniture," Dr. Finklestein said. "Rare, but real."

Harold looked at the psychiatrist's couch, upon which he had refused to lie down when prompted by the psychiatrist.

"But I do sit in chairs," Harold said. "And sleep in my bed."

"And yet you find yourself standing in many settings outside your home."

Harold nodded.

"Most of the time," Dr. Finklestein said, "epiplaphobia can be traced to a phobia of another type. Fear of ornate carvings, for example. There was a famous Hollywood actor who suffered from just such a malady. He was afraid of antique furniture with any sort of animal figure."

"There's no animal on your couch," Harold said.

"Ah, but here is where your hypochondria figures in," said Dr. Finklestein. "You imagine there is some animal head lurking about, hidden perhaps to the naked eye."

"I do?"

"Do you see what is on the wall above the couch?"

Harold looked and saw a framed diploma, a plaque of some sort, and a photograph. The photo was an 11 x 14 of a tiger.

"I took that picture myself," Dr. Finklestein said. "On a nature tour in Myanmar. What I believe happened is that you came in and saw the photo, then filed it away in your subconscious. When I asked you to lie down on the couch, your mind associated the animal with the furniture. Tell me, did you recall any traumatic experiences with animals when you were young?"

"We had a dog," Harold said. "It got hit by a car."

"Go on," said Dr. Finklestein.

"Go on?"

"I feel like you're wanting to say something more."

"You do?"

"I ask the questions here, Harold. What aren't you telling me?"

"Noth..."

"Come now, I can't help you if you don't open up. Is it something related to animals?"

Harold pressed his lips together. He didn't want the words to come out. But they did.

"She scared me with animals," Harold said.

"Who scared you, Harold?"

"My mother."

"Go on."

"She used to tell me, if I was bad, I'd get eaten by wild animals."

"That's terrible, Harold."

"You're telling me! She'd describe how I'd be ripped apart and blood would be all over the place."

"Your own mother?"

Harold felt his shoulders and neck tightening into twisted ropes. "She..."

"Don't stop, Harold. Let it all out."

"She fancied herself a witch."

Doctor Chandler Finklestein stroked his chin in a Freudian manner. "You don't believe that, do you, Harold?"

"I do! Maybe this is a mistake. Maybe I should go to a witch doctor!"

"Now, now, Harold. Let's keep this rational. How long did your mother's threats go on?"

"Until I was ten. My father took me away from her. She screamed the night it happened. She said I would come to no good end. She said I was a bad seed."

"Where is your mother now?"

"I don't want to know."

Dr. Finklestein paused, then said, "Pentheraphobia."

"What's that?"

"Technically it is fear of one's mother-in-law, but the literature is trending toward including the birth mother."

"Oh, man!"

"Easy now, Harold. There is a way out of all of this."

"Tell me!"

"Baby steps. Face your fears. Start by sitting down."

"Where?"

"On the couch."

Harold sucked in a breath. "Do I have to?"

"No, Harold, you don't have to. But do you want to get better?"

"I...do."

"I'll wait."

His nerves fighting him like wild animals—the irony was not lost on Harold Rumstack—he took small steps toward the psychiatrist's couch. When he got to it he almost ran back to the corner. But the look on Dr. Finklestein's face was forceful.

A moment later Harold was sitting.

A long silence ensued.

"How do you feel, Harold?" the doctor said.

"O...K, I guess."

"Breathe easy now. Well done!"

With a smile breaking across his face, Harold started to relax.

Then a roar shattered the silence, the loudest sound Harold had ever heard in his life!

The tiger jumped out of the picture frame, as big as a car, snarling, teeth bared.

.   .   .

***

When the police showed up they found Dr. Chandler Finklestein catatonic in his office chair, blood spattered over him. The body on the couch was little more than raw, mangled flesh.

It was a week before Dr. Finklestein came around. A detective from downtown, Kennedy, questioned him in the hospital.

"Can you talk?" Detective Kennedy asked.

"I...I..."

"Easy now. We're just trying to figure out what happened in your office. Your patient, how well did you know him?"

"Know?"

"Drake Henry," Kennedy said.

"Drake? No, Harold."

"An assumed name," Kennedy said. "His real handle is Drake Henry, wanted for several murders committed twenty some odd years ago. You didn't know that?"

Dr. Finklestein opened his mouth, but no words came out.

"Look here," Kennedy said. "If you'd like a lawyer with you, we can get you one. Or you can call your own. I have to tell you that you have the right to remain silent, and anything you say can be used against you in a court of law."

Silence.

"Would you like an attorney present?" Kennedy asked.

"N...no," said Dr. Chandler Finklestein. "Please...get me a witch doctor."

FORBIDDEN TEXT

"Shhh," Pal said. "We gotta keep our voices low. The sensors."

"The sensors of the censors, you mean," Kelli said, and laughed.

"This isn't funny. If they find us with this it'll mean the jolts for both of us."

The jolts was how they and their friends referred to the AI-electroshock therapy approved by Congress in 2082, for all federal "counter-cogitations." In 2089 they defined all counter-cogitations as "federal" for being a danger to the social order.

"So how'd you get it in the first place?" Pal asked.

"My grandfather," Kelli said. "Before he died he covered it in oil cloth and buried it, right before the great confiscation."

"My mom was a little girl in the great confiscation. She told me they ripped a book right out of her hands."

Kelli said, "My dad told me the story of his dad burying this book by a magnolia tree across the street from their old place, just before they came and cleaned out his house. My dad's always been afraid to dig it up, for obvious reasons."

"So why aren't you afraid?" Pal said.

"At some point you just can't let them scare you anymore," Kelli said.

"That's jolt talk."

"Big deal."

"I wanna go," Pal said.

"You sure you don't want to see?" Kelli said. "I bet there's part of you that wants to."

Pal said, "Did you open it?"

"Just once. I looked at the cover. Then I heard a censor van outside and covered it again."

"You're scaring me," Pal said.

"Get over it," Kelli said.

"So ... what exactly is it?"

"It's some sort of medical book," Kelli said. "I think it has pictures and diagrams. Want to see?"

Pal swallowed, his Adam's Apple bobbing. "Okay, but hurry."

Kelli put the book on the table and slowly removed the oil cloth.

"See?" Kelli said. "It's by a doctor."

"Dr. See-uss?" Pal said. "Funny name."

Kelli ran her finger along the title. "It looks like his office was on Mulberry Street."

"This must have some of his cases."

"Ready to have a look?" Kelli said.

Pal said, "I dunno. Maybe we should burn it, just to be safe."

With trembling fingers, Kelli opened the book.

ON THE CAMPAIGN TRAIL

"Now you understand you're speaking to a crowd of rabid Bible believers," Willard Earwicker said.

"Yes, yes," said Lamar Maggs.

Earwicker adjusted the candidate's tie, a subdued burgundy to go with Maggs' dark blue suit. Having been brought on to lead Maggs to the finish line of the campaign, Earwicker was not leaving any detail unattended.

"You need to get on the same wavelength with this crowd," Earwicker said. "A surefire way is to tell them what your favorite verse is."

"You mean, from the Bible?" Maggs said.

"I don't mean from *The Journal of Forensic Dermatology.*"

"You don't have to be snarky about it," Maggs said.

"I just want you to realize how important this is, as a first impression." Willard Earwicker, at age 63, was considered by most to be the top political consultant in the country. Lamar Maggs was 45 and making his first national run—for a seat in the United States Senate.

"Of course I understand," Maggs said.

Earwicker almost said, "*I don't think you do.*" But in the few weeks he'd been with the campaign, he'd learned that Maggs had a very thin skin. This called for delicate handling.

"So do you have a favorite verse?" Earwicker said.

"I don't know anything about the Bible," Maggs said.

"Everybody knows *something* about the Bible," Earwicker said.

"Sure, okay. Fine. How about, 'God helps those who help themselves'?"

Earwicker, who had grown up Baptist, said, "That's not in the Bible."

"It's not?" Maggs said with an astonished look. "It should be, shouldn't it?"

"That's not the point." Earwicker looked at his watch. "You'll be on in a few minutes. Now—"

"How about 'The road to hell is paved with good intentions'?"

"Not in there, Lamar."

"'Honk if you love Jesus.'?"

"This isn't funny! This audience is serious about such matters."

Lamar Maggs flashed his famous smile and patted Earwicker's cheek. "Just tell me what I should say. That's what I pay you for."

"Tell them you're glad to be with them, and that it warms your heart."

"Warms my heart. Got it."

"And that you're glad to share with them—*share* is an important word with this crowd—glad to share your favorite verse. Then say John 3:16 and wait for the applause."

"John what?"

"3:16," Earwicker said. It was the first verse he ever memorized in Sunday School, all those years ago. "'For God so loved the world, that he gave his only begotten Son, that whosoever believeth in him should not perish, but have everlasting life.'"

"Oh yeah, that's a biggie," Maggs said.

"John 3:16, got it?"

"Got it."

"Off the cuff, to set the mood, then you launch into your speech."

"You worry too much," Maggs said.

"I get paid to worry," Earwicker said.

The audience in the large church applauded wildly as Lamar Maggs made his way to the podium. He smiled and waved to the crowd. When things quieted down he said, "So good to be here tonight. It warms my heart just to be able to share a few thoughts with you, to be with a group of people who share my feelings, as I share theirs. In fact, I'd like to share with you my favorite verse from the Bible. John 16:3."

Maggs waited for applause. But there was only silence. Some in the crowd looked confused. Maybe they didn't believe him.

"Believe me," Maggs said. "John 16:3 speaks to me. It speaks about me! That's why I wanted to share it with you tonight."

Crickets.

Must have bowled them over with my sincerity, Maggs thought. Best to plunge ahead. "We gather here tonight as our country faces some severe challenges…"

———

Joining Willard Earwicker in the wings after the speech, Lamar Maggs said, "Boy, tough crowd! It's almost like they didn't believe a word I said."

"Oh they believed you, all right. They believed John 16:3 speaks all about you."

"Isn't that good?"

"The verse is John 3:16!"

Maggs swallowed. "What's the difference? It's still in the Bible, isn't it?"

Earwicker picked up a church Bible from a backstage table, and flipped to John 16:3. He handed it to Maggs.

"Read it," Earwicker said.

Lamar Maggs looked at the page and followed the numbers to the verse. He read it aloud. "'They will do such things because they have not known the Father or me.'"

Maggs looked at Earwicker. "Oops."

———

Lamar Maggs lost the election in a landslide. He returned to operating his Ford dealership in Phoenix.

Willard Earwicker received a six-figure advance for a book on politics entitled *The Well-Versed Candidate.*

THE LAST HUSTLE

Benny McMillan liked to hustle people. Ever since he was a kid, pitching pennies and dimes, he found his greatest thrill in a little lying and a little cheating, especially with money on the line. His mother told him, "Benny, you're too clever by half. Someday this will all catch up with you."

"Not me, Ma," Benny would say. "I got the juice."

Then one day the juice ran out. A check kiting scheme bought Benny a five year stretch in the pen.

When he finally got out he had a choice. Go on as he always had, hustling for dollars. Or do as his gray-haired mother always wished: get an actual job.

The thought of manual labor made Benny shiver. Hustling was his game. If he still had the juice, of course.

With two twenty-dollar bills in his pocket—the same two he'd gone into prison with—Benny decided to limber up with a little hustling at a bar.

The dimness of the place matched Benny's mood. He ordered a shot of Jack from the beefy bartender, who seemed friendly enough.

"Down on your luck?" the barkeep asked.

"Don't know," Benny said. "Haven't tested it yet."

"You a gambler?"

"In a way."

"You like to make bets?"

"Sometimes."

The bartender smiled. "How'd you like to bet me?"

"On what?"

"That I can make you sound like a train."

"A train?"

"Yeah. A great big train."

Benny snorted. "Sure, I'll take that bet." Why not? Silly as it was, it was a good test, a way to get the juice flowing again. In fact, Benny made a little bet with himself right then. If he walked out of the bar with more money than when he came in, his hustling days would go on. If not...oh, boy, he did not like thinking of the alternative.

"Twenty bucks?" the bartender said.

Benny fished out one of his twenties and slapped it on the bar top. The bartender took out a twenty and laid it on top of Benny's.

"First," the bartender said, "a joke. Just to lighten things up."

Benny drained his whiskey, smiled, and said, "Sure."

"Knock knock," the bartender said.

"Who's there?" Benny said.

"Chooch."

"Chooch who?"

The bartender snatched up the twenties.

Hustled! Benny McMillan had just been taken to the cleaners by a stupid joke he should have seen from a mile away!

"Don't take it so hard," the bartender said.

"You don't understand," Benny said. "I needed to win tonight. My life depended on..." Benny stopped when he saw a nicely dressed man sit down at the other end of the bar. He looked rich, successful. In other words, he looked like a perfect mark.

Benny went over and sat on the stool next to the man. "Say buddy, how'd you like to make a friendly little bet?"

The stranger looked at him quizzically, but with seeming interest. "Bet?"

"Yeah. You and I lay twenty bucks on the bar. If I can make you sound like a train, I win. If I can't, you win."

"A train?"

"That's all."

The stranger thought about it a moment, then pulled out a money clip. He plucked off a twenty and laid it on the bar.

Benny took out his last twenty—his *only* twenty—and put it on top.

The bartender sauntered over to watch.

"First," Benny said, "a joke. Just to lighten things up."

The stranger nodded.

"Knock knock," Benny said.

"Who is there?" the stranger said.

"Chooch."

"Who is this Chooch?"

Benny slapped his forehead.

The bartender said, "This guy's name is Gunnar. He's from Germany."

Taking the money, Gunnar said to Benny, "You are looking like you need a drink. I will buy it."

Benny McMillan now works as a fuse tester for a demolition company.

BEHAVIOR MODIFICATION

"Thank you for coming in today, Mr. Swanson."

"It wasn't exactly voluntary."

"Yes, but we are trained to be polite, and might I suggest the same for you?"

"It is a little nerve-racking to be hauled...I mean, asked to come in to a BM office."

"We at Behavior Modification never use that abbreviation."

"I...well..."

"You hesitated there. Let me just make a note of that."

"Wait a sec—"

"We don't need to take up much time here. The Program picked up something we need to talk about. Would you like a glass of water?"

"Let's get on with it."

"Surely. You watched the President's address to the nation last night."

"As I was ordered to."

"All citizens were so ordered, Mr. Swanson. We are not singling you out."

"It certainly seems...I understand."

"A good first step. Now, at thirteen minutes, three seconds into the address, you winced."

"I did?"

"Let me show you on the monitor. You see? A wince. And the Program immediately flagged it as distaste. Which is, of course, a misdemeanor."

"Wait...wait..."

"Strong distaste is a felony. You were very close."

"May I say something?"

"Of course. We here at Behavior Modification believe in monitored speech."

"I'm being monitored?"

"As we all are. Now, what is it you wish to say?"

"I know why I winced."

"So do we, Mr. Swanson."

"You don't understand."

"Accusing Behavior Modification of not understanding is a misdemeanor."

"I mean...I just want to tell you, I winced, but not because of distaste."

"No?"

"No! I have hemorrhoids!"

"....hm....let me input something....ah, no, the Program distinguishes between winces of distaste and winces of low-level pain. Here, see for yourself."

"But I'm telling you!"

"You are not here to tell us anything, Mr. Swanson. The Program has never been wrong."

"How do you know that?"

"Excuse me?"

"Who monitors the Program?"

"It self-monitors."

"Then..."

"Yes, it can never be wrong. That's the beauty of the system...Ah, you winced just then."

"Hemorrhoids!"

"Afraid not, Mr. Swanson. And lying to an officer of Behavior Modification takes us to a Grade B Felony. That will be two years in re-education in, let me see...yes, there are several openings in our North Dakota camp."

"Wait, what?"

"We're finished here, Mr. Swanson."

"You can't do this! It's...un-American!"

"Now it's a Grade A Felony. Good-bye, Mr. Swanson. We will notify your next of kin."

THE HUMAN CANNONBALL

For twenty years with the Dangling Brothers Circus, Harold Stackhouse was known as "The Human Cannonball." No one knew exactly how he had acquired his skill, though Harold dropped some curious hints to newspaper reporters from time to time.

"My big brothers used to sling me out of giant slingshot made of tire rubber," he said. Some reporters were loath to take that as fact. But how else could you explain a serene Harold being fired out of an exploding cannon into a net, night after night and twice on Sundays?

He was the show's main attraction, along with Lila and her Wonder Horse, and Lefty Mancuso, the one-armed trapeze artist.

But all good things must come to an end. One Sunday, after the last show, Harold Stackhouse knocked on the trailer door of Clyde Dangling, the owner.

"Enter!" Clyde Dangling said.

Harold burst in. He did not know any other way.

"Excellent show tonight!" Clyde said. "You did a triple somersault! I've never seen the like!"

"That's because it was my last time," Harold said.

"I beg your pardon?"

"It's time for me to retire," Harold said. "I figure I've been fired out of that cannon 31,999 times."

"That exact?"

"I missed one show in Toledo, back in 2010. I fainted from trichinosis after eating at Charlie's Midway Hot Dog stand."

"I remember that day," Clyde Dangling said. "We had several sick folks."

"Changing the expiration dates on the hot dog packages doesn't solve the problem."

"That Charlie." Clyde chuckled. "He's out on parole now, did you hear?"

Harold cleared his throat. "So thanks for everything."

Clyde got up from his desk, came around, and put his hands on Harold's shoulders. "You can't quit. You just can't!"

"Sorry, Mr. Dangling. But my mind's made up."

"Truly?"

"Truly."

Clyde Dangling sighed. "Ah, well. We'll have to try to replace you. But I can safely say, when it comes to someone being shot out of a cannon, we'll never find anyone of your caliber."

ALL GLORY IS FLEETING

JSB: In October of 2021, Chris Taylor of the L.A. Dodgers hit a dramatic, bottom-of-the-ninth home run to win the Wild Card playoff game against the St. Louis Cardinals and advance the team to the NL Division Series. Naturally, he was mobbed at home plate. Really mobbed. Which got me to thinking about a baseball player named Stan Knobler...

Stan Knobler was in a slump, a big one, an October slump, the kind they talk about after you retire. You know, "He was a good hitter, a darn good hitter, but he choked in the playoffs. His team never made it to the World Series, and part of the reason was Stan. Come cooler weather he was just a plain old .230 hitter. Just can't explain it. He might've made the Hall of Fame if he could've hit in October."

So there he was, age thirty-five, and he had the chance to end that talk forever. To send his team to the Fall Classic with one swing. They were down 2-1, bottom of the ninth, a runner on first base.

Game 7 of the championship series. It was win now or go home.

Stan Knobler had butterflies for sure, for on the mound was the league's best relief pitcher, Manuel "The Monster" Castillo, and he was ready to rumble.

The city, nation, and many parts of the world were watching.

Castillo got Knobler down 0-2. Then a pitch in the dirt that Knobler almost went for.

Now the count was 1-2.

Knobler fouled one off.

Then Castillo tried to fool him with a big, roundhouse curve. Which did not fool Stan Knobler. He'd been known early in his career about his ability to hit an Uncle Charlie, and now all that experience paid off.

He lifted the pitch high into the night air.

The right fielder, Brad Palaver, went back, back, back, to the wall ... jumped ... as the ball sailed over his glove by a foot.

The sell-out crowd exploded with wild cheers.

The dugout emptied as Stan's teammates and manager charged onto the field.

As soon as Stan Knobler crossed home plate, they mobbed him. It was a joyous, jumping, laughing, yelling gaggle of testosterone, and Stan went down screaming "That's right! That's right!" before disappearing under a pile of players.

The last player to jump on top of the pile was the back-up catcher Buck Finchley, who weighed 260 pounds.

A minute later they began unpiling and stepping back, only to see Stan Knobler's face and body planted a solid inch into the dirt around home plate.

Later that evening, the manager, Mack "Happy" Westlake, said to a room full of reporters, "He crossed home, then he went Home."

The room grew quiet. A reporter brushed away a tear.

"But we're goin' to the Series!" Happy Westlake said.

A MOTHER'S LOVE

I know people say a boy can be too close to his mother. Especially if he's 21. But I beg to differ. Especially when you consider my mom.

She is an overachiever.

Tall, beautiful, magnetic. My dad ran out on us when I was just a baby, and she raised me all on her own.

"I will love you forever," she used to say, comforting me. She was my rock all through my growing up years.

And just because I found out she was a killer, should that have made a difference?

I first became aware of Mom's "other activity" when I was in high school. Gradually, I came to accept it. I didn't want anything to get in the way of my mother's love.

So I joined her in her, um, doings. We became partners, so to speak, but always first and foremost mother and son.

Like the other night at Mr. Johnson's house. Elbert Johnson was an old kook, the neighborhood eccentric. All neighborhoods have at least one of these. They somehow get fixated on somebody else on the block, and start making wild accusations.

Johnson became fixated on us.

So a little after midnight we paid a call on Elbert Johnson. The old fool shouldn't have left his window open.

He screamed when he saw us, but Mom made short work of him. I marveled again at her effortlessness, how artfully she implanted her fangs.

When we got back home, I told her, "I'll love you forever."

"And I you," she said.

We got in our coffins.

"Sleep well, Mother," I said.

"See you tomorrow night, my son."

BORDER INCIDENT

JSB: Several of you will recognize the comedic basis for this little story. I have shamelessly borrowed it. I do so to offer my fresh take for the entertainment value to those unfamiliar with source material. Shakespeare, after all, took a well-known story of the time and turned it into *Romeo and Juliet*. Why can't a pulp fiction writer, in this respect at least, emulate the Bard?

Juan Francisco de la Santísima prided himself on being the best border agent in all of Mexico. It was said he could smell a smuggler the way a hound dog sniffs out a rabbit.

But he was flummoxed one day when a young man rode up to the border on a bicycle, with a backpack on his back.

"What do you have in your pack?" Juan asked.

The young man said, "Only dirt."

"And why do you carry dirt on your back?"

"To help me stay in shape."

"Hand it over," Juan said.

Juan Francisco de la Santísima opened the pack wide and poked at the dirt with an iron rod. He felt nothing. He dumped the dirt on the ground and spread it.

Just dirt.

Giving the pack back to the young man, he said, "You may go. The dirt stays."

And the young man rode his bicycle across the border.

A week later, the same thing happened. The young man rode up, Juan Francisco de la Santísima stopped him and examined his backpack. Again, nothing but dirt!

The young man rode on.

The following week it happened again! The young man on the bike with the full backpack rode up, and an angry Juan Francisco de la Santísima yanked the pack away and dumped all the dirt on the ground. He almost screamed when he came up empty again.

Feeling that he had lost his touch, Juan Francisco de la Santísima quit his job with the border patrol and became a bartender in Tijuana.

Some six months went by. One night the young man stepped into the bar. Juan Francisco de la Santísima recognized him immediately. He pulled a beer and set it before him.

"Do you remember me?" Juan said.

"I do indeed," said the young man.

"I no longer work for the border patrol. And your drinks are on the house if you will just tell me one thing. I knew you were smuggling something, but I could not find out what! Please tell me, what was it you were smuggling?"

The young man took a sip of his beer, then leaned over and whispered, "Bicycles."

MISSION TO PLUTO

It had been five years since the last message from Trask.

The only signal coming in was from the tracking system of his spacecraft, indicating what they all feared—that Trask had crashed onto the surface of Pluto and was dead.

Now, finally, NASA was sending a combination rescue party and exploratory team to see if they could find out what happened.

A hundred years ago, during what some historians call "The Virus Epoch," such a mission would have been impossible. But since then much knowledge had been gained about space travel in general and Pluto in particular.

Once called "The Ice Planet," Pluto had been downgraded to a "dwarf" in 2006. That's because it had not become "gravitationally dominant" in what the astronomers call its "neighborhood."

But a shocking discovery in 2098 upset that solar apple cart. Astronomers had either missed it, or somehow, some way, Pluto had developed a hospitable atmosphere along with gravitational pull. Further, a heat source outside of our solar system indicated that the "ice" on Pluto's surface was not frozen water. Rather, it was some sort of granulated, crystalline compound, like sand on a beach.

Which was when Guy Trask went up on his seven-year journey to Pluto.

Which was twelve years ago.

Which meant that the rescue party would land on Pluto nineteen years after Trask left the Earth.

The crew—Captain Derek Stallings, First Lieutenant Amanda Freed, and First Officer Lionel Hall—broke out the freeze-dried champagne when they were one day from landing. It was a 2087 freeze-dry, a very good year.

The ship landed without incident, and the three stepped onto the Plutonian surface. It took an hour to become fully acclimated, but during that time they were almost speechless at what they saw: Three magnificent structures, spaced approximately fifty yards apart. Multi-colored, made from some sort of alloy. They looked like mini-castles from a children's book about knights and dragons.

As Captain Stallings began to communicate a plan of action, a figure appeared out of the "castle" to their left.

His hair was long and gray, and his beard stretched down to his stomach. He wore a robe of some kind. It had to be!

"Guy Trask?" Captain Stallings said.

"You made it!" Trask said. "Fantastic!"

"I can hardly believe it," Stallings said.

"Pretty cool, eh?" Trask said.

"There is so much we want to ask you before we take you back."

"Back? No. This is my home now. I'm perfectly happy living alone. No crime, no riots, no totalitarianism, no taxation, no hassles. Well, almost no hassles."

"But how did you build these...structures? What materials? What tools?"

Trask smiled. "There are more things in heaven and earth, Horatio, than are dreamt of in your philosophy."

"What?"

"A pity they stopped teaching Shakespeare a hundred years ago," Trask said.

Stallings cleared his throat. "What exactly are these buildings?"

"Well," said Trask, "the one I came out of is my house. And that one on the end is my church."

"And what is the one in the middle?" Stallings asked.

Trask sighed. "That's the church I used to go to."

ABOUT THE AUTHOR

 JAMES SCOTT BELL is a winner of the International Thriller Writers Award, the Christy Award, and the ACFW Lifetime Achievement Award. He's also the #1 bestselling author of books on the craft of fiction. He studied writing with Raymond Carver at the University of California, Santa Barbara, and graduated with honors from the University of Southern California Law Center.

A former trial lawyer, Jim writes full time in his home town of Los Angeles.

For regular flights of fancy from the author, sign up for his newsletter by going to: **JamesScottBell.substack.com**

Visit his website: **JamesScottBell.com**

www.ingramcontent.com/pod-product-compliance
Lightning Source LLC
Chambersburg PA
CBHW050119030726
47505CB00007B/1934